Blue Burneau

BLUE BURNEAU

Glyn Maxwell

Chatto & Windus
LONDON

for JOANNA RYAN

First published in 1994

1 3 5 7 9 10 8 6 4 2

© Glyn Maxwell 1994

Glyn Maxwell has asserted his right under the Copyright,
Designs and Patents Act, 1988 to be identified as the author
of this work

First published in Great Britain in 1994 by
Chatto & Windus Limited
Random House, 20 Vauxhall Bridge Road, London SW1V 2SA

Random House Australia (Pty) Limited
20 Alfred Street, Milsons Point, Sydney
New South Wales 2061, Australia

Random House New Zealand Limited
18 Poland Road, Glenfield
Auckland 10, New Zealand

Random House South Africa (Pty) Limited
PO Box 337, Bergvlei, South Africa

Random House UK Limited Reg. No. 954009

A CIP catalogue record for this book
is available from the British Library

ISBN 0 7011 6071 3

Designed and Typeset by
SX Composing Ltd, Rayleigh, Essex
Printed in Great Britain by
Mackays of Chatham plc, Chatham, Kent

Contents

Here are your waters and your watering place.
Drink and be whole again beyond confusion.

Robert Frost

I

Burneau's Plight

I

Me? Don't look at me. Don't look at me though I strike you as ever so strange. Don't jog my arm, don't offer me drink, let me sit up here on my stool at the bar with no drink at all, slowly drawing my fingers through a puddle of beer while I wonder what is next for me, what is left for me. Let my appearance pass you by, make no impression on your day, my smart grey suit be no surprise, my sunglasses no talking point in this blue smoky dark, nor my face awaken the remotest recollection. Whoever you are, I will not be a part of your experience. If the god, the god who reads men, the god who wants to know them, if he will swing his spotlight along the faces in this bar, rest assured that it will neither pause upon nor return to the shaded face of Maris Burneau. Do not look at me, because I cannot look back. Do not make me talk to you, because I will tell you nothing but lies.

But something will tell all. I have no words for him except 'the death', and I call him that because he is not here, and because he is here, but mostly because he makes it his mischievous business to nudge me from all the paths and passes of my life towards the pits, the ditches and sands. The death it is who will make me think of what I have determined to put from my mind. Why does he do that? Why does a thing so besotted with emptiness rush headlong to fill all the spaces in the world with his needless reminders?

Why not? You are lost utterly. I am lost utterly.

Don't think about your plight, Burneau, I have said. I have said this every few seconds since I stumbled out of the sunshine into this bar, to sit here hunched, one hand upon the standard-issue gun in my pocket, the other trailing limply through the spilt beer. Don't cry. Don't think about your plight.

No, goes the death. *Do both.*

Think about your home, which is a simple cottage on the high slopes of the Folded Mountain, far away on the Mainland. Think about how you have left behind your beloved family and friends from the village. And about how you are now on the island of Badeo, a place of which you know nothing and where you know nobody. Think about your job, which is to guard the Viceroy Lagland on his inaugural tour of this dangerous colony. About how you lost him in the crowd. Lost him in the crowd. Paid to protect his life from death and you lose him in the crowd. Think hard about that. Why did you lose him in the crowd? Think about a vanishing girl with flame-coloured hair. Think about how you have lost your master and so your job and so your livelihood and so your home in the time it takes to eat a lunch, because you set eyes upon a girl with flame-coloured hair. And about how now they will hang you by your wandering mind because you lost him in the crowd. Now cry, because at least you can't think as you cry.

Then don't cry. Think.

Think about seething, implacable Badeo, full of bandits sworn to attack the representatives of the Argeline Domain. About how you have abandoned the gentle Viceroy to those dangers with only three bodyguards. And don't forget how they hate you, those three men. How even now they'll be saying 'I knew it, a traitor at heart!' How secretly they'll be hoping that harm comes to the Viceroy, so their hostility to poor Burneau is revealed as well-founded: 'Some witless mountain-man — first sniff of danger and he evaporates quick-time!' Try to imagine the Security Force ever forgiving your dereliction. Not easy, is it? *Is it, eh, Burneau?*

That barman is looking at me. He'll ask what I want. I have no idea because I'm not from this island. What do they drink? What do they talk about? I have no money. He must

4

leave me alone. It is impossible for me to accept or agree that I am lost utterly.

You are, though, remember.

– What can I get you, sir?

– *Hanged.* Well. What drinks are you serving today?

Look at the way he looks at me. He has a kind face, he must have family, friends. He wipes his brow. If I don't have a drink he'll throw me out. If I have a drink I'll have to run out when he asks for money. I have a gun. What was it for? To protect the Viceroy. I lost the Viceroy. I'm done for. Dereliction. There's a blackboard! A blackboard? I can chalk up my drinks. *Well, there's your life saved, matey.*

– Can I chalk up my drinks?

– If you're banking on a long stay, sir.

– Very much banking, yes. *Dereliction.*

– We got Royal, Spezial, Tretners, Grinzal, Frosch . . .

– Frosch please.

– Frosch it is, Mr -?

– It is, yes, Frosch.

– Frosch is your name there, eh?

– (What?) Yes it is. (Oh mercy.)

– One Frosch for Mr Frosch, eh, Magnick lad? I do like that, I do!

A plump blond boy at the far end of the bar pipes up:

– Well then fill me a glass of Magnick Magnifico and I'll always be your friend!

He lifts his drink to salute me – now that's a thing we do in the mountains of the Koborol! But I'm not from there. My name is Frosch. I'm from – I'm from – I'm from here.

– You not from these parts, sir? (says the barman, placing my drink before me, still chuckling at how my name is the same as it).

– No! I am! Very much from them. Thank you.

– There's you on the board, sir, Mr Frosch. Initial F. There. Seven markers and fifty cents, but all on the board. I'm Cyrille, and I must say it's always been a pleasing thing to see a new face, if you'll shake my hand here.

– Yes! *Hangmen do that*. Yes.

– Woh (cries Magnick, who looks like he should be in school somewhere) you're one of us now, Frosch. One of the Friends of Magnick, as we say.

– You say (says Cyrille) on account you're him, Magnick. I just say here's my friends all a-drinkin' at All Afternoons. My new friend Frosch here, he's got his drink on the board.

I drink. I have a name and a drink. *Same word though, Burneau. You only got one word.* It's a beginning.

Between Magnick and me are two customers, a broad-shouldered man smoking a pipe, and a striking woman in black, whose hair seems purple at the ends, illuminated by the light of the television screen which her head obstructs. Everyone else in the bar is grouped around tables, but nobody is watching the programme that's on. *Oh I am*, the death reminds me, *in case the Viceroy gets shot dead 'cos you lost him in the crowd.*

– How's the Frosch, Mr Frosch? (enquires the barman Cyrille).

– Well. It's up to its usual.

– You from Allalong then, or St Sperice?

– *I'm an Argeline*. Oh, Sperice. That region.

– Which street down there?

– *Ha-ha-ha, got you*. Oh, I'm between places.

– Ah yes. He's between places, Mme Maricolo.

The dark woman turns her head abruptly, so her purple-black mane dances and settles, but the brightness behind her still shades her face.

– Between places, is he, Cyrille, hmm?

– This is Mr Frosch, Mme Maricolo. Like the beer, he is.

– That's a ridiculous name. Is he foreign? He sounds like a Mainlander. I'm going to come and talk to him. Or is it 'go' and talk to him? Who knows until I get there? I'll investigate.

Mme Maricolo gets down off her stool, but brings it with her to squeeze between myself and the smoking man. Up close I see she is strong-featured and about forty, attractive, but her skin rather caked with make-up. Her eyebrows are dark, her eyelashes long, her eyes warm and deep. She seems a little drunk, and fixes me with a misty look.

– Here I am then. Are you a Mainlander?

– No. *Yes he is.* But I've spent time there. And that's where I began to sound somewhat as if –

– Did you come with the Dignitary?

– The Dignitary.

– What is he, the Dignitary? A Vice-count?

– (Magnick says with a yawn) A Vice Roy. A fresh marionette to dangle over our homes.

– The Viceroy (I wonder). Was there a Viceroy coming?

– He's out there somewhere (says Mme Maricolo), he's out there meeting the people of Badeo Town. That's why all the children are home from school. I've got two, and they are.

– Not Magnick (laughs the barman), he's never to be found in no school!

I stare, and learn as I listen. Here in All Afternoons they are unhappy with the rule of the Mainland over Badeo. Well, I was told of all this, I was briefed on the boat as we sailed to the island, but my colleagues said the capital city itself was quite safe: only out in the regions were the tough, intractable crews. The word in this dark bar is that it might not be so simple. The Viceroy is out there somewhere. There will always be people who hope to harm a Viceroy. I'm drinking in a bar. The voices of the customers lower as they mention the group called the OLB. No one goes into detail, they talk elliptically. The death hovers near the bar, pointing me out: *bodyguard, bodyguard, lost him, lost him, watch him.* The smoke rings and whirls through the blue air, and Mme Maricolo buys me my third or fourth drink of Frosch. I feel able to say:

– Nutty, this is. In flavour.

– So you're between places, Frosch. I'm between husbands as it happens, at least I do hope so. In the meantime, it is

7

good enough for me to meet here with my friends. I live on the Avenue Hali. That's your part of town, isn't it?
– Yes? Yes.
– Yes.
– Sperice. (I remember.)
– St Sperice, yes. But you're on the move?
– I am. (St Sperice, dammit, concentrate.)
– Out of the city?
– No, I'll stay in the city. Here. It's what I know. *It isn't.*
– That's good. We may meet again then. I never like to meet people I may not meet again. People always ought to tell you, you know, Mr Frosch. They should say, 'You may not meet me again.' If they said that to me, I'd say, 'In that case let's not meet at all!' And I'd walk away just like that. So you'd tell me, wouldn't you, if you were in that category?
– That's nonsensible (says Magnick). Everyone is someone you may not meet again. No one's bound to meet anyone again. Best thing, Violet, is to stay where you are, like I do, then it can't be your fault if people never meet you again, do you see? They call this corner The Magnick Corner.
– The balls they do (she whispers to me), only *he* does.
– Hey Mr Beers (he calls across), you watch yourself with Mistress Malagala, she's thirsty these days, you look.
– He's a terrible boy (says Violet), the way he calls me Violet and him so young. And the way he calls me Mistress Malagala and him so young. He doesn't know half of what some men know about me, but that's not much. He should just shut his face really, if I was his mother. You Badean born, as they say, hmm?
– No. no, in fact, no.
– Where then, tell.
– *Mainland-born, Badean-hanged.* Guess. *Clever boy.*
– Gamor.
– (Fishing-town) No.
– Saldeo.
– (Other side of the island?) No.

8

– Laquilla.

– (What the hell.) That's right.

– I knew it! I worked there for years.

– We travelled. We were never there.

– Oh neither were we! Never!

The afternoon wears on. Young Magnick becomes absorbed in a newspaper, which I resolve to read when he finishes. He never finishes. Violet reminisces about her childhood and buys me some more beer. The quiet smoking man, whose name is Stromberg, walks out suddenly and is replaced by an elegant silver-haired man, who orders a long glass of white Fortified and suggests it is time to watch the television.

– Is it *Carli* already? (Magnick queries him.)

– Go home for *Carli* (says the new man). There's news on now. Almighty commotion down on Avenue Maldeau. Crowds.

– Sod the crowds, Dr Fencile, what about Carli stuck in the Tomb of the Damned?

– You missed last night's (says Violet Maricolo). She got rescued from there by her real father. But the only way you can tell it's her real father is if he opens his –

– Shush! (cries the doctor, now working the volume control on the television set). I want to hear what's happening outside!

– (Cyrille says with a chuckle) You doctors, ain't enough you listen to our hearts, you want to listen to the whole world's hearts!

Violet mutters to me that he could just go outside to hear what's happening outside, but he gets his wish and we hear this.

'Residence officials are mystified as to what the Viceregal Party was doing on the Avenue Maldeau at all. The projected route of the Viceroy was out of the Hotel Marine, south along the Promenad Furasol, along the north shore on the

9

Way of Salute, then south along the Porodo and eastward on the Avenue Marchant. This would have taken the Party along the south perimeter *of* the Viceregal Gardens and the Residence itself, skirting the poor market district of Allalong, where the Avenue Maldeau is situated. What seems to have happened is that for reasons known only *to* themselves, the Party, consisting of the Viceroy and four Argeline security agents – a surprisingly small number *in* these volatile circumstances – took an unexpected right turn deep into Allalong, where we presume no police cordon had been erected. This is Roger Golli outside a very confused Viceregal Residence. Gordon.'

'Thank you, Roger. I'm Gordon Capka on the Porodo. There's still a great deal *of* bewilderment here, you might say panic. I don't know if you *can* see behind me but if you *can*, Roger, what you'll see is a large security presence for presumably, well, security reasons. Some officers have begun rounding up eyewitnesses *to* what appears to have been the apparent incident here this afternoon. We'll keep *you* up to date with the news as *and* when we have it. This is for now Gordon Capka for *Newshour* on the Porodo.'

– Ta and Ra to you, Vice-arooga (says Magnick, lifting his glass) Freedom for Badeo . . .

– Shut up! (the doctor hisses) We don't know what's happened!

Violet turns away from the screen and back to me. I'm sitting here sure in the knowledge that I do know what's happened. I have a right to. If it's true, I'm a dead man. *Probably is*, goes the death, shaking out some nuts, *so ya probably are*.

– Oh yes, we *do* know what's happened! (says Violet) They've put on a lot of ridiculous commercial breaks just when they were about to tell us something!

– Good Lord (says Dr Fencile), it's sounding like they took a shot at him.

10

– Four bodyguards? (cries Magnick in wonder) Four? Those Argelinos think we love 'em! That cheese couldn't have stayed on his feet with four *hundred* of the bleeders! For the last time, We Can't Stand You Bastards!

– Hey and that's enough in here (the barman says roughly): my people ain't all red-cheek rebels, boy. Here's Mr Frosch here, who we don't know what about.

– Let's ask him, shall we? (Magnick demands) You a flag-waver, Mr Beers? You like us being someone else's dominion?

– Well. I think it's a pity if there's been a . . . I hope no one's too injured.

Now leave me alone, all terrible strangers. My name is Burneau, I have a Papa and Momo, I live as a crossing-sentry in the uplands of the Koborol, patrolling my crossing in the shade of the Folded Mountain. We drink white-flower juice and dance with the shepherdesses in the fire-barn. We walk the high ridges. We talk of the great Argeline City. I took Jessigo and Laora to the cliff-edge and pointed out the smoke on the far horizon, though I couldn't really see it, or not until they said they could. I –

Am none of it no more. Not now the crowd closed on the Viceroy. Best bet is what? Go back and stand trial. Dereliction. Abandonment. Those if you're lucky. Else treason. Else high treason.

I'll go back and tell the truth. I was knocked down by the crowd. *Only it's not the truth. Tell 'em about the flame-haired girl.* I was lost in the crush. *Damn right you are, Burneau: you are absolutely lost.* The Viceroy will understand.

The Viceroy will understand, he's a gentle man and he liked me. *Well, let's hope he's conscious, then he can register his affection. And don't forget those other three bodyguards: remember they hate you. Adzell, Mace, Yung.* I know they do.

The news comes back on the screen now. I'm going to run

from this bar. I'm going to take my chance outside. I'm armed and I can run. I do not mean to die. Violet grabs me by the elbow.

– They're back! The *Newshour* team!

Magnick snorts into his cocktail.

– All liars and drunks, those Mainland hackers.

'Roger, why do you think the Viceroy chose to forgo the traditional motorcade for a new Argeline dignitary for this some might *say* foolhardy as indeed it now appears walkabout today?' 'Residence officials are talking guardedly Gordon and I stress guardedly *about* the Viceroy's stated intention to "get to know the simple Badean folk". What *does* remain as yet unclear is why having decided on this walkabout the Viceroy and his four bodyguards moved off the intended route and plunged one would have to use the word into some of the narrower and I think you could safely say more dangerous or problematic *from* a security angle streets *of* the Allalong district Gordon.' 'With only reports indicate four bodyguards?' 'Gordon, in fact we *have* been hearing only three bodyguards that's one *less* which would of course have been inadequate in the context *of* the, this, this thing that appears to have happened Gordon.'

– I can't remember (says Violet) have they said what thing happened yet?

– It's somethin' (says Cyrille). They got it way up high in the News. You OK there, Mr Frosch?

– Oh. I'm here, and there. You know me. *Ha! Nice one. Very well blended.*

– 'Simple Badean folk' (mutters Magnick) I hope they blew his brains out.

' . . . very much a sense of shock and to a certain extent disbelief. Earlier I could hear behind me a young woman saying "I can't believe this" which in a very real way says it all.

What we have here at the Gate of the Residence is families gathered here to wave to the new Viceroy as he was *to* have reached the Gates, very much a sense *of* loyalty to the Argeline Mainland and now not all that surprisingly a very *real* fear that the Mainland's suspicions about Badeo Island *in* the light of the recent attack on the New Badeo Excelsior are well-founded. Obviously a sense of anxiety about how the Mainland government might respond to what appears to have been the work *of* its opponents possibly and I do *say* only possibly those based around the south-west of the Island. Eyes to a degree are on the mountain if you can see it behind me, Mount San Timotheo, home to the bandits of the notorious Organ Liberat Badeon or OLB. Already some of these bystanders and I stress this *is* their opinion only are blaming this bandit group for the apparent outrage. There is I would have to say a feeling of anger directed at Furasol, the Island's second largest town, thought *by* many Badeans to be a haven for OLB guerrillas. Of course at such a time imaginations run riot so I stress this *is* only speculation; we would however advise Argeline citizens to avoid *if* possible the town of Furasol in the coming weeks. Meanwhile all we know for sure is that Viceroy Wallemire Lagland of Badeo is not going to be passing *through* these Gates today. This is Roger Golli at a subdued and I would have to say disappointed Viceregal Residence.'

– You all right there, Mr Frosch? (asks Cyrille to my face) You taking it bad?
– We don't know what it is yet, stupid (says Violet). We can't take it bad or even well till we know what it was. You have another drink, Mr Frosch. Have you got a first name I can call you?
His name is Maris. He looks pale because he deserted the Viceroy and something obviously happened to him. And because it means they'll shoot him for desertion. Which means, even you must know, you stupid gypsy woman, he'll

never get home to the Mainland. And, er, he'll never see his
people again. What else. Oh yes, his home, his friends, er . . .
Give me time, lady, there's oodles more.

– I should buy you another drink so you remember!

– Thank you. It will help me to.

– Why do you wear sunglasses in such a dark place as this,
I'll ask you while I'm buying your drink . . .

Take them off. You won't look like a bodyguard. *That's
right, take them off. Great disguise.*

– That's much better because you have nice eyes, you
know.

– Thank you, Violet. They're a little weak.

– Now you don't look like a security man!

– Oh. Good. Thank you. My eyes, you see, they're a
little –

She turns to barge the doctor on his stool.

– Oi, do we know what happened yet, doc?

– It's other news. They'll be coming back to it. Then
Lucien will marshal all the material back in the studio.

– Not today (says Magnick), today it'll be fat old Starbert.

– Oh I like him (says Violet), I've met him. Did you know
that, Frosch, I've met him.

A young man of about my age (I am a young man/*you
were a young man*) has rushed into the bar, and shouts:

– I saw it, boys, I saw it! Give the eyewitness a Tretners!

– *Sshh!* (says Dr Fencile) we're trying to watch the news
here!

– I was there, I tell you! History, boys!

– Will you be quiet?

While the regulars at All Afternoons watch a commercial
presentation for the gentlemen's clothes firm Fabilo, Violet
pulls the young man in his pale suit towards her at the bar
and murmurs:

– We're listening, Conny, what did you see?

– Viceroy, they shot him. Dead? Dunno. But he fell, like,
Madame Maricolo, he like fell and didn't get up.

– Who shot him?

– They did. Dunno. Suddenly there's guards everywhere.
Dr Fencile turns around angrily:
– *Not* according to the reports, young man.
– We got Roger (agrees Cyrille), he's sayin' there's only
three guards. No wonder they got him.
– Only three bodyguards! (pants the young man) But then
there's police all round! I saw bodies, I did. Whose? Dunno.
– Perhaps if you'd be quiet (says Dr Fencile loudly), we
might find out *exactly* what happened.
The regulars, who had begun to pay heed to the young
man, now turn indignantly back towards the television.
The death is the guest presenter.

' . . . main points of the news again with Starbert Loss.'
'The new Viceroy of Badeo was shot and wounded this
afternoon on a market street in the south of Badeo Town. He
remains in a critical condition in the Hospital Infanta. Three
bystanders were arrested at the scene. The Viceroy, Wallemire Lagland, seventy-seven, was on his inaugural visit to
Badeo Island, conducting an unscheduled public walkabout
in the commercial district of the Town when three shots were
fired at close range. Early reports suggest that one of the
Viceroy's personal bodyguards is unaccounted for, leading to
speculation that he may also have been shot, or even have
been connected in some way with the assassination attempt.
Residence officials will neither confirm or deny this. More
news will follow as *and* when – in fact it would appear – if
you'll excuse . . .'

– He's put his finger in his ear (Violet nudges me) that means
he's listening. It could mean there's more.
– She's right (sighs Cyrille), always with the ear.

'Reports just coming in we *think* and I stress that we only
think at this stage – no, is that confirmed? We are now receiving confirmation that Viceroy Wallemire Lagland has in

the last few minutes at the Hospital Infanta as a result of an attempted assassination we've been calling it sadly not just attempted any more I can confirm died in the last few minutes without regaining consciousness. And that, tonight, is the very latest report from the troubled Island of Badeo. Our thoughts are with, obviously, it, and the relatives of Viceroy Lagland, out to whom our hearts obviously go at this time. This is Starbert Loss at a very sad seven o'clock in the Argeline Domain wishing you a good night though perhaps in the circumstances for once not a very good one. Good night, all Argelinos.'

Good night, Starbert.
Good night, Maris. Sweet dreams.

II

I am lying in bed waiting for my lover, whose name is Violet
Maricolo, to enter the room. You could not say that our
affair has lasted a long time, but there is no denying the intensity of my feeling for her, this woman, my lover, Violet
Maricolo.

Go ahead. I'm not saying anything. Update me, do.

We met in unusual circumstances. We met at All Afternoons, that popular bar we both frequent, or were both
frequenting at the time we met. How do I remember the day?
Because it was the day they assassinated that dignitary sent
from the Mainland. Why can't they leave us alone? (is what I
think, along with all right-thinking Badeans) but yes, everyone seems to remember what he was doing that day. I, for
example, was drinking many glasses of Frosch, a beer of
which I have always been fond. People laugh when they hear
that my name is also Frosch, but it's really not surprising.
That's why I drink that beer. And that's what I was doing on
that day. Just another day on the Island of Badeo.

Uh-huh. Go on.

Well, all right, it was today, or yesterday. Yesterday, I suppose, as it must be gone midnight here. Here on the Avenue
Hali. Where we are. We met over beers, as we heard the terrible news, Violet and I. He was shot by some assassin and he
died in the Hospital Infanta, without regaining consciousness. I met a man who saw it happen, we both did. It's a bad
night for the Island, for all of us Islanders, because the Mainland won't be happy. But who wants to think about it? Better
to concentrate on the good things in life, like love, like my
lover: Violet Maricolo. 'Mr Frosch,' she always says, 'you're

17

just never going to tell me that old first name are you? To me you're Mister, and I call that fine!' Oh, how I love her, the things she says.

Finished? Well. Where on earth to begin? Your name isn't Frosch, it's Burneau. You're not, as you claim, a Badean, but a Mainlander from Gispar in the Koborol. Nor are you a poet, which you told her. Yes, you bloody well did. So you don't live in this City, you're not between places, you don't know where you are, you've got no papers, you've got no money, no way of sailing back, you're already a suspect in the killing and – what was the other one, tip of my teeth -

– Long time away, Mr Frosch! She rustles in in what sounds like a lot of material.)

Oh yes, you don't love her.

– Asleep, are we? Surely not so (she rustles near my side of the bed) when we've hardly met!

Don't be asleep, man, be dead. Call it practice.

I'm asleep, fast asleep. The day was too much, though I'm sorry to disappoint my lover Violet Maricolo, who has been so kind to offer me a roof over my spinning head in this time of great danger. What with the curfew they imposed at nine. What with the prospect of house-to-house searches without warning. What with the things I heard on the television, in those wretched abysmal hours that followed the announcement of the death of the Viceroy, as Violet ordered me more and more drinks, and we sagged and swayed together on the bar, gazing at history boldly and crudely in the making . . .

'What do we think about this man they're calling the "Lost Bodyguard", Gordon? Any ID on him?' 'No ID as yet though obviously when it comes we'll have a name for you in the meantime we have Colonel Delavila, who was with the Viceroy just prior to the incident and was lucky enough not to have been in any way, er, scathed . . .'

'I'm hearing reports we have a name now. Is it Bruno, Roger?' 'We do have a name Gordon but it's not Bruno it's

"Burno" I've got here, B-U-R-N-E-A-U, apparently, pronounced "Burno", but the Security Force perhaps not surprisingly have revealed few details about, um, Burno, other than that earlier confirmation that he has *not* I repeat *not* been accounted for . . .'

' . . . Going back to General Papler's point, is it possible that the OLB might have infiltrated Argeline Security to the extent of placing a terrorist among Viceroy Lagland's bodyguards?' 'Nothing has been ruled either in *or* out at this stage, Jorge, but I will say that there is some speculation concerning the origins of this Guardsman Burno. One of the surviving bodyguards, for instance, a Guardsman Adzell, is already on record as having had what he terms "grave suspicions" about the missing man, though he was not specific *about* the suspicions or indeed the gravity of them . . .'

Let me go on the television. I'll lay it all to rest. I'll take my gun and I'll – my gun! *Don't fret, I got it. I put it behind some books. This lady don't talk like she reads books so she'll never find it there.*

– You're not *really* asleep, are you, hmm? Poor Frosch. Too much Frosch! Or too much history!

She's touching my shoulder. If she tickles me I'll wake. *If she tickles you kill her. No, screw her then kill her.*

– I'm going to go and check on the children, I can hear them giggling through the wall. When I come back I'm going to wake you up, even, even, even, if it's just to say Good night, what with us so tired . . .

She rustles out. The death goes tinkling after her, imitating her walk. I wonder where the god is.

This is the god I have. Let me tell about the god I have. To whom, though? To the god I have?

The god I have I must have because of the death I have. I am aware of him most keenly when the death is at his most cutting. He is earnest, the god I have, and that irritates the death. The god I have is not always with me, I think, but he

19

never quite forgets me, and he leafs back through the book he reads to find my name. I always hope he does. I don't think it would make him happy for my thoughts to cease. I think he would look up from the book and say 'Oh' in a disappointed voice – like my father would in a similar situation, if his encyclopaedia failed to explain a problem to him – and a crowd would gather around the god I have, but not before he had closed the book, so they too would be disappointed, and resume their seats and their own books or tasks. I have always had much faith that my thoughts would continue, that my life would continue, because I cannot clearly imagine what the god I have would do without them. I see him trudging round the woods, stooping to pick up a branch, believing in nothing. What would happen instead, I am sure, is that one of the crowd would run out after him with my book in his hand, and, riffling through the pages, say, 'Here he is, you missed him, he's there, he's just in bed! He's tucked up in a bed in the Avenue Hali with some woman!' The god I have would soon be back in his seat, frowning, or smiling, in this case I would think frowning at the distance I have come from home, but either way engrossed and not to be disturbed.

Well, it makes me unafraid. Other people talk to me of gods who see everything all the time but I don't think mine does and I don't think he would want to. He seems content from time to time to follow my adventures. I hope he will follow this one; I think he will if he hears of it. I would like to be alone with him, but it's that that is impossible. The death, who is illiterate, will not have it so.

So I am alone for a while, truly alone. I hear Violet speaking to one of her children, then a pause, then her whispering to the other. Paol and Juilla. I saw them only very briefly, when we got back here before the curfew. The boy Paol, who is about fourteen, was watching television. He jumped up and said '*Pkaow*! I shot you!' Violet imposed her own curfew at once. The girl Juilla I glimpsed very briefly, as she opened her bedroom door, saw me with Violet, and closed it. I noted that she was pretty, had much softer, rounder features than Violet, and hair that curved about her face in an almond shape. She was recently seventeen. Violet mentioned that Juilla would probably hate me for ever but that was her choice. I agreed absolutely. Their father is in jail on the Mainland, and Violet has not said why. 'It can't be easy,' I said, meaning for them. 'It's his fault, he did it,' she replied.

We sat in the bright kitchen and ate the remains of a fish stew ('I love this,' I ventured. 'It's Jula's. She hasn't a clue,' Violet said, spilling some down her chin. But I did love it, I wasn't just saying so.) Then we drank two mugs of red Forti-fied in the living room, on different chairs, until we got too tired to talk or hear each other. She showed me to the bed, then she went to the bathroom. I'm lost but I'm still alive.

Not only am I still alive, I am in warm pink sheets in a nice little flat. Without the death, and without the god, and with-out Violet Maricolo, who in my loneliness I confess I do not love especially, I am going to have to concentrate on the level plain of the details. What else can I do? I am nailed here like the Island itself, and past and future wash around like black oceans charring white where they meet me.

She turns three keys and we walk through the door, 16 on the Avenue Hali. And there's a dark tiny hallway, with four doors to choose from. I think, and I may be wrong about this, that the children's rooms are the ones on the left, the kitchen is straight ahead, and the living room is on the right. This bedroom is reached through the living room. I have noticed a small handful of things. For one, there are no fitted carpets, only huge rugs lying about. Violet is a cloth trader, I remember. There are great cushions all around, and fashion or bridal magazines everywhere. The kitchen machines are all different colours, which Violet stressed was her own idea. There are posters on the walls, some for fashion displays, some for exhibitions. They all seem to be from a long time ago. There's no clue about the father, except that his name is Gando Maricolo, because it's printed beside the door. Only the living room and this bedroom have windows on the outside world, two floors down, the darkness of Avenue Hali under curfew. If you almost shut your eyes you can see the pale markings of three great lanes on the street and the elongated words GAMOR, CENT., UNI. The place is not so clean. It's not like home. It's not home.

Home.

What have I got to my name, that I can say it's not clean? But it makes me melancholy to stumble on strange lives. It does not lessen my despair that I can despair in safety a while. I wonder where the flame-haired girl is. She could explain why it is I had to see her. Why it is this has to have been. If she could explain why I had to catch her eye, she could explain to the Viceroy why this had to be his last day in the world. It was his last day in the world. Sleep, Burneau. Roll down the green slope, watch the cottages spin through the sky, roll through the fanflowers, roll and rest panting in the soil, feel sunlight. Keep moving. Mustn't burn. Mustn't burn now, Maris.

In the morning, when the curfew lifts, I will make my way across the city to the Viceregal Residence, surrender myself to the Viceroy's Chief of Staff, and explain to him that I was kidnapped and maltreated by the cruel bandits of the OLB. Organ Liberat Badeon. Those must be Badean dialect words, like the helmsman spoke on the boat that sailed here. *Ca ci ta Bathean inciul!* I wonder where he is, on the ocean or at a port. I'll tell the Chief of Staff about the bandits. They knocked me down on an avenue. Which avenue? Way of Limes, I remember. That's my plan. I toss and turn in this great bed, and there must be one or two potential flaws to my plan but I can't think of any.

Violet is whistling through the flat. Why, when she wants her children to sleep? She comes in with everything. The death has borrowed her husband's green gown so it can go: *One. You have to get across the city and there are police and security agents everywhere. Two. You have only your bodyguard suit, and they'll find your gun when they search you.*

22

*So they'll arrest you. Three. If the OLB shot the Viceroy
they'll want to claim responsibility so they'll say they don't
know who the hell you are. Four. If the OLB didn't shoot the
Viceroy but still want to claim responsibility they'll say the
same because you'll merely be in their way, and the Domain
would prefer to believe them than believe you. It gives them a
reason to bust that town Furasol, and it lets their crappy
Security off the hook. Five. If the OLB had nothing to do
with it and want nothing to do with it, then the last thing
they need is some loser slinging their name about. Six. If they
are professional terrorists, they don't want anyone claiming
he escaped from them, or that he was maltreated, for that
matter. Seven. OK, it gets easier. You don't know your way
across the fucking city. Eight. This smashed old cow saw you
and so did her kids. Nine. You've got no balls. Ten. Oh I'm
tired. Go to sleep. Shit plan.*

    – You're awake. He's awake!

She does it. She tickles me under the arms. I scream and sit
up. She is, remember, my lover. We are always doing this!

    – You were awake all the time!

    – Well, you know me. I'm always awake all the time.

    – I'm not going to bother you now (she says as she climbs
over to her side of the bed. She wears a long nightgown of
red silk, and her black frizzy hair tumbles around her
shoulders.)

    – No?

    – I'm not going to bother you because I don't really know
you yet, hmm? That's surprised you, hasn't it? That.

    – Well, it's very late. It's been a long day. (When it began I
was standing on the same land as my family. Now the ocean
is all around for miles, oh mercy.)

She pulls me towards her, hugs me and kisses my cheek.
She smells of some wild flowers, scarlet I think, that grow
further down the mountain, but the colour might be her
nightgown. She smells also faintly of the drinking, but she's
tried to scrub that out.

– Tomorrow we'll start (she says, whatever that means) tomorrow we'll start to learn things, hmm, but for now, dreamland . . .

She sinks back upon her pillows, with her dark eyes staring at the ceiling. She asks me:

– Why that bar, Mr Frosch? Why d'you find me there?

– You know me, Violet. Always searching (I say, whatever that means) always searching . . .

When I next look at her she has closed her eyes. I think she is asleep, but as I sink back myself she asks me to switch the lights off. I get out of bed and do so, groping back to the sheets. When I ask her if I might stay a while, she makes no reply. I am left completely blind as to whether I have offended her or asked a question of somebody who is unconscious.

Ask me questions. I'm unconscious. If I'm Frosch, I have no past. If I'm Burneau, no future. So ask me questions, do your sarcastic, clever-boy worst, for I'm nobody and I'm frightened but I'm far away and the hours last for ever.

What you tell her? I told her I was a poet.

– You're a what? (she said with a glare as Cyrille passed up a cloth to mop up our mess).

– Oh yes, that's my trade. Poetry.

– Can you live like that?

– No. I survive on my inheritance.

– Oh yes? (she leaned very close) You have an inheritance?

– I do, Violet. From my parents.

– How much, if you don't mind me?

– Oh enough.

– Oh enough he says, and me buying him all his drinks.

– I mean enough to live on without food or heating. Drink is all I ever buy. Oh and of course paper and writing materials. For the poems, obviously.

– You look well on it. Another inheritance, hmm?

– Well, yes.

– Say a poem.

24

– What?

– Or is that work? Saying a poem. Just one?

– It's work.

– That's a shame.

– I'll say one later.

– Do as you please, stranger, do as you please.

I've thought of one now, just in case I face that situation again. After all, she won't know it's just my life I made it out of:

> I stand high up on a mountain! I fold my arms in the
> > wind!
> Then I wave them both! At someone who is on her way!
> Towards me, with her sheep beside her!
> And her dog, Trapper!
> What a lovely sight she is! What a lovely sight it all is!

That's the style of our village poets. She'd never recognise it. She might enjoy that one, I think, because I remember her saying how she wished she lived in the mountains some-where. Maybe I can think of some others that involve things she wishes.

The death taps me. He's got one:

> *You stand against a wall!*
> *Ten soldiers are pointing bolt-action DK-85s at you!*
> *Never mind! At least you'll get a poem out of it!*
> *Bang!*

Oh, sleep. Oh, sleep. Then what, though. Daylight. Searches. News.

Your picture on the television.

Oh, mercy. Oh, sleep.

Manhunt.

Oh, mercy.

– I'll not make it home (I told her, as *Newshour* reported

25

the imposing of the curfew and All Afternoons began rapidly
to empty of customers), I'll not make it home to my hostel,
Violet.

– Where is that, Frosch?

– It's in – the extreme north region (I incoherently
hazarded).

– The docks, you mean?

– Miles, miles up there. Freezing, it is. Woo.

– No, you won't make that. *We* . . . are going to settle up
with *you*, Cyrille, and *we* are going back to mine. *Not*, I'd
like to say to the assembled (who weren't listening) for any
unseemly purposes, but to protect poor Mr Frosch from the
ghastly police and his cold cold bed!

– It's very kind of you (because I'm dead if you don't do
that) and of course I'll pay for everything next time! (There
won't be a next time.)

– You will, Mr Frosch, though this has been my *treat*!

I remember very little right after that, but we were on an
underground train. There was a station called UNIVERSITY in
blue letters and then a plaza to walk across, where young
policemen were everywhere, and flower sellers being hustled
away, then a station called CURO in red letters, where Violet
had to wake me up and march me out into the city. The night
was nearly down by then, blue and misty as if enacting the
curfew, with well-fed men hurrying home, lamps going off in
warm-looking upper rooms, and all, I remember, being
filmed with this acrid van-oil stink, thick tobacco smoke, and
rain freckling the air. When Violet told me it was the rain she
had seen coming, I was quite swallowed up by a sense of
enormous loss and displacement, and had to cough to mask
the onrush of tears. For it was then that I thought of the Viceroy in the sunshine of his cabin that morning, cheerfully
expounding his theory that all islands were like women, and
it was then that I thought of everything, which I have
realised, I really have realised regardless of all my choking,
laughing, gracelessly squabbling voices, is gone now.

26

Not everything. Burneau. Not everything. Not you. You ain't come so far from home to be hauled off to some dungeon. But, oh, you will be, matey, and that'll be that'll be that. There'll be other crossing-sentries, there'll be other lonely ladies sleeping in silk red nightgowns, other deaths, other gods, other men like you. But they don't end. Only you end. Love doesn't end. Your love ends. Here, here on the edge of that cliff here's a lady in a silk red gown, a drunken lady who bought you drinks and all but carried you here. Touched you on the thundering train, your leg, thought you forgot? Was staring when you glanced. Kissed you here in the bed. Lying here, here, here, breathing, barely sleeping. You going to lie here till the arclights find you? Accomplice. Assassin. Virgin. Fool. Do her. Touch. For me. For me now.

– Violet.

Louder. Louder. Die happy like I do.

– Violet!

– Wha – ? (she sits up, blank, she was asleep.) What?

– It's me, it's Frosch?

– Oh! Love. Hello. What's the time . . . oh but it's hardly – mister, you have a bad dream?

– I'm – I'm – *He's a virgin.* I'm – I mean my name isn't –

– Isn't what? Isn't Frosch?

– No! No – yes, it is Frosch.

– So. What isn't it?

– Well. Nothing. Nothing really. I did have a bad dream.

– Was I in the bad dream?

– No. You weren't in it. It was a thing I was alone in.

– You're not alone now, though.

Violet draws me to her and we embrace. My face is buried in her tickling hair, then I feel her relax away. I expect to be able to kiss her, I am filling up with excitement, but her eyes are closed again and she is gone, quite gone. I believe it is right for me to stay here in her arms, so as not to wake her.

The death thinks so too, whose joke it was.

So I am lying in the arms of my lover, Violet Maricolo. The

air is dark with wine and red flowers. The whole of the Island of Badeo is under a curfew because the Viceroy was assassinated. It's my curfew. The only sound in it is my breath and Violet's. I believe I would have saved him. I believe I would have been a hero. As things have turned out, I am a murder suspect, and could be hanged in time. Fine. Could have been one thing, turned out to be the other. Good first day? *No, bad.* Saved him? *No, abandoned him.* Hero? *No, hanged.* Oh well. *Drink?* Thank you. *Frosch?* Frosch. Frosch it is. Frosch it is. Frosch it is then.

III

– Let's stop here, says the Viceroy.
  – Let's not, says Adzell.
  – Why ever not? says the Viceroy.
  – A million reasons. Look at it.
  – It's a lovely old square, that's what I see.
  – There's people, sir, there's people. Those kind of people.
  – I want to meet those people.
  – You don't want to meet those people. Believe me on this, sir.

– Then let's stop here, says the Viceroy.
  – Jokin', sir? says Mace.
  – Dead serious, young fellow, right here in the shade.
  – Better keep movin', sir, don't you reckon?
  – On the contrary, Mr Mace, I should like to stop here, take a breath, get my bearings, meet some folks. It's new to me.
  – It's new to them, sir. They don't all like it.
  – Who says they have to?
  – Don't stop here, sir.

– How's this feel, Mr Yung?
  – Lonely, master Viceroy.
  – Dangerous in your opinion?
  – Lonely, master Viceroy.
  – The oracle has spoken, says the Viceroy. On we go.

– Here then, by this exquisite fountain. Exquisite, Mr Burneau, do you think would be the word?
  – Yes that's just what it would be.
  – Well said, Mr B.

29

– He would say that, sir. He's new to this business.

– Is life exquisite only when one is new to this business? What a notion. May I stop here, Mr Adzell?

– I'd incline to No, sir.

– Mr Mace?

– Dead not. It's unexpected, sir.

– Mr Yung?

– No wise. Dangerous and lonely.

– Mr Burneau, surely you? I mean, smell the leaves here, will you only smell the leaves? Valecunda, that's called.

– I imagine it's safe, sir.

– Then I'm decided.

– But you die here, sir.

– Valecunda. Hmm. 'The sobbing tree . . .'

– You're shot. I saw it. It's already happened.

– I'm nevertheless decided. Will you only smell those leaves? Valecunda, that's called, 'the sobbing tree . . .'

By the time I know where I am, I am aware I am alone. The gap in the curtains shows the day low and cloudy and I get out of bed, returning to read the note that Violet – the woman whom I befriended in the bar All Afternoons – has written and left for me.

'Taken J and P to school then at work till 5. Make my home like your home. There is no need to wake up yet. Your friend Violet M xxx.'

Make my home like your home. Well, I'll just push open your door then and run through the meadows! I'll be at the high crest before you can say Frosch! Make my home like your home. I'll just live here for ever then, I'll wish away the ocean. I'll pick . . . valecunda. No such thing. Like Viceroy Wallemire Lagland. Maris Burneau. xxx.

My gun is where I hid it. I pick it up, check its action, put it back behind a fat book called *The Examination of Candidates in Law*, and a tall book called *Fish Cooking for High Numbers*, and go to the kitchen. There's some lemon drink

in the fridge, a half-good apple and some bread, which I but-
ter and eat four pieces of. Make my home like your home.
My head is aching, and my heart beats terribly fast. Make my
home like your home. I am seized by an uncontrollable desire
to know everything about the people who live here. I do not
see how otherwise I can make their home like my home.
Though this desire is uncontrollable, it is superseded by the
desire to delay doing anything. I go into the living room, sit
down with my lemon drink, pick up this remote controller
they've got and switch on the television.

'Don't believe a word, Josefina. More from our duckbilled
friends a little later. Plenty still to come. You're watching
Lora Cato and *Network Argelino* first for news and first for
stars on a very cloudy yuk brr morning *over* the Domain
good morning to you out there *it's* just coming up to 9.30 the
latest news on the half-hour you're looking very dapper this
morning Rodney?' '*That* was no ordinary launching, Lora!'
'Sounds like me all over!' 'Get back to you on that one. This
is Rodney Toll *with* the latest headlines from the Network:
Security Spokesperson Dagmar Frock appeals for calm on
the tragic island of Badeo, as a curfew imposed in the wake
of the murder *of* Viceroy Wallemire Lagland is broken in
Furasol, Saldeo *and* the capital last night. Some three thousand troops are arriving from the Mainland to restore order.
The Security Committee are interviewing the two men
wounded one seriously *at* the scene of the shooting. And, *no
news* this morning of Mystery Missing Man a few ems there
who just *might* hold the key, as agents travel to the remote
Koborol region in search of information. That's our lead
story coming up a little later *I'm* Rodney Toll here comes
Morona Plack on the Highway Gamor I hope not *on* the
Highway Gamor it's just gone 9.30 . . .'

*You live in the Koborol. You wish you were those agents.
You know where they're going. They're going to Helder,*

where the Central Authority for the regions of the Koborol keeps birth certificates and photographs of all who reside there. You were born there. There's a picture of you. There's a picture of me, only they glued your face on it. They'll be back from Helder by the end of the day with a black-and-white death-warrant. We'll be stars at sunset. So that's the time you have. Let's hear your plan.

I am going to hide here, here on the Avenue Hali. This woman will help me. *She don't know you need help.*

Then I'll tell her who I am. *She'll panic and blow the whistle.*

I won't tell her. I'll stay here because she likes me. *And what about the house-to-house searches? Soldiers come when nothing happens.*

We'll think of something. *Do, by all means.*

The death changes channels. Different people telling the same story. It's like a camera gliding through a graveyard, only not yet focused enough to show that every headstone has my name on it. I meet the Viceroy, interviewed in his garden – perhaps a year ago? – with his wife Elesse behind him, raking.

– Oh it beats politics. Thing is, I like it too much. I have to be if you like prised away from here! Look at this. This is called Flowering Wild, but it's after a man named Wild, it's not actually wild at all. Wilson Wild. A man from Creekford, I believe. Wilson Wild. Lavender petals, see. Spring blossom, I think, Lessie?

– That's right, says his wife without looking up from her raking.

– A spring blossom, look.

A white-haired old man is beaming in a library. He has in front of him an illuminated manuscript, like ours in – in our sanctuary.

– He could tell you truths that were unpalatable, you know, but the way he told them, he rather found a way of making them sound quite acceptable, even friendly, and in that way, yes, he was very much the politician.

The Viceroy in uniform, blue and gold and black, shaking hands with some Ptopolino chancer.

– Lagland took little credit at the time for his negotiations behind-the-scene with the Ptopoline businessman Srahi Mneppe during the Glass River Crisis, but it is now generally accepted that his diplomacy was significant in –

The death instinctively switches stations and I meet my erstwhile colleague Mace, standing there right where we were yesterday, one of those shady plazas in Allalong.

– . . . whether he was.

– But you think he had dropped behind?

– First thing I notice, right? There's Adzell, right? There's Yung. And my Man is, like, there, so like Burno should be like, at that point, at this angle, facing that way. Right?

– And he's not.

– What do you reckon.

– He's disappeared at this time?

– Is what I'm sayin'. Is what I'm sayin'. Is what I'm tellin' your Island people. Is what I'm tellin' the Investigatress, right? He's gone. Dust. Nowhere's where Bruno was, nowhere and quote me.

– Does this not lend credence to the theory that he was in fact in some way assaulted *before* you reached this point – rather than suggest he was an accomplice, or indeed that he –

– No it don't. No. 'Cos also, like there's too many things about the guy that just, don't, you know? Add up?

– So you never actually saw him on this plaza?

– Well, I weren't lookin' for him, was I? I's lookin' out for my Man the Viceroy. Now, you tell me, where was he hit?

– Further along, yes? Towards the Avenue –

– No, on the body like.

– The Viceroy was hit through the back, on the right side.

– Blind spot. That's Burno's wall, see? Walls, we call 'em. Right and rear he was. I's left and front. Burno's right and rear.

– Guardsman Mace, you must be a very angry and disappointed man.

– Tell me about it.

– I'm sorry?

– Tell me about it.

– Well, absolutely . . . Now where, just for a moment putting yourself in the same position as Maris Burneau, if indeed he was let's say for the moment instrumental in the execution of this attack, and this I stress is only speculation, where do you think he might be now?

– Now? Makes no odds. You'll find 'im.

– Ye-es. What about the wider issue. Do you think an armed uprising is likelier now than it was say at this time yesterday?

– Makes no odds what I think. I'm paid to save lives. I don't like to see my Man go down. That's all. Don't like it.

'An interview recorded this morning with one of the three loyal bodyguards who survived the assassination of Viceroy Wallemire Lagland. Out there, somewhere, the fourth is hiding. The Security Department expects to produce a likeness of the man *in* the next hour or so, and an actual photograph later in the day *from* the remote region of the Koborol *from* where hailed this we only speculate murderous traitor Maris Burneau. General Papler, if I might bring you in here . . .'

The telephone rings! Don't touch it. You're not here. It must be Violet! Don't risk it, don't risk it. It rings sixteen and a half times. I sit here, not here. Then I wander, exhausted by that terrible cannonade of bells, back to the room I awoke in. Here's the window that affords the best view of the city. I stare down, trembling, at the street below, see people walking briskly by, a couple of black vans speed through, changing lanes from CENT to GAMOR. A man sells pale green newspapers. Then I look across the rooftops and aerials opposite, at chapel towers and living blocks in most directions, even some tall red trees not far away to the right. To the left is the cluster of high buildings, the centre of Badeo Town. Allalong must be beyond that area, the harbour even further. The ocean, however, is visible straight ahead, perhaps just half a mile off, a grey leaden strip with a highway skirting it below. I remember from the maps we were given that this city lies on a headland, a jut, with the ocean north and Badeo Bay to the south. The centre, the markets, the hotels, the Viceregal Residence and Gardens, that's all towards the western extremity. That's where we docked yesterday. This time yesterday I was on the sea, with the Viceroy reminiscing and the three bodyguards hunched together in the corner of the foredeck endlessly playing their games of Scissors-Paper-Stone. They would not let me play with them because I sometimes won.

Out of the living room, though still in earshot of the television, I feel myself succumbing to terrible curiosity once more, and soon find myself at the door of the room with JUILLA written on it. I open it.

The death is sitting on the bed.

You'll like it in here. Hot and sweet. Cute little person. Take a look at this diary. All crosses and love hearts. 'Round to num 72 for goodbye party for Karil. G there dresses like Carli but did no gd. Met Reba from Av Glazi said I cd come on Forest Laq trip. PG going? Shame! Strawbry hat. ND/JM yes. Mom late with pale man.' *You, dat man.*

A framed photograph of a grey-haired gentleman, thin, moustached, bespectacled. Her father Gando? He doesn't look like a man Violet would like, or a man who'd be in prison. There's a poster of some young men, all in black jackets, standing in a group scowling. There are signatures across all of their legs. They must be a close group of friends. A clock with the cracked face of a moon. A glass of some kind of pale pink fluid. A bracelet. A silver-white dressing-gown crumpled on the unmade bed. Black socks and light blue underwear on the dizzying carpet. Up there there's a calendar with pictures for the months: some brooks, a water-fall, a well, all in a gentle, grassy region, unfamiliar. Nothing written on the oblongs of the days.

Ain't it just like home, eh, save it still exists. And look through this wardrobe, you ever feel so warm, old pale man? You ever feel so keen on getting home unhanged?

I'm getting out of here. *Why not wait for the searches?*

I'll get out into the countryside. *So pick me some Flowering Wilson.*

There's a person in the corridor. *That'll be them now.*

I duck out of the girl's room and go across to the living room. The television screen reads WALLEMIRE J. LAGLAND, LAST OF THE PEACEMAKERS as I switch it off and hear a key turn in the lock. I sit down in one of the chairs and stare, frozen, at the blank screen. Whoever comes in puts something down in the hallway. It clanks like bottles. The person goes into one of the children's bedrooms and I feel I should have a gun in my hand. By the time I have stood up and begun to walk across to the bookshelf, the daughter Juilla, whose room I was just standing in, is standing in the door-way. She's wearing an amber shirt and black skirt, and her hair is tied in a ponytail. So recently was I in her room, look-ing and reading through her things, that I find it impossible to believe that that is not the explanation for the filthy look she is giving me now. What it's easy to forget is the might of untruth. Give me some time and I will make this girl believe a hundred lies, like her mother does. If she says I was in her room I am going to say I was not. She sniffs.

– I'm ill. I'm not at all well. Go away from here. Unless maybe you want it.

Then she turns and goes back to her room, locking the door behind her. I find myself taking the telephone off the hook.

Want It, want It, want It! IT is the illness. Fool. Virgin.

I don't think she looks ill at all. She looks very well. She's a truant. She's lying. *Well, ain't that thoroughly evil?*

When I switch the television on again a man in a red jacket is presenting the newscast in front of the words NO NEWS in great black letters with cracks all down them like they were old slabs.

' . . . return as soon as we can to that story. This is Dennis Flames and Midday Roundup there is *no news* on the whereabouts of missing Security Guardsman Maris Burneau, the Koborol uplander wanted in connection with the assassination of Viceroy Wallemire Lagland, *no news* on his possible membership of the terrorist group known as the OLB, and *no news* on the so-called Wounded Two, still seriously injured in the Hospital Infanta . . .'

Off it goes so I can think. Off it stays while I sit here and fail to. Nothing from Juilla's room, and even the death is quiet. His quiet, it *means* though, always. This time it means *Listen to your chance of making it through this shit.* His way of making a 0 with fingers he hasn't got. Your chance? 0. Your chance? 0.

The god shakes his head. It is not a number he understands. Three, yes. Seven, yes. A hundred and one. Nine thousand and nine. Whether he is near the beginning of the book or the end, he can find no record of a page 0. He is prepared to accept that it can be believed in, but he shrugs and says alas he cannot. The other people look up for a moment, then go on with what they were doing. They hear a page turn.

There are ways.

If I stay here and do nothing, there are two things that may happen first. Someone in the Maricolo family will see my likeness or my photograph on this television. Or soldiers will arrive on the Avenue Hali and arrest me for having no documents.

Taking the first one first: I could disconnect the television. But I need to see it. I need to know how close it's getting. And out in the town, the children or Violet could see my picture anywhere. So: they see me, they recognise me.

If they see me I have to draw the gun on them, then they'll do as I say. Would I use it? No. But do they know that? No. So they would do as I say. When they recognise me I'll draw the gun on them.

Then what? Sun's come out. I'm tired. I'm only just up! but no I'm tired all right. So . . .

Then what. Then: keep them together. Be kind. Be pleasant. Don't frighten them. Then they'll do the next thing. The next thing is obvious, isn't it. What. What. Force them, force them, to provide me with an identity. Visiting relative, caught in curfew. Papers lost. They can change my hair, I can grow a beard, yes. Violet can go out and buy me clothes.

What if she calls the police? Easy. I keep the children with me. Hostage. If one person goes out, two stay in with me. Easy. She's not ill at all, that Juilla. I wonder what she's doing. Writing in her diary, probably. 'Pale man watching tv. Hate him f'ever.' It's wrong to hate someone for ever when you've only just met them. Sorry, but that's what I think. Perhaps she is ill, though, and that lessens her tolerance of strangers. Fair enough.

Three? Four? Whatever. Is the phone off the hook? Yes. Cut the wire. No, pull it, there. Nothing too drastic. Just won't work now.

Now, if I fool the soldiers with the new identity, I can stay here for as long as I like, keeping the family hostage, keeping them happy. That's good, that. I'll be someone else, not Frosch. Not even Frosch, who I'm not anyway. Just have to stay out of that bar, keep the little secret with the Maricolo family. Fine. Good!

Oh. What about sleep? My thoughts will wander, the sunlight get to my cheek like now, my eyes will close, open, close, and that'll be it! They'll tiptoe clear of me, out of 16 Avenue Hali and straight to the first Security Post. So . . .

I do have to love her. Sit up. I do have to love her. She has to want to save my life! Somebody has to want, that much, to save my life! They all do! Then, then, if they all love me, love me – if they all love me – I won't need the gun again, I'll have the new identity, I can move about, get new papers somehow, sail back to the Mainland when the search is called off! I will see home again!

Is it my turn yet? No!!! *OK, keep your head on.*

I'll take the rickety old Journeyman coach, five days to the Vale of Koborol, take the funicular up the south side of Mont Adepte, joking with the farm workers, stroll the last ten miles to the Gispar Plateau, by the high crest, home on the seventh day after starting! The wood smell of the porch! The logs piled up, the fire lit inside!

. . . etc . . .

The table set, the plates hot, the oven . . . Well. I need these Maricolos. I won't make it alone. If the police come before the family knows who I am, they won't protect me because they won't know I'm wanted. I'm just some man from a hostel in the harbour. So – might as well tell them now, tell them, draw the gun on them and say. Sooner I do that sooner I can work on some – some convincing disguise, some credible identity . . . Tell them. Go, knock on Juilla's door and tell her you've something to say . . . but that's too soon, I mean she doesn't even like me. I'm alone, I'm a man, I have to sleep, don't forget that – they have to love me first. They have to love me first.

That's going to take a million years, with all due respect.

Go on then. I'll sit here. I'll sit here in the sun, bloody mortal, bloody doomed. You do and say it all, friend, you suck me out from inside.

Thanks. Have you any idea how much dosh the Government is going to offer yon ordinary citizen for information about aforesaid Maris Burneau? Enough for a rocket-launcher for the boy, three thousand strawberry hats for the girl, plus silk knickers laid end to end nine times round the

globe, and for Violet, well, a sea of Frosch, a lake of red For-
tified, a prince for a second husband, half the Viceregal
Gardens. They all have to weigh those little incentives
against the love of a drunken stranger, also penniless, jobless,
homeless, hatless, documentless, mapless, hopeless, gutless,
what else, help out here . . . anyroad. You think about it.
Also, also, yeah you drop off in the sunshine, you do that,
Burneau, you doze, you burn, but also, also: what kind of
love is it that draws a gun on a woman and two kids? True,
in normal circs I would give not a flying fuck, sir, but you
cannot call this the act of a lovable man. No. I've got a plan.
You want to pick up that shooter of yours, tiptoe out the
door, check all the soldiers and policemen and agents in the
world are on their lunch break, then go haring out through
Badeo City and chance it like a hero! Ha!

— What are you laughing at?

I open my eyes and Juilla is where she was before, in the
doorway, now wrapped in the silver-white gown I saw
draped across her bed. Her eyes are blazing, her hair is all
plastered, electric, she's been sleeping on it.

— Was I laughing too loudly? Did I wake you up?

— No. I stayed asleep. I stayed in my room. I'm not here.
Huh.

— I'm just — waiting for Violet, your mother.

— So that's her name. Wondered.

— She left me a note, saying she'd be back at midday. I
didn't expect you home.

— It's my home, mister. I'm always expected. You're not
expected. You'll catch my fever.

— How are you feeling?

— Pissy. I hope you don't get it. Who are you?

— My name's Frosch.

— You from that drinks bar?

— Yes, or no, but I met your mother there.

— I hate it, it's dark. Everyone there, they're finished. Pch.
Na more.

– But they're friendly people.

– Don't matter if you're finished.

– Am I finished, do you think?

Juilla rests her upper teeth on her lower lip and contemplates me for a moment.

– Mm-hmm.

– Oh well.

– Sorry, you asked me. Why's the TV off?

– I was sitting here thinking.

She frowns, then sniffs. She looks perfectly all right.

– Thinking about what then?

– Death, mainly.

– Death? (she says as if the concept is new to her) death you were thinking of? Sign of being finished. Press the blue switch.

– That's On, is it?

– Mm-hmm.

– It's mainly news programmes just now. All very boring!

– You think? So do I.

– All those faces and reports.

– Press blue then press 4. It's a music station. Then press Up on the sound so I can make my lunch and listen.

– You feel up to some lunch?

– You got to feed a fever, mister.

– Is that right?

– It's a rare fever. Got a long name. Lasts days. Press blue then press 4 then press Up. Hey I'll do it –

– I'll do it.

I press blue.

' . . . possibility of two separate assassins firing from – '

I press 4, and I see Juilla's group of five friends in black jackets all wearing those black jackets and singing a song together on a windswept hillside. They keep singing 'So la raina, so la raina'.

– So la raina! (sings Juilla Maricolo) So la raina mi mi oo!

– Do you know them? (I wonder, as I watch the death dance all around her, matching her steps.)

– So la raina! Yes, I love them! He's my favourite, in the black?

– Oh yes. He looks nice.

– My friend likes that one.

– I prefer your one. How do you know them?

I ask, but I look up and she's gone through to the kitchen, opening cupboard doors then singing loudly in her rare fever. The death is on the screen again, donning a black jacket like Juilla's friends, singing 'So la raina mi mi oo!' then creeping conspiratorially into the foreground to say:

Brave start, Burneau! I think she really loves you! Cake, it's going to be from this point! Cake! Cake! Cake!

IV

It is the exact middle of the afternoon. How do I know that? This is how I know that:

Everybody is elsewhere. The satisfaction of eating at midday has worn off, but has not been replaced by a desire to eat any more. Midday seems an afternoon ago, the evening seems an afternoon away. I am alone in a bed. It is cloudy in such a way that it is neither light enough to improve my mood nor dark enough to rouse me to initiative. The girl, the god and the death are absent, one in her room, one in his woods, one plucking souvenir postcards from the pavement cafés of Badeo Town. These absences remove the three possibilities of an extreme conclusion to my plight, and make the likeliest outcome dull, predictable and yet wholly impossible to foresee. In retrospect it will have been the obvious thing to have happened. But now, it is the exact middle of the afternoon. Time is snoring deep in men's hearts. Everybody is elsewhere doing the thing that he is paid for. Everything is true, but what's true is beside the point. Everywhere are places where something must happen soon.

Somewhere the Viceroy is, for the first time, restless in Heaven. Those who died yesterday and are safely installed in the Other Place, they have realised right now.

This is not a time to catch a neighbour's eye. It is not a good time to hope or pray, but nor is it appropriate to fear the very worst. Memories are inevitable, but their scenes are poorly enacted, unconvincing: it doesn't seem likely that things came about that way. The future is no more skilfully presented. It is so flimsy as to be cartoonlike. Even its protagonists have trouble believing the speeches the heart has

43

written them. The air is just too thick with the present, and that is almost touchable, bulging at the senses, endlessly, gauchely repeating its one idea. In the middle of the afternoon the names of folk and objects all but liquefy, or reconstitute into black marks here like filings, or tiny choices of my tongue. They become mere ways of making do until their real natures are known. This is why it is a time when decisions are pointless: nothing's constant enough. A sum can't be made out of rising and falling numbers.

This is the point where light and darkness circle one another, so that often it seems to get lighter later on. And it's the one time when the weight of the body exceeds the weight of the mind, so that citizens sleep if they can do so where they are. And the one place where the old are herded up, the children gathered together, and the people in between left lone and bewildered. The middle-aged people and the young men and women, lone and bewildered, are most likely to speak the truth, but least likely to address it to any. Only the self is listening, and the self is half listening. It is the closest day gets to being the middle of the night. The middle of the night is all this but with more love. Love present, love absent, but either way, more love.

I, Maris Burneau, innocent of the crime of which I have been suspected in my absence, lie alone in bed with a gun I believe I would never use. I am a most accurate image of the exact middle of the afternoon.

As a van drives past, formally marking the end of the exact middle of the afternoon, I open my eyes (which were already open) on the stiff white squares of the window panes, very slowly retrieving their dimension of depth, after a long spell of complete blankness. Outside has become outside in the city, outside on the Island, the outside world, the future. During the middle of the afternoon nothing was outside.

Because the exact middle of the afternoon is over, I can hear sounds from Juilla's room again. She is bestirring herself, moving about. I know what she is getting ready for. All her munching conversation over the loud music, as she despatched three great sauced rolls from a picnic box and I asked unanswered questions about the singers and the songs, was of a drama serial, *Carli and the Stranger*, which I believe I heard mentioned by the plump assured boy Magnick at All Afternoons. *Carli* is the favourite of the Badean citizens; Juilla is getting ready to enjoy its next instalment.

Carli and the Stranger tells of the adventures of a young girl, Carli, who ends every episode of the serial in a situation of dire peril, only to be spectacularly rescued at the beginning of the next. At first that was all Juilla told me. She was chewing, looking at the music programme. It's not so rude of her. She thinks I should know these things, because she thinks I have spent my whole life on her island, instead of not quite one day.

– Always (I wondered, looking at Juilla) always rescued?

– Of course. Else she'd die or something. Then what?

– There's never a surprise though. Is there? You could miss the first five minutes of the show, because you'd know Carli was always going to be rescued. In fact, you could miss the last five minutes as well, because you'd know Carli was always going to get herself into a situation of dire peril. You could just watch say the middle twenty minutes of it, between rescue and peril, to see how she copes with life when she has some say in the matter.

– What you on about? (she said, staring at the next song, which was being sung by a beautiful girl sitting in a tree with a ginger cat on her shoulder).

– Well, I was thinking, why not begin each episode with Carli in a situation of dire peril, and end it with her being rescued? That seems a more satisfying drama, Juilla.

– You never watch any TV, mister?

– Oh no (I say, truthfully, in fact, for we receive only the Farmers' Station on our mountain) no, we never got good television. In Laquilla. (Where I recall I was born.)

– What? You get the same television in Laquilla as here. I

45

know, 'cos I've got a mate there. Livia Mauser. You get the same.

— Oh, but you didn't in the old days, when I lived there. We just had, well, news.

— Just news? (she exclaimed with commendable scepticism in the face of this feeble lie). That's awful. News is the worst. It's just to fill in. I don't believe you. No stories?

— Just news. This is going back a long time, obviously.

— Why, what are you, old?

— I've been around (I conceded, glad the death wasn't around to hear this one).

— Now you're around here though. Who do you know in Laquilla? Do you know the Mausers? I do.

— The . . . Mausers? No, I don't think I –

— They live in the rich part, on La Lagonda. They're rich.

— Oh. I lived in the poor part.

— Yalloa?

— Mm-hm. We just called it 'Yellowtown'. That's what we did.

— I know that. Everyone does. You must know St Gaud then?

— Oh, tell me about it! (Eh?)

— Tell you about what?

— Er, tell me about *Carli and the Stranger* . . .

She told me. Eating every last crumb from her plate, then wiping up yellow sauce with the tips of her fingers while still fixedly concentrating on the endless string of numbers being performed on the television – it turned out to be a song cycle, for her five friends singing 'So la raina' were back about every twenty minutes to sing it again – she explained not only the general plot of the saga, but also some interesting behind-the-scenes information. I have been passing all this through my mind ever since, passing it backwards and forwards and committing it to memory, so that if anyone still doubts my Badean credentials I can reassure them with my mastery of and enthusiasm for their most cherished cultural institution. This is the story, as I have pieced it together from the details Juilla gave me.

Carli and the Stranger had begun a few years back. Juilla proudly remembers watching its very first transmission. With a skeleton cast of five, it began with three knocks on the door, an old man saying to Carli, 'There's a stranger to see you' and then no one being there when the door was opened. Now every episode begins with that reminder of the serial's humble origin. In those days it was a simple drama about everyday life on a secluded lane on the eastern outskirts of Badeo Town, in a comfortable imaginary suburb called Old Hanslip. *Carli*'s appeal had been immediate and enormous, with the leading actors and actresses becoming important local figures, snatches of dialogue being repeated and remembered, and various regions of the city, indeed the whole island – with the exception of what Juilla calls 'the rebel corner, they don't like anything we like' – laying claim to being the region upon which Old Hanslip was based. These claims would turn swiftly to denials, however, when life was not so good around Carli and her friends and neighbours. ('I don't know anywhere like that,' said Juilla. 'Why do you watch it then?' I asked. 'To learn what places I don't know are like are like,' she said flatly, and I must say it sounded rather like a rehearsed response.) But this popularity, unsurprising given the generally sunny atmosphere in which the affairs of Old Hanslip were conducted, started to create some curious offshoots for both the stars and viewing citizens of the capital city. Curious, I say on reflection, though the way Juilla told the story these curiosities seemed the most natural developments possible. That girl's confident tone lends a certain plausibility to her view of life, I must say, and I do accept that it is hard for me to be sceptical, given the instability of my own position in relation to reality. Nothing she – or Violet or the television – has told me of Badean life is any more preposterous than the fact that I am being at this very moment hunted down by most of Badeo's soldiers and

47

policemen for the assassination of a venerable and distinguished man I admired as much as anybody, when my only crime was to be distracted from my task and lose him in the crush. Or the fact that my only hope of survival is to be loved by everybody in this flat on an alien street, so that I can assume a new false identity even newer and falser than the one I have already assumed. Or that even my survival here on Badeo does not guarantee my ever returning home to my beloved Koborol. In the face of this and the thousand other small difficulties I believe I am going to have to overcome, the tale of the making of *Carli and the Stranger* is indeed a mere story of everyday life. So back to that story, Burneau, until you can tell it like a Badean. Otherwise you won't have any life, not even an everyday one . . .

As the show's starring actors and actresses became more and more famous, they became better and better paid, and developed a taste for finer things. They tore up their contracts with the Badean Network and became serious actors in adventure films, or piano singers who could fill concert halls with their names alone. One young woman (who played Gilla, Carli's best friend, in the very first episode) became the Mayoress of Gamor. One girl had twins and became twice as sought after as any mother on the Island, on account of her expertise at childbearing. One young man, who played a confidence trickster, has his own morning slot on the Badean channel, advising early risers on investments. The more popular the show became, the quicker its actors and actresses were to vanish and re-emerge in other walks of Badean life, as if nothing had happened.

At first, Juilla explained, the team of scriptwriters coped with the phenomenon of disappearing young stars simply by replacing them at once with others who, though they might possess no talent whatever for acting, bore a close physical resemblance to the lost face. 'Though some of them were nothing like. Maria Sonsa was nothing like Gabrielle Roon.' (See how I store these things? I can hear myself saying them!)

The problem was, the replacements soon became as loved and prized and recognised as the stars they had replaced, and they too cast their eyes upon serious art, or politics, or the worlds of fashion and music. Nothing for it then but to call up an actor or actress who was, literally, third-rate, or who barely merited the title at all. The popularity of the series evidently waned then, as one by one the Badeans noticed that not one single participant in the drama had the means of conveying the slightest impression of real life. Juilla's schoolfriends used to gather in a nearby park after each programme, to reminisce about the better days. 'Sometimes,' she said, reliving the time, 'we just shook our heads for hours. Once when I said "There's a stranger to see you", Luisa Firol just burst out crying!'

Then she told me about Tolbert, a thoughtful young cameraman, who provided the idea of genius that was required to save the series, and was these days the producer, director, chief script editor and an occasional actor in *Carli and the Stranger*. 'I've seen Tolbert,' said Juilla Maricolo. 'He was getting into a green van on the Avenue Strauber.' 'Did he see you?' I wondered with a genuine interest I had somewhat bizarrely developed. 'Why would he see me?' Juilla said blankly. 'Because you saw him.' She looked thoughtful, then unimpressed. 'Yes but he's who he is, mister.'

Evidently the brainwave of this Tolbert was to have noticed how many babies there were in the show, for the coming of a new infant among the characters was highly popular with the loyal fans of *Carli*: only a wedding day or a death drew more attention. Tolbert suggested that, whenever an adored young couple abandoned the serial, instead of replacing them, the writers should allow the action to vault forward fifteen years, from the birth of the latest child to the tense and significant teenage difficulties of that same newborn. This way, not only could the best child actors and actresses be introduced to a rapt audience, but the best of

49

Badeo's older stars could replace the youngsters who had moved on, by playing their characters blossomed into middle age.

So Tolbert took over, and the beloved show took off on its daring, headlong surge into the Island's future. By now it was two centuries ahead of real time, and the probable technological advances of that dim and remote age were sorely taxing the imagination of the Badean Network's overstretched creative departments. Juilla pronounced herself happy with the idea that people could vanish and reappear somewhere else in a flash, and prepared to believe that all illnesses could be cured by then, but pretty sceptical about vans and trains that could fly in the air, and totally unconvinced by the 'third sex' idea. 'No way!' she said, giggling in a blush. 'And you'll notice they never show you their parts!'

Then she put her plate down on the carpet, hitched herself up cross-legged on the sofa, and explained the latest plot developments, 'because we'll be watching later'.

– Oh will we? At what time? (I said in real excitement).

– Five it starts (she said cheerfully, her rare fever quite abandoned) but Mom will want to watch the News, so we have to put up with her moaning.

– You mean, we could watch *Carli* instead of the News?

– Everyone does. They watch the Mainland News, it's later.

– I saw the News before, Juilla. There's nothing. Let's watch *Carli*!

– At school, before I got so ill – I hope I'm better soon, it's not nice at all . . . they said someone was shot! Some important man.

– In *Carli*?

– No, no, in Allalong yesterday. In the News.

– Oh yes, yes, but that's all over now. There's 'no news', it said.

– Oh. This is a good song. It's called 'Blue Pines of Laquilla' – will you get homesick, mister?

– I imagine so, Juilla.

– As long as you don't cry. I read somewhere that Kosta –
the singer – has never even *been* to Laquilla!

– Is that right?

– He *looks* homesick, though.

– Not really.

Now ask me anything, I won't shoot you. Who was the
first actress to play Carli? Clea Luckmer. Who plays Carli
now? True Garrison. Why does Carli never get any older?
Because in Episode 52 she discovered the Blue Elixir. What
dire peril does she presently face? She has been imprisoned in
the Black Forcefield by deranged Automaton Xavik-85. This
looks like the end for Carli. Why would it be ironic if she
were unable to escape? Because Automaton Xavik-85 is a
direct descendant of the old man who first developed the
Blue Elixir: Mr Davis, the chemist, who lived at number 85.

Now, do I not sound ready to adopt the life of a Badean?

Violet is back, I hear her coming into the flat, or rather I
hear the commotion of Paol returning, complaining of some
injustice in the classroom: 'They're dead, they are, next time,
Mom, they're dead!'

– I'm sure they are (she is still saying indifferently as she
comes into the bedroom and sees me sitting up, clothed in
her husband's dressing-gown, in bed. I have not moved since
the end of the middle of the afternoon.) Glad to see you recovered from our drinking bout, Mr Frosch! Barely!

– Right! How was your day at work?

– Don't ask, I might answer! And now I've got Jula down
with her fever again. Just what I need.

– Yes, we met. What fever is it?

– She spoke to you?

– A little, yes.

– She's moody, you know. Sometimes one thing.

– Well. It's been quiet, otherwise.

– Yes, I heard the searches haven't started. They've been
setting up roadblocks and interrogating people in the south-
west.

– (Furasol: rebels.) Ah, Furasol, yes. Might have known!

– Not arrested anyone yet. We'll look at the News. Are you going to join us, Mr Frosch? There'll be no beers served at Afternoons tonight!

She throws her overcoat down on the bed and goes out, sighing about some next task. With a grave expression, I very slowly get out of bed, slide the gun into the pocket of the dressing-gown, and follow her out of the room. Two steps behind, the mimicking death walks with exaggerated gravity but is right – for once – about ceasing to breathe. The god sees the both of us: his breath is first to be exhaled.

In the living room, which is illuminated only by the television, sits Paol in his blue school blazer and Juilla, glum and sallow in her silver-white gown, together on the sofa, watching a programme about hunting birds. Violet passes through the light and on into the kitchen, from where she calls:

– Wine, Mr Frosch?

– Yes please, I will, Violet.

– I will as well! (cries Paol).

– I won't (Juilla says, however) I'm not really up to it.

I sit down on one of the two armchairs facing the screen. When Violet comes back, she has poured two glasses of what looks like red Fortified, and continues the conversation where she left it, though everyone else has finished. My own mother does that.

– Not up to wine, she says, but she's quite up to chatting away with my friend all day . . . Here you are, then (she says, passing me one of the glasses and retiring to the other chair) here's this for your busy day I don't think!

– (Juilla retorts) Wasn't *all* day, was it, mister? It was hardly at all. He didn't know *Carli* so I had to tell him.

– He don't watch *Carli*? (the boy demands of his sister) What is he, some kind of Dead Man???

– Well, no one's watching *Carli* today (Violet announces crisply) because the News is too important.

– NO!!! (cries Paol) –

– Mom, I *have* to! (cries Juilla) 'cos I was nothing but sick all day and I had *nothing* to look forward to, and I was telling the man about it, and telling him what would happen, and so now *he* really wants to watch it, not just me an' Owli and you *said*!

– I'm sorry, Jula, but I'm sure Mr Frosch would agree that the News is far more important than *Carli* tonight. The police are looking for the bodyguard who killed –

– More important than *Carli*??? (bellows Paol) Nothing's more important than *Carli*! (He punctuates this by bashing the nearest cushion with his fist.) No nothing!

– Now be sensible, Owli, it's only a silly story.

– No, 's not! She's in the Fourth Field!

– Forcefield, stupid (Juilla rebukes her brother, then turns and murmurs with great urgency) Mom, listen . . . it's not fair, is it, 'cos I got my fever, and also because there's News on later, but *Carli*'s *not* on later, so if we don't watch *Carli* now we'll never see it again, *ever*, but there's always News. So –

– Jula, it's serious what's happened! There could be a war because of it!

– Could there? (I hear myself wonder.)

– Well, who knows? Oh I don't know. Mr Frosch, you decide. Do you want to see this silly show they watch –

The children explode in frustration:

– Silly? You watch it *every night*! (shrieks Juilla).

– It's your *favourite*, you said! (yells Paol).

– You're changing your mind 'cos the man's here, that's all!

– Mr Frosch (Violet says wearily) that's the trouble in this place. Always outnumbered. We may not hear about the bodyguard till tonight, when these horrors are asleep. Do you mind that too much?

No, that's fine then I can shoot you all with this.

– Mr Frosch? Is that all right? To watch *Carli* and the News later on? Do things that way round?

– (Juilla says hoarsely) I'll be your friend for life, mister.

– Don't influence him, Jula! That's quite enough out of you!

– Is it all right, Mr Frosch? The next News is at eleven.

– (Six hours to be loved.) That's fine.

– *CARLI*!!! (cry the children in triumph, Juilla embarking on some committed coughing, Paol arching his back on the sofa in a demonstration of his pleasure.)

– I'll make some lemon greyfish toast (says Violet Maricolo) then we can follow the day's events in peace.

The four of us watch *Carli and the Stranger*, Episode 507. Or rather, at first I watch alone with the two children, while Violet clatters loudly about the kitchen. After a minute or so she joins us, and watches from the door.

Carli is saved from the Black Forcefield by the timely intervention of the Golden Airtruck, piloted by an especially heroic and popular character called Gadison, who spends a lot of time protecting Carli, but also seems to enjoy the company of an icy woman named Lexos, the real intentions of whom are the subject of some fierce whispered debate between Juilla and her brother.

– Silly cow (says Violet) I was at school with her.

– Don't say that (Juilla pleads) I hate it when you say that.

Half-way through the programme, history is made. I know history is made, because as they break the transmission of *Carli and the Stranger* and replace it with a blurred picture of me and a Special news Flash, Violet actually says:

– That's odd, they never break into *Carli*.

'This picture was released by the Security Wing of the Argeline Defence Bureau at 4.44 this afternoon. This is the man wanted in connection with the assassination of Viceroy Wallemire Lagland yesterday. Maris Burneau is of medium height with brown hair and a pale complexion. He is likely to be armed. Do not approach him. If you see him, contact the police. He is thought to be making his way towards Furasol.

He has a slight Argeline accent. Any information leading to his capture could result in a Citizen's Gold Award for the informant. We apologise wholeheartedly for this unprecedented interruption, and now return you to this afternoon's instalment of *Carli and the Stranger*. Dr Waganao has sworn revenge upon Gadison, in the mistaken belief that his real father – '

I switch off the television. Only now do they really look at me. Violet switches the light on. Only now do I remember to draw the gun on them. The death is saying *Look fuck I was watching that*, and now saying *He won't shoot, people, he's all heart, I'm afraid.*

I gesture the staring Maricolos to sit close together on the sofa, and then, finally:

– I don't really know how to start.

– Start how you like, mister (says Violet steadily) we're doing all right here.

– Can I say that I didn't do it?

– You can say anything you like, Maurice.

– Maris.

– Maris.

– Maris Burneau.

– We're pleased to meet you, Maris Burneau. Your hair's not really brown though, is it?

– I'm pleased to meet you, Violet Maricolo, Juilla Maricolo and Paol Maricolo. You're my best friends on the Island. So I'd very much like to tell you the truth.

Oh brother, goes the death, levering himself into the empty armchair and picking up a magazine. *Spare us that old thing . . .*

V

Anyone could walk in here, neighbour, visitor, soldier, ring the bell, be let in, sit down, meet the family. Here's the family: kids on the sofa, watching television. Mother in her armchair, reading a magazine. Father in his own armchair, just sitting there, thinking, maybe pondering his good fortune, how he met his wife, how their children turned out, so beautiful and different. All their belongings, their rugs and photographs and books everywhere, their many books. *The Examination of Candidates in Law*, they have. *Short Lives of Three Badeans*, *The Adventure of Good Fran Gader*, *Caught in the Headlights* by Roger Golli, *Fish Cooking for Even Higher Numbers*, *Dragonfeed: The True Story of the Crime of All Time* and *White Wines of Badeo, A First Companion*. Then there's this large one Mr Gando Maricolo is reading intently at the moment: *Stippler's Superscale Atlas of Badeo Island*. Three others are piled by his feet on the floor: *The Politics of Possession. League Standings Quarterly. Alien's Guide to Badeo.* The neighbour, visitor, soldier could tell this was a broadly educated, interested, lively family group at peace with one another. Gando stirs and politely questions his attractive wife:
 — Badeo Town is the only harbour then, it says here.
 — That's right. To stop the smugglers. They used to run narcotic drinks out of Saldeo. They used to crash the boats a lot. It's all in *Alien's Guide*, Maris. The orange one.
 The children are watching a film. They are very quiet, and concentrating very hard on where they look. From time to time, each of them looks very hard at Mr Maricolo, as if to ask him something, and then they look at each other, and

56

resume watching the film, *The Rains of Tamaru*. The girl murmurs at the screen:
– This is where Lucio dies.
– Isn't (goes the boy).
– You've never seen it.
– Have.
– It's on too late. You never been up this late.
– Have. Always am.
– All right, what's he die of?
– Shot.
– Wrong.
– Is.
– Not.
– Was when I saw it.
Violet Maricolo, the mother, goes out of the room and comes back with a tray. There's a jug of wine and some greyfish on toast.
– More wine and toast, Maris?
– Gando.
– More wine and toast, Gando?
– Thank you, Violet.
And she fills his glass full of strong dark red Fortified, hands him two triangle-shaped pieces of toast, then resumes her seat, sighs contentedly, and goes on reading a magazine called *Your Home Your Life*. Her husband glances across at her, and takes a considered bite of toast, as he recognises the face on the cover of *Your Home Your Life* as being that of a young actress by the name of True Garrison.
– Violet . . . that's True Garrison on the cover, isn't it?
– Mm-hm. Well done. Gando.
The children glance across together at the magazine, both nod, then glance back at their father and stare so hard at him his death appears between them on the sofa, staring equally hard and enquiring:
– *Gando . . . That's Blue Burneau in that chair, isn't it?*
The children both look at the death, between them, where he shrugs *only kidding*. Family life goes on.

Why Blue? Why Blue Burneau? Get this. There's four bodyguards sitting on the deck of a boat. Three city men and a mountain boy, all relaxing in the sunshine, all looking confident in their silver sunglasses. The city men are playing some hand game, it's called Scissors-Paper-Stone, it's three ways to die, right? The mountain boy's on his own, smoothing down his grey suit and sort of contemplating it on him. He looks up with a frown, like he's got something important on his mind, but doesn't really know if it's important enough to say. Inside the main cabin there's this man they're guarding, and he's drinking tea with the ship's captain. (He dies, by the way, not the captain the man, so don't get involved.) The mountain boy finally gets enough sunshine to have to say what's on his mind and what it is is this: 'We always wear grey suits.' Let me flutter that by you again: 'We always wear grey suits.'

Yeah, well, vital. The city men look up, one by one. The first one says, 'And?' The second one says, 'So?' and the third, a giant, looks down again.

'This dark grey colour,' he says, the mountain boy. 'I wondered if anyone had ever considered a change from it.'

'Stone,' says a city man. 'Paper,' says another, while the first says 'Seventy-six plays sixty-five.' 'Change to what?' says the second.

'Blue, it could be, for example. A blue colour.'

'Oh yeah? Like why? Blend in with what? The sea? The sky? Birds' eggs? Blonde's eyeballs? You do your work for the years we done it, Burno, then you can tell us what colour and all.'

They laugh, at his expense.

'Blue, he goes. You hear him? Gotta put in the years, boy. Gotta do ten years no blood on your grey suit, then you can start sortin' through fuckin' colours. Eh, Adzell?'

'Perhaps he'd prefer rose-red, or butterflower? They'd make a change.'

'Where I come from,' the giant says, 'Blue's no luck, Mr Burno. We got rhymes against it.'

'Paper.' 'Paper.' 'Eight-one–sixty-nine and right behind ye.' 'Blue, he goes.' 'Blue Burno.' 'Yeah. That's right. Blue Burno.'

And you know what the punchline is? That same mountain boy is being manhunted across the whole of Badeo in connection with the assassination of the man he was supposed to be guarding and guess what he ends up in? Right first time, clothes belonging to a jailbird named Gando Maricolo, who has only one suit. Blue. Oh they won't catch you now, sir, you can call yourself Grey Gando.

What do you think I was trying to do? I was trying to make friends! I was trying to make a conversation! With my brand-new colleagues! So then we could work better! *They hate you and he died. Belt up and read your atlas.*

Badeo is somewhat rectangular in shape, about twice as long east to west as it is from north to south. A big sea monster took the bite of Badeo Bay from the north-west corner, and he bit as far inland as the centre of the Island. The northernmost tip is the jut of land where the Viceregal Party (that's the late Viceroy Lagland, his three surviving bodyguards, and the vanished fourth one, who I would think is safe in Furasol by now) landed – yesterday morning, was it? – and upon that jut of land are situated the Hotels Royale, Marine and Imperion. Badeo Town itself is a narrow spit of land with the Ocean to the north and Badeo Bay to the south. Right: in the west are the docks, then Allalong and Nuneval, two districts where the streets are cramped and crooked, suggesting poverty or age or both, the Porodo, a wide, significant boulevard (this atlas has flags all along it) and the Promenad Furasol, that runs south along the Bay. Furasol is, I presume from the scale, visible south across the water. Moving east along the head-land, there's the Viceregal Residence and Gardens, the grander hotels of the centre, Palaz and Sancristo, a park called Dewdrop, the University, then, in the east of the city, the Hospital Infanta, a stadium – where they must play the game for which there are League Standings in this other book – and then tower blocks, factories, more factories. There's a little key: this must be the underground train network.

BLUE LINE north-east to south-east: Port Royale–Porodo–University (been there)–Brade Infanta.

GREEN LINE west to east: Porodo–Sancristo–Stadio–Fabrico. (Words that end in o).

RED LINE mid north to mid-south: Sancristo-Curo (been there)–Brade Infanta.

Simple. Blue–green–red. Nearest to, where is it, Avenue Hali, here, east of centre, is CURO, yes, here. So, for the docks, to get home, I'd travel in this way: Red line from CURO to BRADE INFANTA. Blue line all the way from BRADE INFANTA to PORT ROYALE. Or . . .

Red Line from CURO to SANCRISTO. Green line from SANCRISTO to PORODO. Blue line from PORODO to PORT ROYALE. Wait for a boat then. Have a drink, waiting.

– Violet.
– Gando.
– What's the quicker route from here to the docks. Is it south by way of UNIVERSITY or north by way of SANCRISTO?
– It's south, Gando. The green line's always slow, hmm?
– And it stinks (says Juilla), it stinks of tramps.
– Thank you.
– Watch, Owli, Gonzalo dies in this bit.
– Doesn't.
– He's eaten by a tigress.
– Isn't.
– You two (snaps Violet) behave yourselves. Gando, all those tips are in *Alien's Guide*. The orange one.

Gando, natural as anything. This is the first time it sounds truly natural. They have changed my appearance in the three hours since I told them. Since I explained all the truth to them – my innocence and distraction, my confusion and bad luck, then my immense good fortune in finding Violet in All Afternoons, and discovering my strong attraction to her, at which I hinted strongly – they have been my friends and supporters. At least, two of them have. Paol was excited by the sight of the gun, and took to putting his hands up all the time, no matter how often I asked him to put them down again. And it was Violet's idea that I could actually assume the identity of Gando, and literally assume his Citizenship Card for my own.

– So, you've put on weight, so have I! You've shaved your moustache but you can grow it back – and the rest is only the silver hair! Jula, you've got that dye from Gisella – you know, it really works, Maris!

– Frosch.

– Gando!

– Look that was a present, Mom (Juilla said sulkily).

– Do you want Maris to look like your papa or not?

– Why does he want to look like Papa? Papa looks like a bad moneylender.

– Well, that's what he is, dear, hmm?

– He's got to! (cried Paol). Else they'll hang 'im! High up, probably.

– Jula love, we have to help our guest.

– Yea, 'cos he's got a gun! (said the boy, putting his hands up). And it's loaded.

– It's not like *Carli*, when we know he'll be rescued.

– We don't know that (retorted Juilla), do we? We don't know that because tonight we didn't see it! She might be lying dead for all we know, and all my friends when I've not got a fever any more and I'm at school again whenever that is will know *more than me*.

– He'll shoot you, Jula! (said Paol urgently). You better not annoy 'im!

– Shoot me? (Juilla muttered, looking right at me). I don't think.

61

At that point I decided to be firm. I told Juilla to go and get the hair dye from her room or else I'd shoot her. It worked. She flounced out with a meaningful sigh, and reappeared with a small bottle, with the words GADISON SILVERLINE wrapped around it.

— Hope you like that, making a sick girl walk that distance.

— Gadison (I noticed with confidence) he's a character in *Carli*, isn't he?

— Might be (said Juilla).

— Well, we're not doing this here (said Violet briskly), it's off to the bathroom to turn you into a loving husband!

I have been considering how this will work. I will be able to sleep only by shutting all three Maricolos in Violet's bedroom overnight, then sleeping against the door. The window's too high above the street for them to climb out, and they wouldn't cry for help from that window because I'd of course shoot them, as I think they now realise.

How will I be able to bathe? By taking one of them into the bathroom. The boy, that will have to be. I will have to bathe on the days the boy is at home.

For in the days, I will have to insist that one of them remains permanently with me, as a hostage. We can work on a system of alternate days. Violet takes a day off from the cloth-house. Juilla and Paol take turns to stay home from school. Just until the crisis is over. Perhaps the security forces will arrest anyone. There can't be an indefinite curfew. When the curfew is over, and the search scaled down, and I am accepted generally as Gando Maricolo, it is merely a case of waiting patiently for the right ship going at the right time to the Argeline Mainland. And as for money? It will have to come from here. Whether borrowed or stolen, it's the only possibility. One day, when all this is a remote memory, I will return to Badeo Island with ten times the money I borrowed or fifty times the money I stole, and with a great bouquet of flowers beg forgiveness of the kindly Maricolos.

But the first difficulty was the dyeing of my hair. I requested that Violet and Paol be locked out of the bathroom while Juilla did the work. Violet suggested she herself would do a better job, seeing as how she knew Gando's appearance better than her daughter. Juilla said, 'No, I've known him all my life. You can't say that, can you, Mom?' Violet insisted she could do a much better job. Juilla reminded her, 'This is *my* bottle.' Paol, still with this hands up, frowned and said, 'I reckon this'll end in a shoot-out,' which in turn reminded me that it was in my power to decide. I decided that it was important to get the most recalcitrant member of the family, Juilla, on my side as soon as possible.

– Juilla can dye my hair, I don't mind, I don't mind at all.

– Well, I mind! (said her mother).

– Better let her do it (I said).

– Watch out (said Paol), he means business.

Violet turned and stared at me.

– Do you? Are you threatening us, Maris – Gando?

– Well, yes, I suppose, yes. Not – threatening, but saying well I suppose yes, it's Juilla's bottle.

– You heard it from a man with a gun (said Juilla quietly).

Violet sniffed.

– You'd better do a good job, Jula, or we'll never see him again.

– Oh well, that's scary (said the girl, pushing me into the bathroom ahead of her).

– You better do a good job, Juilla (Paol agreed) or we probably ain't never going to see no sunrise.

– What? (Violet was asking her son as Juilla locked the door on them).

Juilla spun the bathtaps on and had me kneel by the side of the bath, bending over the side. The gun was in my right hand.

– You'll have to take the jacket and shirt off.

63

– I can't, I've got the gun.

– He's got the gun. Then they'll get wet, won't they?

– Well. You stand by the door with your hands up, and I'll take them off.

– That's exciting. All right, mister.

– Papa, that should be.

– Not till you're him.

Juilla slouched against the door in her silver-white gown, with her hands resting on the yellow-brown nape of her neck. She had piled her hair on top, just a few strands dangled down. I could hear her breathing. I could hear traffic, though it was past the curfew by now. Hastily I took off my blue jacket and stiff grey shirt and knelt down again, with the gun back in my right hand.

– You know something (she said, from the door), this isn't going to work, mister. You really are nothing like him.

– You can come back now. I did what you said.

– You can see your skin's paler. Though they don't have that on the card, that's true. So it might work.

– You think?

– No. Not a hope. Shame, though. You're not quite as bad as I thought.

She moved my head under the taps.

– Too hot?

– Too cold.

– OK?

– OK.

– I did this for Susi Cahimo and her skin went yellow. I don't care. She asked for it.

– Am I still finished, Juilla?

– Again?

– You said I looked finished. When you first saw me. In the room.

– I didn't know you had a gun, mister.

– Well, yes. Does that make me less finished, in your view?

64

– Less? No. More. But you'll go out with a crash.

She ran her fingers through my hair for the first time. This was about two hours ago now, two hours twenty minutes. It was the most wonderful sensation of my life. I can still feel it. I can still feel those slight fingers slithering through my matted dirty hair, wringing it, swirling it, smoothing it, everything. She worked in silence for a while. I am proud to have her as a friend. (Daughter, step-daughter, friend, whatever.) We did have this one conversation, I recall.

– How can a woman be flame-haired?

– Did I say that?

– Keep still. No, I did. The woman you saw, the one in the crowd who made you lose your concentration. How can she be flame-haired? You mean red-haired.

– Well, yes. Hair the colour of flame.

– Orange-haired, then. Red's like, you know, hot wood.

– Somewhere in between it was. Embers, you mean.

– Was that love on sight then?

– What?

– You and the orange-haired red-haired ember woman. Was that love on sight?

– No! It was a terrible accident.

– Mmm ... My friend Gisella and this boy Nando in my class. She says that was love on sight but he says it wasn't. I agree with him. I don't think it was love at all. Keep still. This won't work.

– Is it changing colour?

– Sure, it's changing colour. Doesn't make you Papa, though. Too hot?

– Just right. Mmm.

– Have you shot people then, with a gun?

– Oh yes, many.

– Why?

– To protect the Viceroy.

– If it was you who caught the assassin, would you shoot him? I mean, like now it's too late to save the Vice-thing.

65

– Viceroy. No, I wouldn't shoot him. Ow!

– Keep still. Why not? Look what he's done to you. You're stuck.

– Well. So be it.

– So be it? That's you, I think. Mister so-be-it.

– How's it looking, Jula?

– Jula, he calls me. Very grey, Mister-so-be-it. Just like Gadison.

And her hands worked on, soaking, curling, tugging, untwisting, as I fought to keep my eyes open through the drenching water and stinging silver lotion. My whole scalp tingled with where her fingers were or had been. And still do, now it's midnight and I watch her curled there on the sofa, dully watching the end of her film. Paol is asleep, Violet in the kitchen. I go:

– That's it then. News now.

– You again, it'll be. You're famous, but I don't count you as famous. I've seen some famous people, did I say?

– It's not me any more, Juilla. It's some mountain boy, the one who did it.

– He didn't do it. You did.

– I didn't do it. Someone else did.

The black marble slabs of words behind the nighttime newscaster Bob Pool say BOB POOL, as if the most important news of the night so far is that he's still who he is, but then those words rapidly disintegrate and reassemble as OPEN YOUR DOORS.

'Open your doors we are saying tonight open your doors as the capital city is subjected to general security searches *by* the brave young men of the Badean Police Force I'm Bob Pool this *is* Midnight Bulletin on the *Bob Pool Show* and this *is* a photograph of *Maris Burneau*, the Argeline uplander wanted in connection with the murder of Viceroy Wallemire Lagland Yes. Ter. Day. Nice face shame about the shooter. . . bit of a message here I might read: *every* possible precaution it goes it's from the police department *every* possible precaution will be taken *to* ensure the safety of citizens during the hours *of* the search and the police have been asked to extend all courtesy to you *in* this time of crisis that's nicely put nice men those policemen nice men tough *job*! As you know this is them still not me I'm Bob Pool as you know these *are* difficult times and we would ask you *to* bear with us just until this dangerous man has been apprehended now on to lighter things tonight on the *Bob Pool Show* we *have* a young lady we think you may recognise when we cover her eyes like so . . .'

– Look she's orange-haired. Was it her, mister?

    – Papa (says Violet from the door), you have to call him Papa, Jula.

    – He looks nothing like him, Mom.

    – You wanted to do it yourself, didn't you? Well, it's his only chance. If they arrest him now, on your own head be it.

    – So be it, Mom, so be it, Mister so-be-it.

Now starts a nervous time. I switch off the television and ask Violet to take the children into her room. Paol wakes up, raises his hands and goes, muttering, 'Don't worry, mister, I won't give you any trouble . . . ' Juilla goes too, yawning, saying she's tired anyway, and it's unlikely the evening's excitement will have made her fever any better. She reminds me one last time that I look nothing like her father. Violet says I do, then adds that she means it. It's amazing, she says, brightly.

The children go to the bathroom, then the bedroom, dragging mattresses and blankets from their own beds. I wish them goodnight and lock them in the room. 'So be it,' says Juilla, yawning. 'So be it,' says Paol, nodding as gravely as he can. Violet and I go into the multicoloured kitchen and wait for the police.

    – What if they run a check? What if they find I'm in prison on the Mainland?

– Welcome to the Island, love. Nobody works that hard.

– What if they ask about my job?

– You've lost your job. You worked for the New Lake Bank and they laid you off, Gando.

– What do I do now, then?

– You watch *Carli* and sleep, Gando.

– They'll never believe that.

– They will, it's all they do.

When a knock comes on the door an hour later, I open up to two clean-cut officers in dark green uniforms, both proudly sporting the bronze blazon of the Badean Security Division.

– Good evening, sir, you will have been informed that this is a warranted search of the premises. My name is Inspector Will and this is Inspector Fabileu. Are you . . . (and he cranes his neck to read the name on the plaque by the door) Maricolo G?

– Yes.

– Georg, is it? (ventures Inspector Fabileu).

– Gando.

– It says so, Don (says Inspector Will).

– So it does. On we go.

– And you reside here with Maricolo V and two children of school age?

– Violet, Juilla and Paol, yes.

– May we come in, sir.

– Of course.

And everything, to the drumbeat of my tense heart, seems to be going well. They stroll around, they look in on the children, who pretend to be sleeping, they open a few cupboards and wardrobes, they admire the poster of one of the exhibitions organised by Violet's shop. Inspector Will says his wife went to it. Then he moves on.

– Any suspicious folk pass through here, sir, ma'am? (enquires Inspector Fabileu, peering into the fridge).

– No (says Violet) all very quiet since the curfew.

– Ah (sighs Fabileu, slamming the fridge door shut), that's just when you get it, see. No strangers, intruders?

– I know everyone I've seen lately (Violet confirms).

Inspector Will comes in from the hall.

– OK, Don, let's wrap this. Don't want to disturb the family peace. Can we just see your CCs then, folks?

– Our Citizenship Cards? (says Violet, glancing at me) I'll go and get them.

Once Violet is gone, Inspectors Will and Fabileu simultaneously start to tap their feet in the kitchen. Will says:

– What you do with yourself, sir?

– (New Lake Bank) The New Lake Bank I worked at, then I lost that work and now I . . .

– Do other work, eh? (Inspector Fabileu grins.)

– Mainly stay in, watch the dramas.

– Lucky bleeder, one has to say (says Fabileu).

– *Burneau's my real name*. Well, you could say.

– We do, we do indeed say (Inspector Fabileu says).

Violet comes back with the Citizenship Cards. She's lucky. Hers looks exactly like her. Mine's hopeless. It looks like Gando Maricolo. Inspector Will looks at hers and nods, Inspector Fabileu looks at mine and nods. They swap, and both nod again.

– You're a very lucky man, Mr Maricolo (smiles Inspector Fabileu), isn't he, Mrs Maricolo?

– He is, and he knows it!

At the door, in fact just as it is closing, Inspector Will turns and obstructs it with his hand. In his hand is a piece of paper that's dark pink.

– Not quite done, sorry. Would you just sign this, say we were here, didn't force entry, broke nothing, passed the time of day and so on. We have Courtesy Standards to meet these days.

– That's right (says Fabileu with a sigh) you're supposed to like us, in the new dispensation.

– We do like you (Violet laughs). Gando, don't we?

– Pen, sir? (Will says, passing me his dark green and bronze pen with W G WILL written on it.)

I sign and pass the paper back. We say good night and close the door. When they knock again, about five seconds later, the death is with them. Will says apologetically:

– Very sorry, sir, just a double-check. Inspector Fabileu here thinks this signature isn't very like the one on the CC.

– It's awful I know (agrees Fabileu), but I'm afraid it's my training, sir. Can we just see the card again?

– I'll get it (says Violet, abandoning me for ever).

– Damn that training! (cries Fabileu, to make me feel better in death).

– Language, Don (says Inspector Will).

They both start to tap their feet again, and this time the death joins in, skilfully, saying: *Never forget how lovely she was, never forget the look she gave you, never forget the smell of her bedclothes, never forget -*

– Ah, here she comes (says Fabileu) with the evidence, so to speak.

Violet passes them my Citizenship Card, saying:

– There's several years between those signatures, Inspector.

– That there are, that there are.

They both have a good stare, half-way through which Inspector Will turns away as if satisfied, satisfied one way, anyhow.

– You know something, sir (says Fabileu amiably) if it wasn't for your distinctive brown eyes I might have doubts about this!

– I think I'd know if he wasn't Gando! (Violet chuckled with complete poise and truthfulness.)

– Course you would, love, course you would. Tell you one thing, if you ever think it isn't, just let me know, won't you!

– That's not very courteous (Violet smiles sweetly) I might have to mark you down, hmm?

– Any time, love, any time (says Inspector Fabileu with a wave and he's off, catching up his colleague).

They're gone. It's done. They're walking away laughing down the dark landing of 1-24 Avenue Hali. The death stands there frozen in the doorway, then starts to rummage through his pockets for all the forms he can find, but Violet is still smiling when she slams our door in that white disgusted face.

VI

Every man should be married, every man should have children. Every day is different and special, but each has its own unique delights. There are new sights to see, new sounds to hear, new work to be done, new challenges to be met. A husband and father discovers that there are infinite ways to love and be loved, like the sun itself, around which all, though circling constantly, is strewn each day into beautiful, altered patterns for his pleasure. I wake in the morning, go smiling into the bedroom with tea for my sleepy family, help them to prepare for the difficult day ahead. While Paol clatters noisily about the bathroom, and Juilla slides herself wearily from the sheets, Violet makes breakfast to the sound of the radio. Whenever I hear the song 'Lullaby of the Foothills' (sung by Kristof Vaber and the Valley Five) I see, smell, taste the world of we Maricolos in the morning! We prefer the music to the news, the news is always so glum. All riots and unrest and more soldiers sailing here. Whenever anyone mentions the prospect of civil war, Violet switches to a music station, because she worries about the children listening. I don't think they really care, though. Those bandits from Furasol will never amount to much. Violet sings along to 'Lullaby of the Foothills', eats, and laughs with me at the glad simplicity of it all.

> Home to the meadow, home to the mere,
> Home to the maple tree, home to me . . .

What's wonderful about my family life is that I'm never alone. One day I will spend with my wife Violet, walking the streets of my adopted Badeo City, the next I'll be at home with my son Paol, playing the endless and complicated game of Ocean Conquest, then every third day I'll spend with my daughter Juilla, in front of the television, watching, discussing or waiting for our favourite programmes. Each one of the three will star in my day, the other two play supporting roles. But I love to have them all about me. What I say is, and I'm famed for saying it: Every man should be married, every man should have children.

Today I'm spending with my wife Violet, but the whole family leaves together, slamming the door of number 16 Avenue Hali, bustling down the stairs thinking 'What have we forgotten?' and then out into a sunny day. We're taking our children to school. We don't have to, they often go on their own, but it is such a fine green day, and Violet's not at work. The children walk ahead, Juilla in her black jacket and skirt, her white socks, her hair tied in a ponytail with an amber ribbon, her books under her arm. She looks down, or across the road, or up at the tops of trees. She looks anywhere but at Paol, stout and dignified in his blue uniform, as he tries to keep up with her strides: he points at things and wants her approval but she's so conscious of being out in the town. She ignores him or is curt with him. He's just a little brother. Violet walks behind them in her long white coat, with her deep canvas bag over her shoulder, and her wild black hair straggling down. She talks to them loudly, or to me just as loudly but without turning round. I bring up the rear. I'm proud of my family.

We take Juilla to her convent school. It's on the Avenue Pindi, which is really just around the corner. She hates it. It brings on her fever. The religious sisters on the steps smile at us, a young but distinguished-looking grey-haired gentleman and his gypsy-dark wife delivering our lovely daughter into their care for the day.

– How's Juilla's fever this week, Madame Maricolo? (one enquires politely).

73

– Ho you know, the same. It comes and goes, doesn't it, Jula?

But Juilla passes haughtily through the iron gates without saying a word to us, and goes up the steps without saying anything to them. They follow her in and close the door. They shouldn't worry about her. She's very affectionate really. Only her family would know the real Juilla, and that's how it ought to be.

Young Paol is different, he seems to like his school, an old sandstone building on the Avenue Glasz. The cobbled forecourt is full of clean young boys in blue blazers, jumping on each other's backs, writing on their own hands, gaping at cards, or looking in each other's fat red books. He dashes away to be among them, getting out his own personal fat red book to show someone something, then Violet and I turn smilingly back from the gates and are alone for the day.

She says she's going to show me the sights, seeing as it's the warmest day for a while, and we'll start with a sit-down at a nice pavement café, so we can plan our itinerary. We go to the Plaza Muro, where she drinks a tall cold chocolate drink and I drink a Tretners beer. A man comes by selling the green news-sheet called *Klarion*, and I buy one with a marker Violet finds in her canvas bag.

All the usual things are happening. Another flare-up in Furasol, but the army dealt with it quickly. Some students demonstrated in Laquilla, my home-town. Badeo's team was defeated by the fishing town Gamor and there was much fighting among enraged spectators. The island sport seems to excite the Badeans as much as anything. Low on the front page, however, is a brief article about the mysterious Maris Burneau, the bodyguard supposed to have murdered Viceroy Lagland. It suggests that he may only have been an accomplice, not the assassin himself. That happens to be the column I'm reading, so I mention to my wife, who is gazing off down the Avenue,

– Something about Burneau here.

– They not got him yet?

– No. That'd be all over the news. This is a small thing, quite low on the page. It's written by Josai Grumo, and she usually does gossip, doesn't she? Suggests Burneau may only have been an accomplice, not the assassin himself. What do you think?

– I think it means they're fed up with not finding him. It means they'll find someone, anyone, and say he did it.

– Josai says there's a man from San Timotheo helping them with their enquiries (I notice, lifting my beer as if to salute their good luck).

– Sweet of him to help, Gando, but it'll get him shot, you wait.

– His name is Pirir.

– His name is history (sniffs Violet Maricolo) Waiter!

– So what you're saying is . . . this Burneau has actually got away with it? You think they might stop searching for him, admit there was a mistake? Pardon him? Maybe deport him home to –

– They'll never stop searching for him, Gando. They'll shoot some loser to make them feel good, but they'll never forgive Blue Burneau. He wasted their time, Gando. Wherever he is, he'd better stay there while he's safe. The way they'll – Another cold chocolate, please, and a Tretners for my husband? – the way they'll see it is – if they can lose Burneau so completely into thin air, he'd jolly well better stay in thin air. For ever, at least.

– Well. Where do you think he is? This Burneau.

– Where do I think he is? Where do I think he is. Where do I think he is I think he's somewhere warm, somewhere safe, somewhere planning a wonderful day with a friend, hmm? That'd be just like him.

– Just imagine (I imagine) if he, I mean after all that, didn't actually do it . . . kill the Viceroy, I mean. Perhaps he just lost his way in the crowd. They'd surely pardon him for that. For his mistake.

– Nah. Fucking up? No one pardons that one. Drink up, dear.

Off we go then, relaxed and complaining and arm-in-arm towards the clean new underground transport station BRADE INFAN ('Brade' is old Badean dialect for 'bridge', for this is the south of the Town, where the great Bay Highway crosses the River Rumol) and from where we have to take the Blue Line two stops to PORODO. Violet stands right by me, says there's no point in trying to sit down, and sings as we sway with the motion:

– Home to the meadow, home to the mere, home to the maple tree, home to me. Porodo.

This is of course a very good place to commence any sight-seeing expedition (however many times you have visited in the past!) as it places one in convenient proximity to the exotic beauty of the Viceregal Estate and Gardens, the Dew-drop Park beyond them, the lively and colourful market districts of Nuneval and Allalong to the west, and the elegant boulevards of L'Embassade and the University of Badeo to the south-east. And in Badeo Town, remember, one is never more than ten minutes' walk from the Ocean or the Bay. We go for an orientating stroll along the Porodo, looking into the windows of some of the Island's dearest stores: the clothes company Fabilo, the vintner Roschli, the exquisite glassmakers Belligan & Finn. We linger there, the window display is so elegant.

– What would you buy if you could buy anything, Violet?

– That. Or those. Or that. That. (My wife presses her face right to the window.) See all those colours as you move ever so slightly? It's green it's purple it's yellow it's red!

– I'd buy the boat. In a glass boat you can see the bottom of the ocean, see it as you sail.

– Why would you sail anywhere, Gando? You were born on the Island.

– Well, yes I was (I admit), but anyone born anywhere would like to sail somewhere. I'd like to sail in a glass-bottomed boat.

– It's blue it's yellow it's green it's pinkish!

– I'd sail somewhere new.

When Violet's feet are tired of walking, we stop at a small cosy wine bar called The Livelihood, and go inside. It's very dark, and on all the walls are red and black squares. Violet insists I try a grainy brown drink called 'stow'.

– It's what they have here. It's made of bad apples.

– Can I order a beer, where's the menu?

– There's no menu. There's just stow.

– Who wants to drink bad apples?

– These men (says Violet with a wave to them. There are, I see as my eyes become accustomed to the darkness, about seventy men sitting on either side of an extremely long and extremely narrow table that seems to stretch away into the earth itself. Each man is drinking stow from a short glass beaker, and three or four of them wave back at Violet.) You have to try it or they'll never stop looking at you, hmm?

– They're still looking at me. Do they know I'm not who I am?

– They don't care who you are, as long as you drink what they do. And about that being not who you are, Gando . . .

– Yes, Violet?

– Fucking forget it, hmm? How can I believe it if you don't?

Stow is going to be one of my favourite drinks, I can tell. It's one of those few drinks of which one immediately senses the benefit. We're not great drinkers, we Maricolos, only on special occasions really, but we like the old traditions here, and here's to that, here's to that one!

– Here's to freedom! (I pronounce to my wife).

– Freedom, Gando (she says), and the future.

– The future (I say) and home.

– Home (she says) and us.

– Us (I say) and them (I say, raising my third glass to the ranks of Old Badeans in the shadows).

We amble down to the southern shore of the Town, over-looking Badeo Bay. The sun is glinting off the water. Far across the brightness we see two places: opposite is the sprawl of Furasol, in the shadow of snow-capped Mount San Timotheo, the lone peak of Badeo. Away to the right, where the land tapers off at the mouth of the Bay, is a cluster of tall modern buildings.

— That's New Badeo (I say).

— Of course, you know it is. You live on the island, yawn, yawn.

— It's always being attacked, that is.

— You know that too (says Violet). Honestly, Gando, you're always mentioning things you've known for years! We need to get some lunch in you, mmm?

— By the terrorist people.

— I told you (she hisses) my friend was on the last boat out.

My wife's best friend is called Thea. She used to go across on a pleasure boat to gamble at New Badeo, which is a little resort designed for the richest Badeans and visitors from the Domain. The problem was that the only land access to it is via Furasol and the dirt roads around Mount San Timotheo, so the Organ Liberat Badeon kept bombing the harbour and threatening the hotels. Now nobody goes there except detectives investigating the explosions. They go in plain clothes and get fired at from the high balconies. They come back and say 'It was them all right.'

— Think of it (says Violet, when we discuss this at Gheorgi's on the Avenue Rand over slim glasses of white Quiga), think of all those lush hotel rooms all empty, all abandoned! All that comfort and no people! Thea says it's heavenly.

— Heaven's not always being bombed, though (I reason), and it doesn't have casinos.

— It does have casinos. Gando's heaven would.

— There's no Gando. I'm Gando, and there are no casinos in heaven.

— As you say (Violet sighs, savouring the aroma of her Quiga).

— What does Thea know anyway?

– She only just escaped with her life. Then again, most of my friends say they only just escaped with their life. They all seem to have been the last people out of New Badeo! I wouldn't like to only just escape with my life. Would you like to?

– This drink is the most absolutely beauteous drink. Would I like to what?

– (She drinks.) Only just escape with your life.

– I have only just escaped with my life.

– No, you haven't. You've lived a quiet life with me for many years.

– I haven't.

– Look, fucking hell, Maris, you have. We have two children.

– Haven't. I've got two brothers. I'm in the middle.

– Well, you're in the fucking middle now, matey! I'll just leave you here, shall I? See how you find your own way home to my place? Or see how you make it back to your bloody mountain and your sodding sheepgirls, eh Burneau?

She stands up and I reach for my gun, so she sits down again. She glares at me, picks up her Quiga but can't drink it because she's started to giggle uncontrollably. I say:

– I think you are, Violet, apart from being my wife, which you always have been, I think you are also as well my best friend in the world. And it is *that*. It is *that* which has kept our marriage so strong. For so long.

– Tell me a poem, Gando (she sniffs, as her laughter comes to an end).

– Gando isn't a poet. Frosch was a poet. Gando worked in a bank. You should know that, Violetto, you married him.

– You can work in a bank and be a poet.

– You can, Violetto, you can. But I (and I finish my Quiga with a swig so vigorous I nearly choke) I . . . didn't.

We have lunch in a university bar near the station University. Violet orders chicken pie, and I decide to try the Gamoran delicacy shutfish stew. A bespectacled student at the next table peers across at us and says:

— Not from Gamor are you, people?

— My husband likes this dish (says Violet primly, about to giggle again).

— Yes I do (I say) I thought I would and I do. It's not too salty. As a matter of fact it's just how we have it at home.

— Because you see (continues the student, munching a stick of bread) Gamor's not our favourite town today, know what I mean?

— No, I don't! (says Violet indignantly) and I don't care! They make a damn good shutfish stew there, don't they, Gando?

— Oh, the game (I remind her); they beat us 17-10. Women (I snort in the student's direction) they just don't understand, do they?

— They don't (he says uneasily).

— (Violet goes on the offensive) Like what *is* your favourite town today then, sonny, hmm?

— The one I live in (he boasts), today and tomorrow. (Then he gets up and, on his way out, leans over my shutfish stew and says to it): Put *that* on your spoon and sip it!

When he's gone, Violet says 'Fuckwit', and we squeeze hands together across our little table.

We lie down on a patch of grass across the Avenue Marchant from the Viceregal Residence. We lie down and sleep off our lunch a while. By the time we rise again it's gone mid-afternoon. We both have headaches and Violet suggests we leave some of our sightseeing until the next day we spend together, because she has to fetch Paol from school in an hour.

— And Jula (I say).

— No, not Jula. She's eating with her friend Gisella.

— You didn't tell me that.

— It's none of your business.

— She's my daughter.

— She's not.

— All right, but I care.

— All right, but I don't, hmm?

I would think that even the soundest marriages have moments like these. We walk along in silence for a spell, along the busy streets in the University area, then decide, almost at exactly the same time, that rather than board the dirty warm train at UNIVERSITY, we'll stroll back along the Promenad Sperice by the Bay, and have a last drink together on our way home.

– We'll go to Too Late Now, they do a good selection. Plus I know Yuri.

Too Late Now is a bar below street level. It's even darker than The Livelihood. We settle into two very high bar stools and say hi to Yuri, the owner. Violet says I ought to drink the green whatever-it-is because everyone does and I do and we have another bit of a row. Yuri comes over while we're sitting there glaring at our flushed reflections behind his bar, and says:

– Doc was in here for ye, Ma'am.

– Dr Fencile?

– In here for ye. Wonder how you been, Ma'am. Always never in no more.

– Afternoons? D'you blame me, Yuri? Full of sleaze, it is.

– To ze brim, Ma'am.

– Don't tell him you saw me, will you?

– He coming back, Ma'am. Like soon. Wit ze schoolboy.

– Magnick? Oh fuck. We're going, Gando.

– Coming back (Yuri sighs as we drink up whatever it is and move off) coming back to sleaze all ze night and sleaze all ze day!

We hurry out, and walk on through the streets of St Sperice to the familiar trees and buildings of the Curo district. I'm filled with anxieties, I'm frowning about them all.

– Can't always be secret, can I? One of them will see me. You'll say I'm Gando. They'll say I'm Frosch and I don't look like Gando. Mr Beers, that boy calls me, that Magnick . . .

– They never saw Gando. You think I drank in that hole all my life? God, Maris.

– Gando. They'll say I'm Frosch.

– Say you lied, Gando. Say it's none of no one's business.

– It's a terrible world (I decide).

– I didn't shoot him (says Violet).

– I didn't shoot him either (says me). I loved him.

– You love me, husband, is that why you talked to me?

– Yes it's why, Violet.

– Goat's arse is it. I'm nothing but a safe-house.

– No! No, you're not! You're my best friend and wife!

– And you're my husband and you're bad news, Gando, you're bad news after all these years, bad, bad news. I don't intend to love you, I think I should warn you. If I do it's my fault.

– Well. I'll just. I'll just. Go then. The Likelihood, is it called? Well the 'likelihood' is that you'll find me there. I'll have no name at all.

I wander a few yards and stumble, honestly, on the street-kerb. I can hear her sigh from there.

– It's livelihood, you fuckwit, not likelihood.

She strides up, gives me the keys to 16 and stalks off to fetch Paol from school. I get home, let myself in, go to the bedroom and lie down. My head is really spinning. The death it is who is spinning it, spinning it like the globe on its grey axis. Then he stops it with a thump and I sit up like the dead would.

Out of curiosity . . . Who's your hostage now?

I run blindly through the streets towards where I think is the Avenue Glasz. I'm right. I look far ahead along the sunny street for the figure of Violet, or Violet and Paol. I find neither. When I reach the school there are a few children still waiting at the gates, shouting.

– Does anyone know Paol Maricolo? (I gasp as the shouting ends).

– I do (says a boy, with his own little death climbing on his back in regulation blue blazer). He's gone 'ome, sir, with his mom.

82

I turn away. Violet and Paol are gone, but I didn't pass them the way I came. So they went a different way. The death agrees this means they've gone to the police.

To say they've found Burneau. I know. *So the police can come and pick him up.* Yes, obviously. *And shoot him.* Fuck off. *You fuck off.*

Juilla. I run the quarter-mile or so to the Avenue Pindi, and by the time I reach the iron gates of the religious school I'm drenched in sweat, my shirt another skin. A lady is there in a hood, smiling at me.

– Good afternoon!

– I'm the father of – I'm – has Juilla Maricolo gone home?

– Nobody's gone home!

– You mean she'll still be inside?

– Nothing has finished!

– Nothing . . . nothing has finished (I'm panting) so I can wait, I can wait here?

– Of course! You're out there in the world! Out there in the world you can always wait!

I wait. A bell goes. The school doors swing open and dozens of girls come flowing down the steps in the red of the late sunshine, disentangling their ribbons and bows, rolling their socks down as they run, shaking out their brown and white and yellow hair. The lady stands smiling in the river of them, smiling straight at me as they flood past on either side.

They knock the death over. He likes it.

– Juilla!

She stops in mid-stream, and a friend of hers stops with her.

– I've come to collect you!

– I'm going to Gisella's.

Juilla is beautiful, I notice for what I think is the first time. If she doesn't come home with me I'm going to kill her. And her friend, and the lady, and myself. Lie down there with the death, keep my eyes wide open till they're pale blue with sky.

– You have to come home, it's an emergency.

83

– What, you going to shoot me if I don't, Daddy?

– Don't be rude! (The lady smiles at both of us) Don't be rude! He's run all the way to see you, Maricolo!

– Juilla (I hiss at her) it's just for an hour, a bit of an emergency – then you can go with Gisella, all right? Please, it's important.

Juilla asks Gisella, who shrugs then nods. I get my daughter and we walk quickly away, many eyes upon us, the death explaining the exact circumstances to the whole school.

– That was fucking embarrassing, mister, do you know?

– Shut up or I'll kill you.

– You're drunk.

– Shut up.

– Sloshed, loaded, spammed . . .

– I don't care. I don't want to kill you because you're so beautiful, Jula, but I have to stay alive, or there's no god, you see. No book, no god. Then he's in the woods.

– Right. Right you is. Mister's the boss. Save us.

We turn right into the Avenue Hali.

– Do you really think I'm beautiful? (she actually asks).

– I do, yes.

– Would you love me if I let you?

– Let me what?

– Love me.

She rests her upper teeth very gently on her lower lip. I see this because we have stopped to have this exchange and are facing each other somewhere along the avenue whose name I forget. I forget everything. I'm thinking how pleasant it would have been to have had her standing there in my life all the time, for her always to have been there, for me to be able to say 'I have known her for years!' to the yearning, asking faces in the same room. But how long has she looked like she looks now? How long will this be her? I am seeing her, in my giant's detachment, sailing past me on the whole of her planet, sailing through this chamber in which aliens can

84

glimpse each other. The distance between our planets is vast but it looks like nothing. Mine is the planet of death, hers the planet of always. The distance then is nothing in space but everything in time, so I am happy for the instant of recognition that passes between our worlds. From mine comes a voice: 'There you go, sailing on for ever!' and from hers a whisper: 'Remember us when you're gone . . .' It is only when we pass this close that I notice with both love and horror how she too has a death beside her, and it's just as cheerful as mine. I hadn't seen it from a distance, but as our planets pass I feel the two lock eyes. And so Juilla and I go on with our quarrel while our deaths fall in love. The god hears me say:

– Love you how?

– Any old how. Forget it.

– I'm your father, Juilla.

– You're not, though, are you. Like in *Carli*, Carli's always finding out that people aren't who they seem.

– I'm who I seem.

– Hardly. You can't get through a day without changing your name, your face, your story. You're nothing like who you seem, whoever that is, poor bastard.

– Deep down I'm who I seem.

– Deep down I'm who *I* seem.

– Who do you seem?

– How do I know? You can't seem to yourself, mister. You need someone to seem to. How do I seem to you?

– Beautiful. Strange (I add, with the dim honesty of one who's not really a father).

– That's how I am, deep down.

– Beautiful? (I ask her).

– Strange (she answers) and let's get home.

When we reach the upper landing of 1-24 Avenue Hali, she grabs me by the arm and says quietly:

– There's no emergency, is there?

– Not now you're here, no.

85

– You lost your hostage, didn'tcha?

– Yes.

– So now I'm your hostage, aren't I?

– Yes.

She ponders this, then raises herself up, comes towards me, kisses my lips with hers then moves away, wiping them.

– You've been drinking stow. I drank that at Susi's sixteenth and my puke was this colour.

– Juilla, I'm your father.

– So when's my birthday?

– It's, it's – early in the year.

– Fuck me what a loser. It's in autumn, mister. Calls himself a father.

– Juilla, dear, I have to stay alive somehow!

– This is the best way how (she whispers, and kisses me again) but I reckon you want to clean your teeth.

– You don't understand. Your mother has gone to the police with Paol. You have to understand that we're in a hostage situation. I'm sorry, Juilla, but things have just turned out that way. Now. Go into the flat.

She stares at me and shrugs. I unlock the door of 16 and she walks in, then turns and shakes her head:

– You had me for a minute. But Mom wouldn't do that. She's sleeping with you, isn't she?

– No, she isn't, Jula.

– Bet she is.

– How can she be, you idiot, I sleep alone on the floor! You all sleep together in her bedroom!

– I'm not an idiot (she says hoarsely, with a tear in her voice) I'm not, and there's mornings, there's afternoons! I bet you don't just watch *Carli* with her! I bet you rip each other's things off and leap around on the furniture while I'm trying to do my lessons! Trying to do lessons so I don't grow up an *idiot*!

She sobs and runs through the living room to the bedroom door, slamming it shut behind her before I can get there and stop her.

– Come out of there or I'll shoot you, Juilla Maricolo!

– Shoot, mister, I don't give a fuck, I hate you and I hope you die!

– I'll have to shoot the lock off, Juilla, but before I do I'd just like to say that I do find you very beautiful and wish you would kiss me again. Now, make sure you're standing clear of the lock because after I've counted to ten I'm going to shoot.

– I'm standing *exactly* in front of it (howls Juilla) so you'll kill me!

I don't even bother counting to ten. I stand there, no one's father, no one's husband, no one's friend, no one's dream, and wait for the police to arrive and put me out of my misery.

Instead it's Violet and Paol who arrive, wondering why I didn't leave the door open. They are absolutely loaded down with shopping.

– Juilla's here (I answer for some reason).

– Went via the store (Violet wheezes in the hallway) to get some things for supper. Look: what do you think this is?

I think every man should be married and every man have children, but I say I have no idea.

– It's shutfish from the market, Gando. Caught this morning is what they told me. And Jula will do her chocolate cake for pudding, I should expect.

The bedroom door opens, and a voice says:

– Might do.

VII

Sleep, sleep, it's what the god wants to see.

It won't be the end of the world if I sleep. I can see how it might be perhaps a little dangerous to, but she'll wake me up, she'll nudge me in time, as long as she doesn't sleep, but she won't or if she does, I'll wake her up in time. It's the middle of the afternoon, I mean. It's not even very likely that one of us will sleep, and the idea that we both would is frankly crazy. That we both would! When look at what it would mean, Maris!

Sleep, come on now, sleep.

Anyway, you do have the gun. Open your eyes: it's over there on the bedside table, it's inches, inches away. She is ten times further from it than you are! If she grabs for it she's dead. I can hear her breathing. Nothing has happened. I wonder what will, now that we're here and nothing has. I'm hot in all these clothes. It's down my back I'm hottest, it's my back that she's near to. I wonder how near. I'll turn when I'm ready. See how near. Meanwhile me. Eyes wide open, very awake. Head a bit giddy, drank so many things yesterday, not enough water, that was the key area. Not enough water, water between drinks. Then all that red Fortified, no wonder I'm so giddy. Mouth dry too.

Sleep, sleep, it's what the god wants to see.

I wonder what it would look like to see us here asleep together.

Unutterably sacred. Sleep, Maris, sleep. It's the impossible image, the image of all happiness and you could give it to your god so easily this day, this dark cloudy afternoon, you and the beauty curled up in this one place, sleeping, shifting,

88

trusting, sighing. Oh imagine the god ... You know he'd
stare at this page, and his stare would resolve itself into a
peaceful contemplation, then startle into a joy, resolve itself
again into inexpressible peace. All those who are around
your god would gather at his shoulders, Maris, would be able
to read the page for themselves, he'd never notice them there:
shush, they are all miming to one another, shush, shush ...
You know what the god does now? He smooths this page
with his great hand, then turns a little corner over to remind
himself that any time he can be back here, leaf back to this
and see the white triangle that's pointing to the image of all
rapture: see yourself asleep with her, asleep with her, asleep

– Not asleep, are you, mister?

– No! I'm quite awake (and here I am, awake, indeed sitting up).

– All right, only asked, it's just it wouldn't be a bright idea.

She sits up beside me in her white T-shirt. It says CAGLIO
PANTHERS IT'S 101 TIME on it. I don't know what else she's
wearing because when she got into the bed she asked me not
to look. She said that if we wanted to kiss any more we ought
really to kiss in the big bed because else, she said, it was just
like kissing some boy at a dance, and that was 'pretty pointless in the end'.

– You have dances then? (I asked, as I got into bed in my
white shirt and blue suit trousers and socks) We have dances.

– I bet they're not like our dances. Ours are wild. Close
your eyes.

I did and saw them, the stomping dances in the barn at
Gispar, but in the formations snaking along past the log fire I
just saw faces from the Island – Juilla, Violet, Magnick, Dennis Flames, the angry student in the café yesterday, Adzell,
Mace, Yung, all dancing and laughing. This was just after
lunch. I felt the springs of the bed bouncing as Juilla got into
bed with me. As Juilla got into bed with you. As Juilla got
into bed with you. This was just after the news at lunchtime.

'More from our cloven-hoofed friends later this is *Network*

Argelino first for news and first for stars on a very overcast I think you could say where indeed is our summer gone afternoon I'm Lora Cato and I think we *have* Dennis Flames do we yes Dennis afternoon I hear you've had some trouble with your gearstick Dennis?' 'Nothing a little oil can't solve it's one-thirty I'm Dennis Flames *with* the news headlines and it's more trouble for the Bank of the East Argeline as Mr Ricatorio Figel testifies to further irregularities more on that later the President sets out a new agenda *for* foreign policy in the light of recent trouble in the Dominions my name is Dennis Flames this is *Newshour* and *we look* at the rising tension as further divisions are sent *to* the troublesome once had a truly fabulous holiday there island of Bah-deo great shame the time is just coming up to one-thirty-one and now this.'

– I'm not in the news much any more (I tell her now), it's as if I never was.

– I'm not in it ever (she points out sadly) and I definitely am.

– I think I may be home and dry.

– I think I may be home (she says for some reason). If anyone finds us like this we'll be home and dead.

– You think your mother would kick me out? We're just talking though, aren't we. I don't think she'd kick me out, would she?

– Bloody hell, mister. You tell me. You married her.

– I didn't. I didn't even – well, sleep with her.

– Shut up, who cares. Anyway. Paol would kill you if Mom didn't.

– Why? Nothing is happening. Paol? He's a little boy.

– He'd kill you, chum, then nothing would always be happening. I'm sleepy.

– Is it your fever again?

– No, don't worry. You can stay here next to me. It's just sleepiness. I didn't sleep last night much.

– No, I didn't (I say truthfully, for I really didn't at all).

– Why didn't you sleep? Because of anything?

– (Because of you) No.

– That's like me. It wasn't because of anything. I'm going to rest for a while (and she slides down to the pillow again) and you know you better keep watch, mister, else I'll slap you.

Juilla turns over and takes some deep long breaths, really does sound like she's asleep. I look down at her. Her honey-brown hair is tangled and plastered to the pillow, her white T-shirt has ridden half-way up her back. Further down her, in the darkness below the coverlet, I can see the pale gleam of her slip, but nothing else. Then she moves her legs back to lock into mine and I can tell by the feel they are bare. It is possible quite awkwardly to ease myself down to my own pillow, which I do, keeping my face back from her hair, then gently placing my hand on the nearest wisps of it, and testing it like some thread there's never been. I shouldn't be wearing all this. I'm burning.

And I'm phoning. Is that the Ybrul Brothers Cloth House on the Avenue Strauber? Mr Bellamorte here. We think there may be an incendiary problem at 1-24 Avenue Hali. We can smell burning. That's right. Yes. And we think one of your employees, a Madame Violet Maricolo, may be a tenant of the property. That's right, yes. Yes. Yes. Better to be safe than – that's right. If you could. No smoke without. Sorry to be such a. Quite. Cheerio.

Look at her. Look at her. I have never felt like this before. I have never imagined feeling like this, and I cannot imagine feeling like it even at the moment I am feeling like it, and I do not imagine I could ever express it either. I can see the time go by. I can actually see its black pulses on the air, plock, sshh, plock, sshh, I can't even see her face. I don't know her. She's rude and young. I'm dependent on her mother for my very life. This can never be. We could never go anywhere. We have no money. We could only ever travel as father and daughter. Violet would come after us. She'd do better than

91

the Badean Police. She'd hang us higher. Shoot us deader. Leave us for flies. Plock, sshh, plock, sshh. what is it? What is it? I feel nothing. I feel what she feels. I look at her and feel the position she's lying in, feel warmth down my one side, feel the cool breeze on the small of my back, feel I have honey-brown hair spread across the pillow. Feel I'm alone though. What is it? What is it? I could die for doing this, could be found today, tomorrow, could still be tried and killed, never, never see my real home but it is beginning not to matter. I had a surge of home. Then, it was warm, like water, it seems to have slowed down time, made it have to wade, made it not bother and stand there. What is it? She is moving, breathing, knows it's me here. I can think of all the things we can talk about, do together, I can build a whole high city of the to-come on the one tiny page of a past we have. Juilla and Maris. Maris and Juilla. I feel nothing. She is feeling it for me. Now the lower half of her body has pressed back on me and moves, moves very slightly up and down. What is it? Very strange and clear now, very bold and certain. She's no more asleep than I am, is she, and her hair tickles my face. I arch away from that and she turns, turns face down so her eyes glance along at me:

— What, you all right?
— Yes. It tickled.
— What tickled?
— You tickled, your hair.

She turns all the way round and watches me closely. She rests her upper teeth gently on her lower lip, as she has been doing since I have been alive, and brushes a lock of hair from her forehead. She raises her eyebrows and looks very young. Then she looks serious, grown and purposeful. She watches, watches my face very closely as one of her little hands starts to hold me where I thought she would, then undo me, staring, shrug me free and begin, for the first time in this world, staring, gently, deliberately, staring.

Is that the Ecolas Belombre on Avenue Glasz? I'm trying

to get hold of a P. D. Maricolo, yes, he's needed at home. Mm-hmm, I know, but it's important. In other circumstances I'd obviously – that's right. Yes. I mean you got to haven't you sometimes. No, that's very understanding. Yes, I have been in touch with his mother. She'll be home shortly so there won't be a problem. Yes, that's right. Ha, you're telling me, lady! Yeah! Yeah. She's nice, isn't she, the mother? Very trusting. Works at Ybrul Brothers. Do I know Paol's big sister? Do I know Paol's big sister. DO I KNOW PAOL'S BIG SISTER! Lady, she's a doll. Let me tell you, she hops into bed in her underwear, wriggles against you, makes so you can't do nothing, then just goes right to it, staring at you, her mouth wide open and so wet you have to kiss it, lady, I'm sorry am I boring you? No? I mean, she goes to a convent school, don't you know? It's not as if she's from a luckless home like so many these days. Where did she learn it? Who knows where she learnt it but she makes so you just can't bear it, and you lie there, hang on, hang on, xxxxxxx, dropped the phone that's better you lie there and you want to speak but she kisses you you want to touch her but she shakes her head you want to kiss her but she won't that time you want to scream but she says shut up or I'll slap you I mean what would you do, me I think I'd do them anyway I think once it gets to that stage, I think once it gets to that stage, once it gets to that stage, hang on, xxxxxxx, thought I heard someone, xxxxxxx, no it's the wind on the landing, what can you do? Anyway, must get on, you know there's lots of people have to die today, that's right, that's what I do, right, yes indeed, but it's a living – Whoops! xxxxxxx SORRY, LADY! Really couldn't stop myself. Terrible pun there.

– Heaven, heaven . . .

– Cor, the River Burneau. Look you'll have to say you did that. We've no time to wash it.

– I did do it, Juilla . . .

– No, on your own I mean.

– On my own. Why would I do it on my own?

– Why would you do it – hell, mister. Fine father you make.

– Juilla.

– Father.

– Shut up.

– Or you'll kill me.

– Or I'll kill you. But, what I mean is. Thank you.

– Yep. All right. I liked it. I got kind of, well, sticky.

– What are we going to do?

– I'm going to sleep, chicken, you're going to stay awake and keep sharp so we don't get murdered.

– All right. Right. (I love you.) I'll do that. (Chicken.) Chicken.

– Mmmm.

Home to the meadow, home to the mere, home to the maple tree, home to me . . .

– Mister.

– Juilla.

– I don't know what you think, and I know I go on a bit, and there's all your old cock about being my father and that, but I think you should know.

– Know what, Juilla?

– You should know, sort of officially, this does mean we're having a love affair. It's not just anything.

– Oh. Well. Good! I mean I hoped it wasn't.

– He means he hoped it wasn't. Well it wasn't. Your hope came true, boy. I'm not even going to tell Gisella. Even if she guesses.

– Why would she guess?

– Search me. She's incredible (and now she twists round eagerly) – she can tell me what'll happen in *Carli* too! It's brilliant (and she stares at me, as if I should agree).

– Why would you want to know that? Wouldn't it spoil it?

– God, you're useless. I'll kiss you once for that.

– (Does. Did.) I'll keep it quiet too.

– You? You've no friends. Good night, chum.

And she turns away, wriggles, gets comfortable, settles, sighs and is away. I laugh, I do. I laugh loudly, then quietly, and get ready to stay awake, look after her, do what she asked of me. I lie down again so I can feel her warmth. It's very comfortable and with my hands underneath my head there is no chance I would ever fall asleep. I never once have done in that position. I'll tell her that when she wakes up.

I can see the god from here. One of your angels told him there was going to be a page where he'd see you and the beauty curled up asleep together. So he's frowning now, because it hasn't happened yet and he was so looking forward to it. He's turning back the pages, grumbling, perhaps he missed it.

I'm walking in the sunlight, walking with some others: one of them matters.

'Let's stop here.' 'Let's not.' 'Why ever not?' 'A million reasons. Look at it.' 'It's a lovely old square, that's what I see.' 'There's people, sir, there's people. Those kind of people.' 'I want to meet those people.'

– Sweet dreams (I whisper softly so she can't hear and so she can hear).

– Do my best (she breathes).

He really wants to stop. He has walked for hours. The young men won't let him.

'Then let's stop here.' 'Jokin', sir?' 'Dead serious, young fellow, right here in the shade.' 'Better keep movin' sir, don't you reckon?' 'On the contrary, Mr Mace, I should like to stop here, take a breath, get my bearings, meet some folks. It's new to me.' 'It's new to them, sir. They don't all like it.' 'Who says they have to?' 'Don't stop here, sir.'

– Juilla . . .

– Maris.

– You awake?

– No, Maris.

– What can we do?

– Be fucking careful (and she squeezes my hand with her hand and lets it go).

The sun shines in our faces and the old man tries his luck again. 'How's this feel, Mr Yung?' 'Lonely, master Viceroy.' 'Dangerous in your opinion?' 'Lonely, master Viceroy.' 'The oracle has spoken and on we go.'

Sleep, sleep, it's what the god wants to see.

It won't be the end of the world if I sleep. It's light outside, that would wake me up. There's a wiser mind in me somewhere, I've always thought that, and that'd do the job if it had to. Anyway it's early, it's not long since lunch. I don't believe this has all happened. I don't believe this will happen again. No, no! I mean I believe it will, but I don't believe – what? I'm wide awake now. Awake and in love! In what? In love!

How, and when? Yes she kissed me yesterday, on the landing outside, then once in the room, then after that she and Violet were cooking, and I rested on the sofa, while Paol watched television. I was close to sleeping then – my, I drank a lot all day. Violet sat next to me on the sofa when we ate supper. She asked me if she had not made shutfish stew better than the one I had for lunch. I agreed she'd made it better, it was certainly less salty and the shutfish was very tender. Yes. It was better.

– How can we tell? (Juilla said sulkily. I had called her an idiot several hours earlier) we weren't there, were we?

– Take your father's word for it! (said Violet with her mouth full).

– They said at school who were you (said Paol from the floor) so I said you were my dad back from prison.

– He is your dad back from prison (Violet reminded him).

– They didn't believe me.

– Then they're stupid (Violet said, then frowned, but added) they're just kids, after all. We had a super day in the city, you two. I think we just take it all for granted what a super place we live in sometimes. I think we take for granted how great life is, hmm? Sometimes?

96

– How great is it? (said Juilla, fishing something out of her stew). Is this a snail?

– It's very great!

– I hate them. Owli has to have it.

– I don't (the boy protested). Chuck it.

– (Juilla threw him the wet flotsam, which he dropped on the carpet. Then she asked me bluntly) You think life is great, Father?

– Don't ask him that (said Violet) it's not easy for him with having been in prison so long, is it, Gando?

I remember thinking with terrible clarity how ridiculous Violet seemed just then, pretending I was her husband. What I wanted to say was that I'd never been in prison or even committed a crime until I arrived in Badeo two weeks ago, but instead I said with a sort of inebriated seriousness:

– Life has greatly got better in recent times for me.

– Because you're free now, aren't you, Gando? (Violet encouraged me, tearing her bread into bits).

– And you're happy, Father, aren't you? (said Juilla with a mocking smile and that was the difference).

That is the difference! They both play the game, but Violet thinks she can make it true. Violet thinks that by playing the game she will create the feelings that would exist if it were true, that she can make me feel towards her as if I really was her husband. Juilla just says the words. Knows it's all lies but makes the sounds, because she knows what I know. Words can do anything. Get you out of school. Disappoint the police. Change your name. Make schoolgirls cry. Yes I'm happy, Jula. Yes I'm happy.

I was happy later last night as we did the washing-up, and instead of being left alone again with Violet and her exaggerations of the day we had just spent, or Paol and his 'I bet you' or 'I challenge you' or 'I dare you', I was, for once, for a moment only, left alone with Juilla. She had her back to the sink, and lifted herself up with her hands on the draining board so her stockinged feet dangled over the floor.

97

– It's my turn to be ill tomorrow (she said), my turn to be hostage.

– Is it? (I pretended to have just discovered) So you're at home all day?

– I can feel it coming on (she sighed), that rare fever I get. Then the death must have placed its hands on her brow and pronounced her unfit for school, because she eased herself down to the floor again and said:

– Was I hot? I bet I was. I can feel it from inside me and it'll only get worse.

Paol strode in, staring hard at me, finishing his chocolate bar and saying:

– I've got fever too. I've got to stay home.

– You can't (his sister snapped), not if you're eating chocolate.

– The chocolate *gave* me the fever.

– I got a real fever. Don't know *where* I got it (and she glanced at me as she said so, then wandered from the kitchen).

Paol said as he also departed:

– I know where, but I don't have to say. It's not a real fever.

And I was left alone as ever with my death, flapping me a wet cloth, yawning *you wash, I'll dry.*

Violet made sure she was the last to go to bed last night. We stood in the kitchen. We were drinking red Fortified. She said:

– You don't need the gun now. You haven't realised. You don't need the gun now, Gando, you live here. You're back from the Mainland, you're home, you're who you are. Why don't you let it be, now? You and I could have our room back, the children could have theirs, we could live like a family. Instead I hate these nights, when you lock us in one room and I can hear you stomping about in the living room, sleeping alone on the floor. You haven't realised that we want you here with us. Not out there with a gun. None of us think you've ever shot a gun, hmm?

– Violetto. Violetto. I am a professional bodyguard, I am.

– You only think you were, Gando. Prison did this to you. Was it tough, prison, Gando?

– I would rather not talk about it, Violetto.

– I'm not surprised. Still, if you're going to try ripping off Government contractors . . .

– (I started laughing) Is that what he did, your husband?

– Yes, he was quite mad. 'Is that what I did,' you mean.

– Is that what I did. Well. I was quite mad, wasn't I?

– You and your friend Ferris (she muttered, darkly).

– Me and my friend Ferris (I chortled) Ferris and Maris!

– Sods, you were.

Home to the marigold, home to the mere, home to the meadowlark, home to the mountain . . .

– Juilla . . . You awake, Juilla (Chicken) are you?

Violet kissed me good night and said:

– Tomorrow. Tomorrow when I'm home, then we can change things . . .

– We can change things.

There are two machinists standing by a great machine. I'm one of them and the other one is Ferris. It's printed on his shoulder blade. We've been drinking in a bar. Now we're working the machine again. There is no danger. I am aware this is a dream. I even tell Ferris, but he says there's work to be done.

Sleep, sleep, it's what the god wants to see.

There are two machinists standing by a great machine. Neither of them is a man I know. One turns a crankshaft. The other stands back and mops his brow. 'Let's rest,' says that one, 'or we'll be at it all night, man.' 'You rest,' mutters the other, 'you rest. I'll keep at my turning.' 'There's no need to turn it all night, man,' says the one who spoke first, 'you know we could up and go dancing.' 'You do that,' says the other, 'you go. Enjoy yourself.' The first machinist can't see what kind of a machine it is. He looks up and can't see the top of it. He looks down and can't see the bottom of it, just a pale gleaming below. He's suddenly worried about what it might be doing. But the second machinist, coated in oil, he'll turn it all night, doesn't care what it's doing, so long as he's paid money for it, so long as he has to. Both men are in hell.

'So I say,' says the dark machinist, 'dance the jig until morning. But leave me working here.' 'I don't want to leave you,' the first man protests, 'not all on your own here, man.' 'I am often on my own,' says the working man, 'I want you to be gone.' 'I can't dance on my own, man. Let's leave the machine to cool down a while. We can always crank it up come the morning.' But the second machinist becomes angry now, cries, 'Go, go, so I can turn the machine all night!' It all becomes too frightening in the end for the first machinist, now that the dark man is pointing a black finger right in his face and hissing, 'Go, go, get the fuck out of here now!'

So now I wake and it's only the alarm call of the death, stretching a thin finger towards Juilla, where she's night-marish and shaking in her clothes by the light of the window, though the death is saying *Don't fret I've dialled three ones for the Army*.

And now I wake and it's my gun and the very end of it and Violet Maricolo saying:

– Get out of my flat now or I'll blow your blue fucking head off –

II

Burneau's Letter

From: Ministry of Reconciliation, The,
        Palace of Popular Valour, The,
        Avenue Iaio Gabril, The,
        Uerba Badeo

To: Brother (perhaps Father now) Fredo
    (if he is still to be found there)
    Refuge St Hrabal, The,
    Rezion Ospar, The,
    Koborol, The,

Dear Brother Fredo

I imagine that nothing could surprise you more than to hear
from me, a person whom, if you remember at all, you will remember either as a little boy who got himself lost on the
mountainside one day some twenty years ago, or, more recently, as a traitor and disgrace to the country of his birth.
Certain of our operatives have brought to my attention the
state of my reputation in that land, the Argeline Domain, a
reputation which has fallen so far in general esteem that even
my family are rumoured to have denounced me in order to
protect themselves. But that name is my name, Burneau,
which has stood by me despite my worst efforts to discard or
abuse it, and so I write to you in the fond and distant hope
that you may one day, in the course of your godly ministra-
tions, be presented with an opportunity to pass that name on
to those who gave it me when they gave me life itself, and reassure them as to the nature of certain lies which are

103

universally held to be truths, and of certain truths that have never had a chance to breathe as a truth should be free to breathe and tell them, in short, Brother Fredo, if you are yet living, and perhaps by this time a Father of the Refuge of St Hrabal, tell them my story.

No harm can come to yourself through the reading of this letter, or the subsequent relation of its contents to those who know and did once love me. Harm can come only to me, who through no fault of his own, as I shall explain to you, came to do harm to so many innocent others. Read it without fear, Brother Fredo, though it comes to you bearing the insignia of the foes of the Argeline Domain: the new tenants of the Palace of Popular Valour, the rulers of the Free Republic of Badeo. Read it without prejudice, if you can, read it without hatred, if there is room for me still in your great heart. Harm can come only to me, Maris Burneau, poor bearer of that unhappy name.

I wonder if you remember that time upon those beautiful mountains whose purest air and favour we once shared? This is the first of many stories to be told. How I was following the mountain goat that belonged to the clockman's girl Cecile, how, because of some childish slight she ran away home and left me with that awkward animal, and how it led me higher and higher into the mist, always vanishing over a rock or into a cleft. Why I continued to follow I don't know, but perhaps I felt that the blame for her tears was mine, and so the burden of the goat must be mine too. I believed that if I could retrieve the goat (which, it suddenly grieves me to recall, was never seen again) I could reverse the events of the afternoon: my heartless insult to Cecile's manner of speaking (for all her vowels were long and I made fun of that, yawning and saying 'We'll both be old when you finish!') her sobs at that affront, her running away down the slopes, and the goat's rearing away off and up them.

When the goat had slipped finally and for ever from my sight (it was a goat called Browny) the mists surrounded me and it became impossible to restrain my own tears of utter frustration and loss. So misty it was that I could scarcely make out which way was up and which way was down, except by moving my feet, and so I sat on the stone ground, firmly, grimly believing that I would never see anybody again. Many hours passed on that ledge, and the consolation of tears was that they shattered cogent thought, so that while I endured the wracks of crying I could not coldly apprehend the seriousness of my situation. The consolation of silence was that it might herald a sound, some sound other than the wind, or the occasional shrieking of – a baleful recollection! – ringbirds, we called them. Still, the only sound my silence heralded was a fresh onset of swollen sobs. I have been in a few such situations in the twenty years that followed, I have heard air pass through the clear nostrils of a sniper, I have been without a friend in the world. But no time was ever like that hour, that day, that lifetime as a boy marooned on the frozen ribs of the Folded Mountain.

The next person I saw in the world was nobody I knew. I had only barely understood from the conversations of my parents that somewhere higher than our upland settlement of Gispar there stood houses of a god, and in these little stone huts lived the Brothers of the Refuge of St Hrabal, who were said to live on nothing but their faith and the essences of mountain flowers: the wink-in-darkness, the crust-of-a-moon, the frecklemint. You it was, Brother Fredo, as you were then, who heard my cries, and you it was who appeared out of the blue and worsening mist with a stick in your hand and a cloak made somehow of sheep wool. Of course I remember what you said then. You loudly and instantly said, and your voice seemed to blow away the mist itself, 'See, old son, your snorting made a prayer!'

So young and confused was I that all I thought at the time was how strange it was to be called 'old son' by a very old man (as you then were) whom I had never met before. And I was also embarrassed to be told I had been 'snorting', which

105

was a sound I associated with the pigs we kept at Gispar! But somehow all the words stayed with me, though they have been hidden for many years, as I was hidden in the mist, and that poor goat was hidden and is still hidden.

Doubtless, Brother Fredo, with what you now know about me, or what you have heard about me (which if you will only hear my story you will know to be most different), you would have passed by that terrible ledge and let me freeze or plunge to death on the mountain where I was born. Or you would have given me a helping hand in that direction. Either way, I would not have lived to tell the story. As a man of the Argeline, you would cry: 'For then he would not have been alive to murder the Viceroy Lagland in the street, to fight with the accursed Rebels in the War for Badeo, to plan their battles and orchestrate their attacks, and to sit now behind his great blue desk, great in honour of his status, blue in honour of his nickname, and write this letter to me with a platinum pencil, signing himself so grandly Minister of Reconciliation!' No, you saved me, Fredo, you took me to the warm little huts and fed me bean-soup and whey, and you took me home and by doing so rendered possible all the fearful events that brought such disgrace and opprobrium upon the name Burneau, and so much conflict and destruction to the armies of Badeo and the Mainland.

It is because you saved me that I am writing to you, and because you know of my family who still live in the village below the Refuge of St Hrabal, and because you are a man of a god (and there is certainly a god present in my life, though I do not think he is alone), and because I wish to record the truth. I ask you in the name of your god and my god (which is, after all, the same name: god) and on the honour of the Argeline Domain that nurtured us both, and in holy veneration of the Mountain which both gave me a life and offered me a death you interceded to prevent me accepting, I ask you this: That my letter be not read by any other man or woman in this world, and that its contents be related (in spoken

106

words only, and only by you, Fredo) to only the following people – my father Abel Burneau, my mother Marie Burneau, my elder brother Hektor Burneau and my younger brother André Burneau. And that this letter be destroyed by you, Fredo, once you have read it three times, by burning in a fire. Fredo, if you were to show this letter, to show my story, to the authorities of the Domain, or, much much worse, of this Island that has become my home in exile, I would be surely put to death, for reasons that you will come to understand. And I believe you will understand that this, more than any other, is the reason I have decided to write to you. For once you held my life in your large old hands. You were a stranger and yet you came to my aid. You alone, as it seems to me, are the man who must once more take my life into his safeguard, either preserving my name for the happy reassurance of that good family I cannot hope to meet again in this world, or dooming me to the fell powers of our time, powers with which I have co-operated in a manner weak and shameful. If you are no longer living, and this letter has been opened by a different brother at St Hrabal, I have little doubt that he will waste no time in choosing the latter course, for one who never saved my misty, bedevilled life will see no cause to save it again. My letter is to you only, Fredo, because my letter is the truth, and a man of a god will recognise the truth, because his god is there to assure him.

I will tell you tales of war and murder, of love and camaraderie, of kindness and betrayal. I will tell you how it came to be that I was hunted high and low for a murder I did not commit, and raised up as a hero by concealing one I did. I will tell you a tale of shame and magic. And I will tell you how, on two occasions, two years apart, my heart was found and lost. Somehow I will tell you all.

When I think of what the people of the Argeline Domain must feel for me, I tremble, Fredo, for these are Argeline hands that shake, and a pure heart of the Koborol that creaks with the leaden weights of home lost and time gone. My

107

voice is the tired flesh of a prisoner shackled by those two dreadful anchors. There is no rest but to write, and there is no rest in writing.

Outside this grand empty room, with nothing in it but the blue desk and my golden chair, I hear two soldiers patrolling the corridor, their hard and regular walk fixing time as well as a clock can. All the most important rooms in the Palace of Popular Valour (once the Viceregal Residence on Avenue Marchant, which is itself changed to the Avenue Iaio Gabril, as a tribute to our First President) are to be found so far within the walls of the building that we have no windows. Yet, Brother Fredo, believe me, I have no delight in views of the ocean. The Mainland is too far away to be seen, but to know it is there is to see it, and to know what it thinks of me is to feel all the cries of a country's hatred fill this room like the salt, infested sea. No, I belong in this airless and golden hollow, alone with my platinum pencil, my picture of President Gabril (or General Gabril as he was known then, smiling between myself and Battle Marshal Curtens) and my endless and endlessly delayed Plans for Reconciliation.

The claims pile up half-way to the ceiling, and the ceiling is high above, with clouds and sky painted across it, and the sun with seven points, shining out at the same time as a sleepy-looking blue planet and innumerable twinkling stars. When the claims reach the ceiling itself, they will join on to the end of the Milky Way, as if to hold on to its shirt-tails for eternity! There are claims from West Laquillean wine-growers, for damage inflicted by their neighbours who fought for the Domain; claims from Saldeans, for ruination left behind by the Furasolians who were meant to be fighting on their side; claims from Badean citizens evicted on what they say is false suspicion of collaboration; claims from midland hop farmers who reckon their yields were halved by the drawing of the Second Partition; and claims of wrongful arrest from every single POW jailed on the crowded isle of Cobar – as if there can be a mistake when a man is taken in the uniform of the Mainland! But every claimant threatens death to his opponents; nobody will compromise or think twice or listen. Nobody is reconciled. At times the President will step in through the velvet door that leads only to him, and enquire with a chuckle: 'What have you reconciled for me today, Mr Burneau?' I have little to offer him, but he doesn't seem to mind. He will reach up to take the top claim from the pile, scan it in a flash and say, 'Pay the Furasolian' or 'Fine the woman of Gamor', then he'll say something about what an easy job mine is, and how he only wished he could do it himself, 'But I have no time, Mr Burneau, no time!' I don't want to tell him that the claims he reads are quite frequently counter-claims contesting rulings he told me to give in the first place. He never realises. He never sees that the openness he is trying to encourage is a hopeless project. We will be wading in claims, we will be listening to every lie told every day for the two years of the War for Badeo. Perhaps you will understand, as I now see it myself, that my urgent need to commit the truth to paper is my despairing response to passing the working days of my life engaged in the balancing up of contrary and competing falsehoods.

And of course, Fredo, even the attempt must be shrouded in deceit. Every time I hear between the brisk clacks of the soldiers that soft padding of the President towards the velvet door, I must conceal all of the pages I am writing to you within this trembling paper tower of claims. One day I will be found out, I am sure, or else my letter will be picked off the top of the pile by the President, and he will say, 'Have this traitor arrested, Burneau, for writing to the Argeline!' Instead of my plea, Fredo, you would receive from my messenger a letter asking you to pay for what the armoured trucks did to the barley crop of Farmer Timback of Harao, or taking you to task for your failure to relieve the siege of Laquilla three months earlier and save the sharks in the aquarium! I must be careful, my ears must be two guardsmen.

As I have referred above to 'my messenger', it seems a good idea to explain how this letter reached you, all the way from the gilded heart of the Palace of Popular Valour to the misty mountain hollow where, I fervently hope, the Brothers of St Hrabal still meditate in peace. The next exchange of prisoners home to the Domain (how I wish I too could be an unknown prisoner!) is scheduled to take place in ten days' time. We are shipping fifty Argelinos home in the tugboat *Leonor*, and receiving from the Domain the same number of Badeans in a yacht called *Silverlight*. I have responsibility for this exchange, which I hope will be the first of many, for there are countless thousands left stranded by the fighting. President Gabril is happy to repatriate the Argelinos who sailed here to the War (for some suspect he is trying a little International Reconciliation himself!) but he is, alas, extremely reluctant to pardon the Badeans who chose to fight for the Domain. In fact, he wants some of them shot in due course. What a curiosity of the aftermath of war: that an Islander should want to send the Mainlanders, the foreign Argelinos, home to the joy and safety of their families, but line his fellow Islanders up against a wall! Most of the Ministers are opposed to further bloodshed, but Gabril changes his mind and mood almost from hour to hour. Yesterday over dinner he said he could never pardon the Badeans who collaborated. This morning after eggs and salmon he says he is a man who can forgive anyone anything. The boys breaking rocks on Cobar should be praying for sunny days, Fredo, sunny days and good breakfasts for our President. And of course my opinion counts little. Because I am the Minister for Reconciliation, the President chuckles, 'Of course Mr Burneau says "No more death" – he's the Minister for Reconciliation! Now: let's hear the views of the Department of National Security . . .'

You will discover, Fredo, that I have a special reason to plead for the lives of the collaborators. One boy among them is dear to me, or rather, dear to one who is dear to me. But I

110

shall leave that to the story to unfold as it pleases. It makes no sense to dwell on it now.

I had begun to explain how my message got to you, Fredo. The *Leonor* will be carrying forty-nine Argelino prisoners and one infiltrator, who, out of his friendship towards me, has agreed to conceal himself among the group. My high position in the Government has made this possible, but it remains a terrible risk to take. The young man's name is Tragolani, no ordinary man, and he will carry this letter sealed up and unread beside his heart, carry it right across the ocean between us, up into the Koborol to Gispar, and thence to the Rezion Ospar and the Refuge St Hrabal. This loyal and determined young man is prepared to begin a new life in the Argeline Domain, posing as a soldier returned from the War. I wonder whether every man who is obliged to turn himself into another – as I had to, Fredo – finds elsewhere in the world a counterpart to turn the other way! Now Tragolani will live out his days in the high Koborol, in some valley near to my own, maybe passing by my brothers or parents one morning in the dairy market. I have asked him to make himself known only to you, Fredo. Only a complete reconciliation, an enduring peace between the Argeline Domain and its lost possession Badeo, will create the circumstances under which Tragolani can return here, once he has made his crossing with this letter for you. As for me, as for my return in the opposite direction, I do not think even peace will be enough. And what lies beyond peace? Forgetting. Oblivion.

Rather oblivion than the way I am known in my homeland. I know I am the treacherous Burneau, the upland crossing-sentry who enlisted to guard the Viceroy, shot him down on his inaugural trip to the Island, vanished in the Badean throng, then made his way to Furasol to side with the rebels of the Organ Liberat. The enemy Burneau, the sly tactician, the friend to the Generals, their hero of the struggle and, at the end of the fighting, this powerful grandee who can be found always at his blue desk, deep within the lamplit interiors of the Palace of Popular Valour – in the Ministry of Piles of Paper, we call it. You may know little or none of this, Fredo, high up in the godly solitude of your mountain shelter, but I know that all across the wide Argeline Domain – my Domain first and for ever – I am called the 'Blue Devil of Badeo'. I have seen a colour drawing of myself with a sack over my shoulder, and all the dead infantrymen, Badeans, Argelinos, gypsies, vagabonds, crammed bloodily inside. I think that not even the person who truly did kill Viceroy Lagland, and so sparked the War for Badeo – and that is a person who has passed through my life, Fredo – I think that not even that person should have to carry such a sack. But a man must at least carry his own dead, and my sack will never be empty.

I was one of four bodyguards hired to protect the person of Viceroy Wallemire Lagland on his inaugural visit to Badeo. The names of my fellow guardsmen were Adzell, Mace, and Yung, a huge great silent man. I remember little about them except that they were not greatly enamoured of me: at least, Adzell and Mace were outwardly hostile. As Yung rarely spoke to anybody, it was difficult to interpret his wordless state in any way whatever. In the months and years that followed I came to envy such marble impenetrability – when every word I speak is like a brightly coloured finch or starling, winged by the arrows of hunters, barbed and infecting arrows that spin the bird to earth to be examined, classified, stuffed, served up. I felt strongly that the guardsmen resented the suddenness of my addition to their number, especially since my employment was necessitated by the death of one of their friends in the course of his sentinel duties. Both Adzell and Mace baldly questioned my credentials for the work. What answer could I give, but that the Viceroy Lagland had taken his holidays in the shadow of the Folded Mountain many years ago? That the place had romantic connections for that gentleman and his wife, and that he loved the 'loyal and simple folk' of the region? 'Put your heart in the hand of the mountain man, my father used to say,' as the Viceroy cheerfully reminisced. To Adzell and Mace that was no kind of explanation at all! They were hardened professional security agents, they were strong men from the roughest sectors of the Argeline City. Mace was always shoving me from behind, demanding where were the eyes in the back of my head? Adzell was too quick with his slaps to my face. I hardly saw his hand move, neither there nor back, which made me wonder if some great moth had not beaten its wings on my cheek, or that a devilish spirit was about. It was impossible for them to warm to me. The one chance I had to gain their friendship I threw away, by beating them repeatedly at the game of Scissors-Paper-Stone, the favoured pastime of these three men, despite doing my utmost to lose. Their foolproof methods of play – Adzell's intense scrutiny of minute muscular jolts in the hand, presaging the flick of Scissors, the flat stiffness of Paper, or the brute lumping into Stone; Mace's tunnelling into your very eyeballs for the truths he said he could see; Yung's intuitive sense of the moment – each fell in turn to my utterly random guesswork. What shall I do? Stone! (Adzell does Scissors.) I'll switch to Paper! (And it wraps Adzell's furiously trembling Stone.) I retreat apologetically to Stone again (and crush Mace's V of Scissors). I go back to the handshake of Paper (and Yung does the same) so we play a decider, and I snip his hand in two. Well, they went back to competing among themselves, convinced somehow by my success in the bouts that I was a beginner with much to learn. Do you know that game, Brother Fredo?

We sailed for the fateful Island on a hot summer's day, sitting around the glass-covered forecabin, the Viceroy with his assistants beside a table of tall cold drinks, though he himself was, I recall, a man of moderation in all things, a quality I very much respected and admired. (How strange this must sound to the ears of an Argelino, these words of fond respect for that man from his so-called assassin!) We bodyguards

113

were not permitted to drink that day, and, during the five-hour crossing my three colleagues either slept or played their favourite game; that is, one would sleep and the other two would play. Sometimes two would sleep, in which case the other would practise on his own, but I never ever saw them all asleep at the same time. They were certainly very professional. I sat sometimes this way, sometimes that, watching the slow, slow recession of the only shoreline I had ever known, yellow sands and the famed strawberry façades – a coast I thought I would see again in three months only – or, watching the mercury-bright sea finally give birth to a strip, and then a hump, and then a rising green spread of land in the due south. 'Ca ci ta Batheo!' cried the ship's young helmsman in his language, 'Ca ci ta Bathean inciul!' I remember as if it were yesterday how the Viceroy strode to the window of the deck, to take command of the sight. It struck me that he had not once looked backward towards the Argeline Mainland, and I was impressed by this for a moment, by the single-mindedness and solemnity with which he seemed to be regarding his new appointment. Then, however, I felt a tide of melancholy, for I realised that I myself had ceased to look back about half an hour before, when I could see the southernmost jut of the Argeline – the great pleasure pier at Diena – and that now, as I turned to make sure, the coast I had left behind had disappeared over the horizon. I had forgotten to see it go, and experienced for the first time the sense that I was profoundly alone, that not one soul knew me on the land ahead, that not one could see me from the land behind, that I scarcely existed, I was spirit, I was air. This stream of emotion resolved itself into an almost physical, muscular love for the Viceroy, for the crew, even for those three guards who so disliked me. I loved them all because they were alive, but most of all I loved them because they were there with me in the past. Though the Viceroy died that day, indeed only hours later, and though maybe all of those bodyguards perished in the War, and maybe the ship went

114

down one night with the young helmsman still humming obscurely at the wheel, I seem to love them still, and I think it is for that reason.

'There you are, Burneau,' said the Viceroy, not taking his eyes from the window. 'Isn't she just the isle of all your dreams?'

Out of the corner of my eye I saw Mace and Adzell snigger at this, for it agreed with a joke they had – I was the dreamer, the dreaming Blue Burneau. I went to the window too, in my new suit, wondering how I could contribute to the Viceroy's special moment.

'She,' I said. 'Islands are always "she's", aren't they, sir?'

'Ah, well, you know why that is, Burneau.'

'I don't, sir; no, I don't.'

Adzell cut in: 'He's not really one for the old "she's", sir. Not really in his ken, don't you know?'

(Those men were always referring to the fact that I had had in my life only pleasant friendships with girls, with the shepherdesses and dairymaids around Gispar. They thought I should have fathered hundreds of children by now!)

'Nonsense, Captain Adzell,' said the Viceroy. 'You can see in this man's eyes the clear image of three young girls waving farewell, farewell. Whereas all I see in your eyes is blood and sleep.'

'I'm a guardsman, sir,' said Adzell. 'No one waves farewell to me.'

'Not if you see 'em first,' Mace said with a smirk.

'So, Burneau,' said the Viceroy kindly, 'you carry in your eyes the answer to your question. Islands recall to us our essentially lonely nature. Also, they are generally thought to be beautiful. Everyone wants to possess them, but they have a habit of slipping away. All manifestly qualities of a "she", wouldn't you say? And it's because of their feminine re-sistance to possession, that the world of males and mainlands sends in the likes of me. I am, if you like, a shy bouquet of flowers from the suitor to the beloved.'

115

'And we're your gift-wrap,' grinned Adzell, his last word the inevitable cue for a sudden swipe into Scissors, comprehensively bludgeoned by the Stone of Captain Mace.

We sailed by the two tiny islands off the northern shore of Badeo: Kina, which has a luxury hotel on it, and Kinei, which has nothing at all, and landed at the quay beside the Hotel Marine, from where our belongings were to be transferred to the Viceregal Residence. I hadn't taken much with me: a picture of the family, paper to write letters on, silky green notepaper given to me as a present at my leavetaking banquet. Everything that was needed to keep me looking smart and efficient – shirts, combs, suit-brushes, and all that – was provided by the Security Division, and all the rest I was told I could buy in Badeo. Each of us was given a hundred Badean markers to spend, money that would be waiting for us when we got to our four small apartments at the Residence.

The Viceroy had been advised to go there first and rest, before undertaking his tour of Badeo Town, but in this, as in many other things that day, he trusted to his instincts and decided we would go straight into the Town. He kept saying that he wanted to 'get to know the Badeans personally', which I think was a very worthy desire, but perhaps he had not been sufficiently briefed as to the hostility of many on the Island. True, the Mainlanders were at their most welcome in the Capital itself, but the place was full of provincials too, Saldeans, Furasolians, even San Timotheans, though they were easy enough to spot, with their coloured caps and bronzed faces.

'Round 'em up and chain 'em down,' Mace jeered when he first saw some of them.

'Tell them about the march of time,' Adzell agreed.

We set off, it saddens me to tell, four of us in our light grey suits, with our dark sunglasses on and our four right hands permanently resting inside our jackets. Adzell in front on the Viceroy's right, Mace on his left, Yung behind Mace, myself

116

behind Adzell. We walked, we watched, and all the time that decent gentleman Wallemire Lagland smiled at the crowds roped back along the way, and sometimes strolled over to shake an outstretched hand. We came south along the Promenad Furasol, with the docks away to the right and the most expensive hotels and casinos ranged along the left: the Royale, the Imperion, the Queen of Emaio and, all of black glass, the Richesse.

I felt no fear, Brother Fredo. I felt responsibility, and an enveloping love of strangers, that still, spreading pain I have tried to describe to you. I felt also a love of land – perhaps I tried to feel that in a way this too was home, or at least that it knew home, that it had its Gispar and its valleys with their folk like my folk, and that the only other country was the ocean, was the loss of land – but I know differently now. I know differently indeed. I wonder perhaps whether there is no country but the past. In the past you have an identity, a home, borders you defend: everybody there is your countryman. After the past comes uncertainty, chaos, intrusion, expedition. The walls crumble easily, you are walking towards strangers. You think your country has followed you over the sea, but no, it stayed behind. It is the past, and though you claim it as your land, it has forgotten you itself. You are the past's own past. You are the past's own country, Brother Fredo. You yourself must know that to be true. Remember me, and tell me truthfully – is where I live not somewhere far beyond the past?

And when I wonder what is the future I see the god I often do see, Fredo, and the god cannot know the future any more than you, the reader of this page. When I stop to consider what will be, I see always a god with a book, a god who has himself stopped to consider what will be! There is a moment of real stillness. I sigh and go on, and he is glad and reads on.

When I wonder what is the future I see a death, too, this mischievous dawdling figure that accompanies me on my travels, nattering alongside or off on his own jaunts, though

117

when I wonder what is the future he is always back from where he went, loaded with souvenirs, dear things, useless things.

Adzell, Mace and Yung guarded like they played their game. Adzell relied on his extraordinary quickness, his knack of sensing a movement before the person in the crowd had consciously chosen to make it. Mace's strength was his eyesight, which was immensely keen both at a distance and close by. Yung, again, used his mysterious powers of intuition, feeling the whole moment, knowing ahead what the next one would bring. At one point, I remember, half-way along the Way of Salute (which runs along the north shore) an old man in the crowd to our right suddenly produced a little banner, and hoisted it up to show us: WELCOM MR WALEMIRE, it read, but by the time his banner was in the air he had the barrel of Adzell's gun stuck right between his eyes, Mace's pointing at where his heart must have been, and the enigmatic Yung, somehow, standing beside him in the crowd gently holding a knife to his old throat. I was slower to move, but ended up poised between the Viceroy and the danger, my unconscious impulse having been towards protection. We all relaxed when we read the words on the banner, and Yung, towering above the little old man, patted him on his shoulder while the Viceroy walked across to shake his hand in friendliness. So there was a Badean he got to know personally. My, those men could do their work!

Three times have I been lost in my life, and there, then, came the second time. You know well of the first time, Fredo, in the blue mist of late afternoon high on the Folded Mountain, when you and I seemed the only inhabitants of our world. The third time came hard on the tail of the second, for, this second time, this second loss, was to be the cause of all my perils, joys and bewilderments. How can two events so very different, so far apart in time and distance, so opposite in their natures, be experienced with almost identical feelings? No shy and clumsy boy now, but a young man

118

in a suit, with a job in the Security Division! No bare freezing mountainside to bring on terror and desolation, but a burning, glaring day among thousands of people! No silence – cheering and laughter! No wind, no rock, but water sprinkled over the sweating crowds, wine offered from the darkness of every threshold, fights and dances breaking out beside each other, bumping into each other, becoming each other! An old grandmother in mourning throwing flowers to the guardsmen, some twenty little girls in white and green uniforms, singing through the uproar, a boy jumping up on a roof to blow some long silver bugle – the Way of Salute indeed! It was when we turned a sharp left, away from the coast and on to the broad Porodo that skirts the western reach of the Residential grounds, that I thought I saw a flame in the crowd.

Fire in the sunshine: that's a hard thing to see for sure, but I was quite convinced. It was standing still at first, as if someone was holding a brand of some kind, but then seemed to follow us along just behind the back of the crowd. I would glimpse it, turn and stare hard at the place, but it would be gone. As I turned away I would glimpse it again. If I had been on friendlier terms with my three colleagues, perhaps I would have tried to point it out to them, but with their hostility to my being a guardsman at all, and the electric tension of their truly amazing alertness, I found it too daunting to seize the time or manner in which to tell them of this strangest vision. 'Mr Adzell, fire darting along at eight o'clock . . . ' 'Huge torch aflame due west, Mr Mace . . . ' No, I put it all down to a trick of the island sunlight, and we walked on down the Porodo towards a larger, louder congregation.

'Slopers off to the left,' Adzell advised us. ('Slopers' is a city word for mountain dwellers like the San Timotheans. And us, Fredo.)

'Round 'em up,' said Mace again, 'and chain 'em down. No, roll 'em down. Roll 'em down their slopes.'

'You missing your own mountains, Burneau?' the Viceroy wondered, waving at an old lady in a wheelchair.

'No, sir, I carry them in my heart,' I said ill-advisedly.

'I bet they're blue,' said Mace, 'his mountains.'

'Of course they are,' the Viceroy agreed as he walked. 'Beautiful blue high peaks of the Koborol. Do you know – what's its name – yes, do you know the "Plainsong of the Lonely Soldier", Burneau?'

'I don't know that one, sir, no.'

'Slopers moving off,' muttered Adzell. 'Expressions nine clicks hostile.'

'Oh, I adore the Plainsong,' said Viceroy Lagland. 'We used to hear the milkmaids singing it in the morning, in the Rezion Juspar, do you know it? Woke us up every time, it did!'

Yung said something.

'What's up, tall man?' Mace asked quickly.

'Shaved stick, due west.'

We saw a young student holding a stick at the front of the crowd.

'Seven-five clicks hostile,' Adzell guessed.

'Less,' said Mace.

'Falling,' Adzell agreed, as the student lifted his stick, which unfurled a flag of the Argeline Domain. The Viceroy gave him a thumbs-up sign and started to sing softly:

> 'I am naught but a lonely soldier,
> I have naught but my bread and water by,
> I do naught but fight for my lord and king
> But I miss my babies seven, oh, and I
> Miss my lady, oh I do, I
> Miss my lady, oh.'

I glanced off to the left, where I thought I saw the flames again: there was nothing. We walked on.

'That's a corking ditty, sir,' said Mace.

'What happens to this paragon?' Adzell wondered in his unkind way.

'Just that,' said the Viceroy, 'for about a thousand verses. And in the nine hundred and ninety-ninth he gets three Ptopoline spears in the back.'

'That's tough on 'im,' said Mace. 'I mean, like so near the end of the song, sir.'

'He sings on, though,' said Wallemire Lagland, that good man, 'he sings on, doesn't he, Burneau?'

I wonder if you can imagine the disgrace of a bodyguard getting separated from the man he is protecting? How can it compare with your own life, Brother Fredo? You would have to fall fast asleep in the middle of one of your prayers! Worse, you would have to forget the name of your god. I was with the Viceroy at the junction of the Porodo and the Avenue Marchant: we had to turn left into this wide boulevard (which we have renamed the Avenue Iaio Gabril) running between the southern edge of the Residential Estate and the area of the city known as Allalong, the most cramped, dirtiest and liveliest part of Badeo, where the meat, fish and cloth markets are located, and the worst of chancers, and the cheapest of women. Only about thirty yards along the Avenue Marchant there is a turning off to the right. This plunges right into the heart of Allalong. It's called the Avenue Maldeau. The Viceroy abruptly decided we should change our course, and mingle with the people of Allalong at their daily travail. No matter how Guardsmen Mace and Adzell strove to dissuade him from this idea while we had paused at the junction, he wiped his forehead with his lace handkerchief and stood firm: 'To watch over them well, I must know them well,' was something like what he said. By this time we were accompanied by a number of dignitaries, including the Mayor of Badeo, Colonel Delavila of the Badean Civil Guard, and Mr Usham, from the Inspectorate of Free Trade, each with his own bodyguards. Mostly, these men were of the opinion that Allalong was a dangerous zone, and Viceroy Lagland's safety could not be guaranteed. The Viceroy suddenly asked me what I thought.

121

If I had agreed with the other guardsmen, that it was too dangerous to change the plan at this point, perhaps they would never have suspected me of involvement in the murder, but, as I have sought to describe, I was filled with warm feelings of trust and goodwill, and intoxicated with the luxuriance and vigour of all these city lives. So I – awful moment to go stinging across the memory – I told the Viceroy I thought it was a good idea.

'They'd like and respect you for showing an interest. They'd remember it, I think. They'd tell their children. I would if I was them.'

'We'll all bloody remember it if we screw up in there,' snapped Adzell. 'It's urban jungle, sir. All sorts, I tell you.'

'Slopers, hixies, whores,' added Mace.

'Citizens, eh, Mayor?' the Viceroy grinned at that gentleman, who creased his sunburnt brow and said: 'Not what you might call model, Viceroy, if my drift is as it were got . . .'

Delavila, the Colonel, a fearsome man bolted together with gold, demanded some swift decisions: 'In or out, you want? You want in, in it is. Out, out it stays. You tell me, I tell them. Things get done. The army.'

On we went, as Delavila's soldiers in cream uniforms and the police in dark green and bronze hurried on to rope back the jostling citizens, and Mace and Adzell muttered under their breath two steps ahead, while the Viceroy tried to cheer them up by recollecting the infinitely more perilous situations he had encountered in a lifetime's service with the Dominion Corps. 'The evacuation from Rucoi, lads. That's what I call peril. Sweet little girls firing at us from their bedrooms. Why, we could see their rag dolls beside them on the windowsills! I swear they were shooting too. And the Sugar Riots in the Argeline City – they set my car on fire! In the War for Amadul I was ordered to minesweep an entire village in the dark.'

Yung murmured: 'Hear what they say where my mother come from, sir. "Ybai man yvee, na jakara Jhoti" – "You still being alive, that don't scare Mr Death."'

'True enough, Yung,' agreed the Viceroy, 'but I prefer this old gem I picked up in my research into the old Badean tongue: "Humao enamo Enam, Gharei kito esbaram . . ."'

'Yeah, me too,' said Mace, with a new nervousness in his voice. 'Don't it just slither off the tongue, sir?'

'"A man in love with Life, Death sneaks off in shame."'

'Sure he does,' said Adzell, 'then picks you off from the roof of a garage while you're singing the "Lonely Soldier".'

'"Life for the living, death for the dead",' I joined in, and three heads twisted balefully in my direction.

'Well, I wish I'd coined that one,' said Adzell, as they turned back.

'You Argelinos,' sighed the Mayor, walking behind us, 'always philosophising. Here we just say "Karoo, karobbi!"'

There was a pause, during which nobody asked the Mayor what that meant, so he repeated it – 'Karoo, karobbi!' It was many months before I discovered it was pure nonsense taught to children.

The streets were narrowing into shadowy alleys, or opening out suddenly into squares, which were called plazas, and in which we were dazzled by sunlight or turned gloomily green by the shades of high church walls. As our route had been chosen at the last minute, and was now being decided on the spur by the Viceroy – 'This looks very charming!' 'Ah, let's talk to the blanket-sellers!' 'We'll go up these little steps here!' (much to the consternation of Adzell and Mace, as well as the businessman Usham and the Mayor himself) – we sometimes found ourselves almost alone; other times a crowd would mysteriously be waiting for us. This is where Yung's uncanny sensitivity came in useful. 'This square will be deserted,' he would say, or: 'We will happen on beggars here . . .'

Strange detached details return to me, glimpses of those last moments before the old life ended and I lost the Viceroy. I remember watching the material of the back of Adzell's suit being dappled dark and pale grey by the sun through some balcony railings as he walked, and Mace clipping the heels of the Free Trade man, Usham, who spun around with a start of such horror that Mace drew his gun in surprise. Colonel Delavila, our great vanguard of gold, kept slowly circling, so that half the time he was walking backwards and facing us. I remember the Viceroy pausing to look at a sundial, and tracing the line of the shadow with the tip of his forefinger. Dreamily, he asked us: 'Who was the man who made this dial? Time, Man, Sunlight, Shadow . .. was this not the end of all things? Was this not the man who snatched Time from the sky, where it was racing free as a swallow? What was this man's name?'

The Mayor leaned forward to dust the surface of the dial: 'It's probably engraved somewhere, Viceroy.'

'Was his name not Death? Or even – Devil?'

'Oh,' said the Mayor, 'oh, well, I don't know about that . . .'

'Would we have Time if we had no sunlight?'

'I'd have my trusty pocket-watch,' said the Free Trade Man briskly; 'I'd have my trusty pocket-watch.'

And I remember how the Viceroy looked at him with a peaceful, silly smile.

Then the Mayor said he had a rather intriguing tale to tell about his son, but no one asked him to elaborate, and we never heard it.

So that's hidden too, Brother Fredo, with Cecile's mountain goat, with the origin of the words 'karoo, karobbi', with my good name in the country of my birth. But the goat ended somewhere, the words had a purpose, the Mayor's son knew something that we could have learned from. And my evil repute is founded upon misunderstanding, incompetence, error! And the Viceroy's life? Well that's not hidden. The death hides nothing. The death shows everything, displays what's for sale, displays what's not. The death who travels with me is a first cousin of the death who travelled with the

Viceroy. He says that that death is a confirmed pornographer.

Where are the hidden things, the million billion truths? Each single starry truth that would change our world did we know it! What if I had caught the goat and brought him home? What if we had heard what the Mayor's boy told his father, and because of it the Viceroy had changed his mind about something, and just – just, suddenly somehow – turned and glimpsed his death crouched in the green shadows on the Way of Amises chanting 'Buy or sell, buy or sell, buy or sell . . .'

I have met in these two years many people who know the truth, Fredo, many people who claim they know the truth, claim they possess it, like the Mainland once possessed Badeo, claim there are no hidden things. They can look at my questions and tell you the only answers. I suppose they are like mathematicians, like my brother Hektor intended to be. Beside the calculus of a mathematician, outside of his equation, there exists nothing. Once he has equalled everything up, the remainder of his belief must cancel out, must amount to nothing, must equal nothing. To the rebels up on Mount San Timotheo, the answer to the question of Badeo was 'Destroy the Argelinos!' To the Mainland Government, the answer to the same question was 'Smoke out the bandits' And one truth is very mighty, but two truths make war, and war lays the mighty to waste, as it did so many soldiers and armies in the fight for this Island. Those who see only one truth are not mighty, Brother Fredo, they are ill, miserable and ill. And do you know that their sickness is? That they live in perpetual day. They are unresting, unsleeping. Because they live in perpetual day, they do not know about the million billion hidden things that are all true, and they block the one sun they know, like the hand of a sundial, and they bring down the shadow of Time on our world. Because to believe in one truth is to live only so long as all other truths are hidden. So the lives of the believers of one truth last this

125

one day only, and when it is twilight at the end of their day, their hearts turn to ashes in horror that night is falling, and they die, croaking in incredulity 'This cannot be so! This cannot be so!' as a million stars come out. How the believers of one truth are remembered is in a single word, because they lived for so short a time.

But the believers in hidden things, they know that night is coming, and that makes their own day bright and precious as a diamond, and it is neither wasted nor lost nor blackened. They carry the secret of night happily through their lives, because it has made those very lives like marvels to them. You cannot pin them down with a word, nor hoop them with our 'isms'; as they move through their days and nights, glad and unafraid of them, you can almost see, to the right and left of them, high over and below them, behind them and ahead of them, Fredo, floating, the shimmer of hidden things! Believers in a billion truths may die young in our terms, at ten, or twenty, or thirty of our years, but they have had the experience of manifold nature: they have felt endlessness. Time itself is flummoxed by their lives. Fredo, the physical end of our world, what will itself end our world if anything can end it, is perpetual day. At the world's end stands the believer in perpetual day, the creditor of one truth, screaming over the heads of a crowd that is looking into a sunset. But the believer in hidden things? That is the world's child.

Oh, I sit here in this grand, golden room, upholding claims and refusing claims, tick-tocking my life away with my platinum pencil, the worst kind of bureaucrat for an already corrupted regime, and I make my claims for my own beliefs to a Brother of the Refuge St Hrabal! You who must have thought much further in your many years. I wonder what your god would make of my idle thoughts! My god looks mildly up from his book as if to smile at me, but he seems to look beyond me, off into the distance. Is he looking at your god, Fredo? Now he starts to read again. And I notice how quiet the death has gone.

The last time I clearly remember being in the company of the Viceroy and his escort, we had just turned right into the Avenue Maldeau. I did not see how it could possibly be the same street we had started on, but Allalong is like that – streets are broken and begin again elsewhere. The entire area exists on about three levels, a low one some three hundred years old (which includes Avenue Allalong and the Way of Lyres) a network of alleys about twenty feet higher (for example the Avenue Maldeau) and a recent addition of narrower, straighter pathways such as the Paradion and the Avenue Strauber. The same building could have addresses on three streets, depending which floor one lived on.

We had descended from one of the paved modern alleys on to the Avenue Maldeau at exactly the same time as a walking band was rising up from the ancient Avenue Kluy, all in black and old gold, with trumpets, fiddles, pipes and tambourines. They must have been waiting for us on the Avenue Marchant, hoping to play the Dominion Stanzas to the Viceroy to welcome him to the Island, but, once he had made his decision to change course, must have gone in search of him. They had therefore been anxiously seeking our party throughout the bewildering warren of Allalong, and now, as they came across us, they began to run with their instruments, so that they could pass by us and play their music walking backwards before us. Perhaps, deep within their immortal musical souls, something was telling them that History was about to be made, and would soon require their services. At any rate, suddenly they were everywhere.

You can imagine, from what I have told you about the acute sensitivity of Guardsmen Adzell, Mace and Yung to rapid movement, what dreadful chaos was provoked by the sight and sound of the black-and-golden bandsmen bustling towards our party! Adzell's quickness scarcely served him then, for every movement he made to aim his gun at the temple of a piper was cancelled out by as quick a motion to fix his sights on the heart of a drummer-boy – he simply could not pinpoint the source of the most pressing danger. Mace's animal eyes blanched like the Milky Way itself, perplexed by shimmering light and shade. 'Chain 'em up!' he yelled in confusion. 'Chain 'em *all* up!' Yung seemed to take on the properties of stone, as if to balance this apocalypse of action by assuming the eternal stillness of its opposite. And Burneau? Burneau blinked and panicked and forgot for all time what he was supposed to be doing. If you ever see a man at such a point of crisis that he seems utterly unaware of his surroundings – say, someone who has been informed of a death, or somebody about to be dealt one (or somebody stuck on a mountain ledge in a freezing blue mist at dusk, Fredo!) – that was how I must have looked to a bystander: dim, slow, and clownish, a sleepwalker in a functioning day-lit world.

Then I thought I saw the flames again. I turned to see what they were, and they were nothing but the bright hair of a young woman, that was all. But there are not so many red-hairs on Badeo. For when a thing becomes rare on this Island it becomes prized, followed, hunted almost. Certainly, the red-haired have to fight for their privacy. Everyone wants to be seen with them! Some of them wear their red hair in scarves; others turn it black with anchrosyne, but this woman wore it out and flying, red like blood-oranges, yellow as sunshine and melting the air beside it.

I know this woman. I knew this woman. But I won't tell you that until I reach the time I found her for myself. You must understand and share my bewilderment. She was nobody I had ever seen! I wasn't to know the part she had to play!

Our group – the Viceroy, we four guardsmen, the Mayor, the Free Trade man and Colonel Delavila, plus all the burly miners they used as bodyguards – had stopped in the middle of the Avenue Maldeau while the band streamed past on either side. I had backed my body up against the Viceroy's (so I thought) to protect him until the ruddy and perspiring

128

bandsmen had flowed past, and was watching the flame-haired woman as she walked quickly away from us, downwards into the sharply declining Avenue Kluy. I watched her as she gradually disappeared over the hump of the cobbled road into the shades below, her black stockinged legs, her pale blue dress, then her crown of flames that seemed to hold the sunlight longer than all things around her, as if her hair could catch the light through chimneys, houses, walls. Then she was gone. I edged backwards to make sure I was still touching the Viceroy, still capable of shielding him from the unexpected.

But who was ever there to shield me from the unexpected, Fredo? The person I was backing up against was a bandsman, a puzzled trombonist in glasses, who was himself lagging behind the people he was meant to be part of. He turned and frowned.

'This is all very good of you,' he said, 'but I'm one of plenty.'

And now between the trombonist and the band streamed a crowd of both cheerful and fretful citizens who had just recognised that a man of importance was among them and could be seen by them in the flesh, in person, if they only pushed hard enough! Which meant that between the bodyguard Burneau and that man himself was the trombonist in glasses, the crowd of ever more and more loudly demanding, drunken Badeans, all the rest of the black-and-golden bandsmen, the beleaguered and hopelessly outnumbered remainder of the bodyguard and – somewhere among those countless individuals – the one who wished that that mild, decent and capital gentleman Wallemire Lagland was dead, and very soon afterwards executed that wish.

Who killed Wallemire Lagland?

Well, I know who killed him. But all that mattered then was that I did not, did not know he would be killed, though the sickening possibility spread through my very organs all the rest of the afternoon until it washed across the television

129

screen and turned into the truth. I know who killed him, but I am telling a story of confusion, and trying to place the things I knew at the points when I knew them, Fredo, the better to explain my deeds and delayings. And there is a lower, darker reason for my reticence. I am writing from the heart of a world that has celebrated me for that one deed I did not do. All the grandeur and respect that is about me is grounded in the general knowledge of my selfless revolutionary daring. In the wrong hands this note is a suicide note, but still, the later I reveal the darker truths, the better for my trembling soul. I will, for now, remain with the truths upon which I acted, and the configuration of the world I knew.

What that world itself knew was a series of connected fictions. After my public accusation I was hunted unsuccessfully across the capital and the countryside. It seems that as the Mainland authorities lost patience with their failure to find their one suspect, they decided they had better have some suspects they could find. One of the two people wounded at the scene of the assassination (one bludgeoned half to death by Guardsman Adzell, the other bludgeoned the whole way by Guardsman Mace) incriminated a simple San Timothean called Pirir, who happened to be in the vicinity. Both Pirir, who was shot after a brief trial, and the surviving half of the so-called 'Wounded Two', who mysteriously disappeared and was never seen again, were soon beyond the reach of enquiry. And I was downgraded to the role of an accomplice, a contemptible upland mercenary, the hired infiltrator who ducked away to leave the hardened killer Pirir a gap to shoot through. My erstwhile colleagues did nothing to dissuade the Investigatress, the Prosecutor, the press and the public from this version of events, and, until the War began in earnest, I was all but forgotten, though I had been charged with conspiracy to murder, undefended, and found guilty in my absence.

This is to blunder on into the lies of the future. At the moment I lost the Viceregal Party on the Avenue Maldeau I was too busy suffering the desperate reality of the present . . .

130

Where was I, Fredo, oh agony to tell! The man who would stand accused was lifted off his feet like an effigy, but innocent and unregarded, and borne by the sheer pressure of the crowd along some other alley, where I fell down among the yellow lizards and the sandalled feet, scrabbled for life in the dirt, like life was some precious memento I'd dropped – not expensive, but paid for now and intended for someone – and which I must have snatched up intact, for I was heaved against a dark wooden nameless wall, which gave.

Brother Fredo, I have now related to you the circumstances by which I became innocent of the crime at the same hour I seemed to become guilty of it. I have told no lies, I have made no exaggerations. I have written you this letter one hundred and seven times. That is many times to address a man who may pick it up from a glass-topped table in Heaven! But I swear to you, my reputation for evil and treachery in the country of my birth is founded upon absent-mindedness (mine), confusion (the crowd's) and corruption (the Government's). Now I know that I could write a world of lies one million and seven times, and all those boastful zeroes could not add the least speck of truth to it, but believe me, Fredo: I owe my position in this youthful Republic – and I owed my position in the ranks of the Organ Liberat fighters who harried the imperialist Argelinos off the Island – to the rebels' belief that I did assassinate the Viceroy. Be sure what is at stake as I write, for, let me presume to teach you, if somebody makes you a villain for nothing, his enemies will raise you up a hero for the same. Entitle that the Tale of Burneau, and bind it in the little library of the Refuge! Only, understand that I can have no motive for telling the truth now, other than that it is the truth, and that I dearly wish the family Burneau (who I believe and pray still abide in the village of Gispar below the Folded Mountain) and only that family, to know it for the truth.

They will need to know how the lost and frightened young man who stumbled into an all-day drinking bar turned, changed, crystallised into this honoured, chauffeured Minister twinkling with medals but dwarfed by the world's tallest edifice of paper. They would want to know why I rose like a fabulous monster in the rebellion, the legendary strategist whom all collaborators saw in their dreams, standing on the horizon with arms akimbo, both mascot and brain of the OLB, whose life General Gabril would never risk in combat! They will want to know who is the girl I love, who is the boy I am looking for, whose murder I drag behind me. Our Minister of Health wants himself to live for ever, our Minister of National Security wants to sleep well in his mansion, our Minister of Finance – well, I think you know what he wants. But I am the Minister of Reconciliation. I'll reconcile myself to what is.

The tale of my time in Badeo is easily told. Picking myself up off the dusty floor of a dimly lit drinking parlour, I walked steadily to the bar and sat on a wooden stool. I was in a state of considerable panic, as I knew that my abandonment of the Viceroy was irreversible and that however unintentional it may have been it would be viewed as desertion, but, with the help of the amiable crowd there, and not a few bottles of a lively drink, I began to piece together an innocent identity for myself, a name, opinions, prejudices that would convince the Badeans around me that I was merely another of them. I became a man named Mr Frosch.

Now, with terrifying, grinning inevitability, the shooting of the Viceroy was confirmed on the bar's television. Confirmed, I say, for I had already played it many times on a film in my mind. It was the worst that could happen, and so it had to be envisaged. When the outrage was announced, I worked desperately at my identity – assuming a love of the sport they all loved, then the trade of a poet, of all the things there are to be! – while further reports told of the Viceroy's coma, deterioration and death. Then came the rumours that one of the personal bodyguards had vanished, then the cold infuriated face of Guardsman Adzell, displaying his hatred of me

132

for all the world to know; then came talk of curfew, crack-down, random searches, arrests on mild suspicion. Then came my real name in capitals on television.

What saved me that night – for, remember, I was without my name, without any knowledge of the Island, without documentation or money, without possessions or a roof over my head – was the curiosity and friendliness of a woman named Violet Maricolo, who frequently drank alone at that bar, and who was glad of some company for the evening. By which I mean just that, Brother Fredo. She was no cheap woman such as flourish in the undergrowth of cities: she was sorrowful and somewhat adrift, a wife abandoned by a roguish husband (jailed on the Mainland for repeated fraud), left to bring up two children (a girl and a boy), and slowly running out of money in a small flat in Curo, a quiet, declined neighbourhood of the city. She worked in a cloth-house, but that was going out of business, what with the vogue for a silvery mass-made fabric which was ruining the weavers and their dependants. But Mme Maricolo still had her spirit, and I liked her at once. It is not true to say I would have fallen at the feet of a gnarled hag if she had offered me a roof over my head. No, I should have taken my chance on the streets. Mme Maricolo's sociable nature, and her sense of humour and adventure, made me happy to grasp the one straw that I could see being dangled at me.

I went with her back to her flat and was introduced to her two children: Paol, who was fourteen, and Juilla, who was seventeen. On the whole, they were decent and well-behaved children, and I would have been proud to have called myself their father, though in fact I was not all that much older than the girl.

What Mme Maricolo did for me I can never repay. The years are not so rich as that. Once my picture began to appear on the television and the whole family knew who I was, she went out of her way, at considerable risk, to shield me from the authorities and the prying of her neighbours.

She helped me, along with her daughter Juilla, to change my appearance so that I resembled the picture on her husband's Citizenship Card. (This convinced the policemen who came to search the flat, and, when we walked out in the Town – though we took good care to avoid the bar where I had been seen – we very much looked the part of husband and wife.) She took me under her wing, she sheltered me, kept my secret, fed me and clothed me out of her husband's wardrobe. She did what I asked.

Her children too, they were helpful and kind. The daughter, Juilla Maricolo, a girl of seventeen with honey-brown hair, taught me much about Badean life and culture, all the things that might help me to go about the city in my new identity: about the topics of conversation, the clothes and the fashionable phrases. We developed a good relationship, considering the strangeness of the circumstances. Without my physical disguise of moustache and grey hair, I would not have passed for her father: we were too close in age for that. Then again, I am a few years older, that can't be denied, so I was able to exert some kind of decent authority during the short while I spent in the flat on the Avenue Hali. To tell the truth, I miss her indeed a little, because such a relationship was new to my life. But I must not speak further of Juilla Maricolo at this point. I have not come so far in my missive to you, Brother Fredo, as to be able to believe that – no matter what incidents or emotions I revealed – you would continue to consider my person and my deeds with sympathy. In this case, I can imagine that the revelation of my ignominious acts would turn the very pages crisp and smoky, even before you had the chance to consign them to the fire that must be their final destination. Let me say only that I miss the daughter of Mme Maricolo as today misses yesterday. No idiocy nor infamy committed on a yesterday can diminish that loss. Loss is the past that's got into the room. But that's only my way of bringing her here, making her present – the loss that arrives through a window may indeed be the past, but it may also be the future, who is a mere masquerader. He too brings her here, he too delivers cheap pain and cheap pleasure, and he too dwindles to nothing when I turn to greet him.

But it brings me more pain than pleasure to remember the Maricolos. When I left the shelter of their roof in the Avenue Hali – Mme Maricolo decided it might be better if I moved on – I did not expect to see them ever again, and had tried my best to forget about them, put them behind me. However, after the War I would – as I shall describe when the time is right – stumble back into the life of one, and pledge myself to the improbable salvation of another. Such is the Minister of Reconciliation, spinning out the past from the heart of a web of confusion and contradiction. How will he reconcile the differences of an island people, when his own past and future tug at him from their sentry posts by his side?

It was a warm and wet day, late afternoon in the middle of the summer, the day I took my leave of the Maricolos. I did not have time to say goodbye properly to any of the family. I thought it would be best to make good time, and I was in a hurry to formulate my plans, the better to cope with the perils ahead. For without the shelter of that family, or the mask of my identity as the grey-haired reformed Mr Gando Maricolo, father of two, I was, once again, nothing but the fugitive missing Guardsman Burneau, object of an island-wide manhunt, loathed perpetrator of a deed still fresh and garish in the minds of the people. During my stay at 16 Avenue Hali, I had made long study of an atlas of the Island, and this had helped me to ascertain the safest route towards the southern town of Furasol, and Mount San Timotheo.

Full well I know what horror those names will evoke in the patriot soul of an Argelino, with their terroristic and revolutionary connotations, but surely you can see what kind of a grim sense it made. If I was the enemy of the people, I must find their other enemies and seek protection among them – think of it! I, so proud of my work as a protector of that venerable man the Viceroy, now forced to flee for my life into the arms of his vile and desperate foes, to duck my head among them, to creep east away from the Capital, south along the shore of the Bay, then west through the woods towards Furasol, creeping like a thief all the way towards the men who probably had him killed! My life has not been inhospitable to such ironies, as perhaps you begin to observe.

The safest way was not the most direct. A good citizen with no crimes on his conscience – and you may raise your benevolent eyebrows and muse that I was indeed such a citizen, but no, the pressure of public opinion had loaded my private conscience with the crime of murder as well as that of dereliction – would have joined the Avenue Infanta at Brade Infan, crossed the Rumol and headed south. So straight is that road that with his car pointed due south, a car driver could almost doze at the wheel, or – once he had passed the TV Tower on the left (highest and most conspicuous of the Capital's landmarks) and the last factory piles and workers' blocks on the right – he could sit back and take in the view of boats on the Bay, so long as he was ready for the Great Fork. There he would veer right, away from the lake town Laquilla, and follow the curve of the Bay towards Furasol. Once there, a gentle climb up the foothills of Mount San Timotheo, and he would be where he wanted in little more than two hours.

With neither car nor citizenship, and burdened with a likeness splashed across so many walls that I began to believe that brick had turned to mirror-glass, I slunk out of Badeo Town by way of cold alleys, desolate allotments and waste-ground between the highways, running under rail-bridges, with the echo of my footfall every bit as loud as the screeching freight above me, or hiding face-down in the grass on the deep banks of the River Rumol. It was under the elevated section of the Highway Infanta that I slept until just before dawn. It was awfully cold, and when I woke after what sleep I had, the world was cloudy, misty and damp. I learned then that summer and winter were thick as thieves, went everywhere together, thought the same of us.

136

By mid-morning I was clear of the Town and walking through farmland, through some thick brown crop high enough to soak me to the waist without affording me much shelter. I kept the Highway Furasol parallel about a mile to my right, with the Bay dull and leaden beyond. Through the mist and drizzle that sheeted everything, I could just make out the grey cluster of abandoned buildings far across the Bay. They were hotels and casinos built by Mainland speculators on a jut of land a year previously. They were opulent and glittering inside, it was said, but the incessant bombing and menacing of them by the 'terrorists' of the Organ Liberat Badeon had caused their complete evacuation. Now they were said already to be infested and crumbling. The Argeline authorities had washed their hands of the matter. The speculators had stolen quietly back to the Domain. Across the Bay, New Badeo went on dying, a daily reminder to the Badean citizens of the foolhardiness of their wealth and the slow exhaustion of their power, at least upon that dangerous promontory.

Feeling a desperate need for fellows in my plight, my tired imagination, rattling with love and hunger, fixed upon those mysterious columns, victims of a struggle that was no more the business of glass, cement, marble and velvet, than it was that of a poor crossing-sentry from the Koborol. It was at this point, in a paralysis of sympathy and pity for the hotels in the drizzle – emotions the only cause of which, I now see, was the sense that they might be reciprocated and felt by glass buildings for a man twenty miles away being rained on in a field – that I was arrested.

Two soldiers eating huge sandwiches suddenly appeared, and without freeing their hands to employ any of their several weapons, told me I was to be charged with trespassing on the land. They asked to see my papers. Seeing as how I had left the Avenue Hali in something of a hurry – it's always best to move fast between episodes in one's life, I do find – I had no papers. I was charged with that as well. Once again, observe how pure absent-mindedness and oversight are grievously punished, while cheats and thugs and bullies all tread our world smiling!

The two soldiers, still eating, led me towards the Highway.

'Normally,' munched the older of the two men, 'we wouldn't bother with no vagrant on a beanfield, that's mere footwork, that is.'

'Yep,' said the other, swallowing, 'we'd leave that to the likes of Plagini. But we have to run you through our file. See what bleeps, see what buzzes.'

I meant to begin the detailed explanation I had worked out (that I had been robbed and beaten up by a marauding gang) but what I said instead was: 'Where can you buy such colossal sandwiches?'

The younger man made a sort of cackling noise, as he finished off the last crumbs of his feast and dropped the paper by the roadside, but the older man said: 'In Tatri. At Louisa's. Get in the van.'

The younger man and I got in the back of a little black van that the soldiers had parked on the stones at the side of the Highway Furasol. The older man started the engine and we headed south. I reflected silently, in the direction of my dumb friends the distant skyscrapers, that I was at least motoring in the right direction. Then again, as I have told you, my death is a constant companion of my travels, Brother Fredo, and, in the costume of a young Badean soldier wiping his lips, he pointed out that what I referred to as 'motoring in the right direction' actually meant (a) moving at seventy miles per hour away from my only source of love and friendship on the whole of the Island, and (b) proceeding at the same velocity towards the discovery that I was none other than Maris Burneau. By combining (a) with (b), the kind of sum at which the death is so expert, we achieved the result that not only would I never again set eyes upon Juilla or Violet Maricolo, but that I would never again see my real family so far away in the Koborol, and that I would be put to death by hanging or

138

firing squad in a matter of days; (c)? said the death; (c): And we were motoring in the right direction.

We reached the Fork, and took the right – right again – towards Furasol, gathering speed, while the two soldiers discussed sports (they were supporters of Saldeo, who had made a 'so-so start to the season', drawing a game with Furasol and defeating 'them godforsaken suckers on Cobar') and I composed inside my ringing head a colourful and impassioned plea for mercy, then developed several alternative versions of it, for use in the face of ordinary soldiers, colonels, generals, prosecutors, judges, and finally, executioners. I observed that the greater the authority of the imagined auditor of my speeches, the greater the number of lies that I would be forced to tell. For the presiding judge at my trial I should have to invent all sorts of falsehoods about my being attacked on the day of the Viceroy's death, or being held hostage ever since, until I was found in that field, starving, shivering and so on, whereas my humble executioners, I foresaw, would lay down their rifles if I merely described to them the beauty of the shepherdesses at Gispar, a truth as true as any I have known.

When the first dreary shacks at the edge of Furasol were clearly in view, the soldiers themselves were stopped at a checkpoint. It was raining quite heavily now, and my mind, sure it had found the words by which to save its life, had become satisfied and drowsy. So it was more than ever a shock when the three men manning the checkpoint asked my two soldiers to step out of the black van, and, once they had done so, shot them.

The three men – two of whom were women – now got into the front of the van themselves, and started it. We were quite a few yards down the Highway – still on towards Furasol – before they noticed me in the back. This had all happened too suddenly for me to be afraid, or else the contemplation of my trial and execution had eroded any such capacity on my part, but, for their own part, they were too surprised to take any immediately murderous action. The two women (the man was driving and hadn't turned round) just looked at me.

'I'm under arrest,' I told them.

Now the man looked, for the van swerved half-way into the empty opposite lane, then swerved back as he calmed his nerves.

'What for?' said a young woman with bright eyes and lots of curly hair escaping from her grey peaked cap.

'Trespass and having no papers,' I said, 'but I'm innocent.'

'Stop the car, Stoackey,' said the other woman steadily, 'Let him out.' She turned away.

As the van slowed down, I leaned forward. I had only one card to play, but you know every hand has an unbeatable card and, I assure you – a man perhaps unfamiliar with the sin of cards! – there is no moment like the moment that card is played. The world is there to be beaten. It's like a hand that is Scissors when the world is Paper, Paper when it's Stone, Stone when it's Scissors. My card was the truth. I am well aware that that truth had implications that were wholly false: in fact its implications were the most powerful falsehoods of that instant in Badean history, but nobody can deny that what I said to these people was nothing but the truth.

'The bodyguard. Burneau. I'm him.'

This brought the van to a complete halt. The driver now twisted round and stared. The curly-haired woman frowned and looked sceptical. It was the other woman, the one who had actually killed the soldiers, who turned, gazed deep into my eyes, breathed deeply and whispered in what I can only describe as awe: 'He is. You are. Let's go.'

She must have been their leader, for this seemed to settle it as far as the others were concerned. The two women got out of the van, and the curly-haired one jumped in beside me, slammed the door and began roughly knotting a blindfold around my head. As I lost my view of things, I heard the front door slam and felt the van start up again, accelerating in whatever was now the right direction.

These are all the important facts of my capture – or rather my rescue from probable execution – by the guerrillas of the Organ Liberat Badeon. It seemed a stroke of extraordinary good fortune, but these were days of many such assaults on Badean soldiers by the OLB. I had been surprised by the emptiness of the Highway Furasol: this was the reason. It was a notorious stretch of road. General Gabril – or Doctor, or Teacher, as he then was – spent all his resources on menacing this supply line between the Island's two largest settlements. My rescue was merely the latest offensive by one of the two cells operating in the region. The woman, their captain, Nunez, had – though not until she looked deep in my eyes – recognised my face from the wanted posters. She knew, as I did, that there was only one place for me now. She had found me. I was her triumph, and she was taking me home.

I spent that long, winding ascent concentrating on my present identity, and realising that certain key elements of it would be easy to assume, simply because they were true. Above all, I had my name again – I was Burneau. I really had been a bodyguard in the Argeline Security Division, I really had abandoned the Viceroy on the day he died, I really had lain low and suffered disguise. So no, I was not a poet named Frosch, I had not lived on the Avenue Anywhere or Way of All Things, I certainly did not drink at a bar that stayed open all afternoon, nor were my best friends its regular drinkers. On the contrary, I hailed from the high country of the Koborol, had been a humble crossing-sentry and had sailed to Badeo from the land of the Argeline oppressor, with a hated dignitary. This was what was new about me, this was what I now had to change, this was where it would have to begin. What struck me as fortunate about the new circumstances was that instead of having to describe a set of experiences I had not had, all I would now have to do was adopt a set of attitudes I did not hold. It sounded much simpler to me. Yes, I abandoned the Viceroy – but *yes, I meant to*! He died

141

because of me and *that was the plan*! I was born on the Mainland but I *love FREEDOM*! Yes, to all outward perception, my life had been like any other humble life on the remote rural heights of the Argeline Domain: inside was where seethed my implacable hatred of that nation, where blossomed a passion for *all things Badean*, and – above all – for the heroic struggle of the legendary mountain guerrillas of the Organ Liberat Badeon and its enigmatic leader, Doctor Iaio Gabril! Easy for me to rise up silently, monstrously, through the ranks of the Security Forces, nurturing my animosity, lying in wait for the day I could *strike a blow* against the oppressor, until, at last, on a summer's day in the heart of my beloved Badeo Town, my opportunity came. Working under cover as a bodyguard protecting Viceroy Wallemire Lagland, that symbol of *arrogant imperialism*, I had seized my chance when it arose, shooting him down in a scene of confusion (this was all very easy to reconstruct, since my former colleagues Adzell and Mace had speculated many times on television that this was how I had done it) then making my ghostly getaway into the dives and darknesses of godforsaken Allalong, to reappear – as if by magic – in the mountain hideaway that represented, for me, *all hope for the future*, and for the people of my adopted country!

While I conceived this history, noticing how the torchlight of my hatred for the Argeline and love of the glorious OLB reilluminated the facts of the past in all sorts of curious ways, I was being hooded, crammed into the stinking back of the van, pulled out again, marched for two hours up a steep track, given some water, marched another half-hour or so, and finally, as I felt the blissful cool of some high-ceilinged interior, I was sat down, unhooded, unblindfolded by a man who was not familiar, and left alone.

I was sitting on a comfortable faded settee in the exact centre of a large and largely unfurnished white stone room, very cool and still, very empty. Apart from my settee there was nothing but a low table several feet away with a bowl of blue flowers on it. The room was brightly and naturally lit, but from above, from the light through the ceiling itself rather than any windows. And the sides of the room formed a perfect octagon.

You must have been in such places, Fredo. I was to learn that it had once been the chapel of an order of nuns. The ceiling had been stained glass, but its depictions were all of weather, so that if it rained on a bright enough day, the brightness could still activate the deep blues and hot yellow of sunlight; or if the sun really did shine outside, it could illumine rolls of purple cloud, or daggers of lightning. And lightning had done for it one day, a pine tree smashing the entire spectrum of weather down upon the praying sisters. The chapel was abandoned to the elements. When the guerrillas found it – two years before my arrival – it was more like a great canful of entangled plantlife than a building for anything. Now it was clean and fresh and bright, but had a numb ringingness about it, that I attribute in my professorial retrospect to the scars of its spatial memory: the whispering of someone's gods, the transfiguration of daylight, the rain made of glass, the glass become a killing rain, and the vengeance of Nature in the guise of healing.

I would spend all of the next two years in Camp Liberat, and much of it in this white octagonal room, or Hall of Weathers.

If Time had passed for those two years at the pace it was passing at that moment, alone in that unique chamber, eternity would have ground to a halt before I came down off that mountain. I sat, I stood, I walked in a line, I walked in a circle. I waited, I sat.

I have been doing the same things all this afternoon, with only the writing of this letter to remind me that Time has passed at all, that I am a Minister now, not a fugitive, that the War is over, not about to begin its hottest phase. What other differences are there? Few. This room in the Palace, the room in which I write truths that would, were they widely

143

known, fill its corridors with wild accusations and its dungeons with soft cries, in its emptiness and echo and the way it focuses mind upon life until mind is exhausted and life explained, how different is this golden glorified shed from the octagonal soundlessness of my first hours on San Timotheo? The regular clock of my guards' progress away and back, away and back, is reflected all that time ago by the violent swings of my mood from a dazed, dreamy forbearance to an almost frenzied passion of panic and wonder. A man with a continually amended past, and without a clear image of a possible future, can feel only those extremes, for his blood takes over in the absence of thought, it lights and blazes and beats and burdens like the past, while the work of the future is seized upon gleefully by the nerves – jangling, infinite in sensation and possibility, recording only pleasure and pain, for who foresees a future of eternal balance and placidity neither suffered nor enjoyed? The elements of my insides circled and sparred, while I was left trembling, cold, weakened by the white ten-faceted nothing that was always happening next. As I would be trembling and weakened at this moment, were I not at my desk, engaged in my letter, or rather, looking for all the world as if I were deep in the greatest labours of Reconciliation. Lies against the silence, Brother Fredo, lies and truths together warding off the silence, like the soldiers of two weaker forces allied against a fate worse than defeat, uneasily piling up sandbags together, or watchfully trading jokes and cigarettes.

Presently the door that had closed so long ago opened, and in walked the woman who had identified me as Burneau, with a new man. I stood up, not through politeness or anxiety so much as through a desperate dogged happiness that the waiting was over, that my mind could be refuelled again with sounds, words, things that change.

Nunez walked briskly across to face me, as if to record as emphatically as possible that my presence in the world had been noted, that I was back in the world of real time, and I

144

could begin right now with hers. Her face was sculpted and hungry-looking, her eyes deep and tired and aware, she wore a loose-fitting, shiny black running outfit and her teak-brown hair was short. The man stayed by the door.

'The Child Behind A Wall,' said Nunez, looking down at her nails, then looking through them at me: 'The Master Of The Game. I was expecting you, Burneau.'

'I had nowhere else to go,' I said, truthfully (I might have to say 'truthfully' from time to time, Brother Fredo). 'They were all over Badeo, those, er, imperialist sons of bitches . . .' (And much as it worries me to relate, especially to a religious man, the infinite number of times I said 'er' to my captors, it was nevertheless probably my chief means of communication.)

'Home is the Bolting Pig,' she said, 'in Torchlight.'

'Well. I'm very hungry, ma'am. Those soldiers you – er – they had these large, large sandwiches. They're gone, obviously, but when did I last eat? I couldn't say.'

'Where have you been, Burneau?'

'Where have I – ? I was in a disguise, ma'am.'

'Captain. Nunez. A disguise? So the Bolting Pig was in the Deep Blue Sea . . .'

'I'm not, er, much of a poetry reader.'

'No. What are you much of, Burneau?'

'Hungry, Captain Nunez. Tired. Lost, desperate to – if there's a place here – that first. Hungry mainly.'

'Why did you kill him?'

'I'm sorry?'

'Lagland. Why? Who asked you to?'

'The Viceroy? No one. No one asked me to. I just, er, took my chance and – did it.'

'So it seems. But you're an Argelino?'

'Well, I don't see it that way!' I said, rediscovering with great joy my talent for brazen untruthfulness. 'Frankly, Captain Nunez, I'm from the Koborol. Up there we don't call ourselves Argelines at all. We believe in freedom, all of it. Any of it.'

'"Likewise is seeded on a slope far-off, and wine is made/Of word and wonder anywhere. Down, hope against all hope/That every word you said to me has been and is said there . . ."'

'Well. Exactly.'

'Who sent you? What's the name of your unit on the Kolorbore?'

'That's Koborol. Oh, we're not organised. We don't have a struggle. I mean, we would have if perhaps there were more soldiers about, but we're so, sort of, high up that no one comes that far, except religious orders and those people rich enough to charter balloons. They come for holidays in them. In the balloons. Which then, er, go again. And come to collect them. At the end.'

Nunez stared, nodded and confirmed: 'So it was the cultural imperialism of these people that awoke you to the injustice and arrogance of the Argeline nation?'

'That's right, it was. It was them. The balloon people.'

'So. How did you get so close to the Viceroy? How did you get the work as a bodyguard? We've been trying that for years.'

This became easy. Both truths and lies seemed as welcome in the bright octagon as sunshine and clouds in the sky, and it was exciting for me to have this bold woman taking such an interest and believing everything. I told her about the Viceroy's arrival on our high crest in his balloon, and his romantic feelings about the Koborol, all about the urban thugs Adzell and Mace, and the still and terrible Yung, all about their extraordinary sharpness in the security field.

'We knew all about them,' said Nunez irritably. 'You were the blank, Burneau. You were the cipher, the Child Behind A Wall. Now you appear in Stormlight.'

'I had to, really.'

'I know you had to, I know you had no choice. The cards cannot lie.'

'The . . . cards.'

146

'Cannot lie. Or, not to me.'

'Ah.'

'Why didn't they catch you?'

'Why didn't who catch me?'

'These bodyguards – you say they were so hot.'

'I'm hot too, Captain Nunez. I was out of sight.'

'Where did you go?'

'I don't remember names. I lived on my wits, Captain Nunez.'

'Did anyone get your name?'

'I had a false one. Frosch.'

'That's a beer, isn't it?'

'Might be.'

'Why did you choose a beer?'

So it went on, with the Captain, who could look quite fierce and quite childlike in the course of one sentence, questioning my motives, my actions, my latter movements, while I eagerly responded with the full story, or rather, *a* full story. I thought it held up well, as Nunez nodded more and more frequently, and gradually seemed to take less interest in my answers. I thought this was because, using both the truth and my talent for make-believe to construct my account of the assassination, I was developing quite a convincingly detailed narrative.

I was doing nothing of the kind. I know now that she was perfectly aware from the very beginning that I had no more been the assassin than you had, Brother Fredo. She had her private reasons for allowing me to play that part. And, indeed, nothing could have given the OLB greater satisfaction than the fact that the Police, the Security Division, the Island Council, the Army, the Investigatress Dagmar Frock and the Mainland Government would all have to admit privately – whatever public show they could mount around the scapegoat Pirir – that the genuine assassin was the Viceroy's own bodyguard Maris Burneau, who had not only accomplished that audacious act but had also managed to elude the keenest

147

manhunt in the Island's memory and slipped through the fingers of them all to his only possible place of safety: Camp Liberat and the octagon-shaped Hall of Weathers. So Nunez nodded one last time, and snapped her book on my thousand lies.

She summoned an elderly mountain couple, Mr and Mrs Fulbahli, and under their guidance I was shown the way to some food, a shower, and what passed for a bedroom in Camp Liberat: a tiny dark closet of a place at the end of one of the four corridors which led away from the octagon. The room had the word CORPORAL chalked on it, just CORPORAL, CORPORAL nothing, a curiosity which in two years of trying I never once remembered to enquire about at the right time. The shut blinds were made of straw, green straw which made the room seem like a glade in a jungle. There was one small hardboard box for my possessions – which consisted only of the clothes I was wearing – and a simple electric light with a yellow bulb.

'Don't forget,' said Mrs Fulbahli as she left.

I sat down alone, clean and naked on my cool sheeted bed, and waited for the Creature of Blood and the Creature of Nerves to screech back into me again like the implausibly fierce reptiles that used to fly the skies over the Koborol. Instead, I must have keeled over at once, like a body, and slept long and deeply, with my feet on the pillow and my head as spinning and still as the planet's.

If you have read this far, Brother Fredo, it is time for you to break from my letter. You are an aged man, if you are still living. You have read enough to pass the message on to my family about my innocence in the matter of the Viceroy's death, and about the comfort, status and relative security of my post here in the Republic of Free Badeo. So rest now. Where better to leave me than on a mountain, exactly where you found me? Still a boy, still lost, still surrounded by cloud, but still living in hopes of a second Brother Fredo, to hear the cry, to part the mists and show him the way home!

*

148

Now, while you rest upon your simple cot in the shrouded Refuge of St Hrabal, and I, the rescued Burneau of my strange years on San Timotheo, sleep my first night in that mysterious cramped haven, I will describe to nobody – for nobody should hear such shameful human histories – how war came to Badeo, and how I played a part so significant that it was my dubious reward to be elevated to this Ministry of Reconciliation. I will talk of lust and error, of ignoble nights and days quite dissipated, of love, of fear, of triumph, of murder. Of Confusion and Hopefulness, my constant companions, and of the god and the death, theirs.

Iaio Gabril was the Senior Doctor of Viniculture at the University College of Furasol. He had been appointed twenty years prior to the War for Badeo, and was a wise, diligent and widely respected teacher of his subject. His theories on the cultivation of vines had been turned into successful practice by winegrowers from the Forest Laquil to the slopes of San Timotheo, and, within about five years, Badeo had developed from being a producer of mere exotica for the Mainland for use on special celebratory occasions, to being the largest exporter of wines among all the Argeline Dominions. Wine, more than timber or tourism, was what had generated the prosperity that made Badeo Town – for a while – such a flourishing little metropolis, and had brought the Argelino merchants and chancers swarming south across the Ocean. What with the increase in confidence and business, Badeo itself turned from being a distant and exotic idea, notable primarily as a cherished inclusion in the stamp collections of Argelino children, to being the major holiday resort for wealthy Mainland families. As bottles of red Saldean Mauette or the pale Xerai from Laquilla moved from the special corners of dusty cellars to daily pride of place on the supper tables of the Argeline, the island, though far away, established itself close to the heart of the huge, rich Domain. Now hotels reared up on the North Shore – the Imperion, the Sancristo – the wild grassy spaces of the Capital turned to quaint fenced parks full of fountains and statues, and the dusty roads became three-lane highways, linking Badeo Town in the north-west to the rest of the Island: to Gamor in the north-east (small fishing village dubbed 'Badeo's Best Kept Secret!' in a holiday promotion, and subsequently its worst) to Furasol on the Bay (quiet university town turned gambling den and crime haven) and to distant Saldeo (sleepy mining town invaded by the young).

There were other changes. As rich tourists arrived, so did soldiers. One incident in a Furasol nightclub, when a Mainland businessman was roughed up by some peasants, brought a troop of infantrymen into the town. An attack on them brought more. Soon, Furasol was more or less garrisoned by a battalion recruited not only from the Mainland, but also from Badeo Town, Laquilla, Gamor and the Isle of Cobar, a whole troop of young Badeans tempted by boredom and a steady wage to hang about the other towns of their Island in the chocolate-brown uniforms of its occupying power.

Slowly, imperceptibly, day by day, in peace and quiet, the War began. As the value of Badeo rose in the eyes of the Argeline, so the profile of its 'guardians' was raised. For those to whom the 'guardians' were intruders, the need for resistance grew. The attempt to safeguard money brought attacks on money. The cost of the attacks raised the cost of the safeguarding. Death, made curious then jealous by the power of money, soon became its equal as a unit of currency, and Badean television was the nattering bourse where soldiers' deaths were traded against those of rebels: one week at 1-for-3, when 'soldiers' were fighting 'bandits', the next at 1-for-7, when 'heroes' were up against 'animals'.

No one visited Furasol now. Speculators moved their assets further up the coast to the promontory where, with the folly of avarice, they built the ill-starred Casino New Badeo – a place one could travel to only via the dangerous Highway Furasol! The rebels made it unreachable by land, a risk by

150

sea, and the tourists and socialites fled with tales to sell. The Mainland continued to ship craftloads of soldiers into Badeo Town, while the Organ Liberat Badeon (emerging as the toughest, best equipped of three rival groups that had fought bitterly over the right to liberate the Island) intensified their attacks on what they saw as weak links in the chain around Badeo – the cargo boats, which they pirated, the hotels, which they threatened, and the highways, which they attacked suddenly and swiftly, by day or by night. Once again the Mainland fattened the army, once again the rebels, from positions on the dark side of Mount San Timotheo, got the army back in their sights. Meanwhile, on the Mainland, the Argelinos wondered who on earth could be co-ordinating such a skilful campaign (one so skilful that it at times re-minded them of the salient achievements of their own glorious history) and yet, each time they found and jailed a rebel, assuming they had thereby lessened the resistance, the resistance heightened. Every time. Every time Nothing hap-pened, it was followed hotfoot, powerfully and surprisingly, by Something, and, although these violent Somethings were always preceded by Nothings that could, if intelligently read, have been interpreted by the Mainland as warnings of impending Somethings, they were instead repeatedly inter-preted as Victory. Primarily, this was because Victory is a pleasant and quite cheap interpretation to make; secondly, because a considerable number of speculators, businessmen, newspapers across the Mainland and newscasters for the Argeline television networks were constantly pressing the Government to interpret Nothing in this manner.

The cause of the recurrences of Something, the co-ordina-tor of this lurch towards out-and-out conflict, was the Senior Doctor of Viniculture at the University College of Furasol: Iaio Gabril. The man most directly responsible for Badeo's prosperity, and thereby indirectly responsible for its conflict (for the love between money and death is a strong, strong love, beside which humans hang about like first husbands) was also one of the main protagonists and intensifiers of that conflict. Yet all he appeared to do throughout these years of escalation was teach his classes, write his papers, and publish such fundamental industrial volumes as *Wine from Water*, *Wine from Sand, Good and Evil Viniculture, Wine from Nowhere* and *The God, the Grape and the Golden Falls*.

Though he was first and foremost a scientist, Dr Iaio Gabril would interleave his technical wisdom about soils and insecticides with short passages of his own poetry, written in a form which became known as the gabrilette. Here, for example, is the one with which he began that first book, *Wine from Water*, written when he was a mere twenty-seven:

You know, know grape, know blood, know mind.
    Believe, become. The island soil
Is green as water, green as soon, so furnish from the sun
    and wind
The globe of wine and sup its oil. Before, below, the
    moon.

Innocent enough, I am no poet. But, over the years, Dr Gabril developed a teaching style which was based entirely upon the principle of metaphor, the subtlety and craftiness of which he had so perfected that he could lecture about the various soils of the Saldean Plain for two hours, then leave behind him, wandering through the corridors of the University, a little group of shaken young students quite convinced that they had just heard a diatribe against the Mainland. He made the striving for a perfect wine such a resonant and ringing concept that in the ears of his auditors it stirred thoughts of liberty, justice, and an ideal place to be. His lecture room was his amphitheatre, his blackboard a tablet of ultimate truths, his time as precious as the oldest and rubiest Castel Karol-Lajessi. He taught wine-growing: they learned Revolution.

This will sound extraordinary to Brother Fredo, if he reads

152

it, but if a man of a god can believe the absurdities of how we start our wars in the world, perhaps he will credit this singular marvel. He knows better than any young revolutionary that belief, like disbelief, is a habit of thought.

But I heard many accounts of the phenomenon from rebel fighters who had studied viniculture under Gabril. Nunez, who had gone to the University at Furasol to learn how best to grow sparkling wine in the huge vineyards she had just inherited near Foretto, told me that the first time Gabril lectured to her about effective spacing of seeds in a chalky soil she drove straight back to her home town, where she later found herself spraying anti-Argeline slogans on a quiet residential street. Woodkind, another of Gabril's operatives, once doodled aimlessly through a lecture he found dull, only to discover that by the end of the two hours he had written a cogent and detailed plan of how best to incapacitate an armoured truck, armed only with a rope and club. There were diagrams, too. Another former student of Gabril's got himself arrested in Little Fura for throwing stones through the window of the tourist office. The police were wholly mystified but equally unimpressed by his claim to have been working on his 'spumante assignment'.

Dr Iaio Gabril continued to teach his classes, write his papers, publish his books. Neither the police nor the army once so much as questioned him, though they arrested many of his students, and incarcerated a few. Far from harassing him or his faculty, they applauded his efforts to get this deluded and volatile generation to learn a trade so vital to the Island's continuing prosperity as viniculture. When the Mainland authorities suspended and finally closed the Faculties of Politics, History, and Dance (after one notorious instance of incendiary choreography), they expanded Viniculture, establishing further and higher courses, encouraging richer and more students, pressing Gabril for assurances that he would stay on and grow with his famed department. In any case, most suspicion was expended not on the University

153

at all, but on the poor farmers and loggers around San Timotheo, the demonised 'slopers' of the Island's imagination. Indeed, many of these were swift to join the ranks of Gabril's vinicultural shock-troops in the early seasons of the conflict, but the original plotters and perpetrators – whether they were rich farmers' sons from the hinterland of the Capital, dark bookish lads from Laquilla and the interior, inherited country daughters like Nunez and her friend Rabaiette, or poor boys from Gamor and Saldeo – were students in the faculty whose senior lecturer was Dr Iaio Gabril.

Imagine what you imagine where, but over the iron lip
Of what's to come there flows a wine so cordial and so
  clear
No mind can sip the meanest sip but he has sipped from
  mine.

I do not know, and will never know, to what extent Gabril sanctioned the increasing violence and mercilessness of some of the OLB's acts as the time wore on. The students who left started consciously to fan the revolt, without wholly understanding the wellsprings of their fury. Innocents began to die, when tightly planned strategic assaults on army patrols and garrisons gave way to indiscriminate bombs, uncontrollable conflagrations. Probably the wilder students broke free of Gabril's influence, creating their own little cells of joyless diehards. Faction fighting broke out in the OLB, and there was certainly a time when the whole uprising could have been left to burn itself out from the friction of its inner antagonisms. But the Mainland Government, its bankrollers nudging it to proclaim Victory, decided to do Something, and, when the Viceroy Bize was blown up near Furasol late in the spring of Gabril's twentieth year in the Faculty of Viniculture, they took action no less decisive than it was foolish. They closed the University down.

Dr Iaio Gabril was tipped off about an hour before the army arrived, and, famously concluding his final, curtailed lecture with the words 'We have planted, we have grown, let us harvest, let us drink', he strode towards the high ridges of Mount San Timotheo, his adoring and intoxicated acolytes singing in his wake, and the villagers of the uplands receiving him, then following him, with gifts and shouts in their many dialects. It is said that the first platoon of soldiers into the abandoned lecture hall was never seen again, at least, not in the form of Government soldiers, for, so affected were they by a record of wine-growers' worksongs that the Doctor had left playing, that they shed their uniforms and climbed the mountain naked after him, each extolling the pleasures of the grape of his own province.

The OLB regrouped around its leader, restored to the very heart of the organisation, aloft in his eyrie on the mountain. Those who set up Camp Liberat, on a meadow just below the snowline, did so with the full conviction that they were following a man who had been teaching them Revolutionary Studies for the last four years. Of course in believing this they were wrong, but they were young and wild, and they drank the wines of the angels, and would argue their various merits until dawn.

After Viceroy Bize came Viceroy Lagland, and let the history books tell it bleakly: shot down on his first day in Badeo, in the sunshine of a dirty Allalong market, by his bodyguard, it seemed at first, then later – without a doubt – by a sloper named Pirir. With the University already shut, three-quarters of its students in jail but the treacherous accomplice Burneau still missing – something drastically successful had to be done. The Mainland Government was being advised either to declare Victory or declare War, both of which would be preferable to the prolongation of Nothing. So next the Argeline artillery fire-bombed the mountain itself. Camp Liberat moved into an abandoned hermitage, just above the winter snowline.

The day after that, three weeks after the death of Viceroy Lagland, two members of a patrol were shot dead on the Highway Furasol, and an iron cordon of more of them was dug in all the way from the Great Fork to the south coast of the Island. Badeo's three warships took care of the Bay, the sea to the west and the sea to the south, until the peninsula that included Furasol, Mount San Timotheo and the ghost of New Badeo – some quarter of the Island in square miles – was effectively besieged. I believe it is not improbable that the very last person to enter that stranded quarter of the Island, before it became impossible for civilians either to reach it or to escape it, was myself, hooded and crouched in the back of a stolen, bloodstained van, and on my way to Camp Liberat, where I would remain for two years, sometimes a prisoner, sometimes a lover, sometimes a listener, sometimes the war's greatest strategist (through no fault of my own), but usually, most of the time, merely waiting to be any of them.

This may be where Dr – General – Iaio Gabril first enters my story, but it is not where I first enter his. In my early days at Camp Liberat, I felt I was little more than a vagabond given shelter by sympathetic outlaws. Indeed a special vagabond, the Island's Most Wanted Man, after all, but a secret starting to become a problem. That was how I felt most of the time. I passed my days sleepily, dully, lying awake in my bedroom, or sitting in the Hall of Weathers, being endlessly and repetitiously questioned by three interrogators in turn. They never seemed to compare answers among themselves, for the same questions always came back: who sent me to Badeo, where did I hide for two weeks before Nunez found me, why did I use the name Frosch – the rebels being understandably sensitive to the possible connotations of using the name of any beverage as a cover – then, how had I infiltrated the security services, who were my contacts in the OLB, on and on through what I believe were humid, grey but rainless afternoons.

In the first days, I was dependent on the glass ceiling not only for light, but also for knowledge of the weather. I was not allowed out, and peeking through the blind in my room offered a view only of a sheet of corrugated metal that had been nailed over my window some time after my arrival. I ate alone in the octagonal space, letting the clatter of my fork on the floor take a whole half-minute to sink back into the silence. I used a primitive lavatory next to my bedroom, making every possible sound that could remind my environment of the presence of a human, and looked dully forward to the next series of easy questions, or to a rare reappearance of Nunez, who occasionally asked things a bit more taxing, questions I could feel my brain contemplating like a creature – it was a while since I had had any sense of a brain. I wondered if it would ever be possible to tell Nunez about my past, my real past, for now it was coiled right about my heart, and was no bigger than it.

About a week into my time, the questions suddenly ceased. Nunez strolled into the Hall of Weathers one sunny morning with a bronze tray bearing two crystal glasses and a green bottle of unlabelled wine. This had been opened but not begun. She drew up two of the three chairs her comrades had left behind them, put the tray down on one and sat herself down on another. I remained on my settee, blurrily watching. She started to pour the wine, softly reciting a gabrilette as she poured. It was the one that starts 'Imagine what you imagine where' – Number 314, I believe. But to me then it was strange and not a little threatening. I was determined to learn all I could from Nunez, but my week-long languor was such that I felt hazily inhibited, floating, enfeebled. And then, on a sunny morning, to sip that milk of a wine . . .

'We don't think you can leave,' she said, holding a glass up to the sunlight, then passing it to me because it was my glass, 'but we're not sure what to do with you. We're besieged, you see. What do we want with another mouth to feed? Then again, as I tell them, here he is, here you are – the killer

157

Burneau. They know, they have to shelter you. We're that kind of people. "We have to do the possible with all we cannot be",' she intoned, swilling the wine about her own glass. Then she downed it.

'You won't be disturbed. This is excellent. It's almost like a Fortice, but I bet it's not a real one. No, nobody lives here, Burneau. Just Teacher, the Lady Mnam, myself. I live here. My people live outside in the Camp.'

'I thought this was the Camp.'

'It's the beacon and tower of the Camp.'

'It is a good wine, it is.'

Her eyes narrowed: 'What do you mean by that, Burneau?'

'It has a good, you know . . . taste, to it.'

'Just say it: you feel something.'

'It's dry? Is it? Yes. Dry and, well, oaky.'

'It's not oaky at all. It's peachy. Don't be ashamed, Burneau, don't be ashamed to admit certain feelings. Anything that happens here doesn't really happen at all.'

'Is it dangerous?' I asked her.

'It's strong and dry, it's almost a Las Gideu.'

'The Camp.'

'The Camp . . . ' she murmured, filling her glass again.

'Is the Camp dangerous?'

She stared hard: 'It's the Nest In A Whirlwind. You should know that. It's a sliding card in your spread. That means it affects its neighbours.'

'So it's dangerous.'

'So it's not. It's not, Burneau. Drink, Drink, assassino . . .'

'I'm getting the peachiness now.'

'Yes? Do you know much about wine?' she asked pleasantly.

'I've never drunk much of it. I like the white stuff when it's very cold.'

She blinked at me for a moment, then put down her glass and said frostily: 'Oh. Do you.'

158

A long pause, a great hole opened up in the day, a hole I had to fill with wine before speaking again.

'Nunez . . .'

'What?'

'What's happening out there, I mean down below, what's happened? It's so quiet here. Please say.'

She resumed her clinically professional poise, and strode around as she spoke: 'We're locked in, that's for sure. Land, sea, borders. So: supplies. We're on our own. We're like you. We have Furasol and some villages. The boys and girls down there are bringing everything in, everything up high. Else we don't eat. Are you warm, Burneau?'

'I'm warm, Nunez.'

'I'll ask you again this winter. Then see what you say. We have to chop trees to keep warm up here. We chop trees, we can see for miles. What's that mean? From miles they can see us. How's the wine?'

'It's getting home.'

She stopped and blushed like a teenager. 'Look, I'm sorry about what you said. I'm sure you never meant it.' Then she walked on, once more like a troop commander: 'Here's the cork and dreg, Burneau, here's the cork and dreg. You stay here for now. I mean here, in this room. Or your room. I'll be with you when I can be. The Fulbahlis will bring meals, change sheets. And such. The Teacher will see you soon. Pay no attention to the Lady Mnam. Don't worry. Remember, you have no choice but to conceal your true feelings. You are the Child Behind A Wall. I'm very much the same. I'm the Fire-Fish. But you knew that, else you wouldn't have found me. Would you, Burneau?'

I agreed, of course. Whatever belief she pursued through whatever strange dispensation of playing cards, I had no idea, but I had come into their world without much of any-thing, Fredo, like the world of the Maricolos, and the whole world – I had to wear the clothes they wore. She made several such visits, Nunez, always bringing a bottle – always

159

a different wine, never labelled, always finished – either in the middle of the morning or just before the end of daylight in the octagonal room, but I never saw her at any other time.

One day, the same door opened and a long-haired slender youth I had not seen before wandered in with three bottles wedged under his left arm. I must have been at Camp Liberat about six weeks. He set the bottles down on the three chairs, one on each, and said with a sniff: 'Sod it, would you look? Nowhere for me now.'

'The floor,' I believe I said.

'Of course, never saw it there,' said this youth, sitting down cross-legged between two of the chairs, and proceeding to open one of the bottles.

'Are you one who's been here before?'

'Can't tell you that. I've been everywhere before.'

'Are you with Nunez?'

'Woh no. Can you imagine? Me neither. Are you?'

'I'm Burneau. I don't know what's going on.'

'"Burn-eau", is it? I figured "Burn-you". But I know who you are. You're the hitman, goes the rumour. I'm Tragolani, F, Wine School, UCF. Best days of my life so far. You try this, this is an absolute blinding beauty of a drop. I'd march through the Arselicko for this. Talking of which.'

I drank. 'Talking of which?'

'The March, the March, that's what we'll drink to, Burn-you. The March on Skeniche.'

Who's marching, where's Skeniche, why are they marching, when are they marching and what's it got to do with anything, were some of the questions to which I might have progressed, but I was quick to learn that, with this singular character, patience often paid off, because left to his own devices he would eventually get to the information you wanted. The thing to do was keep sipping and keep up.

You will know this yourself by now, Brother Fredo, for this is he, Federico Tragolani, the young man who has brought

160

you this letter. I grant that he looks wearier now, but his energy remains undiminished and his appetite undimmed. Perhaps as you have done, I now received from him the first details of the outside world since the salvation of my kidnap by Nunez and her cell. He told me that Mme Dagmar Frock, the woman sent by the Domain to investigate the assassination, and Extraordinary Envoy Boris Brew, sent to advise upon the restoration of order to the Island, had agreed that the next step after the establishment of the Organ Liberat's guilt in the matter of the Viceroy was to consider the use of force to 'liberate' the ordinary people of Furasol from the talons of that desperate 'bandit crew'. But those same ordinary people of Furasol, Tragolani explained, were heartily sick of the fighting – whoever started it, and for whatever reason – and were beginning to commingle in the main square of the town, prior to marching slowly all the way to the cordon that the army had thrown across the countryside. This was nine miles out of Furasol, at Skeniche. The intention was to shame the young soldiers into letting the whole of the Furasolian populace through the barrier, so that the puppet government would learn clearly and without resort to violence that there was a mighty will towards insular unity. It was fully believed by the organisers of the March on Skeniche that most of the Badean cadets would turn a half-circle and join the walkers, arm-in-arm, join in their songs and mountain rhythms, walk all the way to Badeo and confront the authorities there. Tragolani readily admitted, when I pointed it out to him, that this March was a blatantly pro-Liberat manifestation, in that it was only the OLB who ever appealed for Unity, meaning Unity independent of the Argeline shackle, and, indeed, the ranks of the 'ordinary citizens of Furasol, voicing their fatigue' were sure to be swollen by the extraordinary and far-from-fatigued graduates of the Wine School sporting the false beards of slopers – not to mention the feared highlanders themselves. But the young man countered my accusation of bias by stressing the unanimity of the People against the Cordon, which, left in

161

place, would slowly strangle and starve Furasol and the south-west of the Island.

'And after all, friend, they go in peace, you know.'

'But the government will see it as anti-Mainland, won't it?'

'Call it anti-this, pro-this, but call it *this*: mothers, children, grandmothers, grandchildren, boys, girls, doctors, lawyers, stokers, players, poets, cooks and dressmakers, all Badean Islanders, Burn-you, merely wishing to pass from A to B. Isn't that *the* fundamental right of an Islander on his Island? And if an Islander is prevented from passing from A to B on his Island, we must look hard at who is preventing them . . . The Organ Liberat? Is the Organ Liberat preventing them? Go on, you answer . . .'

'Is it? Oh, well – no.'

'Doctor Gabril? You answer again. It's how he taught us.'

'No. And it's Burneau.'

'The army?'

'Yes.'

'In threes,' he said. 'Ask two questions to which the answer is No, and it'll be easier to say Yes to the third. That's in *Wine from Nowhere*. I'll lend you it. It's in it.'

'Thank you. Have you ever heard of a game called Scissors-Paper-Stone?'

'A game? Can't be. There's no game you can teach Tragolani. I'm champion at most, best at the others. You can . . . try though, if you want to.'

None of my work in the Ministry of Reconciliation, tortuous and labyrinthine as it is, has ever been as difficult as teaching this young man this simplest game of this or probably any other world. Any game requires just one quality of a man: honesty. Without skill or strength, there can still be points, if the players are matched in ineptitude or frailty. Without space, there can be tournaments of the mind. Without language, simple bouts of brawn. Without company, a game against Time itself, or its artist, Memory. But without honesty and accordance with the established rules, there can be nothing. A game without honesty is war. It is not merely like war, it is war. Two best friends can play the simplest card game, but if one denies to himself the sanctity of the rules, then he denies them to the other player too, and he is fighting a war. It takes only one to begin a war: now both must fight a war. Now their honesty can be only to themselves. It is in this sense alone that war is not a game. Democracy is a game, law and sex are, art and work and health are: they have rules, they are all fair games for humans. As a general rule – I have rules, in which case the conduct of my life is a game – those things which tend towards general happiness, or an equality of joy, are games, while those things which tend towards the achievement of victory, trailing defeat, decline and inequality of joy in its wake, are wars.

Oh, but please, do not look upon this Tragolani – who has done me such a service and walked so far to find you – as the harbinger of all martial ills, just because he can't play a simple game like an honest man! I preface my short description of the game in this manner, merely in order to explain the circumstances of my only defeat in the game of Scissors-Paper-Stone – my proficiency at which I have alluded to on many occasions – a defeat suffered ostensibly at the hands of a beginner. Well – a beginner at honest game-playing perhaps, but an old dodging veteran of chicanery and bluff, a real battle-scarred mercenary between the lines, I can tell you.

I showed him the three possibilities: fingers, palm and fist, let him practise a while and then suggested we start playing. He frowned and looked wary.

'I'd say you have the slight advantage of experience, no?'

'I'm no expert,' I said.

'Well, I'm a quick learner, and if I win, the victory will be all the more glorious, and your loss I would imagine almost unbearable.'

I shrugged, thought about a game-plan, and made Stone. He made Paper – it started out as Scissors, I swear, but it changed. I kept quiet. I made Stone again. He made Stone. I made Scissors, and he made a flimsy page for me to cut to ribbons, evening the score. I went back to Stone (we call that the Koborol opening, by the way) and he removed his hand completely.

'Stone,' I said. 'Two–One.'

'Absence,' said Tragolani. 'Absence beats Stone. Absence is the end of Stone.'

'No, it isn't.'

'It is.'

'There isn't any Absence. It's not in the game.'

'Oh get real, Burn-you, there must be. Otherwise how can there be Presence? Dear me. What's your degree in?'

'All right, all right. What beats Absence?'

'Nothing. You can't beat it. Try beating Absence. No way.'

'Then why not always use Absence? You'd never lose, would you? And it's Burneau.'

'Surprise is one reason, obviously. Skill, variety. Those are key elements, Burneau. Burn-Hohoho. Right, play. My two crap on your one. I like this. First to a hundred?'

If any man had a day to spare, I had it. My days had become so indistinct and futile up there on that mountain, pacing the octagonal room. I'd think to myself in the morning, 'Today's the day I break out, I find their leader, I find Nunez, I plead for a passage home, I demand better treatment – I killed the Viceroy!' Then in the afternoon: 'Tomorrow's better, start fresh and early,' and in the evening, 'I wonder what's for supper tonight?' and by the end of the day – 'I must get the Fulbahlis to change this lumpy pillow . . . ' How leadenly was Time on my side, like a huge great clumsy boy in the playground – no, I don't want him on my team, I don't mind! You have him, you take him! But there stood Time, plumply awaiting instructions.

164

I accepted that Tragolani's conduct of the game was going to be warlike and inappropriate, but felt that some hours in his company represented a good opportunity to find out more about the OLB, and about Camp Liberat, Nunez, the March on Skeniche, and the future for us all. So I nodded, sat back, drank another glass, and began to play him. And yes, there was worse to come. He developed a fifth variant on the hand position: the Eye, formed by thumb and forefinger.

'My Eye reads your Paper, friend. That's seventy-two.'

When I formed Eye, he was waiting for me with Scissors, and jabbed it out.

'Bet that hurt! Next frame. You're an old-school player, you see. But Tragolani, he's always boxing, always thinking . . .'

The score is not important. Suffice it to say that after about seven hours of play, the best of seven hundred hand-frames, with a huge yawn he called a halt, offered me the last of our eighth bottle of wine and said he was off to bed.

'Tragolani,' he said, 'What you are is a cheat.'

'What's this then, Arselicko manners? Play the game, eh?'

'What am I doing here? Why don't they let me out? Or let me join, let me do something?'

'See, that's been on your mind all day! Showed in your game-plan. That Triple-Paper you do just doesn't wash. So now you're making excuses for a lousy attack. Passable defence though, I'll grant you.'

'What defence? There *is* no defence in Scissors-Paper-Stone, Tragolani. You make the hand at the same instant. You don't change when you see what I'm doing!'

He sat back.

'You don't – you don't . . . no defence, huh? Hah! Now you're going to say it was beginner's luck, aren't you, you Arselicko hitman, you're all the same, you are . . .'

'I'll come on the March, Tragolani. I'll hold a banner, beat a drum, do anything – but I'll die here in this place – of drink, if nothing else!'

'No, you can't come.'

'Why?'

'You know why. Best-known face on Badeo these days. Famous man. Bastard. Truth is, we haven't the least idea what to do with you. Nunez'll keep you here so long as she can. At least until she's had her, you know, way with you. Sorry, oughtn't have said. My big mouth.'

'Way, what way?' I demanded, my innards turned to melted chocolate in contemplation of different ways.

'The kind you live through, friend. The kind you live through and live through and live through. There's another way, which is just the same except change "live through" to "die through". One more for luck? *Yne, tvar, tvigo . . .*'

Stone, I did, as if to affirm some solidity and strength in the region of my bowels. And at first I thought Tragolani had invented a sixth confounded invincible gesture, but no: his hand was held out as if to shake mine in greeting, which, when we shook, it did seem to do.

I couldn't sleep that night. I got out of bed, felt for the window and pulled back the blind. Blind I might as well have been: the corrugated metal sheet was now, clearly, nailed to my window. On my way across to the corner to switch on the lamp, I tripped on my own shoes, stumbled and smashed it, cutting myself. I squatted in a darkness so total it seemed final. After a hopeless time, I crawled out of the room, perilously relieved my wine-barrel of a body in the tiny bathroom, and then set off, like a determined infant, crawling along the cold polished corridor towards the octagonal room, in the vague hope that for once a door might have been left open to the world's last conscious self.

It had been. As I felt it give, I slowly stood up, and knew a surge of excitement, the intensity of which reminded me of when I had last felt it, when Tragolani had told me of Nunez, whose face I now remembered clearly, her 'way', her sculpted face, her searching eyes!

Constellations had flooded the Hall of Weathers with dizzying bright air. I moved to the centre of the room, with those eight walls glowing softly around me, and I looked directly up through the pinnacle of the glass ceiling. Days of rain had cleaned it so well that it seemed to vanish from sight, and let me stand unfenced from the starry firmament. I swayed, nearly overbalanced, and sat down cross-legged where I was. Suddenly, with extreme and quite shocking clarity, I had a cogent thought.

Don't march.

I shook my head, not to disagree, but as if to dissuade some insect from settling on me – why should I be telling myself not to march, when there seemed to be no question of the OLB allowing me to anyway!

Don't march.

It came from somewhere deep. If I closed my eyes, I had to own to it, but if I opened them up to the heavens again I placed it somewhere there, out there. It was not a voice that seemed to have made a sound in the Hall of Weathers – which usually contained sound like it was as captive as I was – but only within me, where it echoed for a while. At last I believed it had died away, and, as if to make sure I had rid myself of this frankly disconcerting phenomenon, I began to stand up again, to throw off the stars as well – then it happened again, clear as a chime, but altered to its final form.

DON'T LET THEM MARCH.

Then I swayed and staggered, and visions crowded me like crazed birds – joking marchers and pale soldiers, shouts and boasts across a line of trucks, banners blowing wildly, fingers holding trembling cigarettes, confusion and heads turning, guns lifted in the rain, then thunder, blood on shopping bags, shoes on a highway, somebody crawling – 'DON'T LET THEM MARCH!' I cried out – the Hall trumpeted my cry – then I looked up at nothing but stars. Silence, blood beating at my temple, then dead silence. I don't remember how long I stayed there on the floor, but I know that sleep came before I was gone, and I woke up with the sky dull grey over my head, and rain streaming in tatters across the sloping glass.

I had woken possessed of an acute and steady awareness, and knew that my mind had spent the hours of early dawn frantically rationalising the sight I had seen, while my worn eyes and drunken limbs slept and refreshed themselves. Like a rolling newspaper to the random feel of the world was my spinning mind to my heart. The truth was as clear as daylight, and as soon as my cries had alerted somebody – a shrunken old man whose only job seemed to be taking the labels off the bottles of wine, and who happened to be passing on his way to the kitchens to see the Fulbahlis – I gushed out my story to him:

'It's the weather, you see! It rains on the boys' faces and they hate that! And the teams – the boys are from Gamor, Badeo Town, Saldeo – and Furasol have beaten them all this season, so they're itching for a fight! And because the marchers are laughing to keep warm – well, they think they're laughing at them! And the thunder comes at the wrong time, the warning shot is drowned – the wet banners blow in their faces – that's what starts the panic! And they're drunk, the mountain men, so they don't take any notice – and because they're only thirty feet from the barrier, when they do hear it they think it's the soldiers – because the wind is north-westerly and it makes them seem nearer – and oh – it's the rain on the boys' faces – it's that that they can't bear!'

The label-removing man adjusted his glasses and frowned, but when it became clear he was not going to respond, I shrieked out the point as I saw it – 'You have got to stop them marching on Skeniche! Nunez, Tragolani, Stoackey, the people – you have got to stop them marching!'

'A dream, was it, sir?' muttered the label-removing man, reading the label of a slender brown bottle, and dusting it with his thumb.

'A vision!' I blurted out. 'A vision over there in the centre of the room – in the middle of the night – it was starlit, but look . . . I was right about the rain, wasn't I? See?'

'Ho, then,' said the label-removing man, 'You were right

168

about the rain. You were right about the stars. Sir, we have had nothing but clear nights and wet days for a fortnight. I am not about to elevate you to the status of a seer, sir. You are not a seer, sir. Now, I must take these bottles to the kitchens. Our people must be provided for on their return tonight.'

'Sir, they won't return alive!'

Now the label-removing man began to get irritated, and starting picking expertly at the edges of the label.

'Ho, then. Are you saying we may be wasting our wine?'

'In essence, yes, I am!'

'In essence, yes, you are. Well. Perhaps you might go back to bed, sir, in essence, and dream more dreams, and tell me exactly what I should open, and what I should store, and perhaps what temperatures are best for every vintage! Good day to you. Now I have to lock this place. You are not meant to be here at this hour.'

'I couldn't sleep – it was open – it was then that I had the – '

He made a move to open the door, and I grabbed his arm so that he dropped one of his bottles. It rolled unbroken against the wall. The label-removing man watched it come to a standstill, then he turned on me with a look of icy fury and introduced himself.

Dr Iaio Gabril, former Senior Professor of the Faculty of Viniculture at the University College of Furasol, was in appearance small, bony, bespectacled, possessed of scrutinising hard blue eyes and a beaked nose, wiry of frame, slightly crooked with perhaps seventy years on him, shabbily dressed and completely bald. He was also, in appearance, quite angry.

'A dream? A dream? You think that a half-year of intricate calculation is going to be derailed by the hallucinations of an Argelino killer? You yourself are lucky to be alive! You leave these matters to me, my young friend, and keep your dreams corked in their magnums!'

169

As he vented his imaginative spleen upon my vision, I stooped to pick up the fallen bottle, the label of which was still half-attached. I gave it to him.

'Break upon the day the wine of night and as the time
Is swilled about the glass between the rim and the deep
    bell,
Remember what's to come will drink its fill of your
    delight.'

He didn't say that, I did. Nor do I know why that one, or then, except that it seemed to concern the future. As he heard the words of the 19th Gabrilette (collected in *Wine from Sand*) he perceptibly brightened, and, by the end of it, was nodding in profound accord.

'Ho, then, Mr Burneau, you are a memoriser of works?'

'Some,' I said, 'yes, from childhood.'

'A child indeed when I composed that one.'

'A child indeed, sir.'

'Mr Burneau, it has been a fascinating pleasure to make your acquaintance. But do let me remind you that you must stay here in our Hall until we come to a decision on your own "what's-to-come". In the meantime, try to eat better, sleep longer, and sleep sounder. Dreams are for children, prophecy for prophets. You are mistaken about the March on Skeniche. The Government has already conceded that it must let the women and children through the cordon. You might as well prophesy the conversation we have just had, Mr Burneau. You would at least be closer to the truth. I do hope to renew our acquaintance when I have more time on my hands. Morior, Nagel!'

As those two familiar patrollers appeared at the end of the corridor, I racked my brains for one more piece of his own work that might make him tarry longer – something about things being not what they seem?

170

'White's not white, and red's not red, and the dry's not
   dry. The grape
Is soft and contrary as hope. All words are gathered in
For crushing on the bloody stone. The wine is what is
   said.'

'Indeed, Mr Burneau. But that's a mere draft. In the re-
vised edition I altered "The wine is what is said" to "The
wine is what is lost". Now that's quite a different story.'
   'But you spoil the rhyme, Dr Gabril. It's not, with respect,
a gabrilette any more.'
   'Mr Burneau,' he said testily, 'the vine is not yours to cut.'
   'Please believe me!' I cried, as the patrollers parted us
firmly, locked the Hall of Weathers and escorted Gabril
away down the corridor, but my heart had long given up the
struggle to convince him, and my thoughts were left miserable, listening dully to the rain. I wandered back to my little
room, and cleaned up the broken glass.

I will not describe to you the March on Skeniche. Not only
because I was not there, and so did not witness it, but also
because I have said enough. Early that afternoon, about 120
Furasolian civilians were shot down by a panicked regiment
of the Badean army. Many were injured, many killed. It happened in a dark thunderstorm. The army blamed the
marchers, whom they accused of being drunken and dangerous. Many of their bodies were found under the heavy,
soaking remains of their banners, which seemed to have
blown back in their faces and made them start running. The
only aspect about which I was mistaken in my foresight was
the danger to Nunez and her cell, who had at the last minute
been ordered – by Dr Gabril – not to march. Those who did
return came back up the mountain wounded, bedraggled, enraged or in despair. When Gabril, in an implacable fury, saw
that there was – on top of everything else – far too much
wine to go round, he remembered me.

171

The first I knew of any of this was late that night, when my door suddenly opened. It was Stoackey and Nagel, two of Nunez's men, who took me to the Hall of Weathers, pulled up a chair for me in the centre of the room, and told me to wait. Then they left. The centre of the room was so vividly spotlit that it was impossible to tell whether the sky was starlit or overcast, but as my eyes gradually adapted to the sudden and specific brightness I perceived that about me there was nothing but mist.

Soon several people walked in, Gabril among them. Chairs were scraped about, whispers and murmurs filled the air, the atmosphere was urgent, fractious. Then the clear voices began, at an approximation of the four points of the compass, around the edge of the ring of light. There was the dry academic crackle of Gabril directly behind me, the husky rasp of Nunez to my left, Tragolani's lazy drawl to the right, and, dead ahead, emanating from a vast shade wrapped in an army greatcoat, the ineradicable growl of Battle Marshal Brangeon Curtens.

'He knew the soldiers would fire,' Curtens was saying, 'because he knows the hearts of Argelinos: murderous, hollow . . .'

'He mentioned details,' said Nunez. 'Is that not right, Dr Gabril? The north-westerliness of the wind? The thunderstorm?'

'So he's a weatherman,' grunted the Marshal, 'as well as a gibbering drunk.'

'Quaff it how you will,' said the Doctor, 'but accept my word that the wine is poured, and by this man.'

'Who told him about the March?' smouldered the Marshal. 'Who told him anything?'

'I told him about the March,' said Tragolani. 'He asked me. You should try spending a day with him, Marshal. Nothing but questions. He's a bad sport too.'

'They're rotten through and through, comrade! I say it's time we make an end of him off our own mountain!'

'Out of the question,' said Gabril from behind me. 'Nunez rescued him from certain murder. If we do to him that same evil from which she saved him, we are negating her act of revolutionary fellowship, and we don't do that.'

'Thank you, Teacher,' said Nunez quietly.

There was a silence, then Gabril spoke: 'Perhaps you are curious, Mr Burneau, as to why we allow you so openly to listen to our deliberations. But we wish all things to be plain to you. We pride ourselves on the openness of our dealings. Even Battle Marshal Curtens, who is of the opinion that you should be killed, if possible tonight, respects the honour which has been accorded you by your merely being considered a matter worthy of our discussion.'

'Thank you, Marshal,' I said into the light.

Gabril's voice stiffened. 'We have suffered a terrible and serious reversal in our fortunes today. The seriousness, terror and pity of my heart is heightened by my recognition that our disaster was largely foreseen by you, and, therefore, could have been in some way avoided by fuller action on my part. I am of the opinion that we should question you regarding the circumstances under which you saw a – let us say, an "illumination" of the day's events before they came to pass.'

So I told them what I have already set down. That I had spent the day idly with Tragolani, that we had drunk numerous bottles of red wine, that I had been unable to sleep. Then, how I smashed my lamp by accident and crawled to the Hall of Weathers, how I looked at the stars, how I heard the voice say *Don't let them march*, then saw the images of the day to come. How I fell asleep and woke up in daylight.

'Because the only alternative,' said the Marshal crisply, once my account had petered out, 'is that he knew his fellow recruits and collaborators would shoot at innocent civilians, because he knew it was in their battle orders – because he still works for them!'

'No he doesn't,' said Nunez, 'he's a Horse Alone, I assure you.'

'I have been considering deeply,' murmured Gabril, 'and now I should be attended. Tell me, my friends, what did this man foresee?'

'The wind direction,' said Nunez.

'Banners soaked,' said Tragolani, 'thunder drowning the warning shot.'

'That the soldiers would fire because of their hatred for Furasol's heroic sportsmen?' Nunez ventured.

'Ho, now,' said Gabril. 'No. Those were his rationalisations. He did not foresee any of those things. His rational being worked retrospectively to create them. Yes, the wind was north-westerly, but it *had* to be so, otherwise it wouldn't have made the drunken San Timotheans at the back of the crowd think that the soldiers were advancing on them. The banners *must* have been soaked and plastered to the faces at the front of the crowd, because otherwise those people would have seen the soldiers lift their rifles in warning, and would not have panicked and run at them. The thunder *must* have drowned out the warning shot, because nothing else would have been loud enough. So. There must have been rain, north-westerly wind, and a thunderstorm. This was not in itself the illumination granted to our friend. The illumination he had was, in fact, aural. The words *Don't let them march*.'

'Absolutely,' said Brangeon Curtens. 'Therefore he's nothing but an Argelino infiltrator confusing us with his bad conscience! I say we end it now.'

'Ho, now, on the contrary,' said Dr Gabril. 'Now we begin.'

'Begin what?' said Tragolani.

'None of Burneau's rationalisations diminishes the fact that he did indeed visualise the massacre at Skeniche. But, according to him, he visualised it only after hearing the words *Don't let them march*. Now ... what did he know before he heard that voice?'

Tragolani pondered. 'That ... Furasolian civilians were marching?'

'That they were cadets, young,' said Nunez, 'that they were mainly Badeans themselves, but from other towns? Did you tell him that, Federico?'

'Did I?' Tragolani asked.

I agreed he had done.

'Where's all this leading?' the Marshal wanted to know, as if it was not at present leading in any direction he hoped it might.

'Here,' snapped Dr Gabril. 'Here and now. Everything Burneau warned us about was merely a rationalisation of a vision, which was in itself the visual staging of a set of words. All the details – the rain in the faces of the cadets, the banners blown back, the thunder – followed on from the original premise, which was an aural intuition that the march would end in a massacre. So. All that intuition required for its creation was what?' There was silence, shuffling. 'Knowledge. Essential, basic, factual knowledge. The age and nationalities of both marchers and soldiers. The likelihood that the marchers would be drinking, that the soldiers would break under pressure. The observation that the pursuit of trivial sports is not so trivial in the hearts of young Islanders as we might have believed. So.'

'So what?' boomed the inevitable sceptic.

'So what we do about Mr Maris Burneau is feed him.'

'Feed him?' the Marshal spluttered.

'Feed you,' said Gabril, and I felt as if the hot bright light on the back of my neck was the beam of his attention, 'feed you information, knowledge, facts, history, Mr Burneau. Feed you, as much as is humanly possible, the world.'

'Call me a stupid growling old soldier,' growled Curtens, 'but what the devil do you mean, Gabril?'

'Think, my friend, think. Burneau's gift, if such it is, is for synthesis, not analysis. For insight, not intelligence. It is we who must supply the intelligence, feed him the ingredients for him to ferment the wine. He will observe, absorb, process, and finally deliver. The more he knows about the world

175

outside, the more he can tell us about the way that world will turn.'

There was a long pause. I was aware of Tragolani, off to my right, stirring uncomfortably in his chair, suddenly abandoning it for the comfort of the cold floor. Then I felt the warmth of Nunez, to the left, almost tangibly considering the words of her beloved Teacher. Even the Battle Marshal subsided for a few minutes, at least until he rumbled:

'Dead meat if he's wrong though, eh?'

At first light, the four of them – Gabril, Nunez, Tragolani and the Marshal, along with three or four of the ubiquitous ex-students, led me, at last, through a long curving corridor and three small store-rooms, out into fresh air so unfamiliar it made me stagger. We walked along an overgrown mountain path for about a mile, then suddenly, unforgettably, walked clear of the trees and stopped on a wide grassy ledge from where all was visible. Through the grey misty light I gazed in great excitement, away down the side of the mountain, dotted with little settlements among pine forests with white flashes of waterfall, right the way down to the steamy crawl of Furasol, out to Badeo Bay. And, there beyond, was Badeo Town itself. I could see – I remember thinking instantly with an acute jolt – the city where Juilla lived: her movement, wherever, whatever it was, at least was held in the giant eye of my vision. Remember, Fredo, that I felt a responsibility towards the family I had befriended, especially to the children, and they were often in my thoughts. I saw the thin silver height of the TV tower to the east of the Town, the hotels on the western shore, as lifeless and desolate-looking as their eerie counterparts away to my left on the promontory, New Badeo. I remembered how I had associated my plight with theirs on the morning of my capture by the OLB, which reminded me again of the circumstances of my sorrowful hasty departure from the Avenue Hali. My nostrils flooded with painful cold air, my hull of a mind with overpowering bright memories.

Soon the commanders took me back, but now installed me in the Hall of Weathers like a little prince, with several comfortable chairs – so that I had a choice of where to sit – a cabinet of books, a wooden dining-table, some tasteful spreading plants, pictures, ornaments, shelving. I was given the freedom to place all things as I wished, that I might re-create for myself the sense of north, south, east and west that I had lost in the great whiteness. My bedroom remained the same, small as it could be, but they tore down the corrugated sheet outside, so I had my view, which was of a little court the sunlight discovered only in the early evening, with an old well between a couple of silverwood trees growing through the cobbles, and, above the dilapidated outhouses opposite, the looming head of the mountain.

Above all, they fed me. Into the Hall of Weathers every morning poured newspapers, magazines, newly published books, intercepted letters, maps, sports results and theatre programmes, gossip from the entertainment industry, financial news, popular recipes, transport tickets, histories, calendars, almanacs, and any news of advances in scientific fields, medical, chemical, technological or military. Television and radio were denied to me, not by the rebels but by the Argeline forces, which had knocked out the receivers in Furasol in a rocket attack; one, I should add, which was suffered before my elevation to the status of Extraordinary Adviser to the Organ Liberat Badeon.

My first success came very quickly, the night after the interrogation I have described. A rapid scan of the newspapers available to the rebels (*Liberada!*, their own physically flimsy but beautifully phrased pamphlet; *The Good Badean*, the puppet regime's predictable propaganda; and *Dawn of Day*, the Mainland's colour spectacular), coupled with a browse through an atlas salvaged from the threatened university by Gabril, and an old painting of 'Furasol Harbour,' which Rabaiette, the curly-haired girl, had insisted I have in my bedroom – these things had given me, as

I stood that morning through the small hours in the Hall of Weathers, a distinct sense of vulnerability around my right shoulder. When I moved directly underneath the central pinnacle of the glass ceiling, the feeling intensified so much that my arm twitched and pointed at the north-eastern facet of the room.

Big from below. Big from below.

No mistaking it – *Big from below.*

I shouted out, the sloper Morior ran in – for a guard was always posted outside the octagon from that time – I spoke and he went to fetch Nunez. She, looking dishevelled and strange in the low red blaze of the corridors, muttered some orders to people I couldn't clearly see. My information having been communicated, I was forgotten, so that while the rebel commanders and soldiers milled and clattered around the passageways, I was left to make my slow way back to bed, clutching my sore shoulder which, I soon realised, was perfectly all right.

Nunez's people (Stoackey, Rabaiette and Woodkind) were sent north-east from the Camp along a narrow, sheltered path, from where they witnessed distinct movement about a quarter-mile below. They had only just finished their reconnaissance when a sniper-shot cracked off and they all started to run. Or all except Nunez herself, who hissed to them to get down and stay where they were. 'Big,' she told them 'Big from Below,' meaning that my words had suggested there was something more to come. After about an hour Rabaiette spotted a clearing in the trees and the unmistakable sight of a rocket launcher being towed into place. By first light the cell, with the support of a second cell under the command of a black-bearded man named Overot, had encircled the clearing, and by sunrise both the artillery team and their rocket launcher were in rebel hands. The rocket they had intended to fire was trained on the north-eastern wall of Camp Liberat. Battle Marshal Brangeon Curtens roared 'Coincidence!' through the corridors all day and all night, but Gabril sent

178

Tragolani to the Hall of Weathers with a bottle of his best Karol-Lajessi, the slopers made sketches of me to wear around their necks for luck, and Nunez stood that evening in the doorway of my bedroom, in a plain black dress with a green belt and a short skirt, her arms folded and her feet bare.

'There was a space for you, Burneau, and now it is filled. Last night I cast the spread for Fire-Fish – me – and you know what? Blue as the spring is in Foretto. Bluer, even, bluer.'

'What did you learn from the artillery men?'

'How not to beg. How not to bargain. How not to lie.'

'Did you, well, kill them?'

'We don't, well, kill anyone, well, Burneau. We wine and dine our enemies. Until they're, until they're . . . wined and dined. Let me in. I can't abide being outside a room. Spaces beckon me in.'

'Right. Come in, Nunez.'

She sat on the bed and crossed her legs. I sat down quite nervously on the other side of the room, below the window, but the room was so small that we were not so far apart. My legs stretched across the carpet almost as far as the bed.

'And now you will stay,' she said softly. 'Now you will stay until the vine is grown, the fruit crushed, the juice in bottles and the label stuck.'

'It's the strangest life, Nunez. Reading, sleeping, staring up at the stars. That's a poet's life. I'm really just a crossing-sentry.'

'You were. And I was a frivolous country girl. Such is life, Burneau. The cards fall, we fall. It is your duty as a revolutionary to deploy the talent you have in our cause. Badeo will be free, as sure as the sun will shine tomorrow. We are merely to be ready for that shining.'

'The sun may not shine tomorrow,' I said. 'In fact, preliminary forecasts suggest – '

'It will. Clouds may cover it, they cannot put it out. Is that some Karol-Lajessi in that jug?'

'How can you tell?' I wondered, for of course it was, though Tragolani had won half of it from me already, playing a card-game called 'Ask the Dwarf', which I had never heard of, and which he had not explained before he started dealing.

'It's on the air,' said Nunez as I poured her a glass, 'it likes me and it swims my way. My legs are cold.'

Her legs were bare, dark smooth legs but with a long scar running from her left knee to her anklebone.

'Barbed wire. Nothing.'

'You ought to,' I said, 'wear something over them. For the cold, that is.'

'You know I do, Burneau, I do. I wear my black stockings that keep me warm and snug, but I have lost them. Where? I do not know. I do not know.'

'Hmm. Did you wear them on your mission?'

'I did not. I work in overalls, like the others. I wear them around this place, when I'm waiting, and walking about, and I take them off to go to bed but that's not where they are. There's nothing in my bed but me these days.'

'So nothing at all just now then,' I said blandly, unable to cope with her.

'The Child Behind A Wall, Burneau, you are. Look behind that wall and maybe we'll find everything.'

'And you're the – Fire-Fish?'

'I'm already found. Now, you have work to do. Rabaiette says there's something you should see.'

Rabaiette met me in the octagonal room and fixed me with her eager green eyes.

'There's been a twist!' she declared.

Immensely popular with the people of Badeo Town was a television drama called *Carli and the Stranger*, featuring the futuristic adventures of a young Badean girl. This programme, which was screened four times every day, was followed with fanatical devotion by most of the Island's population, with the significant exception of Furasol, where it was regarded contemptuously as a symbol of the Capital's decadence and triviality. None of the students, soldiers and slopers of Camp Liberat had the remotest idea of how very important was this drama in the daily existence of the Island, and it took my experience, gained on a plumped and comfortable sofa with Juilla Maricolo resting her head on my shoulder, it grieves me to remember, it took my experience to apprise the revolutionaries of this fact. Even before they brought me my newspapers to scan, I requested that I be brought daily summaries of the plot of *Carli*. Though this request puzzled the students, Nunez, to her credit, had enough faith in me to make sure I got what I asked for. It was one such summary which Rabaiette excitedly thrust into my hand that night. It read as follows:

'Carli escaped from the Plane Gund-77 with Officer Bogel, but refused to accept that he was her long-lost brother Ronde. The real Ronde declared his love for Gazella, but she was unable to forget what happened in the Support Podule. Zyrex and Norma argued over custody of the Miracle Changeling. The Sex Force began to ascend the Mount of Gloom. The Entity threw a party.'

'So everyone will be happy, won't they?' Rabaiette exclaimed, 'because that girl Carli escaped! And there's a party! I thought you should know, Burneau, so I immediately and without delay – '

'Just feed him the print, Rabby,' said Nunez coolly from the door. 'Leave him to interpret.'

So, of course, far from getting a proper night's sleep, or being able to ruminate upon the odd pronouncements of Nunez, who could be a hard-bitten fighter one moment, and a sulky girl with no stockings the next, I was up all night again, reading the first imprints of tomorrow's papers, scanning weather reports, screwing my eyes up through pages

181

and pages of young men from the cadet schools and drama colleges, studying recent fashions and theatrical styles, swotting up bestsellers and measuring precise distances between towns. At about 4.45 the next morning I tottered into the arms of Tragolani and was heard to murmur: 'The new wine is not wine, the new wine is not wine . . . ' before I fainted on the floor.

At about eleven, a group of five cheerful young men arrived at the gates of Camp Liberat, claiming to be soldiers of fortune anxious to serve the cause of Badean liberation, full of stories of their scrapes and perils. They were instantly arrested, searched and interrogated, after which they were exposed irrefutably as students from Badeo's College of Dramatic Art who, short of money to ply their trade, had each accepted a large secret payment from the Government to infiltrate the Organ Liberat. I learnt that under intensive wining and dining they had conceded they were part of a whole army of impostors intended to flood the OLB over the coming weeks, and what's more, over dessert, they agreed that the glorious ascent of the Mount of Gloom by the Sex Force in the drama series *Carli and the Stranger* – in which they all dreamed of participating one day – was what had inspired them to take the money. Dr Iaio Gabril himself came to my room to pin a medal on me as I slept.

But that was not the only surprise waiting for me when I awoke. For one thing, it was disconcertingly dark again, for I had slept undisturbed all the way into another night. Then, when I tried to sit up, the better to examine whatever cold, pendulous honour had been bestowed upon me since I was last conscious, I felt something soft tangled up between my bare ankles. On closer inspection, it turned out to be a flimsy black stocking. Its twin, which I thought I would find somewhere, was entwined around the door handle. I untied it and held them both in my hands, while my medal was already forgotten upon the upturned box I kept beside my bed. Had Nunez done this? Why?

182

I made my bewildered way back to the Hall of Weathers, outside which lingered Woodkind, the mournful, philosophical ex-student who worked with Nunez. He related all the details of the thespian impostors, and how valuable all my information had been. He also told me that 'our esteemed Educator' had not only honoured me with the much-coveted Red Grape of Change, but had been singing my praises all night to his disciples. Even Battle Marshal Brangeon Curtens had improved in his mood, since Tragolani had pointed out to him that if my Advice continued to be this Extraordinary, his chances of winning battles and eventually the War would be greatly enhanced. Gabril himself was reputed to have been so jovial that he had dispensed with metaphor in the case of the treacherous drama students and had actually invited them to dine and drink with him. They, in turn, enthralled as so many before them by his wise counsel on the subject of south-facing vineyards and the repulsion of the Coldball Beetle in the event of a rainy autumn, had volunteered for active service in the ranks of the OLB! He had actually laughed out loud and called for another twelve bottles of Mauette Regale before pointing out to them with a smile that they had got to be joking. I had missed quite a night, by this account, for even Woodkind was in a rare good mood, but he had no idea where I might find Captain Nunez. I went back to my room, while Woodkind shuffled in a circle round the polished floor of the Hall of Weathers, composing a hymn to someone also called Woodkind.

When I got back into bed, I first thought the Fulbahlis had put another sheet down – but why in the middle of the night? They were an eccentric old couple, but their eccentricities always erred quite emphatically on the side of idleness as opposed to extra labour. Stumbling out of bed again and turning my new lamp on, I realised that the material in my bed was a dress, a short blue cotton dress with mere straps for shoulders, and the stockings – which I had rolled into a ball – were now stretched out in the shape of two skinny black legs, with the 'feet' at the bottom of the bed and the elasticated tops of the 'thighs' disappearing up into the dress. The clothes all were warm, as if their wearer had simply vanished in the air, but the warmth, I supposed, could have been mine. I folded up the curious arrangement and hid it under the bed. Then – acting under a firm and inexplicable compulsion – reversed that action completely, tucked the phantom woman into the sheets, and strode back, wide and wonderfully awake, to the Hall of Weathers.

Woodkind had gone, though his song was still fading on the last word ' . . . sea . . .' The sky was cloudy on the glass and I had so much work to do.

The Hall of Weathers was an awful mess. It had only been a matter of hours since I was established as its lord, but heaps of back issues, novels, cuttings and folders were piling up already, some high enough to topple over, as two of them did when I stumbled into them on opening the door. Brother Fredo, if you could see in your mind's eye the room in which I write this letter, and the chamber I now describe herein – you would think that here is a man who was cursed at birth to be followed all his life by mounds and mounds of paper, clean and white, then curled and crumpled, but forever at his back while he walks, while he sleeps, while he loves – flocks and flocks of them dancing through the air! Is that, do you think, the life of a humble crossing-sentry! Documents, files, articles, stories, letters, apologies, poems, threats! And what for? Did they save me from my brief life as Frosch, the dipso-maniac poet, or Maricolo, the ex-bank worker with a family to support, or Burneau once more, the fugitive innocent assassin, or my third existence as Burneau, the captive heroic rebel strategist – or my life now as the despised and, who knows, ludicrous, Minister of Reconciliation? Have they found me peace or prolonged happiness? No, indeed not! And you, Fredo, I doubt that you have ever written a word on a page, but you live a life high up in your eyrie with all that you need or want. One day I shall burn a mountain of paper so great that everyone in the world will breathe the smoke, so high that the smoke will change the weather like an erupted volcano does, and everyone in the world will know that I, Maris Burneau, crossing-sentry of Gispar in the high Koborol, thought *that*, wholly *that*, and only *that* of words and pens and pages, and if they wonder where he is, the man who burned a mountain of paper so high that it rained more often, or so high that it rained less often, or so high that the sunsets were marvels for a considerable while, or the sunrise a sensational colour on just one legendary morning, the wise ones will know he is above the snowline, above the treeline, patrolling his crossing and beyond words for ever.

Can you blame me for such sentiments as I relive this weird history? For, once again alone with the night and the few stars bold enough to pierce the mist, I read a million words in order to be assailed by a mere three. *East one day*, which was rapidly followed by a vision of rebels – Woodkind, Stoackey, Rabaiette – strolling happily through the streets of a dusty town. This, when I described it to Captain Overot, was clearly Furasol, and turned out to be my most successful foresight so far, being founded not upon verifiable history, like my intuition about the rocket launcher, or my anticipation of the masquerading mercenaries, but upon the surest hope of every Liberat rebel from Gabril himself to the wildest sloper. For Gabril, this was the absolute clinching evidence of my gift. 'He has seen, my friends, what we all know to be true!' he cried out hoarsely to his commanders and soldiers, not apparently concerned with the fact that anybody could have said they had a vision that one day the Organ Liberat would hold the Island. I was being elevated to sainthood on the strength of my envisaging free access only to Furasol, which we held anyway! Words again, Brother Fredo, it was always words that got to Iaio Gabril. There and then, at a drunken banquet thrown to celebrate my arrival in the echelons of revolutionary lore, he composed the Thousandth Gabrilette, having sworn at the abrupt end of his

185

tenure at the University College of Furasol that he would not advance beyond 999 until the day the rebels entered the Vice-regal Residence in Badeo Town! That, Fredo, was some honour.

> East one day and east for good, from out the mouth of
> one
> Who journeyed far and journeys on, Burneau the wise
> and blue
> We shall remember you when you are buried in the
> wood.

I noted that Dr Gabril's strict sense of form had returned to him, for he would not consider any alterations to the last line on grounds of structure, but it was a point I felt it might seem churlish of me to press. I sat at the celebratory banquet, smiled at the accolades of admiring young recruits, and prodded at my mounds of irreducible black meat.

I had not spoken to Nunez since she told me about her missing stockings – I had no idea how many nights ago that was, that deranged was I by days of sleep and nights of none – so I was taken aback when she sat down beside me at the banquet. We had been sitting many places apart. I sat at the right hand of Gabril, with an exotic old lady called Mnam on my right. The Lady Mnam said nothing to any purpose and when she did I had to ask her to repeat it. When she repeated it she addressed it to someone else, so I spent much of the time listening to (or nodding in agreement with) the Doctor. Nunez sat at the far end. After too many glasses of the best dark wine, I turned to face Lady Mnam, and found she had changed into the beautiful Captain, as if some story-book prince had kissed her. What was curious about the exchange that followed was that I did fully intend to tell Nunez I had chanced upon her stockings in my room. Only, because the first thing she slurred to me was 'Now I've lost my favourite little dress, Burneau ... ' I took rather against her, and decided to ignore her mad game.

'I only wear it for special occasions,' she murmured, 'like when I had to be in a crowd of crowds . . .'

'You'd better find it then,' I said crossly, turning back to hear Gabril.

She tapped my shoulder.

'Burneau.'

She tapped my shoulder harder.

'Burneau.'

I sighed and turned: 'What is it then now?'

'I wanted to say, is only . . . cool shooting. Cool shooting.'

Understanding her to mean my uncanny instincts for future developments, I thanked her for the compliment. She stuck her tongue out – the most girlish thing I had seen her do, and in front of Iaio Gabril had he been facing our way!

Nunez said in a long sigh: 'Stormlight tonight, be there, be there . . .'

Then she was gone. I felt very much alone again then, and could not summon the courage to question Gabril about her idiosyncrasies, so, shortly after he retired to his rooms, I too made my excuses, declining Tragolani's persistent demand that I make an all-night four for a rousing game of Scissors-Paper-Stone-Eye-River-Rabbit-Fox-Moon (which had become popular with the mountain men) and slouched from the banqueting hall, their drunken pleas and coaxings at my back.

I went to my bedroom, picked up Nunez's things, threw them across the room, climbed in between the sheets, switched the light off, and, Fredo, for the first time in my life since the time when you rescued me from the mountain ledge high up in the Koborol, swallowed hard and then cried like that very boy, because I could see everything but understood nothing, loved everybody but knew no one. Perhaps, as you see me fall, dried, numb, into sleep, you too should sleep, Brother Fredo, for it is no accident that I now speak of love. The saddest hollow of my heart was where I was to be found cowering on the same night that I, for the first time – I admit it with both a pride tinged with shame and a shame fringed with pride – was summoned into the unbelievably delightful dark haven of sexual love.

'Sexual love'? What a strange thing for a monkish man to hear, or maybe not so strange. I am sure you have lived ten lives to mine. I call it love only because sex is all that sex can do, like a river has to run, a flower to bloom. Nothing denied or defied, and nothing unreal. For two people to let one desire do all that it is capable of? For me that falls in the world that is ruled by love. So I say 'sexual love', and do not speak of 'sex', Fredo, not because I am afraid to disturb the remote peace of a godly brother, but because that dog, sex, loves its owner, and if the owner cannot love it, it is not the fault of the dog.

I must have woken at about four in the morning, certainly before the beginnings of first light, for I was in complete darkness. Instantaneously I was both horrified and petrified by the itchy sensation of someone else's hair across my face. There was a moment of sensation, a moment of realisation, a strange lost moment of total unsurprise – which emanated from who knows how deep inside my soul? – and then a moment in mid-air, as I leapt out of the bed, landing just far enough away from it to bang my head on the post and fall on the floor.

'Help! Who is it?' I think I moaned, and there was no answer. I listened for breathing, heard some, realised it was mine, listened for more, heard some, realised it was mine again. There was no other. I waited for my eyes to get accustomed to the darkness, which they did, in the sense that they could reliably assure my brain there was only darkness and not a trace of light to accustom them to it further. This meant that the provision of light was down to me and my electric bulb, but I was paralysed by panic and could not cover the inches required for me to switch it on. I have no idea how long I waited. Dawn did not come, so not that long.

I crawled very slowly to the edge of the bed, and, tensed beyond recognition of myself as a reasoning person, stretched a trembling tentacle of a hand towards the pillow, feeling the air give slightly, like a membrane. It was my left hand that was doing this, presumably because I regarded it as more dispensable than my right, but I do recall telling my left hand that I would never once in my life force it to do anything dangerous or unpleasant again, if it would only consume the last inches towards the horrible revelation.

It found hair, moved a fraction and lost it, then found it again, and only it.

I stood and switched the light on. There was a head of hair on the pillow, just that, no head, only hair. It was the colour of flames.

This, Brother Fredo, may not remind you of anything. Let me assure you it did not strike a chord with me either. I associated it with Nunez and her deplorable pranks. I did not associate it with that vision I hold chiefly responsible for my tragic distraction from duty on the day the Viceroy died – the sight of a flame-haired woman in a world of blondes and brunettes. When finally the trapdoor of my memory fell open, the real door opened too and in walked the real murderer of Viceroy Wallemire Lagland, in her blue dress and black stockings. She put on the flame-coloured wig. Thus transformed, Nunez sat down on my bed and laughed.

'Now tell me how you shot him, Captain Blue.'

Let me pace around the room like a detective explaining all, if only to try to unpick my own tapestries of lies.

I did not kill the Viceroy. I saw the woman in the crowd. I lost the Party, then someone did shoot him, twice, and he died. Now I know that although I wasn't the killer, somebody must have been. A man called Pirir was executed for the crime, but only after the Mainland Government realised they could not catch the suspect Burneau, who was duly downgraded to the role of accomplice. I learned enough from

189

the OLB to know that Pirir was incapable of the crime, and that the so-called 'Wounded Two', beaten senseless by my erstwhile colleagues Adzell and Mace, were unlikely culprits: the one who died was a drum majorette from the beach island of Melao, and the one who disappeared was ninety.

So I knew, all the time I was running from Badeo, and all the time I was taken in by the OLB and sheltered in the Hall of Weathers, that there was a possibility someone else might come forward and denounce me as an impostor. Why did this not worry me? At first, after I was rescued by the Organ Liberat and singled out, by Nunez herself, as the wanted man Burneau and therefore a revolutionary hero, I realised that the imposture was my only hope of survival. If another man did claim the credit, I could have denounced him in turn – after all, mine was the face hung on every wall in Badeo Town – or I could have thrown myself on the mercy of the rebels, but Time seemed to have diminished the threat of exposure. Something else was at play, perhaps a burgeoning inner conviction that I had indeed killed the Viceroy. I had spent so much time admitting to it that answers and lies flowed naturally from my alienated heart without recourse to a rational point. Then, of course, once I had established myself as an Extraordinary Adviser, I was able to work at the core as an active strategist, as opposed to a harboured fugitive. I felt unassailable, untouchable, I felt myself beginning to believe myself! Down with the Argeline Domain, free all Badeo, shoot all collaborators, bomb the dignitaries back to the Mainland! It mattered little, after a while, what happened or didn't happen in the blazing marketplace all that time ago. I was part of the future, I had a task to fulfil.

And then this. My rescuer, my salvation, this starry-brained mad Captain, now terrifying and lovely in a wig of flame, sitting staring on my bed, knowing – as nobody but the Maricolos knew on the whole of the Island – that I was not a killer, that I was a liar, that my credentials for acceptance in Camp Liberat were as false as those of Badeo's mischievous play-actors. Do you really wish to know how demented I had become in that camp? As I stared back at her, it never once crossed my mind that I should hate her for being the person who killed the Viceroy or the person whose murderous cold crime plunged me into this spiralling abyss: instead I admired her, feared her, bitterly loved her for striking a rebel blow against the Domain! And whatever happened, I knew she wanted me with her, upon her, wanted to put me through something I could not help but have.

But she killed him, all right. Though I saw her walk off down Avenue Kluy, somewhere in the labyrinth of ancient lanes of Allalong she stowed the wig, changed into grey, met the Viceregal Party as it was regrouping after its encounter with the confused street-band, shot Lagland, then clambered down into the lower lanes and changed back into the orange-haired lady, whom eyewitnesses – I saw them myself on *Newshour Badeon* – remembered seeing walking away from the scene of the crime. In the event, Nunez was never even questioned. She got a coach to Laquilla before the police had closed Badeo, then stayed there working in a bar for two weeks, before being collected by Stoackey and Rabaiette. The three of them were on their way back to Furasol when they saw their chance to take out two soldiers on the Highway. Having done so and stolen their van, they heard a man say 'I'm under arrest' and thus I entered their story.

Nunez was convinced she had accomplished the perfect crime. When she had first seen my face on television, ringed and stamped as the killer, she said, 'I thought it was perfect – now it is!' Then, when they picked me up on the Highway, she said again, 'I thought it was perfect – now it is!' When I confessed I was the Viceroy's killer, she said again, 'I thought it was perfect – now it is!' For here was somebody else to take the burden or, if the worst ever came to the worst, take the blame. Gabril didn't care whether Nunez or someone else had got the shots on target. The symbol of colonial authority was slain: his excellent student was back in San Timotheo with her team.

'So I thought it was perfect,' she said again, wiping her lips with the back of her hand, 'but now it is . . .'

'You understand, Nunez,' I stammered, 'I had to stay alive here – '

'You are alive, Burneau, you are very much alive . . .'

'And you couldn't have done it without my help – '

'I could, but I'll let that pass for now . . .'

'You see, I did want him dead –' (For, shameful as it is to admit, I omitted one truth – that it was the sight of Nunez that distracted me, and perpetuated one lie – that I ducked out of the line of fire because I too wanted the Viceroy killed.)

'I know, Blue, I know . . .'

'And now I love my work as an Extraordinary – '

'Adviser, yes, we all love it, Blue . . .'

'And the people, I also like, all the – '

'People, yes, all our people, mmm . . .'

I was now kneeling before her on the carpet, my eyes at the level of her crossed dark stockinged legs, with the paleness of her upper thighs and her slip in shadow beyond them, and her hands smoothing her dress again to hide what I was hiding from seeing. Then I looked up at her face, which was quite soft and vague in the light, not at all the face of Nunez in the hard grind of her days, and which was looking back at me with something between a sense of purpose, as if it were a face that had not long to make its mark on the world, and one of complete vacancy, as if it was itself surprised so little to resemble its owner. Its owner, Captain Amadora Guiva Nunez, swayed forward and put her hands on my shoulders. Then she whispered these words: 'Twin Princesses Face Down In The Black Lake' (which relates to a pack of playing cards she was wont to consult, and which had the mystical property of always confirming her hopes and beliefs both before and after the event), then she kissed me on the mouth, with the wet inside of her lips. It reminded me of nothing for a spell, then something I was reluctant to remember clearly, then nothing again. We were still, and our stillness was intolerable.

Fredo, you will have to be an extremely old man to have received this, and an exceedingly patient one yet to be reading it, and a man of great kindliness and compassion to forgive the intimate heat of its wretched recollections, but I believe that two of those things are things that you are, and, if the only factor inhibiting you from reading further, as I stumble on into the woodlands of love and sexual love, is your lamentably having passed away, then so be it. I shall continue to proclaim in this great towering silence my love, my sexual love, my joyfulness, luck and horror at what happened to me. May these wrinkled sheets of government paper be scattered from the side of the Folded Mountain, may they circle and settle on its slopes far below, providing a thousand sleepy shepherds with a thousand separate mysteries, or a hundred venerable brothers with some notes upon worldly vanity! May this very page on which I proclaim my love float gently down upon the grass at the feet of the clockman's goat that I lost upon the mountain on the only day of our lives in which we met, Brother Fredo. May he test it with his horns, may he think it is food, may he eat it all.

I love Juilla Maricolo, the daughter of the house where I was sheltered in Badeo. Though her mother took me in and saved my life by doing so, I saw her honey-haired daughter in the threshold of the living room, ill and home from school, whereafter life was not the same again. She sulked, she cooked meals, explained the plot of *Carli and the Stranger*, she ran her slight hands through my filthy hair and turned it all grey while saying it would never fool anyone. She kissed me in the corridor, twice and the next afternoon said we would have to get into bed together, which we did, and where we kissed many times, and where she said we were having a love affair, and where we fell asleep and were found. We *were* having a love affair, we were, and we would

193

have continued to have it, and grown together as lovers do, and made the world revolve about us, had I not awoken the next morning to the sight of my own gun pointing at my temple, and the mother of Juilla (Violet) saying not 'It is time you moved on', Brother Fredo, as I told you, but words to the effect that I would be dead if I did not. Seeing the two of us in her bed together, Violet Maricolo must have assumed a thing that was not true, as well as many things that frankly were. In the light of that, her decision makes very good sense indeed, and made me anxious for the fate of my young beloved. These things are why I ran from Badeo, why I joined the rebel army, these things are why I am reckoned the fourth most powerful person in the General's infant regime. But it helps me somehow to know that the train of events has the words 'I love' at its head. Hopefully I place them at the end as well, because it does a man nothing but good – and no man any harm – to take his platinum pencil and finish a paragraph with the assertion that it is Juilla Maricolo I love.

My lies to you are those of omission. I know I have mentioned this girl before, because her help in many things was relevant to the account. But I have not previously explained how relevant she is to everything that's not in the account. Because until now this was not necessary. But the love I made was to the Captain that night, and many times after, and to somebody else as well, and something is making me say this in this order, so here I remember Juilla, who was in my thoughts so often, in such colour, in such a strange staring poise, and whom I have seen since in the actual world, in a smashed-up derelict room at the end of war. But let us abandon that pain to the future. Let it huddle with the things we wish for and don't have. The story is far from over. We must shiver and hope.

Picture me in that crowded flat on the Avenue Hali. I fell in love, Brother Fredo. I imagine I did not look much like myself, even before she dyed my hair grey and my eyebrows black. Did I mention that every time I turn my head I can feel her fingers slithering over my scalp? Well, that's true: every time, I do it now, there, though my hair these days is the colour it was. I have felt other hands upon me, everywhere upon me, making me arch, making me buck and coil and sigh, but never are they so close and feeling as those in the oily water. Last week I saw those hands so chill and rubbing each other in the ruins of a house – those very hands! It was like seeing a timeless portrait come alive, like being admitted through the curtain that separates us from the nearest god, just once, just once.

The love that happened to me happened without warning or delay. Or, I say there was no warning, only there had been if I had only had eyes to see it. You know by now that my plight and peril were wholly the upshot of an unfortunate glimpse of a flame-haired woman, who would reappear later in my life as Captain Nunez, the true assassin of the Viceroy, loyal and true soldier in the service of Iaio Gabril. I have looked back from a great height and distance upon the circumstances of that fleeting vision, and it is my contention that I was being prepared for my initiation into sexual love. Prepared by whom? If I survive and love prospers, I will say 'by Love', but if I die before that happens, I would have to conclude 'by the death'. Other than waiting for Time to toss me cheerfully in the air to decide the issue, it is impossible to choose. About all beautiful chances are smeared the prints of Death and Love: chance never seems to present any other real suspects. Look at that example. My sight of hair the colour of flame would bring death to the Viceroy, and love to Juilla Maricolo, and love, for the least instant, to myself Maris Burneau. It is difficult to rid myself of the sensation that I was being prepared for something. As Time has replaced me on the world the right way up, I will settle for love! Looked at another way – what is there in this world that has ever prepared me for death?

Love altered the colour of everything. The recollected images and sounds of the period (mere days, really) can be perceived only through a filter made by (how I imagine him) a long-gone glassmaker, the last of his guild, whose secrets died with him. The filter affects the light itself. It diminishes the world's population to a handful, its tribulations to a murmur. Every movement I remember making, every sight I witnessed, every conversation I had, all are garlanded with lights and the glow of realised, relished joy. Everything happened as if scripted by we two to whom it happened, as if something was demanded and something delivered up! The glances we cast at each other were glances of complicity – that we alone knew our every act was expected, awaited! The room, the people, their names, all names – all is suffused in a miraculous brightness unique to that which has no inclination ever to return. A golden age! For I recall it like an old man must recall a golden age. Now that's a great wonderful accomplishment of love, to make golden ages of single hours, storytelling ancients of young men. When I remember the hours with Juilla, Brother Fredo, I feel older than you are, I feel wisdom beyond you, I feel I could rescue *you* in a fog! I am become part of a regiment that has been marching for ever, has lost untold generations by the wayside, has bled hot and scarlet medals of deep wounds, but can never stop, will never turn, will do nothing but obey, walk on, bleed, obey, one infinite file of good men from a bottomless blue well: the men in love, requited and unrequited together, the million male lonelinesses arm in arm in arm.

The god thinks that's interesting: love is the one thing that makes him thoughtful. Love makes the death sullen, but his love is unrequited so he behaves accordingly, never admitting to anything, scorning and shrugging. But you know and I know, he carves names on gravestones when nobody is watching.

I can see Juilla disappear into her religious school on the Avenue Pindi. I can see her sighing with frustration at the thrilling trials of Carli – with whom I believe she identified in some way – and I can see her peeling tomatoes in the kitchen while it rained all afternoon, glancing up at me and saying 'You can also eat them yellow.' I can choose from a limitless gallery of pictures, from each of which there is only the merest detail missing: I have no idea what Juilla Maricolo looks like.

That may sound improbable or foolish but, I tell you, the god ticks it off as a mark of something. I mean it does flash towards me, her face, but always a blur, always too quickly, like a lampfly, and I'm left flailing about, toppling nearly on a lone tiny planet, loving one so beautiful she has no looks whatever. Her voice presents a similar problem. I know it was quite low for a girl, quite breathy, sometimes rasping, but I cannot really hear it anywhere, just hundreds of others. Hundreds of other girls' faces and voices, scurrying to the empty space to fill it with their youth and their 'Me now!' When I saw Juilla last week she looked nothing like I expected, and sounded different too, fragmented and slow. She looked and sounded like an approximation of a memory of her, but not like mine, I am frightened to say, not like mine. And if I try to define what I saw so recently? I can get no closer than these words can bring you. Do not think me vague, then, in my sparse descriptions of one who means to me as much as I avow: that quality is the truth of it, she is everywhere, close by, and she is far away, gone forth. Even were I to be granted the utmost of my desire, that I should live out my life with Juilla Maricolo, truly I know that among the people I shall never see again is the girl I fell in love with.

The guards have walked back, reminding me of the rest of the world. That is another accomplishment of love: to erase all things but one, even to erase yourself from the picture – or at least to reduce you to the state of an empty vessel alone on the ocean. She becomes the world, merely. The water is all memory of her; the wind her breath wherever it may be; the sky the record of your future with her or without her. And if a bird should suddenly alight on deck? Well, that's nothing

197

but a minute you spent by her side. Approach it and it flies, ignore it and it flies, approach it and it flies. Oh Brother Fredo, old on the earth or childlike on a heavenly meadow, the pain and sadness is consumed by love, for love loves even its own absence, even its own loss. Nothing does that. Not even my god does that, though he's glad that something does.

Well, my minutes with Juilla Maricolo form a tiny flock indeed, and, to pursue the implications of my metaphor (as Gabril to this day exhorts his students) I do believe they have migrated way south and are warm there, but my hours, my nights with Captain Nunez of the Organ Liberat Badeon, they crowd in the water as far as the eye can see, feeding, fighting, squawking. Understand that I could not describe the demanding restless love of this violent individual without first confessing to the nature of my heart's cornerstone, admitting to the measure of my joys, identifying the one existing person – aside from yourself, were you to exist, as I firmly maintain you do – to whom my truth can be spoken. Truth dwells in the heart, is my belief, and therefore it is only to the keeper of your heart that you can speak truth. All else is gossip, flattery, or other effects of our language.

Nunez bade me stand and strip myself of my clothes, while she contemplated me at first with the stern concentration of her fighter's life, then the familiar listlessness that seemed to afflict her in my company, softening her face and sloughing off her years. She made numerous allusions to her pack of cards, the details of which are unimportant. Suffice it to say, they determined without argument the sequence of manners in which we were to behave. First, simply, I was to wear nothing while she wore everything, everything she wore when she destroyed Viceroy Lagland. She sat cross-legged where she was on my bed, as I stood in the desert of the carpet, weak and wordless and with that thing happening to me that a man of a god would be weary to envisage. Then, we seemed to be in the opposite places, the opposite shapes, the opposite clothes, then neither wore a thing and we clasped coldly then warmly together on the bed. All those things marshalled by Love for the purpose of its completion – strength and heat, wetness and blindness, threats that are not, disguises that are not, the dispersion of the senses, the actual loving language of the tongue – all rose and flowed and uttered and were real, and love was made where it felt like being, neither mine for the woman nor the woman's for me, but our own loyal and adoring tribute of bliss towards the thing itself, the thing that makes and loves what happens, ornaments it with sound and odour, and will not permit it to lie itself away.

And I spilled happily into the world of sexual light. The pale disinterested truth fountained out of me into the life of the unreally flame-haired woman and I lay spent and lodged in her arms and exhalations, Nunez, Amadora, the Captain, who is dead, Brother Fredo, and whose murder I am afraid I can no longer prevent myself from confessing.

Now I think I know what I have been describing to you. I had to let go the remembrance of my love and desire so that I could unearth the one foul truth below it. There was no other reason to tell you how I made love long ago to a woman now dead. Do you want to know how subtle were her lips, how clever her fingers, how soaked and wiry the hair between her legs? What is it to you, high on your mountain slope, that a guerrilla woman took my face where she wanted it, and touched me in places I did not know were mine? I have been made to want all things, to worship or waste them as I please, but what possible interest is that to a man who neither has nor wants any earthly thing at all? Sex is not a secret, but it is made of what secrets are made of: privacy, power, and the relish of mortality. That's what it is like now, to write a series of words that I could press into the bony hands of Badeo's most powerful man, hands that are prob-ably within twenty yards of my desk as I write, hands that would see me dead by dawn for the killing of a revolutionary heroine. I murdered Nunez. In time I will tell you how and why. In the meantime, now I hear the guards stepping by the door again, I have learned that writing these words is made of what sexual love is made of.

Nunez got out of the bed, came back and stroked my hair.

'Now win the war,' she said.

I opened my eyes. She was dressed again, looked herself again, had found her cold sculpted face in some corner. I noticed it was almost first light.

'By the way,' she said, fastening her belt, 'we need you in the Hall as soon as possible. Don't go back to sleep, will you.'

Back to sleep? There was no hope of that.

What I wanted to say was something like 'We're having a love affair', something that would remind me that I had once had one – however desperately briefly – but of course the completion of that thought cancelled itself out. Nothing felt like a love affair. So I just lay there for an hour, dulled with pleasure and the dry ragged sickness of lacking sleep, and touched myself where I had learned new sensation, and flattened every emotion I could possibly feel into a clouded featureless plain of contentment. This was the beginning of a long ritual existence I shall attempt to depict in the pages that remain to me before I strip the world of paper for good. I wonder if I have ever slept a good night's sleep since the night I awoke coughing on the red hairs of a wig. I lay there for some two years, really, was made to love, to tell and retell lies and truths, to console and flatter, to squirm and laugh and spurt and keep secrets while, in the endless bewildered hours between the onslaughts of Nunez, I did their work, planned their actions, helped win them their war, and finally made it back to a new Badeo, to love found and lost, to death found and done, to my pointless ticking existence in this huge golden-plated room. So have patience, Holy Brother, with Burneau, irredeemable child and Minister of Waste

Paper. I will attempt a prayer for you meanwhile – or rather, for me, for I think I hear the General's footsteps!

See if my writing has not caught a little cold here, and shivered on the page? It's the General's moods. He did what he Generally does, Fredo: he saluted me without a word, as if I was doing any work that sound could disturb, crept to the File of Unreconciled Claims Subsequent to the Expulsion of the Imperialist Possessor from the Golden Brave Island of Free Badeo (my staff call it the Shitheap) and plucked a sheaf from the top. Next, in a loud whisper, he gave his personal opinion: 'Find for the husband, Mr Burneau, I don't like her tone at all . . . ' Then he tiptoed back towards the velvet door. Then – unusually – he stopped and spoke in a clear voice:

'This prisoner exchange, Mr Burneau.'

'It's scheduled for next week, General Gabril,' I said as matter-of-factly as I could. 'The *Leonor* is taking fifty Argelinos home to the Domain. The yacht *Silverlight* will embark on the same day, returning fifty of our Islanders.'

'That's the plan, yes.'

At this point it occurred to me that General Iaio Gabril had not eaten well lately. He had that strained resentful look of one whose body is making its grievances known. I feared for the prisoner exchange. Without the prisoner exchange, Fredo, my loyal friend Tragolani will never get this message to you! Praying for us both, I did my best to protect the plan:

'It's fifty and fifty, General. It has a sort of fairness to it that seems . . . sort of fair.' (I am no orator under pressure.)

'We, Mr Burneau, are about to return to their loved ones *fifty* men who would have given their lives to see Badeo enslaved for eternity, and you call it "fair"!'

'Ye-es, sir, but also, they're prepared to send back fifty of our men who would have given theirs to free it. That's the fairness I referred to, sir.'

'Fairness? Fairness? "Break the seal and sip the froth and

cry the vintage sour!/Weep the grape a berry, howl in un-deluded wrath!/For trust has died upon this hour. The taste is old and foul."'

That's Number 474, from *Wine from Nowhere*, the dark-est volume, where the lines of the gabrilettes are often broken in half by full-stops or even exclamation marks. This is not a good sign. He breathed deeply and significantly.

'Fifty murderers freed.'

'Fifty comrades home,' I said.

'But fifty murderers freed.'

'But fifty comrades home to Badeo.'

'But fifty murderers home to the Domain!'

'But fifty – . . . well, yes.'

'Find me the list of the names of murderers, Burneau, and I shall go over them with the utmost scrutiny.'

And he left. I have sat here for an hour, quite still. If you never receive this letter, Fredo, this last conversation should explain why. I have concealed Federico Tragolani among these prisoners, under the Argelino identity Lavis Quentine (an artilleryman killed at the Battle for New Badeo). Every-thing will depend upon the extent of the General's 'utmost scrutiny'. He knows Tragolani well from the War, when he worked as a runner and scout for Captain Overot's cell, and, later, for my own 'research' department. Were Gabril to examine a photograph of the prisoner-of-war Quentine – well, that velvet door would open with a good deal more force than necessary, and the old man move more rapidly than he has for years. Alternatively, what if he were to check the names of the prisoners against the names of the dead? He should want to meet this Lavis Quentine, he should want to talk to this resurrected gunner. And there he would find Tra-golani, head shorn in inadequate disguise, no Argelino at all. The deceit would be exposed and that would be that, for me, for this, for my memoir.

I had better proceed with my own 'utmost' in order to con-clude this letter, Brother Fredo, for, sure as day, it is written upon the thinnest, most fragile surface. Who knows what I may say now, now that I fear greatly it will be an unread letter, my confession of love and murder to nobody but myself! Without a man of goodness to receive and read it, who knows through what murky silted delta it may trickle? I shall continue nevertheless, testifying into the space, into my reflection on the page, if only to experience the splendour of being addressed, the wondrous surprise of receiving the truth from a human hand, albeit mine. I will be the last lonely crossing-sentry for human recognition at the ultimate customs-post. 'Halt!' I shall shout to me, and wave through the window at one who passes in the freezing cold: wave so that he pauses, then wave so that he passes on.

The winter was dreary and damp on Mount San Timotheo. My routine was more or less the same every day. I entered the Hall of Weathers at about noontime, to be greeted by the huge heaped deliveries of data covering half the floor. Two operatives would be there reading already: Stoackey, who turned out to have a photographic memory, or the girl Rabaiette, who had special responsibility for developments in the field of entertainment, or Woodkind, who was by and large so lazy as to make his attendance pointless, or Tragolani, restless and playful, who would combine our work of sifting and learning with as much drinking and gaming as he felt we could get away with. It was up to me to control the work, telling the day's assistants the substance of any recent visions I had had, and deciding which elements of the world's factual weight would be most valuable to explore. We would work until about nine at night, munching as we leafed through newspapers, yawning through forests of ancient law cases, carting piles of prize-winning novels to the lavatories. These were communal, rows of cubicles, between which we could discuss items picked up in the day's hoard. No incident nor accident of bodily discomfort was permitted to disrupt our daily business. Our work was considered too vital. The operatives worked in shifts; I did not. At nine I would normally retire to my room, or else join Gabril for dinner. I suppose that happened about twice a week. The Lady Mnam would always be present at these occasions, glazed and inexplicable; Nunez and Overot sometimes joined us; even Battle Marshal Curtens would put in an appearance once a month or so, to see what credit he could take from my foresights, or see what blame he could attach to their occasional imprecisions. There was a succession of intense young men who seemed to be in favour with the General, men who were returning with news of attacks and setbacks, or nervously jovial men who had yet to join the fray. The former would drink to forget their experiences, the latter would drink to talk up their courage. Few of them ate with us twice. Iaio Gabril did not approve of drinking to excess, and he found the efforts of these youths to impress over matters vinicultural distasteful in the extreme. He would hear a long paean to the local white Erailo (which I once heard him describe as 'stoppered acid') and mildly remark to me: 'Drink or speak, the grape will know you,' to which I always nodded with a wise aspect born of months of lying. Otherwise I was called upon to do little, though I was much remarked upon when important guests were present.

You see, my elevation to the status of Extraordinary Adviser to the Organ Liberat Badeon, an organisation wholly committed to Freedom, had in actual fact committed me to incarceration. I was deemed far too valuable ever to leave the Camp, and my visits to the meadow from which the world was visible (heavily escorted by the jolliest, tipsiest operatives available at the end of the day or night) became fewer and further between. It was not considered necessary nor, later, even advisable, that in the pursuit of accurate foresight I should actually see the world at first hand. 'Ho no,' Gabril once said, 'such a thing could distort your wisdom, Mr Burneau, could intoxicate you from the path. You must ferment the world in your mind, not let it spill out down the side of the mountain – for whose does it then become?'

Thus the endless days in the Hall of Weathers, with the earnest students and the cynical students, thus the immersion in the words of the world, thus the life of the very Blue Burneau in those two long (long? the word shrinks against them!) infinite two years of the War for Badeo.

Each midnight I would be back in my little room, the door left open. Some midnights I was alone, I dozed afloat across a lake of wine. Some, though very few, I was asleep. Most midnights Nunez was in my room. She was sitting upon my stomach, doing nothing, glaring. Or she was naked, gripping my ankles with her hot damp hands. Or she would drape her cream sash three times around me until it was so tight that if she merely tugged it could not help but haul us together. Most midnights I was moaning her name, though accurately, bone-drily conscious of everything: conscious when I was obliged to whimper, conscious when I was obliged to shudder to the end. Least conscious then, when my body was voided and held, clutched, and I felt the rare sense of a friend quite near me. At times I have called him the death, but not then. Other midnights I heard in the room the rustle and pull of her underwear as she stood there thinking up things and saying them. One midnight she spat in my face. One midnight she told me I was going to die and, once, she told me she would love me for ever. For weeks of midnights she would never mention love, but would appear in ever stranger, more fantastical attire, take an hour to undress herself, crawl over me with black satin still hanging off her. All of the midnights my body was a thing of hers, and at none of them were my self or spirit any things at all. All the midnights taken together, Nunez completely filled the room with herself here, herself there, with flesh, sweat, silk, lace, blood and spit and the stuff that speaks for me when there is no more space or time, the guileless delible oil that paints 'I must.' Every stroke of midnight from here to the end of me will bloat my memory with the thousand shapes of Nunez, recall to me my rapturous enslavement at her hands, then

205

always, always, cast her up from its foam, stumbling, incredulous, murdered. But it is impossible for me to remember one midnight without the others; therefore this is how I remember her – alive and all around me. In purely spatial terms, with Time hammered flat to Story, it seems impossible that I was ever in that room.

To her, perhaps I never was. She would spray her desires about the night, howl and whisper whatever loped or somersaulted through her mind and do them, find me in the corner of the dark and do them, have them of me, sob whole minutes and be curled to a stillness. I wonder if she had not been doing the same thing every night for years, hurtling along the same illuminated highway that I happened to be trying to cross. Perhaps no one else had ever crossed it. Or hundreds had and died. She would sit up on the bed, or wherever her actions had deposited her, cork all our experience into the phial of her fool tarot – 'The Circle Is Sealed', 'Two Goats Reared A Lion', 'The Wall Is Down And The Child No Child' – then do what remained, kiss me or wipe me, return me to my hunched lonely nakedness and be gone, never once omitting to remind me of my obligations to the struggle. By the first glimmer of dawn light I would have been in the Hall of Weathers two hours already, a dead thing blazing with sensation, shaking with the sudden hurts that I alone could interpret. I would leave my aural message with someone, then stagger back to bed while the Organ Liberat was boisterously waking up all over the outer compound, think of weeping for everything, be unable to weep for anything, and sleep rottenly till noon. I lost my weight, I lost my youth, and I think I lost my spirit, Fredo; but yes, I won them their – won us our – treble-damnable War.

How? You know how. Everybody but me knows how. I became vulnerable to an otherworldly impact that resolved itself first into language, terse and shrouded, then, through our infinitesimally detailed research upon the inner and outer life of the Island, into the probable outcome of each arriving day. I have tried to speculate, and tried harder not to speculate, whereof this gift was made, quite apart from whence and why it came. In the life I had, in the place I was born – in Gispar in the Koborol – I was taught not to open gifts, Brother Fredo, not until the giver was beside me, not until the giver would permit me to do so. I feel that whatsoever gift I had – which has caused nothing but struggle and triumph and misery and no peace – the giver has never been beside me, or, if he has, he will not let me open it. But yes, I have speculated. I imagined, fancifully I suppose, that somewhere by accident I leapt a day – I forgot to have it, or it forgot to dawn on me. While today dawned on the Badeans and Argelinos of the War, I blundered into tomorrow and was unable to find the exit. So all the time I was in the Organ Liberat I was a single day ahead of them, ahead of everyone, and all I was doing was simply reporting on what I could make out through the mist that met me there. Ridiculous as that is, it would explain some things. It would explain why the god and the death seemed more real to me than to others I described them to. They were nearer. It would explain why yesterday seemed so much further away. And it would explain why I experienced today as if through a shimmering veil that showed me beauty but would not permit me to experience it as beauty, that allowed me to love but not to understand, and refused me the human right of claiming my own identity, which I was able to do for mere fractions of time that spun away before they could be savoured.

You know it is gone now, Fredo, don't you? I imagined you guessed. I did find the exit, though I have been slow to realise it. I believe that it happened on the terrible day with which I shall end this letter, the day I entered into Badeo with Captain Nunez, and found Juilla Maricolo on the bombed-out Avenue Hali. Whether or not it happened then, swiftly, or has gradually faded, I receive no impact now, no hurt, no recognition of the form of the to-come. The President's Ministers and Colonels, they still tap me for my gift, but they use

207

it on sports results and wagers on their women. I am right no more often than any man could be right, but still, for now, they trust me. They owe me so much, but their patience will not be infinite, not if war comes again and I hear nothing, no warnings, no voices. Today has come back for me, Fredo, it strode back astounded and hurried me away. I do not expect to experience tomorrow again: yesterday is nearer than it was. The god and the death are mere words with faces, two essentially good kinds I remember, who did each take an arm of mine and seemed happy to proceed in the very same direction, though for sure they had better places to be and better men to know.

But the War now. The War.

Any account of the War will tell you that the first decisive action occurred in the spring of its first year, when three battalions of the Badean puppet army froze to death on Mount San Timotheo, having been repulsed by the OLB. This led to the Treaty of Laquilla in the early summer, in which the Island was partitioned between the 'Badean Dominion' and the New Republic of Furasol, effectively ending the siege conditions under which the guerrillas had lived for so long. What had been a slowly withering limb of the Island was made a nation in its own right, with some limited access to sea trade. Once again the Argeline Domain and its Badean apologists acclaimed a Victory (in the guise of a 'Victory for Peace'), while the OLB, fully aware it had attained only the first of its objectives – recognition and the right to live without harassment in Furasol and on Mount San Timotheo – began to prepare for a further push. Iaio Gabril, ever watchful, refused the invitation to resume his professorship at the University College of Furasol, and remained in his Camp near the summit of the mountain, with his marshals, his captains and his Extraordinary Adviser.

No account of the War whatever will tell you what I am about to tell you – that a ravished and shivering half-naked man alone in a freezing chamber at dawn felt a seizure between his shoulders and heard the words *Cold is the friend* so

208

clearly that he spun round to greet what he thought would be a giant of ice. And of course there was nothing. Yet this was an insight which, after several days and nights of debate, resolved itself into a decision to do just that – Nothing.

As envisaged over the silent months of winter, the Dominion Army was about to run out of patience with the siege and launch what it expected to be a conclusive assault on the Mountain. Several battalions gathered in the foothills and forests above Furasol at the end of the winter. Gabril was absolutely on the verge of giving in to the thunderous promptings of Battle Marshal Brangeon Curtens and Captain Overot to descend and fight – when I, the Extraordinary Adviser, crawled out from under Captain Nunez to receive that cryptic message, *Cold is the friend*. The girl Rabaiette ran to Gabril with the words in a state of great excitement – for I had heard nothing so clear for many weeks – and so the arguments began.

Curtens and Overot were convinced that what this meant was 'Whoever says he is your friend, don't believe it!' But my opinion, supported by Nunez and others, was that the message was more literal, less coded. Sure enough, conventional meteorological research undertaken by myself (with the aid of Nagel, who had trained in physics before switching to theoretical viniculture in his final year) suggested that the phenomenon of a violent cold snap in early spring, though extremely rare, was nevertheless long overdue in the southern regions of the Island. Many of the signs were there: the long wet winter, the stark red sunsets now, birds circling aimlessly – as Rabaiette noted – because they were home too soon. Therefore the best thing we could possibly do was nothing. We should wait and let the weather strike.

And so it did. The Dominion battalions, thinking they had successfully sat out the cold weather, and expecting to march upon a starving and debilitated Camp Liberat, advanced swaggering up the slopes of the mountain. We did nothing but wrap up warm and watch. Before they cleared the winter

209

snowline, the temperature plummeted. Soon stripped utterly of their eagerness to fight, so carefully nurtured by their colonels through the tedious winter, they pitched their tents where they could. The sun withdrew, the crowflowers withered, the frost crackled down and the colonels panicked. One battalion mutinied and retreated, right into the cauldron of Furasol itself. One advanced in a fury and trod on a nest of our snipers. Most sat tight and cursed the unexpected. Only individuals escaped and, being individuals found in a military situation, were duly court-martialled for surviving. The fat fingers of the Domain were burned, frostbitten black, after which time the Partition became inevitable.

Cold is the friend. No, no account of the War will include this. Our enemies would know there was a man responsible for our greatest triumphs, their worst reversals, and they would know his name, Maris 'Blue' Burneau, the wretched turncoat they allowed to slide through their fingers, but they would never know how he did it, what he heard, what he saw. And of course, the greater grew the rumour and the fewer the facts, the deeper was carved the legend of the War Wizard, the Man Worth Armies, the Blue Devil of Badeo.

On went that Devil, creeping from bed to chamber, hearing voices, noting developments, issuing warnings. The OLB made sporadic attacks on border areas around the Great Fork, at Kuara, at Skeniche, at Gruga, in the South Forest (where a crew of young Laquillean collaborators managed to get themselves drowned, as much to my surprise as, I imagine, to theirs) and that tense summer of damp heat and thunder seemed a mere drum-roll towards further clashes.

It was in the late summer, browning over into autumn, that there arose the trouble with Rabaiette, the young curly-haired student who had been among the three I encountered when I fell into rebel hands. Rabaiette's commitment to my work, and the hours she was prepared tirelessly to put in, sorting through cuttings, investigating current fashions, keeping an eye on developments in film and television, had

210

made her quite indispensable to me, and Nunez, who seemed to be her captain (though I never really understood the hierarchy of the Organ Liberat) had released her from military duty. This was much to the amusement of Tragolani, who would often return from a reconnaissance or delivery run and watch the two of us at work, making scarcely veiled observations regarding Rabaiette's personal loyalty, or sometimes just her person.

Rabaiette looked up one day from her digest of the last week's instalments of *Carli and the Stranger* (this was demanding much of our attention at the time, what with the Network's none-too-subtle attempts to depict the disaster of the frozen troops as a heroic sacrifice, setting it against the background of Vice-General Zobarang's evil overlordship of the Light Palace) and she told Tragolani:

'I don't see how you're helping, Federico. I can see you, yes, but not how you're helping.'

'I've done my day, Rabbit, now I'm a free man at leisure. I'm just seeing what's going down in life and love . . .'

'Burneau,' she said, ignoring him. 'This episode 944 has a strong smell of revenge.'

'What's Carli's angle?' I asked, jotting this down.

'Well she's in the love-interest still, with – how do you say that?'

She showed me.

'Oh. Iquyu-bhui,' I pronounced perfectly, 'the Double Horse.'

Tragolani said: 'The love-interest, eh? What am I in, Rabbit?'

Rabaiette sniffed. 'Dead trouble if we tell how you're on that bad juice all the time.'

'Wine for the Little Enamourette?'

Well that was just his way. But I never had any sense that Rabaiette liked me especially. I found her exceptionally helpful and cheerful. I did not foresee how her affection might increase. I never do foresee such things, to be frank. If my mind's eye had in these years the keenest sight of any in the world, my heart was always blithe as a country fool, occupied with one thing at a time, easy to impress, simple to surprise. That hasn't changed. The days of the week line up to say 'Boo!' to my heart, and it jumps every time, I can tell you.

As I said, this was the late summer. It was in fact the official last night of the summer when I received one of the clearest messages I ever got. The oddest, I swear: it was *Fish not funny. Fish not funny*. I could hardly imagine running to the leadership of the dreaded Organ Liberat Badeon with this singular motto. What would that obtuse Battle Marshal say to *Fish not funny*? Or what would he roar to it, rather!

I sat all afternoon with Rabaiette and Tragolani (who, unlike the mystical voice, found it funny for hours) and we pondered the implications. Rabaiette scanned some marine encyclopaedias, but found nothing particularly funny or indeed unfunny; Tragolani leafed through a dozen cookery books, trying to make us ill by reading out exotic recipes irrelevant to our quest; me, I simply stared and puzzled over the words. I was getting no vision.

'Who thinks fish *are* funny?' I wondered aloud.

Tragolani thought they were so funny that red wine gushed out of his nose and made a fresh sauce for the recipe he was admiring. Rabaiette snorted up at me to show her contempt for him, and on we worked, three afternoons, three evenings, three mornings, all in vain.

One of those rare midnights when I was to be found alone in my room asleep (Nunez having led a team down to Furasol to take delivery of some weapons) there came a knock on the wide-open door, and Rabaiette came in in an advanced state of excitement.

'Burneau, it's me, don't worry! I could tell you here or we could go together back to the Hall and I could tell you there!'

Groggily, having at first mistaken her for Nunez, I asked whoever it was who had woken me up to tell me whatever it was here, or something. She stood right by the bed, clutching a piece of paper, and went on breathlessly.

'You know who the fishes are, don't you? Townspeople! It's what the Badeo people call men from Gamor and Saldeo – fishes, or fishmen!'

'We thought of that, but – '

'What we didn't think of was this! An actor, a comedian – who used to be Ronde in *Carli*, before he was Hiram in *Love Among the Meteorites* – Frank Tubayo, Frank Tubayo, he's the talk of the clubs all over the city! His jokes are all aimed at Gamorans, Saldeans, and all about fishes! Here's one . . . ' She consulted her notes. 'What do you say to a Gamoran carrying a fishbasket?'

'What? I don't know. What?'

'And another is . . . why are Saldean women so fat? That's another, and there's hundreds! You know! Those are the fishes!'

'And they're – not funny?' I hazarded, sitting up in bed.

'I think they are,' Rabaiette admitted, 'but no, we still have to puzzle that out . . .'

Soon we were on the floor of the Hall of Weathers and working hard on Rabaiette's lead. She didn't think it was worth waking Tragolani, 'being as he's no use and he's too far behind our current thinking, isn't he?'

But I knew just where to look.

A week ago – BADEO 36:GAMOR 2.

Two weeks ago – SALDEO 21:BADEO 11.

'See that, Rabaiette?'

'I don't follow that game. My sister does, but she would.'

'They're rubbishing both towns. Gamor is hopeless at the game, so the Badeans can't resist gloating. But Saldeo's better, though it's a much smaller place. Both things make the Badeans want to give offence. Both are fishing towns, so both are targets for this actor Tubayo, who's especially angry just now because the plot twist in *Carli* did him out of a steady job. Now other actors are following his lead, finding a scapegoat for their professional disappointment.'

'But – why should you receive a message about fish not being funny? Anyone knows they're not in themselves. But if you made a good joke involving them . . .'

'It's – it's – yes! It's not that the *fish* aren't funny – it's that the fish don't *find* it funny!'

'Nobody likes being joked about. I don't.'

'But a deliberate campaign of humiliating, undermining, degrading abuse, Rabaiette! Who knows if the Badeans haven't – haven't taken it too far!'

Before her frown of puzzlement, that sense of her own breakthrough having broken away from her, could resolve itself into another statement of doubt, I hugged Rabaiette, hugged her with the utter satisfaction of having cracked another code, and when that turned to a couple of kisses and then a complete and mutually astonishing kiss between us, followed by a long stare and then both things alternating for an hour or so until we simultaneously keeled over and slept, the sad story of Rabaiette was on its feet, and limping off towards its grievous conclusion.

The towns of Gamor and Saldeo erupted into anti-Argeline rioting in the second week of the damp weather. Completely taken by surprise, the puppet government – reassuring itself that it had made peace with the New Republic of Furasol – hastily removed several battalions from the makeshift border (a brick wall with some wire on it) to the two fishing towns, at which the Organ Liberat forces, gleefully augmented by the Furasolians who had suffered under siege for so long – and prepared in advance by my foresight communicated to Gabril – streamed over the wall into the central provinces of the Island, and the War, like jokes about fishes in the night-clubs of the Capital, got hotter and harsher.

Gamor was quelled. Saldeo went up in flames. A very bloody and indecisive battle was fought for the central town of Laquilla. We made some gains in the east, Nunez herself leading the attack that retook her birthplace of Foretto back from the Dominion forces. They slouched away north, until they controlled less land than we did: merely Badeo, its hinterland, the north of Laquilla (Yalloa) and the north coast as far as the powderkeg of Gamor. Though the practice was emphatically discouraged, small numbers of wealthy citizens (among them many leading actors, including the child actress True Garrison and the piscatorial humorist Frank Tubayo, as well as the glamorous presenter Lora Cato) managed to get smuggled away to the Argeline in private boats. By then we could pick up television on San Timotheo, which certainly made my job easier, and were aware of the crude propaganda that the once-proud Network Badeon was obliged to broadcast (Gabril, incidentally, was very curious about television, and promised me that when we captured the TV station on the south-eastern outskirts of the Capital, I would be put in charge of programming, a prospect that I anticipated with much trepidation. In the event, it is not a promise he has kept.)

Given the inclination of the Dominion Forces towards idiotic gestures, one of my most significant intuitions was considerably easier to achieve than the one about fishes. *They try to drink nothing* cost me very little anxiety. A rapid browse through the newspapers, a minute with an illustrated history leaflet called *Glory Be: Our Island Victories!* and half an hour in front of the television, and I was able for once to get a good night's sleep, having laconically informed Captain Overot that the Domain was about to launch an assault on the abandoned headland of New Badeo. *They try to drink nothing*: they attack emptiness.

'If you were not who you are,' said Overot, 'I would go piffle in your face, Burneau.'

But I was right again. Some fool in the Viceregal Palace must have thought this would be a surprise move. The only surprise was that their wretched landing-craft got as far as the promontory – or a handful got as far, before being blown out of the water by our guns firing from the roofs of the empty casinos. Some piffle, eh Fredo?

As the autumn took hold, my position was unassailable. This monstrous version of myself, the Blue Devil of Badeo, sprouted in the news media, rumoured, denied, sighted, lost again. A strangely familiar face appeared on my private television screen:

'This *is* Network Badeon I *am* Roger Golli and what we are asking *is* what is this secret weapon possessed by the bandits *of* the so-called Organ Liberat Badeon we ask what's giving them the jump on our superior forces *is* the Blue Devil a man at all or a thinking machine way beyond current er thinking or is it *as* some have said again and again *all in the mind* this is six-fifteen this is Victory News *Genevive*! waltz us through the weather.'

The weather? Ha! In those days, Fredo, I could do that too. The clear ceiling of the Hall of Weathers simply darkened over at the crack of dawn, and shimmeringly displayed the very template of the day to come: warm yellow and golds, streaks of menacing mauves and greys, or plain leaden white. I maintain that this was a natural phenomenon, not a supernatural one. Whatever it was, it was incapable of error.

The rump forces of the Mainland, too thinly spread on the Island, and leaking away in desertion, deprivation, mutiny or covert evacuation to the safety of the Argeline, were confounded time and time again, whatever their tactics, wherever they gathered. We knew what they would do, because we knew what they were like. We knew where they would go, because we knew what was on their minds. And we simply knew what their weaknesses were, because I felt them on my body.

This statement, irreducible to reason, has reminded me of someone equally irreducible: Captain Amadora Guiva Nunez, who continued throughout this period of Liberat advance and Argeline/Badean disintegration to spend five nights a week mining sexual pleasure from the stony soul of her Extraordinary Adviser. One night, when we had cele-brated the consumption of an entire crate of vintage Mauette by dusting each other with sugar, then employing some – well, these are unimportant details of scenery between two points, the Captain's desire and the Captain's fulfilment, as well as being quite inappropriate matters for a worshipping gentleman – the point is that her attitude to my gift, and therefore to my entire personality and point of being, had radically and significantly altered. In short, Nunez was beginning to believe that her violent and extravagant looting of my imagination was directly related to my foresight. She grew to think of her sexual 'self-expression', as she called it, as being indispensable to the Cause.

It is true that the first expression of my gift was roughly contemporaneous with the onset of our sexual congress, or at least with the presence of Nunez's clothes in my room, and, equally, numbly true that it died when she did, but this is not the same as saying that one was the cause of the other, is it? Nunez was always fascinated by foresight because she thought she herself possessed it, though I never saw this mys-tical deck of cards that at an approximate count had eleven Houses and some three hundred Characters: near the end of our time together, she even claimed to have drawn 'The Man of Cream', 'The Whipped Harlot' and 'The Limbless Fool' – none of which I had ever heard of, but all of which were pressed into the service of the Captain's 'self-expression'. I believe that Nunez became obsessed with my gift to the ex-tent that she convinced herself her own joy was intrinsic to its workings. The likeliest reason for the evaporation of my gift is not that Nunez died, but that Badeo was liberated, and that which I could achieve was somehow mysteriously allied to the Island itself, to its soil, perhaps, or its gases. When a room is warm, there's no need to light a fire. When you meet your god, Fredo, you'll feel no need to pray. Isn't that it?

I think Nunez was a demented person, at least by that time. The victim was Rabaiette, who must have loved me, because she became selfless, I noticed, and one afternoon in the Hall of Weathers, some three days after the kiss that had followed our deciphering *Fish not funny*, we found ourselves making slow gentle love (which I had not experienced before) on the pile of holiday catalogues. (I can tell you this, Brother Fredo, because today I believe it is more likely that you are dead than alive. Tomorrow, if I feel differently, I will be sure to pluck out these vile pages.)

You know I love Juilla Maricolo, I told you, and it is not possible to love two women in the same way at the same time, but with Rabaiette I felt a great blossoming friendliness which dilated into physical joy under the pressure of what must have been her affection. I know that I did not love Rabaiette like I love Juilla (but I hope you are not dead, Fredo, because you see the world is still full of us lovers!) – I know this because after we lay together I wanted it not to have happened, I wanted to agree that I would go through life without that kind of love if I could only once see Juilla again. I wanted to make the sort of bargain that one makes into a great emptiness, a deal that the god ignores. I hoped very much, lying there in genuine peril, in daylight, that Rabaiette should feel we should not have done what we had done, and that we were, in essence, merely firm friends.

'I love you, Burneau,' alas, she said, 'now I always shall.'

'Well. You're young, Rabaiette, and it's early in your life.'

'It's not. I'm in a war. It's probably late. But now I love as well. I'll suffer the two.'

'Well. I love.'

'What do you love?'

'Everything really,' I realised.

'Everyone?'

'Well, that's right.'

'Oh well,' she said, suddenly sitting up and reaching for her overalls, 'maybe that explains it.'

'What?' I wondered, reaching towards her, not wanting her to go yet and die in the War.

'The gift, Burneau. And we need it more than anyone needs me.'

'That's not true!' I cried. 'I think you're more important!'

'Well, you see, yes it is true. You don't think I'm important at all. Only as another Anyone, help you show yourself you love us all, make your heart happy. See you're happy now. But you don't care at all. That's what you get, Burneau. You're going to love everything, you're going to have to lie everywhere.'

The sound of footsteps in the corridor outside galvanised us both in the cold and we dressed with blind speed, then stared at each other, clothed. No one had come in. We hugged, and parted without a word.

Next morning at dawn I was standing below the ceiling, my head tilted, my body swaying, receiving tiny jolts of mere troop movements somewhere – nothing our reconnaissance wouldn't have picked up – when I was suddenly, horribly, overwhelmed with coldness. It was literally hugging me, kissing me, loving me. And my cheeks were brushed with icy ringlets of curly hair. In terror I stumbled through the corridors to Gabril's quarters and – not wanting to give away my involvement with my precious new friend Rabaiette – simply requested her services on a permanent basis. To which he quite brusquely replied that she had spent too long in the safety of the Camp and was due for a return to front line duty. 'She is a soldier, Burneau. Until the Island is free we are nothing but soldiers.' When I asked him who had arranged that she be sent back so suddenly, he told me three things: that her superior officer was Captain Amadora Guiva Nunez. That Rabaiette, Stoackey, Morior and Tragolani had left before dawn, to join the advance on Outer Badeo. That it was none of my bleeding business.

So began the blackest time for me on the Mountain. Our military successes had made us over-assured, and none of us was prepared for the reversal that awaited our forces. About four hundred Furasolians were ambushed on the outskirts of

Badeo by the most extreme diehard Badean collaborators, who had lived scavenging like animals in the corners of the city. An awful lot of our people died in protracted fighting, and Tragolani and Stoackey returned with the worst stories. Their last sightings of Rabaiette were contradictory. Tragolani thought he saw her downed by a sniper at the radio station; Stoackey was convinced she blew herself up rigging a bomb. One of Overot's people, on the other hand, could have sworn she made it on to a boat that sailed out of the harbour on fire. We have not found her, but I am not without hope that she somehow arrived, even survived the cold accuracy of my instinct, for, set against the quality of my hope, all other hope sounds like despair. Hope will always wish today to dawn sunny: my hope wishes it will never be otherwise.

Nonetheless, no list of war prisoners sent us by the Domain includes her – though that means nothing, because nobody knew her real name. 'Rabaiette' is a word-game played with two red dice and a white one. Not even Tragolani could beat her, whoever she was.

Inevitably, my failure to foresee the ambush on the edge of Badeo – the worst massacre we suffered in the War – did no good for my status at Camp Liberat. Incandescent with self-righteous fury, Battle Marshal Brangeon Curtens demanded that Iaio Gabril have me shot for dereliction of duty, or treason, or even genocide! Shot, anyway. Gabril, to his credit, calmly cited the victories for which the Organ Liberat had me alone to thank, but privately he was terribly angry. I suppose more than anything else he was afraid, simply terrified that I had lost my ability to see what was round the corner. I mean, Hell! Perhaps he didn't much like the idea that he might have to win the bloody war for himself!

'What happened, Burneau? Or what didn't happen?'

'I can't say, General. I was at my post. I heard nothing and I never felt it.'

'It is of course unnecessary for me to say this, but without

220

your extraordinary capacities, Maris, your presence here is completely useless to us.'

'It is, General. A useless presence.'

'And we need soldiers, numbers, everywhere now.'

'Yes, General.'

'You applied to me for the permanent assistance of the operative known as Rabaiette . . .'

'I did. She died though, probably.'

'Probably. Probably yes she did. But you do need permanent assistance, is that not right?'

'Well, yes, I do. There's so much information, and the stakes are now so high.'

'"The stakes are now so high . . ." That's one of mine, isn't it?'

'Is it?'

'If it is, it's a misquote. Go to Captain Nunez and ask her for help. You know she is a gifted clairvoyante.'

'I was aware of that, General.'

'I think you two are going to have to win us this war together.'

'I'll go to Captain Nunez.'

'She is a very beautiful woman, Burneau. She told me you are "The Child Behind A Wall".'

'I am, among other things.'

'Among other things, yes. I'm "The Great Bird Of Justice". Look, wings.'

'I thought so, General.'

'And "The Wise Mill Wheel". And "The Goldenhearted".'

'Those are the best in the deck, General.'

Then, I remember clearly, when I reached the door of his quarters, he said, 'Maris . . .'

'General?'

'You don't believe any of that horseshit, do you?'

'No, General.'

'Good boy. Still, you work well together. And we need you both now. Good luck. Good day.'

221

It was the worst day yet. For Nunez blamed me too, made furious coded observations about the possible reasons for my oversight: 'You swam The Misted Pond! You saw nothing! You may now be The Ensnared!' At the end of this woeful tale, this wild anguished animal of a woman was explicitly blaming me for the loss of her dear friend Rabaiette and ninety others. It wasn't me who ordered her friend into the fighting!

It would have been quite pointless to explain it as I saw it. For this is how: that whatsoever agency or spirit communicated the messages to me, whether it was the Island, or the god, or my accidentally taking up residence in tomorrow, that spirit had decided that, if there was only one thing I should know about the next day of my life, it was not the blurred details of a faraway slaughter, but that somebody who loved me was about to die. I felt close to the spirit, and to nothing else, because it had made the decision I would have wanted made.

Before I proceed to the end of this story, the end that saddens me so, to my last departure from Camp Liberat, my return to the ruins of Badeo, my rediscovery of the woebegotten love of my life and subsequent destruction of my protector and imprisoner Nunez, I should make note of three messages I received that went entirely unheeded by General Iaio Gabril. And I should explain exactly why they did, aware that the sordid and ignoble truth of the matter is a dark secret, the exposure of which would guarantee my immediate demise at the hands of those soldiers whose icy footfalls clock my hours in this Government. But there is no page of this account that would not result in such demise. After all, I am writing, without permission, to an Argelino, trying to smuggle classified information to him by deceit – the imposture of Federico Tragolani (oh all gods, all gods, let him sail to Fredo on the *Leonor*!) – and whether I confess true love, murder, treason on my part or corruption on the part of my associates in the Organ Liberat, is, as we would say at the old crossing-post at Gispar, neither here nor there nor there nor there.

I am clear in my mind, Fredo. Everything I commit to paper dooms me to death in the existence I know, while consigning me to perpetual existence in the eyes of the reading god. My fond hope is that you yourself shall share in the interest of that god, though all be burned as it must be duly.

The Organ Liberat Badeon (come now, General, come now stealthily out from your velvet quarters and watch me plait my noose with language!) the Organ Liberat Badeon was not quite the thing it seemed.

I had been much puzzled and perplexed by the presence of the lady known as Mnam, neither a Badean nor an Argeline name precisely, who drifted about the Camp nodding and making no especial sense, who always dressed like she had sacked a palace, but whose presence appeared to be important in some respect to the highest levels of the organisation. Each of the ghostly messages that went unheeded seemed in some way to concern her. What I was repeatedly told by Iaio Gabril was that they did not in any way concern me.

The first sensation was that my feet were unbelievably filthy. When I glanced down at them, feeling them squelch and clag in some unmentionable effluent, I had a vision of the entire floor of the chamber swimming in a yellow-brown swirl which glimmered like liquid gold – lukewarm, though – and which stank like, excuse me, shit itself. What I heard was merely *What makes it all it is*.

When I mentioned to Gabril that I was working on this most cryptic of communiqués, he frowned and said quickly: 'War, Mr Burneau, war is that. War is what makes whatever it is all it is. There's our answer. No need to tell us exactly what we know already.' So, suddenly such an expert on the matter of my premonitions, he instructed me to cease all research into *What makes it all it is*.

My second sensation was a good deal clearer. It one morning appeared to be pouring with rain inside, but the rain seemed to have the solidity – and certainly the brilliance – of silver. What it instantly reminded me of was a waterfall. The only other thing that reminded me of a waterfall, setting aside things that more or less are waterfalls, was the jewellery of the Lady Mnam. *No end of it*, was the accompanying strain. *No end of it*. I decided it was time to question General Gabril about the mysterious lady.

He got quite irritated. 'Do you not recall the fate of the holy sisters that once abided here, Burneau? They died when the stained-glass ceiling in the Hall of Weathers crashed down on them in a storm. They were at prayer. They were all killed by falling shards. But. It is a little-known fact that there was one survivor: that is to say, it was not an 'end of it' at all! And that survivor is the very estimable lady to whom you refer. She had overslept that morning and missed the morning congregation. When my people took these buildings over, we retained her in a spirit of tribute to her miraculous survival, in the holy mystical hope that her presence would facilitate our own miraculous survival in the face of our enemies. As it has. Did you realise none of that? Yes. You realised none of it. You see far, you see further than any, but you do not clearly see the past.'

I hope I can say without irony that it is impossible clearly to see anything when it is represented to one wholly fallaciously. This grave account of Gabril's, to which I nodded sympathetically but which I had then to swear to forget, was a tissue of shameless lies. Nobody survived the freak accident in the Hall of Weathers all that time ago. Lady Mnam did not survive it because she was not there. She was never a holy sister. My dreams were not about shit or glass but money, Brother Fredo, money.

The last unheeded vision came very near the end of the War, when only Gabril, the Lady Mnam and myself were permanent inhabitants of the Camp, and preparations were

224

being made to leave it for ever. It confirmed what was by then a strong suspicion, and is now a generally established fact. I simply hallucinated the Lady Mnam standing before me in a great shroud of money. Notes of it, the pink and green hundred-shell notes of the Ptopoline Domain, and they stretched from her shrunken arms away along a street that seemed to open up in a whole wall of the octagonal room, and upon which streets they became the bricks themselves, with the same beaming face of whoever their king is embossed upon each one, and that street wound away down the side of Mount San Timotheo, then forever west across a vision of brown ocean. This one I never even told the General. It was the most obvious statement the foresightful spirit ever gave to me, and it went with the word *Fetch*.

The Lady Mnam was a Ptopoline heiress, the last daughter of a land developer and fabulously rich. The heroic popular struggle of the Organ Liberat Badeon, far from being the glorious vanquishment of a conqueror by an oppressed people, was part of a huge international strategy of the Ptopolinos to destabilise the possessions of its ancient rivals on the Argeline Domain. Our organisation was absolutely heaving with money. This partly explained the growing reluctance of the Argelinos to fight for Badeo. It explains why the influential celebrities who quietly sailed north, abandoning the media to the diehards (*Carli and the Stranger* was in those days a marionette show conducted by a deranged sniper on the roof of the TV station) were soon followed by the politicians, the businessmen, the bankers and, finally, the soldiers. The dawning of that realisation – that the dark secret influence of the Ptopoline Domain was the root cause of the strength of the insurrection, and that resistance to the inevitable was ultimately futile – was the decisive factor in the cessation of hostilities. However much my gift of foresight had accelerated the military process, its fuel and grease was a bottomless lagoon of foreign money, and its source was the Lady Mnam.

Though I do not know how much you know about these things, Brother Fredo, I am sure you understand that this has always been emphatically denied by Gabril and his associates, including, when occasion demanded, his Minister of Reconciliation. And it is true that there is not a single Ptopolino on the Island, nor any evidence remaining of the clandestine funding that was so crucial to our triumph. Officially and diplomatically speaking, we have no more to do with the Ptopolinos than with the Argeline Domain. Less, in fact, since we began talks on the repatriation of prisoners.

The War for Badeo was at its very end. The leading survivors of the Organ Liberat, like Nunez, Overot, and Battle Marshal Brangeon Curtens, their operatives Stoackey, Woodkind, Tragolani, and the slopers and students who had fought from the beginning, all were making ready for the final push into Badeo, from where reports reached us daily of evacuations and surrenders by the last relics of the collaborating banditry. It was at last decided by Iaio Gabril that the time had come to free me from my enslavement, and let me ride with the last liberating truck triumphantly along the Porodo (now the Avenue Iaio Gabril) to the so-called Viceregal Residence (now the Palace of Popular Valour) where I was to be installed – as I duly have been – in a top-level Ministerial position. On the outskirts of the city, I was to join with the battalion that had finally overcome the TV station after a long and bloody duel with desperate marksmen.

The last defender to die was the aforementioned sniper, driven half-insane by fear and a poor diet, but still holding out aloft on the roof of the station, crouched in front of the one working camera, clutching his rifle in his good hand and the strings of the puppet Carli in the other, as he maintained the high excitement of that unforgettable serial to the last. Carli, now in her 993rd episode, was not only the sole survivor of the drama, she was also reading the News and Weather that preceded and followed each segment. And I

226

was lucky enough to see the serial's last classic episode on the last day of my time in the Hall of Weathers, stuck in the place with an inebriated Captain Nunez, cackling her contempt from beneath her flame-coloured wig, with Tragolani, singing as he burned the daily newspapers one by one from yesterday to the beginning of the War, incinerating his way back through Time like a lit fuse, and the elderly tea-sipping Fulbahlis, who were of the opinion that the show had seen better days.

This could certainly be said of Nunez, who in the latter part of the War had become increasingly prone to violent mood-swings and drinking herself unconscious, though that did make my nocturnal life a little easier. I believe Gabril had discreetly withdrawn her from combat until she recovered her fitness for the fight, so that she always seemed to be in or about the Camp – though that made no one's life easier. Such was the weary crew that together witnessed the last ever broadcast of Network Badeon, the ultimate cliffhanging exploit of Carli and her Stranger.

The sniper on the roof of the TV station had no natural ability for storytelling or dialogue, but, having had a bit of time on his hands, he had been learning fast. As Episode 993 began, late one wintry afternoon, even a crew so dissipated and fractious as us, waiting impatiently for the station to fall and clinch our victory, remained enthralled by the twists of the serial. What I saw was a crude bald puppet on six strings. This is what I heard.

'Loyal Ladies and Gentleman of the Argeline Dominion of Badeo Island, welcome to *Carli and the Stranger*, by Alfonse Gau, that's me, who you don't see yet but is my voice, which is today about what happen to Carli when she come to the gate of Paradee. She come to the gate of Paradee on account of how she fight against the rebel from the Black Mountain, no the Evil, Very Evil Black Mountain who threaten her below.' (Sniper-fire, something indistinct through a loud-

227

hailer, more sniper-fire.) 'My name is Alfonse Gau, my voice you hear, and here's Carli on the camera screen, and I do both her voice as well, as well as I do the God of Justice, I do him lower like this. "Welcome, Carli." She's a bit higher, like this "Good afternoon, God of Justice." The God of Justice, now he called . . . er, he . . . no. (Loud-hailer, sniper-fire, cry of pain) *ai ai ai*, he called, well, Mr Just. Mr Just, he says "Carli, you the only one in the world who come to the gate!" (Shots, then very loud shots, as the sniper Gau seems to fire back. Pause.) '"You is, Carli, on account you fight for the good men not the evil men" then Carli goes – you see her she move up and down a bit to show is her talking now – Carli she goes "What about Mr Alfonse Gau?" see that's me in the story too, is my name, viewing listeners. Carli goes "What about Mr Alfonse Gau, on account he helping me here out-side the gates of Paradee!" (Gau fires again, a whole volley returns. Long pause. Voice through a loud-hailer, much closer.) "Yes," Mr Just the God of Justice say now at the gate of Paradee, "yes! I forgot Mr Alfonse Gau, but yes, Carli, him too, account he help you in your good fight." Because, yes, listening viewers, Alfonse Gau, I can now tell it to you, Alfonse Gau is The Stranger. Is now told for all time. And Carli and Alfonse Gau come to go in the gate of Paradee with no single person else than them two, for their – (Shots very loud, a cry) – for their fight. Now the News! Now the News and . . . after, is Episode 997, is it? of *Carli and the Stranger Alfonse Gau* and where we then get to know what happen when they come in the gate of Paradee. This is Network Badeon, Loyal Ladies – and Loyal . . . Loyal Ladies, and – soon is the Weather, and soon –' (Shots. Puppet drops from sight, and point of view lurches to a bright screen, looks like sky. Point of view lurches again. Muffled words. Point of view jolted twice then travels at horrific speed towards Outer Badean suburbs far below, hurtles faster and faster towards a crowd of blurred faces, then swings round to take in vista of sky, trees, buildings. Blackout.)

*

'Got the bastard,' said Nunez.

Memory of that evening dissolves into a sad fog of drunken celebration. Only Nunez and Tragolani seemed especially disposed to celebrate anyway. Gabril was orchestrating tomorrow's journey to the Capital, most of the other operatives were packing things away, and I was a mound of gloom, sitting in a corner of the Hall of Weathers, wondering what on earth there was left of life outside the eight walls and the glass ceiling.

Gabril made just one memorable appearance, clad in the professional robes no one had seen him wear for two years. He drew a deep breath and said for the second time the historic words that had begun the War: 'We have planted, we have grown, let us harvest, let us drink ... ' I remember thinking I ought to have felt much more honoured to hear history in the making at first hand, but somehow I couldn't. It was all that Tragolani could do not to burst out laughing, and the General himself seemed unconvinced somehow. It was a mournful victory party.

My last night in the clutches of Captain Nunez is unclear in my memory, which is no surprise when I consider what a day we had all spent, drinking and shrieking among the charred remains of two years' vital information. I am certain of only three things: that the last thing she did before leaving my room was to set fire to the flame-coloured wig, leaving it grey and crackled and stinking on my carpet; that earlier she had elicited a promise from me that I would remain at her side in the difficult months to come, and oblige her as I formerly had; and the third thing is that, somehow, listless and indifferent as I was, I refused to tell her she was the person I loved most in the world, though she threatened me with expulsion from the Organ Liberat if I did not. But I don't believe she had that power any longer. I can still hear the door shut firmly as she left. She did not say good night or goodbye, and she did not tell me to get up and go back to my post below the ceiling in the Hall of Weathers. She had one belt on, and she was streaked with my blood.

But I went back anyway, one last time. The night was brilliant and clear. Outside it must have been cold as the grave. I waited as long as I ever had for messages and ensuing visions, but nothing came to me except the sensation of freedom and the terrible inarticulate moaning of the future, like the beasts our ancestors made of our star-configurations were trying hard to understand. I decided to say 'Juilla', and I suddenly saw and heard her clearly – that was what she was like! Young, soft, low-voiced, brown hair curving beneath her frowning face to meet below her chin! But this was no illusion, Brother Fredo, as had come to me so many nights for such a time: this was an act of my own mind's eye. It had opened.

The next morning two unfamiliar guards came early to my room, threw a thick blanket over my head and hurried me quickly outside into freezing air. I had hoped to see the Hall of Weathers again, once more in daylight, but nobody was feeling sentimental. Even when I was permitted to remove the hood, I found myself sitting in the back of a dirty windowless truck with five strange soldiers sharing cheese and chocolate. No Nunez, no Tragolani, not much in the way of information, not much breakfast out of them either. That infernal trip took hours – the rough mountain tracks, the noisy streets of Furasol, and the smoother highways with nonetheless frequent stoppages – which was how long it took for me to absorb the fact that I would not see the Camp again. It was a much more distressing realisation than I had expected. And I was much more forlorn than I had been on the day I sailed from the Argeline Domain with the Viceroy Lagland, for that was a tour of duty, and it had an end in sight. This was a journey into a place I had hardly known in peace, let alone in the ruins of war. And those I knew – where would I ever find them? Which side had they taken? I recalled that Gando Maricolo, Juilla's father, was in prison on the Mainland, but I couldn't remember what for, so it gave no clue to their sympathies. I had a strong feeling that the boy, Paol, would have joined the fighting if he had been old enough. (The truth, as I was soon to learn, was worse: he had joined anyway and on the wrong side.) What had it been like to live in that teeming city once it became a battleground, a hell of crumbled chapels and shells of homes? That mad sniper Alfonse Gau, in one of his last broadcasts, had swung his camera through all points of the compass high over Badeo Town. He had called the programme *Look Everywhere With Alfonse Gau*! Somewhere in every suburb there was ruination. The worst area was the market centre, Allalong, near the shore. That was where the Viceroy was killed, that was where I met Violet Maricolo in the drinking bar called All Afternoons. But the camera of Alfonse Gau was too shaky, too blurred, for me to determine the state of the Avenue Hali, my one home in Badeo. All I knew for sure was that I could never return to my real home, to Gispar and the Koborol, because I was about to be made a Minister of State on the Island that had humiliated my homeland.

I was scarcely treated like a Minister in the back of that truck, I can say for sure. These young soldiers all knew each other, had all avoided the fighting (we had that in common) and had no idea why I had been bundled blindfold into that truck. Nor had I, for that matter. To this day, I cannot understand why I was not permitted to look at the exterior of the place where I had spent the last two years of my life. Not to see what it looked like from afar. Some of these young rebels had no sense of what was right and decent.

Yet it was in this truck that I discovered one last extraordinary fact that would be gathered into the legends of Burneau, the betrayer, the Blue Devil of Badeo. I learned from the soldiers that on the first day in two years that I had been absent from the Hall of Weathers, it spontaneously destroyed itself. I regarded this as the final act of whatever agency was responsible for the phenomena I experienced there. What I heard it as was a goodbye.

'Lucky, I reckon,' one of the soldiers had suddenly observed out of the blue, 'to miss it by that.'

'Coulda been you,' said another.

'Coulda been you,' said the first.

'Wasn't though.'

'Same here. Wasn't though.'

'Bad sign, I reckon,' said a third one.

'Good sign, I reckon,' a fourth disagreed, 'like it waited for us all to be out. Before it did it.'

'Not all of us. Not her.'

'Us, I meant. The lads. We was all out. Coulda been us.'

'Wasn't though,' said the one who said that the first time.

Our truck was the last, so it turned out, the last to drive away from Camp Liberat, last in a convoy of seven. Gabril was somewhere in it, Nunez and Tragolani and the others all elsewhere; I, as I say, at the back. In the excitement of departure, with the prospect of public glory glowing at the far end of the day, the operatives omitted to check that everybody had been included on the convoy. It was not until we reached one of our own OLB checkpoints, half-way down the mountain towards Furasol, that an absence was noted. Nowhere on the convoy was the Lady Mnam to be found. Horrified, for reasons I trust I have made clear, Fredo, Gabril demanded that his own truck be turned back to search for her, and that the other six all wait at the checkpoint.

This was the story that filtered up the line into the opaque verbal fragments of my travelling companions.

Gabril and two soldiers had returned to Camp Liberat to find it, as we had left it, shuttered, noiseless. Nothing had altered, except that a wind nine times as cold as the morning was slavering through the building like a wolf, so breathtakingly icy that when it met them in the corridor it knocked them down and left them curled in three shivering balls. When they had been able to crawl further, they had reached the Hall of Weathers, whence the appalling draught was originating. This is what they saw.

The octagon was, as they had found it when they first arrived, open to the elements. Its glass ceiling had shattered into a million murderous shards, exactly one hundred of which (Gabril ordered them counted and removed) had nailed the bloody hide of the Lady Mnam to the floor at a point precisely beneath the centre of what had been glass and was now the sky – my place. The burned remains of our world of information – papers, books, pictures, our televisions – were quite interred by powdered glass. It apparently began then to rain on all this.

Of course the most plausible explanation is that the Lady Mnam had overslept and been passing through the Hall of Weathers on her way to the trucks: doubtless Gabril had plans to spirit her back to the Ptopoline under some disguise. But I observed to myself, remembering Gabril's insultingly thin yarn about her religious past, that she was found in no position of prayer.

If that was a message, it was the last message. It was also the last time the Organ Liberat received any foreign aid. And it was the last of the Camp, which Gabril, by all accounts in an incoherent fury, doused with a fuel so ambitious to burn that not even the torrential rain could save the buildings. By nightfall there was nothing left of Camp Liberat, high up on the Mountain of San Timotheo. One dubious report has it that there was literally nothing left, not a blackened ruin, not even ashes. It's certainly true that no one has since been able to swear exactly where the Camp used to be. And no one can find the meadow that had that view of the world below. So they say.

Gabril, I feel, has never been the same man. He had to explain away the intensity of his grief by pretending to me in private that he had once been the paramour of Lady Mnam, distasteful as that must have been for him to admit, and embarrassing as it certainly was for me to hear. He seemed unaware that I knew exactly what she was doing there, about the money from the Ptopolinos, because, though he had waved away my trio of dreams, the fact remained that I had had them. This is the problem with people who spend so long

233

in positions of power, Fredo. They forget the sensation of being disbelieved, and so do not recognise disbelief though it is staring them in the face. They must mistake it for admiration.

Our truck finally came to a complete standstill, and I heard somebody get out of the cabin and walk around to the back. What was opened up to my eyes was a very different world for me, a disconcerting view of high buildings, huge advertising notices, tight knots of soldiers of the Badean Army standing around smoking. All I had seen of the outside world for the last two years was a misty mountainside at dusk or dawn. It was a long time to have gone without seeing pylons, streetlamps, signposts, aerials, and it took me a while to get reaccustomed to the infinite monotony of their shapes and functions.

Note that for several weeks now we had ceased to refer to ourselves as the Organ Liberat Badeon, but as the Badean Army itself, while the former 'Badean Army' or 'Dominion Force' that had occupied the Island on behalf of the Argeline had inexorably declined through the stages of occupying power, brave troop in a dangerous place, desperate rearguard, and, finally, abandoned by their bankrollers on the Mainland, a rump known throughout even the Argeline news media as the 'Never-Say-Dies' (ironically, really, since die was all they did do), the last ragged phalanx of snipers and mercenaries, who elicited some sympathy among the older Argelinos, but were already considered to have fallen behind the march of History. We of the new Government have been surprised and amused by this process, which we have assiduously monitored. It is clear that on the Mainland they do not find it possible to accept anything called 'defeat'. Venerable professors and military veterans alike are agreed on the essential principle that History no longer required a rich and noble entity like the Argeline Domain to hang on to such an intractable little speck as Badeo. The War was portrayed in their news media as a 'Victory' for this principle,

234

known as the Principle of Historical Redeployment. Having said that, some liberal commentators went a bit far. We observed Professor August Amik of the King Karolin University being arrested for giving a lecture entitled 'Waking up to History: Thanks be to the Organ Liberat!' I remember how Gabril nearly choked to death laughing at this, crying, 'History? You should have stuck to wines, Augustine!' Defence Minister Overot sourly surmised that it was probably the exclamation mark that had got Professor Amik his five years' exile. Nonetheless, we knew that Badeo would be a perpetually sore point for the vast Domain, and that none of the main protagonists of the Reconquest – for example myself – would ever be entirely safe from the poisonous branching tentacles of the humbled Mainland.

Badeo Town, into which I gingerly stepped, blinking in the special intensity of city light and almost stumbling over, was in the process of being slowly, carefully, wiped of collaborators still holed up in certain areas, around the Way of Kestrels and the Avenue Lazard, for instance, which were both key streets because they were near the sports stadium. The students thought it wise to restart the Popular League. There was also sporadic sniper fire reported near the harbour, and from the one hotel on the tiny island of Kina. The central area, where the old Viceregal Residence and the damaged Government buildings were to be found, was said to be safe, and already Gabril's section of the Victory Convoy was on its way there. I noticed that mine was the only truck from the convoy that had stopped here on the outskirts, in what was an unfamiliar sector of Badeo Town.

Among the soldiers milling about in the army truck-park were numerous men in blue suits. One of these spotted me, checked my face against a picture in his hand, strode over, smiling, then quickly apprised me of my next duty, which was to give a short broadcast on Network Liberat. Befuddled and nauseous from the journey, in irritation I asked why me. The man smiled, as if we were having some sort of game where I pretended not to know things.

'You're the man with experience, it says here. The lover of television!'

'I watch it, sir, but I've never worked with a camera.'

The official (whom I know now as Romeo Gapp, the Controller of National Free Broadcasting) smiled even more. I noticed that there were three pretty young women with him, all with the same smile but only one between three so they had to pass it between them, have a break from it.

'You don't have to think, Mr Burneau,' said one of the women briefly not smiling. 'The script is written,' she smiled.

'I don't know the techniques.'

'Here it is,' smiled Romeo Gapp, handing me a folder as if it had the techniques in it. 'Go with these girls.'

'I don't know where the studio is.'

'It's behind you.'

The pretty young women smiled together, as I turned around to face the tallest structure I had ever seen, a building that loomed up for several dozen storeys and then whittled itself to a mast, the length of which was about five times the height of the building. I had seen this mast from a distance, of course, but that is a very different thing. It is something like the distance between seeing a strange girl on the far side of a room and standing next to her in love. That's how much light and space that impossible edifice consumes. I was led away by the 'girls', and soon found myself in a tiny, humming room illuminated only by twelve red points of light. We had reached this room in a pitch-dark, lurching lift, which had deprived me of my sense of where I was, how high off the ground, how far from the nearest friend. Sitting in this room was perhaps the closest I could imagine to sitting in outer space, connected to nothing but one's own solitude, aware of nothing but distant creations that are not explicable.

I know exactly how my broadcast went, because I retained a copy, which I have right here. I knew what to read, for I held the sheet in front of me, fluttering with my nerves in that

236

hot focusing cell, but I had no idea how to. The only clue as to how one was supposed to broadcast when not trained for it was the curious emphasis employed by the old Network presenters and newscasters, so, on the signal 'Three on the wings of a butterfly Two on the wings of a butterfly this is Maris Burneau Victory Day Broadcast producer Romeo Gapp on the wings of a butterfly good luck Maris go. Go. Go!' I set about trying to put my instincts into practice.

'Good afternoon *to* you all, loyal victorious heroic conquerors *of* our Island *of* Badeo. My name *is* Burneau, some of you *will* know me as *the* heroic selfless victorious striker *of* the first blow for freedom *against* the imperial oppressor *from* the Argeline. I have gratefully accepted my new post *as* the Minister of Reconciliation. Oh . . . ' (This was the first I had heard of my new job, Fredo, and it distracted me from my broadcast for a second. A man with glasses started gesticulating wildly, so I soldiered on.) 'I wish to make it clear *that* the city of Badeo has *been* liberated, and is safe now, and *that* any remaining collaborators will *be* dealt with very harshly. The victorious *and* noble General Doctor Iaio Gabril, may *his* name be sung from every rooftop, is at *this* moment liberating the so-called Viceregal Residence and is from *this* moment the rightful and undisputed leader of *the* Free Island of Badeo. For now, stay *in* your homes *and* await instructions for celebrating tonight our heroic liberation *on* the streets of our Capital! Glory *to* General Iaio Gabril, chief warrior *and* architect *and* poet of our glorious struggle! Listen now, people, *to* his great gabrilette, number 23: "When now the glass is empty, raise the glass towards the sun/And fill it to the golden rim with air of many days/Then lower all and fill again with midnight to the brim." And now, it *is* time for the Free Island Weather Forecast with Annabel Vort. Glory be *to* Free Badeo. Annabel,' I smiled.

I was much congratulated on my performance. Romeo Gapp

was convinced I had previously worked in the medium, and declared me a 'natural talent' when I denied it. He then asked me to sign my name on his own copy of the script. 'I was there,' he smiled for some reason, and none of this made any sense until he repeated his comment, but added, 'No, Minister, a natural talent.' Though I had just broadcast to the entire Island that I was the Minister of Reconciliation, it was only at this point that I realised I was therefore a man of some importance. Evidently it had only just got home to the TV people too, because I was treated with the utmost respect thereafter, given wine, a hot meal, escorted down to the grand front entrance of the Station (grand, though pockmarked with bullet-holes) helped into the back of a luxurious long blue car – a little tipsy I was by then – and driven off with a powerful surge in the direction of BADEO CENTRAL, ST SPERICE, PROMENAD, HAVEN.

I was just thinking that if I travelled any further in that direction I would reach the Argeline Domain – maybe even the Koborol if I kept that straight track! – when I realised I was not alone. Not only that, but the person sitting next to me must have been reading my thoughts.

'No more high mountains for you, Blue Burneau.'

Nunez was masked and dressed all in black. The only parts of her that were nakedly visible were her left eye, her right eye, and her lips. She had a gun in her right hand.

'I didn't see you in the convoy,' I said.

'Good radio, Burneau.' She licked her lips, a frightening act, to see a woman's tongue and not her face – 'Good radio.'

'I thought it was TV.'

'It was everything and everywhere. That station can beam to the Domain. The receptors there scramble what they want to, and put the rest on the news. You'll make the news, being the Argelino made good, the poor dumb sentry who got famous killing his own country's diplomats. Not to mention helping us bandits win our Island back. Unprecedented treason. Good TV.'

238

'I didn't kill anyone. You did.'

'I don't mind. You take the shine. Fame, who wants it?'

'You think then, that was . . . broadcast to the – Mainland?'

'Up the highest mountains, duckling. Now they know you're still alive. Now they know you not only helped to do in their Viceroy, but you then stuck around and did so well by us we made you a Minister. Isn't that something? You'll never see the place again. They'd shoot you off the landing-quay. Why do you think Teacher asked you to do that broadcast? Now you're on our team forever. You're the Minister of Reconciliation. Get reconciled. Left here, driver.'

I thought I recognised one or two of the street names in this battered and abandoned area of the city, but I couldn't be sure. The important thing at that point was to keep looking out of the window, gather impressions, be curious, do anything but endure the grave implications of what Nunez was saying. I felt clenched and determined, roaring to myself that I had never once expected I *would* see home again – but what was so distressing about Nunez's cold appraisal was that it made me realise that yes, on the contrary, I had indeed expected one day to return, somehow, some day, to there. And my voice might just have spoken there, in my home, in my kitchen, through my moma's radio and out across the tiles she polished, shame spreading into their lives as they looked up from the meal she'd made. Infinite miles and an ocean away, I stared through smouldering eyes at the death's head of the driver, which spun round of course to grin at me, while still driving, then I asked Nunez through a clotted throat what she was now, was she a Minister too?

'Fuck no. I'm not even a Captain any more. (Keep going, man, to the Avenue Naheen, we can cut through Avenue Hali.) No, Teacher thinks we ladies can be soldiers but not Ministers. But here's the real damned jape, Burneau. I work for you. Go on, order me then.'

'Did you say Avenue Hali?'

'Sloshed soldiers everywhere. We're doing back streets. Left here, man. What do you think, Mr Minister Blue? What can I do for you? I got some ideas.'

'For me? What are you meant to do for me?'

'Fine question. Like I did it all, no? Didn't I? I made you the Child In The Ocean, I made you the Jungle Struck By Lightning. So let's not forget what a promise is, Burneau. If I'm ordered to work for you I'll work for you, but the rest is a promise. You're mine, you are. Remember that. There's daytime and there's nighttime. Remember what you are. Remember that – '

'That's it, there!'

'What's that, Minister? Seen an angel?'

'Stop, driver! That's Avenue Hali.'

'Just cut through it, man, it's bombed out. We're going to Dewdrop and we're late.'

'No! Stop, driver!'

'Minister says stop, so stop!' Nunez cackled, still, for all her snarling and sarcasm, her drinking – which I could smell on her – and her entombment in black, at some level rather enjoying her life.

The long car stopped, and I got out. The street had obviously been abandoned, though only every third or fourth block seemed to have suffered shell damage. Front doors hung open, windows were broken or boarded up. It was awfully quiet. Some way off, I could hear guns of celebration and a brass band playing, but those sounds were coming from ahead of us, the university area and L'Embassade. There was no movement here on the Avenue Hali but for the light wind flapping the papery sheets in the upper windows of the tenement blocks. These stretched away along each side of the Avenue. At the far end was a burned-out army truck with two white flags sticking out of it. It was half in a crater.

Sixteen, I remembered.

Nunez got out of the car and signalled the driver to stay where he was. She came up and stood beside me as I gazed along the street.

240

'Our people haven't wiped this sector, Burneau, there's nothing for us to do here. We have to be at Dewdrop by five for the speeches in the amphitheatre. You're a Minister, you pain, you're not here to sightsee.'

'I lived here, Captain.'

'I'm not a fucking Captain.'

I started walking along the street. Nunez followed.

'So. He lived here. Well, great. Left some milk in the fridge, did you?'

'Take the mask off, Nunez.'

'What? Why?'

'Because then we could be anyone. If you wear a mask someone will think they should kill you. Us as well as them.'

'This is crazy. Listen to him!'

I stopped and faced her. 'Take it off. I mean, I order it. I mean, well, please.'

She shrugged and took the mask off. She looked sick and tired, and stared dully through her hair. I had by now thought of a lie.

'I have a contact on this street, a sympathiser, a woman. She knows everything we need to know about the collaborators, their names, their plans, their HQ, their armaments. I told her if I could ever come back for her I would. I got messages from her, Nunez. We owe her. We all owe her.'

This was still my strong suit, recourse to the mystical dimension, and I was by now so practised in mendacity that my lies generally seemed to be more convincing to people than anything true. Nor was it difficult to say that I 'owed' the Maricolos, who had, after all, saved my life when I was cast adrift in Badeo. Nunez spat on the pavement.

'Very good, Minister. You want the driver to come?'

'I'll go alone. She's another hundred yards up on the right. That's where she lives; that's where she said she'd be.'

'You won't go alone. I'll cover you.'

'I'm going alone. You wait here. It's an order that you wait here. I'm not going to say "please" this time.'

'You can say what you sodding well like, Burneau, but I'm not letting you walk into a strange house alone at the fag-end of a fucking war.'

'Doesn't that mean I could have you – what is it – court something?'

'Martialled. No. This is a civil government, Minister.'

'What's the word then?'

'You tell me. You're the fucking dignitary.'

'Exactly. So.'

'Shit as it all is now, I love you, Burneau. I won't let you go alone.'

'You don't love me, Nunez.'

'I do, chum.'

'Rabaiette did.'

'Who?'

'You don't love me.'

'You're wrong, Minister.'

'I doubt it, Nunez.'

'Doubt away. Take this gun, I've another. I'll come as far as the street door.'

'You won't.'

'You mean you don't believe I will, like you don't believe I love you, Burneau. But I will, for I do. Take the gun.'

'There's no danger, Nunez, I know this woman.'

'How do you know her?'

'She sheltered me after I killed Lagland. I mean after you killed Lagland.'

'What did she do that for?'

'She was kind, that was all.'

'You screw her, Blue?'

'Never.'

'I had you pegged for a "never". She love you then?'

'Shouldn't think so.'

'How would you know? You're garbage, you are, Minister Blue, pure and simple. I bet she loved you. That's what it's about. Like I do, much as I hate you. If she loves you the way

I do, you're going to need a whole fucking death squad to cover you.'

I took the gun Nunez offered me, and we walked on together.

What did I expect now? One finds oneself in situations, Fredo, when everything rational, everything intelligent, everything likely, has been jettisoned, and a great shimmering delusion fixes you to a path. How could I expect that Violet Maricolo, or Juilla, or Paol, still lived at 16 Avenue Hali after two years of war? They were all impetuous people. I could see them having jumped on the first boat out, gone off to the Mainland in search of a new life. On the other hand, I could see Violet manically shopping through the War, or drinking in that old bar-room, trading insults with the regulars and chatting up some other lost soul trying and failing to be ignored. I could see the children still at school – though Juilla I realised would be nineteen by now, maybe working somewhere, maybe cooking, maybe washing clothes, maybe washing and cutting hair, slithering her long soft fingers over the scalps of collaborators – maybe marrying one! Washing his clothes, cooking him lovely meals, then bringing them into the room for him! Nineteen. Most girls on Badeo Island would be married by nineteen. Then I saw her alone somewhere, unreachable, then I saw her a prostitute on the ill-lit jetties of Furasol. That's my abiding trouble. I can see how all things could happen. That exasperates the god. Only one can, I hear him remind me, Fredo, though the death adds evenly that no, also, none can.

We reached the block of flats 1-24. The grey stone building was hardly damaged at all outside, but the lock of the street door was splintered and smashed, as if it had been shot off. I felt like a dead man when I thought that, and believed not one of my hopes to be possible.

'See, Maris?' Nunez said gently. 'Someone wiped this place after all. Your spy's a spy some other where. Spy heaven. Or spy hell, where all her secrets are flashed up in neon, and it's so bright even the dead can read them.'

243

'She said she'd stay,' I lied from the heart. 'She said she would and I believe her. She's either here or she died.'

Nunez sniffed. 'She's not here.'

'Stay in the passage,' I told her. 'I'm going up the fire stairs.'

She took me by the arm and said forcefully: 'Let me come with you. I've always protected you. You don't have to love the one who protects you. One day you'll see. Let me come with you.'

I was touched by Nunez now. For all her wise talk she looked younger than ever, young but washed out, tired, falling. But I couldn't let her come with me. I was walking back into my past, into a time before I knew her. She could not be admitted, because she had never existed in the world I had returned to. Fredo, I could smell my own past, in the dirty walls, off the stone floor of the hallway where the letterboxes were smashed open, breathing to me down the spiral stairwell. I could hear the songs the Maricolos liked, welling up from deep inside my mind like some subterranean party that had outlasted the War; I could hear Violet complaining amidst it, Paol braying with his own battles; I could taste the cheap red Fortified we swigged from chipped beakers. How long had I stayed with them – one week, two weeks? My presence in this abandoned passage had somehow swallowed up two whole years of captivity, and all of my rebel acquaintance. The instinct that I was physically close to one or more of the kind, squabbling Maricolos had accelerated my blood, electrified all my nerves. I felt myself to be beyond danger, beyond the OLB and the Camp, beyond the absurd responsibilities imposed upon me with what I knew to be gleeful cunning by Iaio Gabril. I had a gun in my hand. Just that, just that brought it all right back to me. I shook my head and started towards the fire stairs.

'How far are you going?' Nunez murmured. 'At least tell me that.'

'I can't remember. The number is sixteen.'

244

'I'll come if you're in trouble.'

'I won't be, but don't.'

'I'll come if I hear shouting.'

'You won't, but don't come. Just wait for me down here.'

'If I hear shouting, I'll be in that flat before the echo hits. I won't obey your orders, Maris, I've other orders.'

I turned back, stared at her, and nodded. Then I went on up the stone stairs.

The building was absolutely quiet. At the top of the stairs I turned right: the five doors along the corridor were – as I correctly recalled – numbered 12 on my left, then 13 on my right, 14 on the left, 15 on the right, 16 at the end. I passed very slowly along, never taking my eyes off that number 16, as it blurred and focused and blurred again but always grew in size, took up more of my sight until it almost filled it, for my face was right up close and I nodded my brow against the chill white wood. There was a space for the occupant's name by the side of the door, but that was all there was. Without thinking anything at all, I knocked on the door. When I had done that, I did think something. The thought struck me that I had made no plans for any contingency whatever. Burning with hope that Juilla Maricolo was about to open the door, I stood there and prayed fervently that nothing would happen, no one come.

Someone tossed the sun like a coin and its light fell in a diamond by my feet. Nothing happened. I was acutely aware of Nunez down below. It was as if she could hear my breathing, or could have done if I was doing any. I knocked again.

I waited about half a minute. Down at my feet, the diamond of sunlight went out. I took a step back, glanced over my shoulder to be sure that Nunez had not followed me up the stairs, then stepped forward and gave the door a light push. It yielded, swung the whole way open, and stayed like that.

No one lived there, there were no belongings. Nothing on the walls or floors. It was dingy. Such daylight as there was

245

seemed to emanate from the living room, which is where I went, peculiarly relieved, relaxed, with my gun lowered and my guard down.

What else would explain my comic vulnerability at the instant that I entered that desolate, forsaken room of nothing but old sheeting and a rug hung across the only window – that was the one thought I had, and I had it too late – who hung that rug there? Something yanked my head back, gripped my hair with excruciating tightness, and slid a knife blade against my throat.

'Move and I do this,' croaked a man's voice.

'Don't, don't, it's nothing,' I choked out.

The man stepped round and saw who I was. I saw that he was Juilla Maricolo, haggard, wild-eyed, wrapped in what looked like curtains – because I remember thinking why not put the curtains over the windows and wear the rug? – then she stumbled back away from me and stood there, shaking with whatever, cold, fear, hunger, pointing the knife towards me as if that was as effective as holding it to my throat. She looked very strange indeed, and she couldn't speak. I could.

'Juilla. Listen. Whatever you do, be quiet. Understand? Be very, very quiet.'

She swallowed hard and vaguely shook her head. She looked dreadful. I wanted to look after her now and for always, and felt that it would be difficult not to say so. Instead, I set about saving her.

'Because, downstairs, there is a soldier with a gun. If you speak loudly, that soldier will come in here and kill you. Understand? Nod. Nod if you do.'

She screwed her eyes up as if it was too light, though it was hardly light at all in that cavern of a room. She did nothing that I could discern as a nod to me. I tried again.

'Do you know me? Do you remember me?'

There was a lengthy silence. Every part of her seemed about to shiver.

'Yuh,' she breathed.

246

'You and I, we – ' I stopped in horror that I had started to talk that way. I didn't know how to stop though, so I carried on, prepared for all the things to be said and done at what could be the end of time. 'I love you, Juilla, I loved you through the War. I was a prisoner. I was not able – '

'Prisoner? No, no! Captain of the Evil Guard!'

'Be quiet, for pity's sake,' I hissed: 'I'm with a soldier.'

'My brother, he's a prisoner,' she whispered, the knife trembling with her effort at speech. 'I'll never see him now . . . ' Her eyes filled up with tears. It looked like their natural state.

'Where's Violet, where's your mother?'

'Gone, g-gone, Mainland. Left me . . . My brother's a prisoner . . .'

'Hush, love, hush, please!'

Then I heard Nunez's footfall on the stone stairs. I stepped forward and Juilla jabbed the blade towards me. I raised my palm.

'Put it down, love, put it down, there's a soldier – if she sees you do that – Juilla, love, you're safe with me . . .'

'C-c-aptain of Evil, Black, the Murder Captain Burneau!'

'Shut up, shut up!'

'Killed, all our heroes in the Force! My brother's in the Force . . .'

'Juilla, shut up, I love you, be quiet!'

I was thinking – had I shut the doors behind me? How much time did I have? I edged away from the living-room door, hoping she'd come with me, which she did, gibbering: 'Stop or I'll stab you, Murder Captain!'

'Just hush, just gently, just hush, oh love . . .'

I kept moving, coaxing her towards the corner of the room that was blindest to the door. Then I heard Nunez trying the doors along the landing – how many were there? 12, 13, she tried, 14, then I heard her call out: 'Maris, where are you, which room, you bastard!'

Juilla ran at me with the knife. Instinctively – because I

loved her, I maintain – I dropped the gun and raised both hands to shield myself, my left palm closing on the blade, which slit the skin – then I pulled the thing out of her grasp by the handle with my right and barged her away from me with the full weight of my shoulders. Nunez was at the door of the flat.

'Maris, where the fuck are you?'

Juilla, having staggered weakly across the room, now fell against the window, downing the rug so the light flooded in, and she screamed out into the street:

'Evil Black Captain Devil Burneau is here! Help me!'

I moved towards her, blood shaking from my hand, then I turned – half-way across the room – and saw my gun on the floor. Nunez kicked her way into the flat, shrieking, 'I'll take her, Maris!' as I flung myself back towards the gun. Instinct, all of it, why that? Why one woman not the other? Why, dead brother Fredo, in the names of all our gods, why one life not another?

Nunez burst into the living room with her gun trained on the hysterical screaming girl and I fired from the floor.

Nunez fell backwards against the wall, and stayed like that, staring with a frown at some point on the ceiling.

Juilla's scream had died too, and she staggered, convulsing, backwards into the corner. I was up on one knee now. Then I stood.

What happened I think was that Nunez was about to look at me: her head was lolling leftwards, and her gun was still in her hand. In case her eyes were going to catch mine, I fired again, square into the front of her body, and she went down heavily with her eyes fluttering shut.

I must have stood there for a minute, blood everywhere: my hand, my fingers, my cheeks, my mouth. I saw Juilla pressed into the corner, like her schoolteacher had told her to stay there, but she was burrowing into the wall as if to escape the horror that way.

I went to her and hauled her around with my bloody hands.

'You have to run now, Juilla, get away from here.'

'L-look at your hand, Blue Burneau, it's all red – you're Blue but it's all – all red . . .'

'You have to run away now.'

'*You* have to! *You* do! I live here!'

'No one lives here, my love.'

'Love . . . ' she said dully. 'You killed all the people. You would have killed us. My brother's gone. What you are is the Blue, Evil, Black – '

'Shut up, Juilla! I'm going now. Don't stay here, don't live here – go to Allalong, go to the Avenue Maldeau and I'll find you there . . .'

I heard a car draw up outside the flat, a car with a good engine: the long blue car. I knew the driver had a rifle. I took hold of Juilla with as much strength as I ever remember mustering, dragged her to the door of her flat and pushed her out on the landing. She stumbled and looked back, a terrible shaking figure, and she seemed to want to speak.

'Please run, Juilla, I love you and I'll find you.'

'You go away, you always do. You don't come back.'

'Run, for pity's sake, Avenue Maldeau, there's an encampment there!'

'Black Evil Murder Captain . . . you pretend to love the people and then you kill all of them.'

'It's all lies you've heard about me, all lies, Juilla! Now run!'

She suddenly seemed to calm down slightly, and fixed me with the coldest stare I had ever seen. Then she said clearly:

'You will have to find my brother.'

'What? How can I?'

'You will have to find my brother.'

'I don't know where he is. He might be – '

'Find him. Mister.'

I nodded. I just nodded. Then she ran, and somehow, in the twenty seconds that elapsed before the driver and a back-up team of ex-OLB crackshots stormed the block on

Avenue Hali, she had managed to vanish completely, and I had managed to slash the side of my own body, so that when the soldiers happened upon the heroic rebel warrior Amadora Guiva Nunez shot dead through the breast and the heart, I too was to be found, semi-conscious, another victim, but a fortunate survivor who was on his feet again within a week. No suspects in the attack were found. The Government's response was to bomb the Avenue Hali where the atrocity had happened, but, as I observed, the area was more or less depopulated already. Nunez was mourned with great solemnity in the grounds of the Palace of Popular Valour, and buried at her sister's farm near Foretto, where she had learned to love wine, and from where she had travelled, just five years previously, to become versed in the secrets of its production.

Now, Brother Fredo, the narrative is over.

I sit in my office in the Ministry of Reconciliation. Three days and nights have I sat here recounting to you the facts of my time on Badeo. I began with my plea of innocence, and I end with my confession of guilt. I wanted to tell you how I was not a murderer, and to do that I have shown you how I am. That I murdered the real killer of the Viceroy I was meant to be protecting, and whose death caused me to be plunged into this endless plight – that may hold some hurtful poetry in it for pure aesthetes, Fredo, but I have never in my life sought to harm anybody. Now my first sexual lover lies killed by my own hand. My second, her friend, was sent to her death in the War for loving me, and the one girl I love in the world, she is housed in a refugee centre on the island of Kina. It is well-nigh impossible for me, in my position, to secure a private audience with her, though I have done what I can to ensure that the hostel is at least well-stocked and clean. Of Juilla's lost brother there is no trace. My discreet enquiries have led nowhere, and if he is alive he is probably on the Mainland. At least he will be safe there, having fought on their side. If he ever wishes to return to Badeo to find his sister, perhaps he will be exchanged under the provisions of the deal that will, all gods willing, bring this letter to you. The two boats sail in a week's time, Fredo, and I pray that these words will be aboard it, in the safe hands of Federico Tragolani, travelling as a homecoming prisoner. I will think of your meeting. I hope you will not be afraid when his wild eyes and tactless mouth come grinning up the side of the Folded Mountain. Please, if you can, let him rest a while in your sanctuary, Fredo, but do not be anxious that he will stay too long. I know you do not drink wine in the Refuge!

I see you most clearly now, your old face. You are wondering why I have written these things. You know why I wrote them to you, for I explained at the outset how I remembered your saving me in the mist on the mountain ledge, but you are curious perhaps as to why I have dwelt so long upon the details of my pain, and, sometimes, my delight. I have made no secret of the fact that much of the time, my friend, I doubt your continued survival, even in the clean fresh atmosphere high above the villages of the Koborol, even with your simple diet and peaceful existence. If that is true, why have I taken a risk so grievous as this, to write at my desk, mere yards from the office of the President himself, these midnight secrets? That I was no assassin, that I was not even a sympathiser, that I knew there was no heroic struggle but a limitless influx of sophisticated weaponry from a power even stronger and more cynical than the Argeline Domain. That I made what passed for love with Nunez five hundred and seven times and still I killed her. That I thought, that I think, the President a charlatan and most of his students thugs. That I loved the Viceroy Lagland. That all I wish, all I ever wished, and all I ever shall wish, is that I shall come home one day to the Argeline, my innocence published far and wide, and that Papa and Moma and Hektor and André, and the shepherdesses whose names and faces have all faded, all are still there to attest to who I really am. That when I meet them my

251

wife is on my arm, and my wife is Juilla Maricolo. Juilla Burneau. *Juilla Burneau.*

Those are the whole of it, the whole of it.

But why do this, why say them, why write them? Why have I written these joys and horrors in the splashed colours of a book writer, why have I done the blue sky, the sunshine, the rain and kisses and tears and blood – and all, and only, to you, Fredo?

I have been saving to the end my only recollection of our talk on that day. I think you did not expect that I would remember words from so long ago, spoken when a tiny, frightened boy, a boy shocked to have been saved! Well, all the words I have quoted to you about my life on Badeo, all those words were truly said, but no single talk rings as resonantly and sonorously as what I set down now.

'Why,' I asked you, and I was still trembling with the cold, even though you had given me your extra cloak to wear – and so had one of the other brothers, a much older one who can't possibly be living now, I think – 'why do you kneel on the ground and talk to yourself?'

You said, of course (but I was young) you said you were not talking to yourself but to your god.

'Where is he?' I wondered.

You asked me who had said that.

'I said it,' I replied.

'Then there he is,' you said.

'I can't see him,' I protested, 'so he's not there.'

You asked me again who had said that.

'I did,' I replied.

'Then there he is,' you said.

I didn't understand and so I said, quite crossly, I remember, forgetting my manners in a stranger's hovel: 'There's nobody here but me!'

You stood up and went to fetch my soup off the stove, and when you came back you said: 'I heard him then, clear as a child. Didn't you?'

I didn't understand that either, and I still didn't see him, but when I had finished the soup, and felt warm and alive again, you said, as you were cleaning up the pans: 'I talk to him so he will remember me when he stirs the soup, and so he will hear me when I go into the mist. The more I talk, Maris, the more soup he makes me, the clearer he imagines me. You must talk to him, Maris, otherwise he will not know where you are, and he will not know if you are hungry.'

When we were sitting by the fire again, another question rose in my mind.

'What about if I'm not hungry?'

'Then you should make sure he himself has all he needs.'

'The god?'

'Of course.'

'What if neither of us is hungry? Why should we talk then?'

'Neither of us is hungry. Why are we talking now?'

I thought for a long time, watching the fire.

'It's good to,' was all I could say in my weariness, and I remember you laughing when you finally showed me to the cot for all lost travellers, because you said that Yes, it was good to, even if that had been the last thing I'd said all evening!

Before I went to sleep, I asked you how I should talk to your god. You said I should tell him the truth, because it's all he can hear. I asked if that meant he would always know if I lied.

'No,' you said, 'he won't notice if you lie. He won't notice you at all. Then, when you die, which you may do in a hundred years, Maris, somebody who loves you will mention you to your god, and he will look up and say "Who?"'

'If I'm dead, dead and gone, sir, will it matter?'

'It will matter to him, Maris. He'll look for you in his book. He'll be sorry not to find you. But he will, I know he will. He'll find you in the mist, for you can cry up a storm, and you'll be crying for real.'

That night I did cry for real, because I was not in my bed,

because I had lost the goat on the Mountain, because I was going to be dead and gone. I feel much the same these days, and none of those truths has altered, but I have, after these three days and three nights, told you all the truths I can find in my webbed and abhorrent soul, and I end my letter to you with renewed happiness and hope. I also know with a certainty that is a marvel to me, and is as strange and strong a certainty as any that I glimpsed miraculously in the magical Hall of Weathers, that you are, beyond any doubt, alive, Brother Fredo, and that you are, beyond all doubt, reading my words at this hour, and that you do, beyond all reason, believe me, love me, and forgive me for the life I have led on this Island, the lies I have told, and must continue to tell, its people. If it should be that I come to die before you, Fredo, and I feel too that it is a thing you will know, I ask you as one final favour – my only favour other than that you read and then destroy this – that you be the one in the tale you told me, the one who loves me, the one who tells the god of my passing, so that he looks up.

Let it not be that he frowns in ignorance, nor peers at you in puzzlement. Let it be that he leafs backwards through the book and knows just where to find me, so that he hears me again in the terrible mountain mist that has fallen all around. Let it not be that so many years of untruth have turned my voice to the silent mouthing of the fishes. Let it be that he draws his chair up by the fire with eagerness and begins again, because it is good to. Let it be that way. Let it be that way, Brother Fredo. Let it be that way.

Your young friend,
    Maris 'Blue' Burneau

III

Burneau's God

I

It was a beautiful sunny day!

It was.

One could see everything.

It looked as if one could.

Like the green silk of an island surface, with its darker central forests and its one bone of a mountain to the south-west.

Like the great blue bay cut into the island. Such a blue, and the curving promontory at its north edge, silver with human settlement. Badeo Town, this was, island capital and north-ernmost point. Thin white wakes of ships crossing the bay. Darker water far out.

The melted coins of other places: a sprawling second town at the south end of the bay, its southernmost reaches creep-ing to the mountain; a sliver of town by the sea in the north-east, another in the south-east corner. Threads of roads between all towns. Great green openness too.

Two tiny islands off the harbour at Badeo. Larger islands out to the west, one with a settlement. All islands fringed with the white of broken waves, where one thing meets the other thing and something else becomes restless.

The silence of it all. The permanence. Both permanence and silence diminish as one gets closer, then one bends to the ground to see the creatures moving, and Badeo Town is alive with them, like a burrow, a hive, a bloodstream. So much movement, so many places, so many journeys to be made be-tween them now! Green parklands, broad highways, chaotic patterns of streets out towards the harbour. Much steam and stink from there. Grand in the centre, set in a plot of green, a

Palace. It would be interesting to see who abides there, who it is that presumes to have the power to keep the creatures moving.

One could bring him out here, one could teach him what one knows. That the closer one looks, the more there is, the less one sees, the more one misses. As one gets near, the world gets away. It begins, it becomes, for to look is to make. One should teach this on a beautiful sunny day to a man who presumes to have power over creatures, who presumes to see everything, everyone, everywhere. One should teach it to oneself. For if one does not know this: how can the bony man?

He sat behind a great desk, a bony man with glasses. He had the largest room in the Palace. He had helped to bring about a Revolution, in that there was a different man at the desk, but the desk was the same, and the room was the same, and the Palace was the same. He was the President of the Island, and that was the same Island.

He looked a little strained – perhaps because he had preferred the days before all the new responsibilities were placed on his hunched shoulders. Perhaps he was remembering those days. They were not so long ago. He played with a letter opener.

A young man came to him, was shown that he should sit down opposite the President, and did so. It was evident that the two men knew each other, that they had passed hours of enjoyable fellowship. But now the President had problems to share with the young man, and he wasted no time in introducing them.

'Once again,' said the President, 'this prisoner exchange.'

'It's set for tomorrow, Mr President,' said the young man quickly, bringing his hands together.

'There's a snag, Minister.'

The young man did not look old enough to be a Minister, so he must have been very talented or in some way valuable to the President. The President, who, judging by the name of the broadest thoroughfare in Badeo Town, was called Iaio Gabril, handed the young man a photograph of a thin man without hair.

'Minister, who is this?'

The Minister seemed to draw a sharp breath, then sat back, shrugged, put the photograph down on the desk, and said he didn't know.

'You wouldn't,' the President told him. 'This is a photograph of a prisoner-of-war. His name is Quentine. He's due to be shipped to the Domain at dawn tomorrow, on the *Leonor*.'

'So, he's part of the fifty-fifty exchange then, Mr President? Good.'

'Mr Burneau,' said President Gabril, 'Look again. Look closely.'

The young man, who did not even look old enough to be addressed as 'Mr Burneau', looked at the photograph again, shook his head several times, and sat back. He took out a little white cloth and wiped his cheek. He seemed a little agitated.

The President sighed and leaned forward.

'As I say, there is a problem. Could you not be persuaded that this may plausibly be a picture of Federico Tragolani with his head shaved?'

Burneau looked for a third time. It was sad to see a young important man lose his poise so quickly.

'Well. It's . . . a likeness. A likeness of him.'

'More than a likeness, wouldn't you say, Maris? Surely this is your friend, your comrade, my student, my soldier. Our man. Now can you think of any reason whatever why he should have cut off all his hair and attempted to masquerade as a prisoner-of-war?'

'Nothing immediately comes to mind,' Burneau said quite loudly, 'if it is him. Has he been arrested?'

'As in "stopped", yes,' said the President, sitting back and sliding the blade of his letter opener flat along his upper lip: 'As in "marched away to the deepest stronghold without so much as his deck of cards" – no. He's been diverted from the other prisoners scheduled for the voyage. We had him moved to the Displaced Women and Children's Hostel on Kina. We kept him apart from them, goes without saying. I wondered, Maris, if perhaps you were not the best person to go and have a word with him, find out what's gone wrong. I know he took it hard, losing Amadora, we all did – it was worse for you than anyone. I mean it's clear to me that you loved her, Maris, if not to anyone else. But we really don't need Federico let loose in the Argeline at this stage. He knows more about our organisation than I do. Though that's not saying much these days, I grant you.'

Burneau frowned and nodded. 'You think he – may have lost his mind in some way?'

'Don't you? Sad as it is to confess, that's what I fervently hope has happened. For what's the alternative, Maris? That he's a sane, four-square, calculating traitor of the lowest order.'

'Right. Did he have any belongings with him?'

'Just some papers. Personal documents, forged. Oh, and some letters, I believe.'

There was a long pause in the room. It was possible during that pause to notice what a very beautiful day it was, with the sunshine streaming in through the great arched window, as well as how splendid was all the gilt and crimson furniture in the office of President Gabril. It was a very long pause.

Lightly, Burneau said: 'Has anyone checked over those, you know, letters?'

'Oh no. You see, what we don't want, Maris, is for Federico to think there's anything wrong. He's our friend, our comrade. It's delicate, delicate . . . He's been told that all fifty prisoners are being separated for a final debriefing before their deportation. So, as far as he knows, this is all routine. His letters and documents are all with him.'

'Good,' said Burneau with an odd little gasp, 'it's best not to scare him.'

'Well, I wouldn't, Maris, I wouldn't scare a friend.'

'It would be – bad to, yes.'

'We've all been through a lot since we came back.'

'We have,' agreed the young Minister.

'How's the wound?'

'Healing. Thank you, Mr President.'

No wound was immediately obvious on the person of the young Minister, but, as he walked back out of the President's office, it was possible to see that he had a pronounced limp and seemed very much aware of some discomfort in his side; more aware, in fact, than he had been when he entered the room. One also noted for the first time that his left hand was bandaged. He carried on walking along the corridor until he reached what must have been his own office, which was lit by dim electric light and had no windows. It would be interesting to know why, once he had sat down at his own desk, he shut his eyes, rested his head on his good hand and stayed like that for ages.

There was an attractive sunbleached hotel on the little island of Kina, the first of two islands off the northernmost cape of Badeo Town. The closer one looked at this hotel, however, the clearer it became that this was no hotel at all, but a kind of holding place for people without houses or flats. It must have been the place the President had mentioned to Minister Burneau. It takes only five minutes to sail there in a boat, but it was during the course of this short but invigorating – and indeed recommended – boat trip that one next observed the young Minister, neat and tidy and equipped with a smart briefcase, but staring dully into the sea-spray, getting his light blue suit wet. One could not resist following his progress into a small room in the basement of the former hotel on Kina, where he was taken by warders to meet none other than that thin man without hair, as seen in the photograph, who was slouched at a small table with a green baize cloth on it, and dealing himself four hands of playing cards.

As soon as the Minister was alone with the hairless man he called him 'Federico' and tried to shake his hand. But the latter raised two fingers into a sort of V shape and made a gesture as if to snip the Minister's hand down the middle of the palm. This was not a prisoner at all, it seemed, for the two young men then held a lively and friendly discussion, at the end of which the Minister left the room, went to a reception area, signed some papers, then came back with yellow duplicates of them.

'You're ill, Tragolani, remember,' said Burneau. 'Ill's your one hope. I'll hire you to work for me, then Gabril will forget about it.'

'Work for you?' said the hairless man, arching the area where his eyebrows would have been, 'Sorry, Burneau, but I had enough of you at Liberat.'

'I saw Gabril today. He doesn't want you to be a problem. But, if you're not ill, you're a traitor in his book for trying to skip it to the Domain. So shut up, get your sack and come with me. I've signed for your release.'

'How did he penetrate my disguise?' wondered Tragolani.

'Gambler's eyes,' said Burneau. 'Now give me the letter.'

'What letter's that, boss?'

Burneau blanched. 'The letter for the monk in the Koborol, of course. Give it to me. It's why you were meant to be on that boat. Remember?'

'Monk, letter, hmm ... Quite gone, Maris. Boss. That's the thing with hair, you see. That hair had a lot of memory twined up in it, and what's happened is clear. I've been – '

'This is your release paper, Federico. Give me back my letter or I'll rip this up and throw it in the ocean.'

'Here it is. Only a joke. Really, Burneau, I can see that old ministerial grind has worn out your sense of humour.'

Tragolani took a crumpled little package out of his sack and handed it to Burneau, who shut it in his smart briefcase and snapped the lid down.

'I would have done it,' said Tragolani sadly.

'Done what?'

'Taken it, boss. Taken it to the Land of Blue.'

'Yes, I imagine,' Burneau muttered as he stood up. 'Stay here. I've something else to do in this place.'

One thing he had to do was to ask a uniformed woman in the reception area to allow him a brief meeting with one of the many people being held on Kina. The person he was allowed briefly to meet was a hungry-looking girl of about twenty, dressed in dark green overalls. She was always shaking slightly.

Once Burneau was alone with this girl, sitting across a table from her (in a room identical to the one where he had met Tragolani) and looking at her intensely – compassionately, one would have to say, though it is easy to be mistaken about that kind of expression – he moved both his hands towards hers, and they both darted away. Burneau sat back and sighed. 'Why did you ask to see me?'

The girl said, almost inaudibly, 'Cobar.'

'The island?'

The girl stared.

'Cobar the island?' Burneau repeated in the same patient voice.

She nodded.

'He's on Cobar? He's a prisoner on Cobar?'

The girl nodded, then said hoarsely: 'One of the children, they let him come here, he's a rich man's son. He works there, in a mine. Paol was there. In the mine. On C-C-Cobar . . .'

As she started to shiver and cry, Burneau went round to her side of the table, but when he tried to warm her up by rubbing her shoulders and pressing himself to her back, she shrank away and said no more to him.

This was such a sad moment to witness, because one could not help observing some remnants of strong feeling between the two young people. As the girl was being led away, and

Burneau was heatedly instructing the warders to improve the regime for the Displaced Women and Children, both of them, the young man and the girl, stared hard for an instant. But these were instants that did not match, each staring as the other turned. Nobody likes to see that happen, even with what may be mere remnants of love.

Indeed, so lamentable an encounter it was, that one felt disinclined to witness any further connected incidents for several days afterwards, and sadly rose away again to indulge the most pleasant of all one's infinite pastimes, the mere contemplation of that excellent shining island from the high point where motion becomes caught between shimmering mirage and stillness itself, where silence blooms on the wind.

It would be easy by now to have formed the impression that the inhabitants of the island of Badeo do nothing with themselves all day other than sit on either side of desks or tables and impart or absorb information.

Nothing could be further from the truth. One has seen them in their thousands, dawdling or rushing up and down the great boulevards of the capital, driving their vans at speed along the crowded highways towards the coastal resorts (or sailing to the sparkling new citadel of Casino New Badeo across the Bay, with its newly opened hotels and pleasure houses) or one can see them slouching and spitting in the packed bars and parlours of the market district, farming, fishing, felling trees and milling all about the island, where there are no desks nor offices to be seen for many miles.

It is just that sometimes a story can be followed, and, in the early summer of that year (a lovely year, with every season bringing its most welcome gifts to the doors of the Badeans) one could hardly pass a day without seeing the young Minister Maris Burneau forswearing the sunshine and leisure of his lesser citizens for the anxieties of hushed and hint-filled interviews like the following.

264

'Cobar?' said President Iaio Gabril. 'That's not a prison, Maris. It's a crucial element of the mining industry.'

'No,' Burneau protested, 'that's what you told me to tell the Free Network. You yourself confided to me that it's a prison. I've got a note of it in my office.'

'Tuh, caught out again,' said President Gabril affably. One could tell he had eaten a splendid breakfast. 'Well, what of it, Maris? Shall we send them Federico? Send him down a mine, huh? that'll teach him.'

'Don't worry about him, he's in my flat. He's feeling better. No, what I was wondering, Mr President, is whether you might consider an, er, amnesty for the prisoners on Cobar. Many of them, for example, are young Badeans, not really old enough to have understood the complexities of the conflict. Others are frail, others are potential breadwinners whose wives and daughters are subsisting on handouts in hostels – simply because their men are down the mines on Cobar. We could save money, you see, that way.'

President Iaio Gabril stretched out, his feet pressed up against the legs of his desk, so that his great chair started sliding him away as if on rails. He yawned enormously.

'They're traitors, Burneau, you recall? They fought for the Domain. For our dominion status.'

His feet parted from the legs of the desk and clopped resoundingly on the polished floor. Burneau ventured:

'I believe it would be a popular act of mercy, Mr President. We know there's no prospect of them trying to stoke the flames again. There'd be no support for them, and the people are so weary of fighting.'

'And who, Mr Blue, is going to work the mines on Cobar?'

'Well . . .' said Burneau, shifting forward uneasily, 'that's another thing you confided to me, Mr President. That there aren't in fact any useful minerals on Cobar, just a sort of grey pebble dust that the miners think is platinum.'

'Oh. Did I tell you that one too?'

'You did, sir, that night you opened the keg of Las Gideu.'

'That stuff just lifts my heart up by the handle and fills its four goblets. Mmm ... Good, though, isn't it? Platinum. Ha!'

'Yes, I think I'd be fooled,' Burneau conceded.

'Funny thing is, they keep finding these wretches trying to stuff their pockets full of it and swim for Badeo. So they drown trying to smuggle home pebbles! You have to admit!'

When the President's high, jagged laughter had subsided to a smirk, Burneau spoke again: 'They're young and old men, mostly, and I think you would gain remarkable support.'

Gabril wiped the smile off his own face.

'You don't have to be middle-aged to be a collaborator, Maris.'

'True, Mr President.'

'What would Amadora have done?'

'Captain Nunez would have called an amnesty, Mr President.'

'She flaming would not,' Gabril retorted.

'I suppose she wouldn't,' sighed Burneau.

'She was made of harder stuff. Platinum, yes? Well. You know, Maris. You loved her. No, don't worry, that one will die with me. Have I – have I asked you this before? Did she speak before she died?'

'You have asked me,' Burneau said gravely. 'She didn't speak. She died instantly. We never saw them, sir.'

'How's the wound?'

'Healing. Thank you.'

As Burneau was about to go, the President cleared his throat to halt him at the door.

'Our friend Tragolani ...'

'What about him, Mr President?'

'What was he playing at?'

'Well. Vengeance, sir. Like you said, it was losing Nunez. He wanted some Argelinos to pay, he said he wanted to die doing that. I have him back at my place, he's feeling better. The air is clear to him again.'

266

'Tell him he's a mad dog, tell him I look forward to beating him at any game he chooses, even with his infernal rigged deals!'

As far as one can follow this episode, by observing the puzzling young man Burneau and collating his many interviews, one would have to conclude that the story about Tragolani wanting vengeance for 'losing Nunez' is a falsehood. There is certainly some reason why that man without hair pretended to be a prisoner-of-war, and it is impossible to conclude anything other than that the crumpled package which he returned to Minister Burneau was of some significance. Neither man would appear to be the vengeful sort – one hopes that nobody would be – but neither man could be said to have so far been wholly straightforward in his dealings with the island's chief figure of authority, or rather, he on the island who believes he has most power. One is curious. For now, that is all. One will not let the young man, or the man without hair, or the hungry girl, or the man who believes he has most power on the island, vanish into the crowds. One will listen and learn, eavesdrop into the truth.

If one is curious about something, one can do a good deal worse than the following: take a single word, or a single act, commit it to memory, that is to say, paint its outline quite indelibly on one's inner eye and ear, then cast about the world outside in search of it. One attempts this now, at this point, and two potentially significant discoveries are made.

Passing through the swarming crowds of Badeo Town, listening out for the word 'amnesty', one happened only that afternoon upon a milk-faced adolescent sitting at a dimly lit bar, in the market district of Allalong. He was slurring out some vexation to a patient old barman.

'Forgive 'em for fighting, Cyrille . . . Forgive 'em for killing, Cyrille . . . Forgive 'em for – what else? If you're going to forgive 'em for fighting the rebs, forgive 'em for killing the rebs, you may as well not have a thing called Crime, or a thing called Evil, or a thing called Good for that matter! Just have a thing called Time, and let it heal, Cyrille, let it deal and heal and seal . . .'

'You never been no prisoner, son, you never been hup and em down the p'rade-ground wit no choice in no matter, eh? War's over, son. Now all's healing time and ain't no better than.'

'Forgive the Argelinos . . . well, why not invite them *all* to tea on Badeo, *all* to tea together! Forgive 'em that way. We can drink Amnes-tea. Amnes-tea. Amnesia! Amnesias-tea!'

'Shut you up there, you a no good truant, Magnick.'

'For-give-me, Bar Man, I'll have one cup of Amnes-tea. And you'll have one on me, wont'cha?'

'Well, if it go by the name of Froschem . . .'

Further pursuit of the word 'amnesty' leads one to where thousands and thousands of newspapers are spinning through a monstrous oil-black engine that is printing the day's date on each one, and what they are saying, every one of them, is

MERCY FROM ON HIGH – IT'S AMNESTY FOR COBAR!

Find the heart of power, learn the words that are spoken there, tail them into the world outside, watch what happens to them then. Never let them out of your sight, never.

One does it with a word, so. One can also do this with an action. The 'scissor' gesture employed by the hairless Trago-lani upon the amicable extended hand of Burneau was suddenly echoed several times, with astonishing frequency, somewhere far from Badeo. Coincidentally, this happened on the prison island of Cobar. What was seen here took place at the entrance to a mine.

It was the very middle of the night, and three men were squatting down by a meagre fluttering fire, again and again thrusting out their right hands towards each other, either as fists or palms or that same two-fingered 'scissor' gesture, following each manual confrontation with a hiss of triumph, a cluck of defeat, or the respectful silence of the stand-off. They were playing for heaps of pebbles. The largest, quietest man had the most pebbles. After long enough, all their right hands grew tired. They played with their left hands and their left hands wearied too, at which point the shorter, more talkative pair conceded defeat to their hunched comrade.

'You're this rich giant, Yung,' said one.

'Ah,' said the big man, 'the night dealt that.'

'He goes,' mocked the third man, 'like he always goes. Never no skill with him, never no skill. 'Nother round, Adzell?'

'Nohand,' said the one who had spoken first. 'I'm this tired poor dog. I'm a platinum sleepwalker, I'm crawling to the cabins.'

'Fair enough,' said the mocking one. 'Big man?'

'I carry me off too, Mace, is the time,' said Yung, swaying to his great height.

As the one called Adzell also arose, Mace said evenly from the ground: 'Ain't we all just forgot somethin' there?'

'Mm-hmm,' went Adzell, 'the pledging hour . . .'

'Squat down, boys.'

'Nohand,' said Yung affably, and he stooped to lift Mace bodily off the ground in his great arms: 'This night we pledge our pledge on our feet. Too much of me to be north and south all hours.'

The three men performed the following ritual – ritual, for sure, so practised it seemed.

Mace, the one who had been lifted up, now raised his hand, flat, palm forward. Adzell, as the firelight caught a sallow face with sunken eyes, snipped it with his scissor-hand – just as Tragolani had done to Burneau's – then Yung, the giant, gently crushed Adzell's 'scissors' with his rock of a fist. Then Mace wrapped, as far as he could wrap, that fist in his hand.

'Blue death by paper,' he said.

'Blue death by scissors,' said Adzell.

269

'Blue death by stone,' said Yung.

'When Freedom comes,' said all three together, 'comes blue death.'

This ritual enactment had the effect of making them all nod to each other and move off into the darkness. It had also become clear what on earth they had been doing with their six hands, which one had been wondering.

It is no game for one player, though, adapt it how you will. Now utter dark descended over the stone isle of Cobar.

II

Burneau reacted very badly to seeing the list of one thousand prisoners liberated by the Merciful Amnesty. He slammed the manifest down on his desk and said: 'He's not there. He's not even there!'

He repeated these words to that same underfed girl the next time he visited the Hostel for Displaced Women and Children on the island of Kina: 'He's not there, Juilla, his name's not among them.'

'It is – he was seen!'

'Look for yourself!' cried Burneau in exasperation, throwing the manifest down again.

Juilla picked it up with a slender brown hand, leafed through several pages towards whatever name it was she was looking for, stared at where presumably it was not to be found, then looked up at Burneau, her face crumpling.

'He's not there,' she moaned, and jerked into protracted sobbing.

Burneau did again what he had done so clumsily the first time, and edged around to behind the desk.

The same thing happened. Juilla shrank away with a shriek of anguish, and warders came in and started being kind to her.

Then, however, something happened that was different to last time. Although the girl appeared to be staring at Burneau, as the warders led her gently but firmly from the interview room, he, for his own part, ignored her completely. His gaze was fixed upon the list of a thousand names. He was looking at a name under M. He then riffled the pages right back to the beginning and nodded his head wildly up and down the A columns.

What happened next was no surprise. He flipped the manifest over and began zigzagging his finger across the Xs, Ys and Zs. There were no Xs or Zs. He sat back and did not move at all for a long time.

One can simply wait. Stories leap and settle with their own pretty chronology. This man is ahead of nobody now, the mist is clearing from all about him. What the Minister had discovered had made him afraid. Is there any wonder? For it was certain, when he first greeted the hairless man Tragolani, how weak a player Burneau was at that singular game of hands that would seem to be the prime accomplishment of those three desperate, dangerous, free men.

'What do you mean you don't think there should be an Amnesty?' demanded President Iaio Gabril with much irritation, as Burneau almost collapsed against his desk: 'It was, was it not, you own flaming idea?'

'Sir, sir,' Burneau panted, sweat showing clearly down the back and sides of his light blue suit. 'President Gabril: I saw some of those names of prisoners – they're diehards, sir, they're NSDs, they're the worst of the worst, they're – '

'Tots and grandads, you said before! You can't have it both ways.'

'There's three, sir, three in particular, sir . . .'

'What three? I can't liberate 997 and keep three locked up to dig for pebbles on their own! Who do you think I am?'

'B-B-Bodyguards, sir, I think – '

'You want bodyguards?' spluttered the President. 'You don't need bodyguards. You're the most popular Minister there is, Burneau – you've the eternal gratitude of the People! Now, be on your way and – '

'The Viceroy's bodyguards, Gabril, sir, they were the Viceroy's bodyguards, the time I killed him. They were the ones who were there when he died.'

272

'I see. Well maybe you shouldn't have killed him,' Gabril observed testily.

'What?'

'You're too late, Burneau! Too late!' The President got to his feet and thundered: 'I went against every other Minister's counsel to effect your damnable, soft-boiled, soft-brained Amnesty for Murderers, and now it's done, it's done, and they're sailing to Badeo as we speak, and I'll hear no more about it! It's your Amnesty, Burneau, they're your murderers!'

But the Minister got his bodyguards, four of them, tall, broad-shouldered students from the ranks of what was once the Organ Liberat Badeon. In addition to this taciturn four, who marched or crouched or crept along in awe of the legendary young man, he had Federico Tragolani, whose hair had now grown back into short spikes, and who generally stalked him from a certain distance, looking out for danger. He carried wine in a goatskin flask. He was an unusual kind of bodyguard. He seemed to be Burneau's only real friend. When Burneau wanted to talk to him, usually at night, sharing Tragolani's wine as they strolled along the boulevards, it was his four professional protectors who hung back in the dark. Burneau was never alone now. He was not supposed to be.

He had taught Tragolani everything he knew about guarding a man with one's life. 'Eyes everywhere, Federico, eyes everywhere. Now you might think the danger is a man who flashes a dagger, or a man who waves his stick in the air, or a boy with blazing eyes, who rummages in his pockets, or a madwoman with some – '

'I get this,' said Tragolani. 'I get this. They're not dangerous, you're saying?'

They were walking together, early one evening about a week after the Amnesty took effect and Burneau was given his armed guards, walking down the Avenue Sudin, a narrow, poorly-lit street in the market district. Burneau was wearing jet-black sunglasses, which is how one locates him easily on the island, and he was twitchy, agitated, talkative. He had finished Tragolani's flask of Saldean Red Pilgrim, an especially potent brand of fortified wine that was popular with the market traders, and Tragolani was now looking for a bar where he could fill it up again. Burneau pointed a finger at nothing in particular, as if to remind them both that there was still a question to answer.

'That's it, they're not dangerous! There are explanations for them! The danger is a woman, the dangers are the eyes of a woman, the left eye and the right eye . . .'

'I'll note that,' said Tragolani. 'Left eye, and – what was it?'

'This is serious, Tragolani, serious,' Burneau insisted, looking warily from side to side down alleyways, up into windows, behind him, ahead. 'I know these things to be true!'

'What do they do, then, this team of serious eyes, eh, boss?'

'They look at you, that's one, then you look at them, that's two, then – '

'They shoot you somehow?' Tragolani finished, taking back his empty flask and uncorking it hopefully.

'You follow them. You follow them, you turn, and then . . . you're lost, Tragolani, you're not where you were meant to have been!'

'Hmm. And where were you meant to have been, boss?'

'You were not meant to have got here yet,' the Minister said grimly.

He was no more coherent when they reached a bar named All Afternoons, south of Sudin in the Allalong district.

'We'll have a beer in this hole,' said Tragolani. 'Settle you down.'

'Anything. Anywhere,' Burneau muttered. 'Just keep your eyes open.'

The two of them went in and squeezed on to a couple of

barstools, taking no interest in Burneau's four government agents, who sidled in discreetly and dispersed about the smoky room. Nobody there seemed to think it odd that four men in identical dark blue suits sat separately, watchfully about the place. The pale young drinker Magnick, described earlier as a 'no good truant', was slumped at the corner of the bar, but he piped up eagerly when he saw two strangers, one in sunglasses, take their places beside him.

'Buy these secret police two large Magnicks. Each, Cyrille.'

Burneau suddenly looked up startled, stared at Magnick, stared at the barman, then burrowed down into his overcoat. Magnick went on, 'But softly, softly . . . they are verily in a guise . . .'

'Shut up, kid,' said Tragolani, 'we're on duty here.'

'Oh, you too?' said the youngster sweetly. 'So pleasant a thing is duty, I do think. We any crimes to report here, Cyrille?'

'Young man 'n' old wine,' muttered the barman to Tragolani. 'You'll drink beer, officers?'

'Yeah, yeah,' said Tragolani. 'Wake up, Inspector,' he hissed to Burneau, who was beginning to rock gently, while still subsiding into his clothes.

'How now,' Magnick chuckled, ' 'tis a man whose state makes me sober as a girl is . . . I salute this officer, and note with pleasure this surprising development in the short history of the Free Badean Security Police!'

'Shut your fuckin' head up,' Tragolani snapped. 'He's not an officer, he's a suspect in a case.'

Burneau came to life, crying: 'I'm innocent of whatever!'

The barman Cyrille turned round and stared hard at Burneau. 'Is peculiar now . . . ' he murmured.

Magnick chattered on: 'Of what do you suspect him, officer? Take a tip from an alpha schoolboy – you suspect him of having an identity? Then take off his mask and identify the identity!'

He reached across playfully towards Burneau's sunglasses,

but Tragolani beat his arm away so sharply that Magnick knocked his own tall cocktail over, splattering it across the bar.

'Help, emergency, suspect spillage!'

'We're police, kid – I mean, I am. It means you leave us alone, right?'

In all four corners of the room, the government men, who had risen rapidly in absolute silence, resumed their various activities: sitting, drinking, smoking, watching.

The barman Cyrille, having wiped his bar of sticky white fluid from Magnick's glass, pushed a beer in front of Burneau and said: 'You'll have a Frosch, eh sir? Old time, like?'

Burneau looked up, his head tipping uncontrollably back with the sudden motion: 'Thank you, Cyrille, so I shall do . . .'

Now it was Tragolani's turn to look round in surprise, having hitherto kept his eyes trained on the pouting adolescent Magnick, and he demanded of Burneau: 'How do you know his name?'

'We got no secrets, Mr Police,' said the barman, pouring a second Frosch for Tragolani. 'Mr Frosch here, he safe with us, we talk on old times, eh?'

Tragolani looked nonplussed.

'What is this, boss? You know these losers?'

A silver-haired man who had said nothing previously now observed: 'You said he was a suspect. You can't suspect your "boss", my good friend . . .'

But it was Magnick, the intoxicated youth, who, seized by a great surge of recognition, stood on the base of his barstool and yelled at the top of his voice: 'Well you can smear me with you if it ain't our old pal Burneau, the Blue Devil of Badeo!'

Now there was consternation in the bar, as Magnick made another lunge for the Minister's sunglasses: this time Tragolani pushed his hand into the youngster's gleaming face. Cyrille was shaking Burneau heartily by the shoulders, while

276

the man himself, obviously confused by his own drinking, beamed peaceably and sank lower in his coat. Soon the government bodyguards were everywhere, armed and again in shades, saying, 'There's nothing to see here,' as they hauled the ministerial party out of All Afternoons, Tragolani riled and struggling for a fight with the taunting Magnick, who had managed to bite his finger to the bone, and Burneau waving serenely to a whole host of drinkers who had suddenly, in the way of all drinkers, loved him for years.

But it is the exception who always catches the eye. One man, part of the raucous card-playing crowd near the door, though participating in neither cards nor celebration, made his abrupt movement not when the jostling started by the bar, but when the word 'Burneau' was shouted from there. His abrupt movement caught the eye especially, because it consisted of his hand leaving the pocket of his overcoat, parting two fingers in a 'scissor' motion, snapping them back in place to make 'paper', rolling them into 'stone'. It was a convulsive private gesture that he seemed altogether incapable of controlling, but no sooner perceived than it was over, and he stuffed his hand back in his pocket like a gun. Then he was just another drinker among many, wordlessly watching the disturbance and the strangers. And that's all he was until the government agents had helped Tragolani and the Minister of Reconciliation firmly from the establishment and their noise had been sloshed out into the street like dirty water, at which point the eye-catching man (beyond doubt, as he rose, one of the three who played the Game of Hands on the prison island of Cobar) downed his beer and followed them where they went. It would not be without interest to learn where it was they went, but in the darkness and chaos of this city at night one cannot always be sure. Better perhaps in the meantime to establish the shape of what one has seen so far, in the hope of furnishing some framework for a possibly happy conclusion. One has always been of the opinion that a happy conclusion is best, and, frankly, if matters become excessively daunting for the intrepid and duplicitous Burneau, well, there are plenty of other stories to pursue, many many other ways to grace the unending bright hours. So . . .

It is to be supposed with a degree of conviction that this young man Maris Burneau did not intend that when a thousand labourers were freed on his personal recommendation of clemency from the prison island of Cobar, there would be among them the three men who had said to each other: 'Blue death by paper, blue death by scissors, blue death by stone, when freedom comes, comes blue death.' The liberation of these men had already altered the Minister's facial aspect considerably, quickened his walk but also made it range noticeably from side to side, and minimised in the extreme his public appearances by daylight.

Equally, it is to be supposed that what was intended – the liberation of the lost brother of the distressed hungry girl Juilla – had not been achieved, because her information concerning her brother's whereabouts was not accurate.

The liberation of the loathers of blue, as one may term them, is likely to be the reason for the increased security around the person of Burneau.

The continued absence of the lost brother, one may speculate, and the consequent sustained hostility of his sister towards the Minister, one may further speculate, might answer for his recourse to strong drink. Behind strong drink there often seems to lie a virtuous trapped emotion, and one hazards it may be sexual love. That would explain some phenomena.

What does he have on his side? The protection of four hired bodyguards and idiosyncratic aid of a fifth, the unpredictable Tragolani. In theory, the support of the President. Friendship, in the form of individuals one can presume he knew in an earlier period, such as the kindly Cyrille, the fervent Magnick, and the nodding old men in the bar. Love, then, in the sense that he shows no signs of giving up.

What does he have against him? Love, in the sense that he

278

may make mistakes in his hurry to pursue it. Vengeance, an implacable foe. Adzell – that's his name – whose hands move as fast as a hare bolts from a man. Mace, Yung. One furious like fire, one patient like water. Drink, which may lead him into danger. Danger, which may lead him back to drink. Time.

Which is the stronger suit? Time will tell. Note: Time *will* tell. It never tells. It always *will* tell. By the Time does tell, one no longer needs to know. It is not unlike a drunken man who, attempting to maximise his effects, leaves his anecdote too late to impress the company. This makes Time unloved by many, when it too, bound and innocent, is deserving of pity. What Time does not understand is that Man does not find anything about it very funny. Not the jokes, not the tricks, not the props, not the costume. Time thinks it's just his timing has gone. No, it's all his material. One feels the need to protect Burneau from this talentless gag-merchant, who refuses to tell whether he will live out life in the sweet company of others or die the lone blue death.

But one has to know now!

Oh, there is no need to become personally involved, one does admit that. And this individual may have done atrocious things that one missed while one was gazing out into space.

But one missed them. One was gazing out into space.

I WAS WRONG. NOT COBAR. MISCOBAR. IT'S A SECRET. IT'S A PRISON. PAOL IS THERE REALLY. MEET ME 7 MALDEAU. SUNSET TONIGHT. YOUR ALL I GOT. JULAX. /// TO MINISTER BURNEAU. AND PRIVATE.

Burneau sat down at his desk, and reread this letter. He had picked it out of the morning's pile of Reconciliation Pleas. What there was about the envelope that had caught his eye one tries to ascertain, clearly something had. Among more than a hundred letters addressed to him, the most strikingly different aspect of this one envelope was a little drawing, of a man and a woman saying together, their words wrapped up in a fluffy cloud over their heads, DON'T DO IT, CARLI! It was quite well drawn. It was not what you would normally send to a Minister, and it made no obvious sense. One has met nobody of that name since these persistently connected incidents first caught the eye. Curious how such an intense sentiment, such a shrill plea for life or love, is clothed in a form so childishly comic. It seems in some way familiar.

It was another beautiful and fantastic day over the island of Badeo. One does not mean to keep stressing this, but it seems relevant to that day, because it means that Burneau's excuses for looking as fouled up as he did that morning were wholly of his mind's own creation. His body, left to itself, as one would ideally have it left, should have been singing, or dancing. Probably singing.

As it was, he was able to sweep his one opened letter (the decorated note from 'Julax') clear on to the tiled floor just in time to evade the foam of spew with which he splattered the unopened remainder.

One maintains nonetheless that the sun shone brightly and all around the island its light glittered off the green ocean!

By the time President Iaio Gabril stepped in through the velvet door that led to his own office, Burneau was sitting upright at his desk with a fixed smile. The desk, apart from the twin towers of claims that rose towards the ceiling on the two corners furthest from him, was clean and clear.

'Everything all right, Maris?' enquired the President.

'Mm-hmmm, sir,' said he, smiling his fixed smile.

'What's this I'm hearing about some bar in Allalong? Federico get you in some trouble there?'

'Not so, Mr President. Not so. Urk. Pardon.'

'Maris, stick with the men I gave you. That's an order. You may need them. Some of your settlements are not so popular as I would have wished.'

'No, sir?'

280

'Nobody said it would be easy to settle this chaos. Nor govern this rabble.'

'It's not, sir.'

'They don't know what's good for them.'

'No, sir. They don't,' smiled Blue Burneau.

'What is?'

'What's what, sir?'

'What *is* good for them, Minister?'

'We are, Mr President.'

Iaio Gabril took a deep breath.

'You stick with those four men, Maris. Good men. Crack men. And watch yourself. Maintain a distance from your work.'

'I shall, sir. These are turbulent – ' Burneau's choice of the adjective 'turbulent' was an unhappy one, seeing as how it developed very readily into a huge belch, but he soldiered on – 'times, Mr President.'

'Indeed. Now all the vines are stripped and bare, the grape is in the mind,' said Gabril for some reason. 'And on its branches . . .' He broke off.

'Are you all right, Mr President?'

'Now all the vines are stripped and bare, the grape is . . . ' The President sniffed. 'Someone heave in here?'

'A claimant, sir,' the Minister lied. 'His point was taken.'

'Turbulent indeed. Stick with those men, Burneau. That's an order. We are all responsible for our own safety. Bodyguards have been known to fail. The case of Viceroy Lagland, for example. Shot.'

'Indeed, Mr President.'

'Viceroy Bize. Blown to bits.'

'He was.'

'Our own Amadora.'

'Sad but true, sir.'

'Cases of the dead.'

'That's just right, President Gabril,' sighed the young man philosophically. 'Death came to them.'

'Don't let him come to you, Maris. Who else can settle these claims for me?'

'I can think of nobody, sir.'

'That's who there is, Maris.'

When the President was gone again, Burneau stooped to pick up the fallen letter from 'Julax' (presumably the same person as 'Juilla', the thin displaced girl, though one suspects that it may not have been from her at all, merely because it's made of *paper*, and a man more alert than this might profitably have been as wary of accepting anything in that medium as he would have been of accepting a pair of *scissors* in the abdomen or a *stone* on his head. Just a thought. Perhaps it really is from Juilla or 'Julax'. Time will tell), then he sat for a long time in his chair, reading it and rereading it.

One is reluctant to press the point that it could have been the gateway into a murderous trap, in view of the enormous pleasure it had evidently given him. For the next words spoken in his office were these, three times:

'Your all I got. Julax. Your all I got. Julax. Your all I got. Julax.'

Which reminds one, of course, one confesses with some embarrassment, that X means *kiss* on this heavenly warm island.

III

Seven Avenue Maldeau was somebody's house. Not that of Juilla, one would suppose, from the way in which she passed innocently by it every two and a half minutes, crossed the street a few yards up, came back, passed the house on the other side, crossed the street again and turned. It was not yet sunset because she was covered with golden light.

Clearly she was no longer housed upon Kina with the other women and children dependent on the Government, and, although she stepped along with all the nervousness of the recently displaced, it did appear that she was being better cared for somewhere. At least she was waiting for her meals as one of a small number. Certainly, she had been restored to a honey-coloured simple beauty that is, to be frank, what nature intended. But it was still not sunset, because her shoulders and bare arms were all an alluring amber colour.

She looked frequently down the street, up the street, up at windows, everywhere. She walked, crossed, turned, passed again. What a face went by! It was a frowning face without understanding, but it made one thing perfectly clear. It explained Burneau. Note how one can duel with logic and probability all night in the quest for a man's intent, but day will furnish you with an answer by sunset, and now it did set, stroking Juilla's hair with a brush of red leaves, then finishing its dusting on the Avenue Maldeau, leaving it quiet and warm and rustling busily in excited anticipation of the blue time.

Some plans are better than others. Maris Burneau came walking slowly, highly suspiciously, out of the Way of Limes and on to Maldeau in a long green coat, with a wispy grey

283

wig on his head and a woman's sunglasses. As soon as Juilla saw this figure, she walked hurriedly towards it. When she got there, Burneau said: 'Sshh. It's me.'

'I know. It's time.'

'Sorry about the disguise, Jula. I had to lose my guards. They think I'm ill in the, er, cubicle in my flat.'

'You got a flat somewhere . . .'

'I can't say where it is. I am constantly moved.'

They stood on the pavement, shifting uncomfortably in one another's light. A young couple crossed the street, hand in hand. Burneau watched them go by. He looked pretty miserable, as well as ridiculous, but when one sees a girl such as Juilla in this light, at this time, misery and ridicule are the least one can expect a man to suffer. Juilla said:

'You got a fever, mister?'

'No, they – they think I have. My guards. They think I'm in the, er, cubicle. Ill. I'm not allowed to be without them. I'm in danger, you see. Hence the disguise. I'm actually quite well.'

'I knew you. It was sunset.'

Burneau put his arm gently on her shoulder and moved her closer to him, in the shadow of the eaves of Seven Avenue Maldeau. He murmured: 'You know me because I'm all you've got.'

'What, mister?'

'Like you said in your note? "Your all I got"? That's true, in a way. Isn't it?'

'You've got to help me.'

'Jula, listen. You're all *I* got.'

'What, mister?'

Burneau swallowed and repeated clearly: 'You – are all I – have got.'

She didn't seem to get it. 'No,' she said. 'You're – all I got.'

'All right, all right,' Burneau nodded. 'Yes, I am. I'll do anything, Juilla, just say. You think Paol is on Miscobar? There's no one on Miscobar. It's not got any platinum.'

'What's that, mister?'

'Actually there's none on Cobar either. It's a lie, but never mind.'

'I got a letter.'

'Can I see it?'

'No, he told me burn it.'

'Who told you burn it?'

'He told me he can't tell me.'

'Who was he?' urged the Minister.

'A prisoner. He got out. Got out from Miscobar on a boat he made himself! Like all from wood. Then he said to me – '

'You met this man? He came to you?'

'No, no, in the letter.'

Burneau looked away, relieved, but one wonders if that might not prove rather premature, taking into account one's misgivings about anything communicated by way of paper. Juilla, surprisingly, pulled him back to face her.

'He said how his wife met me on Kina, where we were fed by the governors? His wife is called Sulsi, and we shared what we had. Talked about the folks we got missing in the war. She says about her man, on a prison isle, and I say to her about Paoli, him being lost, how he's so young, so young to be gone! This man, he says like he's thankful for me being a chum to his Sulsi, his wife, so he says he saw someone sounds just like Paol on Miscobar, where's there a little prison of twenty men? They dip in a swamp.'

'Dip in a swamp? What for?'

'Hmm . . . diamonds.'

'You sod, Gabril,' Burneau muttered.

'When Paoli's free, he'll bring some diamonds maybe? like this man – we'll buy a new house on Hali, find our father, our mother if we can, then all of us, and we'll be rich, then – '

'Hush, dear, hush. How can I get to Miscobar? I'm a Minister, there are bodyguards everywhere I go. I got away this time, but it isn't easy. Are you sure about this prison? I think the President would have told me. I mean, it was my

Amnesty. I did it for you, Jula. You know. Anyway, maybe it's a high-security prison, and no one's supposed to know, or . . .'

Juilla was gazing off down the street, not listening. When Burneau's excuses had petered out, she said in a soft, low, even voice: 'I want my brother home, Mister Blue. I want him home with me. He's all I got.'

'He is? No I am,' Burneau said, advancing on her in his long green coat.

'You won't go to the prison isle,' said Juilla.

'I will go,' said the Minister of Reconciliation.

'You go, mister,' said Juilla. 'you go, then you're both what I've got, I've got both of you home. Be like before, whatever that was – whatever that was like . . .'

Burneau simply stared at her. Her eyes still looked off into the distance, west towards the harbour, and yes, Cobar, Miscobar.

'I'll go, Juilla, and it'll be like it was before.'

'We'll see *Carli*,' she said.

'Carli went to heaven,' said Burneau, 'with the Stranger.'

'We'll see *Amador the Wine-Grower*.'

'I don't know that one.'

'It's new. We'll travel about, all over the Island.'

'We shall, Juilla Maricolo . . .'

'But come home to the fire . . .'

'We'll definitely have a fire!'

Now she looked at him.

'A home fire,' she said.

Then, by all that's sacred, after this entirely inexplicable private litany, she lifted up her face and kissed Burneau on the lips. Then she ran off down Avenue Maldeau towards the Promenad Furasol, and the gaily-coloured strung beacons of the Bay.

Burneau, after a considerable stillness, very slowly drew a wine-flask out of a deep pocket, lifted it up into the light of the very first stars, drank it all, replaced it in the pocket, and said very clearly and steadily:

'A home fire. A home fire.'

Then he went one way, and wig, sunglasses and long green coat stayed right where they were, in a heap on the Avenue Maldeau, the accessories of a gentleman who is no longer here.

There's a bodyguard called Cressler running in circles around the University. There's a bodyguard called Broder checking bars on the Avenue Marchant. There's a bodyguard called Paville demanding answers at the Hospital Infanta. There's a bodyguard called Ehew shaking his bullet head on the Avenue Strauber. 'Lost him,' moans Ehew in disbelief. 'Call yourself a bodyguard?' Then he runs off down the dark street, adjusting his sunglasses. One can see them because they are moving faster than anyone this evening, or faster than anyone but Federico Tragolani, who is haring around the Palace of Popular Valour like a fly caught in a jar. One knows all the names of bodyguards because they are written on them somewhere.

One might as well just wait by the door of All Afternoons. One might as well go inside, get a good table, sling one's coat over a chair, stroll up, get a drink, bring it back, and wait. Some things are bound to happen. Not bound to happen like growth or death or the loss of time, but bound to happen though they appear to be random, chancy, against the odds. The one agent that binds things to happen in the sphere of human comings and goings, that makes people arrive on time, reach a certain place, say a selected phrase, perform a determined act, is sex. Once in the long silken tether of that, nothing happens against the odds, nothing is that unlikely. To Burneau, one imagines, even the grave risk he runs by having slipped his bodyguards is diminished in the face of the promised joy. He will go where the people are who remind him of Juilla. He will go where he can drink, so the time will pass elsewhere. He will go where he can talk, so his words go out to the air she is somewhere breathing. He will have forgotten that he is not the one telling his story. So he will have forgotten he can die now, and his death be told by another. Here he comes now, as happy as he could be. Here he comes to the door of All Afternoons, warm inside.

'*Blue Burneau!*' cried everyone there, and the early evening crowd parted for his stately progress to the bar, parted for him but not so far that they couldn't thump him joyfully on the back as he wandered, and offer him draughts from their silver beakers.

He made it to the corner where the young drinker Magnick has always been sitting. He was again, and he was ready with a foaming glass of Frosch, as Burneau squeezed into the same stool as before. The silver-haired gentleman was next to him once again, Cyrille thinking peacefully behind the bar.

Magnick had started already. 'Where's your pal with the nine fingers? Off making an arrest?'

'That's right,' mumbled Burneau. 'Off making an arrest.'

'I thought he suspected you, Burneau,' said the silver-haired man, 'or so he said last night.'

'Idiot *docteur*,' said Magnick, 'that was part of their cover! Anyway, maybe he's not Burneau today. Maybe he's Frosch again! So, Burneau, I never did have the chance to tell you what an absolutely sodding feeble attempt at a pseudonym that was.'

'We all believed it,' said the doctor.

'Three nuns at the wheel of a firetruck did we,' the young man opined. 'I always had Burneau down for a closet reb.'

'Closet reb?' remarked Cyrille. 'You're a closet reb, son. First sign of war and there's you in your closet, eh?'

'Oh, I had a part to play,' said Magnick, 'all strictly of two varieties of hush, you understand . . .'

Further down the bar, a moustached man in a hat said, 'Dead right, son. Hush I'm a-hidin' and hush I'm a-crappin' m'self.'

'Two varieties of ha, Stromberg, with a bloody in the middle. Oh, and another thing, Burneau. You ever see Violet? We lost her in the war. We hold you responsible.'

Cyrille said: 'Out on the Mountain he was, with the rebs, son. Hadn't no time for the ladies. Eh, Burneau? We follow you on the Network, see! They say "Who's the man who's winning the war for the Badeans?" We say "He drank in here once, he did, our friend Burneau, the mystery right-hand man!"'

'Sure,' said Magnick, 'if I spent the whole war away from the ladies on a fucking mountainside with nothing but slopers for company, I'd be a bit of a right-hand man myself.'

'He got no manners, he got no morals, he got no future, I say,' said Cyrille.

'I would like another drink, please,' stated Burneau.

'Woh,' said Magnick, nudging him. 'Got something to tell us, Mr Ex-Beers? Shot anyone famous lately?'

'Belt up,' said the man called Stromberg. 'He didn't shoot nobody. He just did what he had to. War's over now. Badeo for Badeans. I'll stand his drink, Cyrille. The name's Stromberg.'

Burneau turned slowly and nodded his thanks to that man in the hat. Cyrille poured another beer. Magnick stared at everyone in turn. The doctor doodled in some spilt drink.

One imagines, fondly perhaps, that some of the participants in this conversation have the faintest idea what it's about.

'So, Burneau,' Magnick rejoined, 'tell us about the Ministry. Tell me when you're going to answer my claim for compensation.'

'What claim?' Burneau muttered.

'Why, compensation for lost education. I'm taking both the Argeline Domain and the Organ Liberat Badeon to court on the grounds of International Strife Inhibiting the Formal Schooling of Badean Youth.'

'You'll lose that,' said Burneau, obviously confident in dealing with his area of professional expertise.

289

'Oh sorry, sorry,' said Magnick. 'So much for friends in high places.'

Cyrille scoffed: 'You ought to go sue my beer for your lost time, no war, no strife . . . Hey, Blue, you don't recall one against the Security Forces for closing me afternoons in the curfew, do you, eh?'

'Mine's a real one,' said the doctor, 'against Captain Tolbus of Laquilla. Commandeering my operating theatre. Seen that one, Frosch? Cost me five thousand markers, I wager.'

'It was a war, *docteur*,' sneered Magnick. 'Captains shit where they want to.'

Burneau raised his glass and said solemnly: 'To all my companions of my first home on Badeo Island. May you all be as happy as I am now one day soon . . .'

'Happy?' said Magnick, raising his eyebrows. 'What's new to be happy about?'

Burneau, by way of answer, put on a sort of proud face.

'What's new there, Blue?' asked the barman gently.

Burneau, by way of further elucidation, lifted his glass and tinked it conspiratorially against Cyrille's.

'Cash or chicks,' Stromberg called along the bar. 'Cash or chicks.'

The doctor turned. 'You have a lady, Frosch?'

'Uh-huh.'

Magnick drew a sharp breath, then muttered: 'You in – yuk, excuse me, finger securely in place down throat – love?'

'Uh-huh,' said Burneau into his beer.

'Yow!' said the youngster, sinking his upper lip into his foamy white cocktail, 'blrrr . . .'

Cyrille chuckled.

'Hey well, young Minister, you learn something today. All the bodyguard in the world can't save a man from that one.'

'Nohow,' grinned Burneau.

'Nohow,' grinned the other men.

Everybody drank.

'I was in love once,' said Magnick. 'Didn't work out.'

'Met you, did she?' said Burneau perkily.

'Too right. Good one. Maybe you met her. Violet's kid.'

Burneau looked at the surface of his beer, then up at Magnick.

'Drop dead,' he told him. 'Drop dead will you. She's a kid. Was a kid.'

'So, I'm a kid, in't I?' the kid protested. 'In't I a kid nah mower?'

'Granted you're a kid,' said the doctor, 'but Juilla Maricolo, she was a lady. She was always a lady. Just like her mother. Friend of yours, Frosch, as I recall.'

'One night,' Burneau sniffed, 'my friend one night. You know where she is now?'

'Violet took off,' said the doctor, 'her and her loud friend, what was it, Thea. Sailed for the Argeline late summer, not last summer though. Not long after you came here, Frosch. Took a heap of cloth to sell in the great markets. Last we heard, no?'

'Right,' said Cyrille. 'Easy come, easy go. We miss her. We got her picture up on the mirror.'

Burneau turned blearily to look.

'Such is war,' said Cyrille.

'Such is war,' said the others.

Everybody drank again. At the far end of the bar, a bearded man with sunken eyes was looking straight at Maris Burneau.

'She didn't take the children then?' Burneau asked brightly.

'No, left 'em,' said the doctor. 'We reckon there was a fight. She was very proud, Juilla. Something happened, we all reckon.'

'Don't look at me, *docteur*,' said Magnick. 'I never got a sniff of her, thanks to that halfwit brother.'

'He did the right thing by his sister, son,' insisted the doctor. 'She was too young for any of that.'

'Your own cadaver on a meathook hand-jiving was she,' commented Magnick. 'She was aching for the jump.'

'What happened to them?' said Burneau – rather puzzlingly, really, since one had the impression he knew.

'Well, of course they stopped school the moment their mother was out of the flat,' the doctor continued. 'I looked in on them every week or so, and the place got lousier, and the boy got ruder, you know how it can be, and at last I looked in one – Monday evening I think it was, and well he'd gone. Joined up. On the Domain side, though. They sent him to fight in Furasol, and he never came back.'

'Such is war,' observed Stromberg.

The sunk-eyed bearded man in a black coat was now sitting on a bench directly under the television screen, still staring hard at the vaguely nodding Burneau, while grasping his beaker with both hands as if to warm them with its contents.

Burneau, in his mysterious way, asked Dr Fencile about the daughter Juilla.

'Well, she went on living there, selling the furniture of the place for money, we reckon that's how she got by. Then the siege began, then the street battles, and none of us could get anywhere. We don't really know where she ended up. Or if she ended up. Maybe she got a crossing to the Mainland, look for her people there. Always a lady, though. You should see the Avenue Hali now.'

'Bombed to buggery,' said Magnick happily.

'Not at all,' said Fencile. 'They've started rebuilding. Luxury Homes for the Big Rebs. I'm surprised your name's not down for one, Frosch.'

'It is, actually,' said Burneau, that man of surprises.

'Where you meet your lady, Blue?' chuckled Cyrille.

'In the war,' said Burneau.

'Ah yes,' said the doctor wistfully, 'the romance of the field . . .'

'*In* a field, probably,' said Magnick sourly. 'What about a name?'

Burneau seemed to giggle to himself.

292

'Come on, you Minister of All Things Blue In Aspect, who's the innocent beauty you've rubbed your nose all over?'

'It's Tretner,' he answered, 'Amadora Tretner.'

'Ah,' said Cyrille tenderly, 'a Furasolian, is she?'

'That's where I was, Cyrille.'

'Tretner . . . Tretner . . . ' the doctor murmured to himself.

There was a pause, then Magnick snorted with contempt: 'Three babies belching in formation is it, that's another fucking beer from this man!'

They all laughed, and Burneau said: 'But I'll make a Frosch of her yet! Excuse me, gentlemen . . .'

He eased his way out of the group and through an archway towards a door marked FELLOWS, which he opened. There were three grimy washbasins on his left, three streaming urinal panels on his right, and two cubicles in the far corner. He made his way heavily towards the further one and got in, bolting it behind him.

What on earth is one meant to say about this, of all the events to observe on this lovely island? He sat there and so on, he hummed and absorbed the graffiti. He must have heard the next man come in. The next man, who was the man with a beard and sunken eyes, and who now produced from his black coat the two halves of a pair of scissors, one in each hand, walked across to the nearer cubicle and stood there by the door, as if listening.

Burneau stopped humming the tune and grimaced, presumably at the realisation of another person being suddenly in earshot.

Then the man, obviously Adzell pretending to be someone with a beard – though one can testify that his eyes are sunken – moved in front of Burneau's cubicle, right up close to it, so that his difficult quiet breathing stained the already filthy door. The Minister of Reconciliation had gone extremely quiet for a man sitting where he was. Adzell took three careful steps backwards towards the urinals, looking very much as if he was gathering his strength to run at the door of Burneau's cubicle.

The main door opened and in walked the moustached man Stromberg, strolling to the central urinal and unfastening his trousers. He tilted his head back and said loudly: 'I didn't want to mention my own claim in front of them idle blighters, Minister, but I lost a half-year on account of black marketeers from Gamor. Army was cut in, I figure. Could be out of business soon. Then what? No more barometers. Don't pass me over like them blighters, eh? I've worked, I have.'

Burneau declared evenly from his cubicle: 'I will go directly to the S file, Mr Strongberg. I will do that tomorrow.'

'You're more than a Minister, you're a ministering angel, Mr Burneau. I always wanted to tell you as how proud I was when we heard you was on the team struck the blow that day. I was in here, I was. You probably seen me. We was all freedom fighters back in them days, but you was the one lit the bonfire, eh? You was Burneau. Still are, I s'pose! There. Said my bit.'

'Mr Strongberg?'

'Minister?'

'Is that Magnick out there with you?'

'Another gentleman, sir. But he's gone now. Did his time. Now I done mine. Another Frosch, sir?'

'Burneau. Er, no – er, yes, a Frosch! Thank you, Mr Strongberg.'

'I'd appreciate it if you call me Dillfield, Mr Burneau.'

Stromberg opened the door and left. Before it had quite swung to, and it took a while, two fingers caught it and Adzell slipped back into the room. He crept noiselessly across the tiles to that same standpoint three steps from Burneau's door. Then he stooped slightly, like a bull about to charge. His scissor halves were in his red fists, which were trembling very slightly up and down, vital balancing components of a running engine.

294

Voices could be clearly heard outside the lavatory, then Dr Fencile and another man came in, talking.

'Speak of the Devil, Toby!'

'How's that, doctor?'

'He's in there, the man himself! Can't speak of the Devil when he's doing his business, eh Toby? You're in there, aren't you, Frosch?'

'Yes, doctor,' called Burneau, 'I'm in here. Who's out there with you?'

'Old school pal, Toby Kapphammer. I was just telling him about you, about how we know you and so on. I was saying how I remember you the day the Viceroy died. Very cool, you were, I've been telling Toby, one very cool customer indeed. Say "Good evening, Minister," Toby . . .'

'Good evening, Minister,' said Dr Fencile's old friend: 'I consider myself both *honoured* and *delighted*.'

'Good evening, Mr Kapphammer,' said Burneau. 'Is that it out there?'

'How's that?' the doctor asked.

'Is that – I mean, there's no one else then?'

'I think there's someone in the other cubicle. Shall I look?'

'Oh no,' said Burneau thickly, 'it's all right, Dr Fencile.'

Dr Fencile and his friend finished off at the urinals, washed their hands with much hilarity about a joke they could see on the wall, and departed, the doctor chortling. 'We're piling up the beers while you're in here, Frosch! We're leaving you behind! Still, if it's . . . official business, ha! Good show!'

'No hurry, doctor!' Burneau cried out.

'You're right, no law!' Dr Fencile agreed, misunderstanding.

The door swung, slowed, then inched itself shut again. Both the cubicles were occupied.

Burneau cleared his throat. 'That's hardly enough paper,' he observed matter-of-factly.

After a while, his observation not having been taken up, he added: 'Scarcely enough to blow one's nose, that isn't . . .'

The bolt slid on the door of the nearer cubicle, then the door itself edged open. Adzell was crouched behind it, his left hand outstretched and both his daggers in the other, so that they looked no more or less than a functioning pair of kitchen scissors. He started to creep out of the cubicle again.

'Who is that?' Burneau croaked.

Adzell froze, and shut his eyes.

Burneau audibly swallowed and went on: 'Because, maybe, I know you . . . Maybe I could – buy you a drink, or maybe . . . well, buy you a drink maybe.'

Footsteps were heard outside again. Adzell sprang upright and walked quickly to the urinals, as the main door opened.

This time it was Magnick, followed by a man wearing a fox mask.

'What are you voiding in there, Minister?' enquired Magnick solicitously. 'Ye memories of old loves?'

'Oh no,' called Burneau, 'I think I've drunk a little much here, Magnick . . '

'No such as much. No such as much. Isn't that true, boys?'

'Who are you with out there?' Burneau bleated.

'Who am I with out here? Well here's me trying to commence hosing down the walls of the white citadel, but I'm stuck between two bone-dry geysers. Most distracting, I tell you. One wonders why these gentlemen have made the trip. It surely can't be for a sight of me . . .'

'Who are they, Magnick? Friends of yours? We could – have a drink with them or something . . .'

'Friends? I doubt it. One of them is wearing a fox's head, and the other one's – well, staring at me like I'm sort of, anyway. Tell them, Burneau, tell them they have to leave me alone because you say so and you're the Minister of Reconciliation. Do tell them, because I'm working on this theory that they don't like me all that much. I don't think they're here to piss about, in any case, or if they are it must have all been a terrible disappointment. Friends, I'm such a blabbering young thing . . .'

'Magnick,' said Burneau urgently from his perch, 'Why don't you all get your beers and come in? We could – '

'Now there's a suggestion! But I don't think my two friends are all that – uh!'

The man in the fox mask suddenly turned from the urinal, gripped Magnick by both shoulders so quickly that he had no time to return his privates to their lodgings, and heaved him across the room against the washbasins. He slid to the tiles clutching his stomach where the basins had slammed him, bewailing his plight in the most obscure terms. Then the fox man was on him again, lifting him up to punch him in the face, so that he was hurled stumbling against the main door.

'Shit!' screamed Burneau from his cubicle. 'Shit! Murder! Help us! Shit!'

As the fox man opened the main door and dragged Magnick gasping out of it, Burneau staggered into action, pulling his clothes back on despite the serious want of paper, zipping and buckling himself in with all the ineptitude of the desperate. Then he cowered back upon the lid of the toilet, resuming his plaintive cry: 'Murder! Shit! Help us!'

Adzell was clearly panicked into a decision by the sudden onslaught of the fox man. He drew his scissors, one in each hand, stood back and ready to rush at Burneau's door, then, yelling 'Scissors cut Paper!' he charged.

As Burneau's door was splintered off its hinges, Adzell, perhaps deceived by his own momentum, went spinning through off balance and had to use his scissor hands to shield himself from the far wall of the cubicle. The scissors clattered out of his control and he fell heavily on the screaming Minister of Reconciliation. There was no second chance though, because the fox man had come back in, drawn a government-issue silenced revolver and shot Adzell five times in the back with it.

'The last one's for you if you don't tell me what the fuck you're playing at,' said Tragolani, removing the fox mask.

'Do it,' whispered Burneau. 'I don't know either.'

297

'Who is he?'

'I don't know. I'm going to be sick.'

Tragolani pulled the body off Burneau, dragged it out of the cubicle on to the tiles, rolled it over and looked at the shocking white face.

'Some Arselicko hood.'

'Tragolani.'

'What?'

'What did you do to Magnick?'

'Nothing. He's all right. Tosser.'

'Why did you do him first?'

'He bit my finger, boss. He's bad news, that boy. Let's get the fuck out of here.'

Tragolani helped the Minister to his feet, and they hurried out through All Afternoons, hitting the fresh midnight air at about the time Cyrille heard the sound of someone stampeding through his wine cellar wailing 'I have died and I believe with sincerity I am in Heaven!' just prior to discovering the FELLOWS toilet in a quite dreadful state, with blood and urine on the floor and walls, shit on either side of the toilets.

'They damn no good these days,' said the barman, combing his hair in the mirror. 'Them kids they damn no good.'

It was in the mirror that he first saw a man with a fox mask sitting on one of the toilets, blood all over him and clutching what looked like knives in each hand, as if he was about to carve an enormous roast for the entire Badean Butchers' Guild.

'Cyrille,' he said to himself, 'that ain't real.'

But it turned out to be as real when the barman turned round as it had been in the mirror and, once he had established that the carving man was quite dead, he went to fetch Dr Fencile who shook his head and agreed.

'There's nothing we can do.'

Cyrille nodded sadly, as if now there was nothing they could ever do, that they would have to kneel there always.

IV

'It's Captain Nunez, sir, Mr President, I wonder if I ever really got over it.'

Iaio Gabril, who had been standing at his desk shaking his head, now sat down slowly and began instead to nod it understandingly.

'You mean you are still mastering your grief, Maris?'

'I believe I am,' said Burneau mournfully.

'I know how much you loved her. I alone know that.'

'Well. It all happened so suddenly. We never saw them.'

'Hmm,' said the President. 'Hmm yes. And you think it may be that only now can you mourn her, and that this may serve as an explanation for your frankly extraordinary behaviour?'

The Minister slowly nodded his accord. Gabril spread his hands wide, and reiterated in a tone of mild exasperation: 'First of all you beg an amnesty, which against my better judgement I grant. Just as I grant it, you barge in here and try to have it revoked. When I tell you it's too late, you beg for bodyguards. I give you four of the best men I have, and the next thing I know they have to haul you from some pigsty in Allalong where you've got sozzled with Tragolani – who only two weeks ago was mentally disturbed enough to attempt a one-man assault on the Argeline Domain! Now, to cork the bottle, strong rumours suggest that the two of you, both in a state of advanced intoxication, were seen running away from that same dive last night, leaving in your wake one shot-up Argelino and a pulverised boy – a Magnick, of all people. That family is only responsible for insuring half the harbour, Maris, I'd appreciate it if their brood was left well alone . . . So what do we piece together from this night of ignominy? You've become violent, alcoholic, unpredictable, dangerous, irresponsible, notorious . . . shall I go on?'

'No, sir.'

'Slovenly, lacking in concentration, lazy, erratic in judgement, dog-eared, dirty . . . Am I to take it that these are all manifestations of belated grief for our comrade?'

'That's my theory, sir,' Burneau agreed.

'That's your theory. I mean, tell me, do, is your life in danger or not?'

'It is.'

'Because if you don't want the bodyguards I gave you, the Ministers of Defence and Security would be glad of them. The banks could use them most of all. They're hated even more than the Ministry of Reconciliation.'

'I need them, Mr President.'

'Maybe. Maybe not. Now. Explain. This dead Argelino, am I right, Maris, was one of the Viceroy Lagland's guards on the day you killed him, and he came after you to settle the score? Is the Professor on the right page here?'

'Yes, you are. But there's two others. They're terrible men, sir, and they're free.'

'Well, excuse me, but whose idea was that?'

'I didn't think this would happen, Mr President.'

Gabril heaved a profound sigh. 'Oh, Maris. What a fall is here. "I didn't think this would happen". Where are your foresights now? Where are your visions, your glimpses, your dreams? How will we see what's coming our way now that everything catches you unawares?'

'I don't know,' said Burneau miserably, shaking his head, but the President went on: 'What can you bring us now but the memory of your deeds? What more can you bring to our lives than you could as a face in the Gallery of War Heroes?'

'I'm learning fast at Reconciliation, sir.'

'That's as may be, but who is reconciled? Every claim you settle seems to dissatisfy both parties, and brings plaintiff

300

and defendant alike storming to the Capital – either to break each other's noses or if possible ours.'

'That's in the nature of disputes, Gabril, sir.'

'No,' said Gabril, picking up his letter opener and prodding his desk with it as if he was filling in emphasis marks on his sentence. 'It's in the nature of disputes that one man wins them and one man loses them.'

'I don't think that, sir. I try to help both sides in some way. So as to reconcile them. It is after all a Ministry of Reconciliation.'

The President stood up.

'Well, I'm sorry, Maris, but it's not. Hereafter it is to be known as the Rationalisation Bureau of the Ministry of Finance. The restructuring should be fairly straightforward, in that the claimant whose victory would cost the state more is always the loser, the claimant whose victory would cost the state less the winner. The winner gets his fare paid back where he flaming well came from. The loser's fines are paid into Reconstruction Funds. You for one should appreciate that, Maris: it's helping to build your villa on the Avenue whatever-it-is.'

Burneau looked glumly at the edge of the desk. 'I don't know much about finance, Mr President. My experience is all in Reconciliation.'

'My young friend, it makes no odds. You, personally, must reconcile yourself to a holiday. Indefinite paid leave, giving you time to mourn your lost love to your heart's content. When you feel ready to resume government work, I will personally ensure that your talents are deployed appropriately. There is so much to do. Vice-Chancellor Curtens is looking for university professors, and I had you in mind for a Junior Communications Fellowship. Ha! Watch television all day, be just like Camp Liberat!'

'I – I've lost my job here then?'

'You are a very great man, Mr Burneau, I mean, potentially a very great, at least a great – perhaps one day – man.

301

And a good fellow. But you are tired, you are out of control. You are suffering. You must rest.'

The President leaned over the hunched young man, and said softly a kind of three-line poem with all the rhymes in the wrong places, a pretentious message, and an over-reliance on vinicultural metaphors. It seemed to cheer them both up in some way, but when Burneau limped from the room like a dog chastised, one was not much disposed to follow him out. He was lost to view for quite some time.

The weather on Badeo got hazier and hotter, as it always will around this time of year. Burneau's four bodyguards were last seen standing like sweating marble statues outside the wrought-iron gates of the Urban Development Bank.

Sexual love: Burneau went down to the wharves with all his sick pay in his black briefcase, mirror sunglasses, and a peaked cap pulled down. One was getting tired of waiting for him here.

Sexual love: he looked about for a suitable boat, and, noticing a smart little green-and-white two-berther, the *Dantelle*, he engaged its stout owner in conversation, during the course of which money changed hands and Burneau received instructions about the working of the craft. The owner left the wharf bearing an envelope portly with Badean markers, a grin on his suntanned face, and a large dimpled bottle of 100 per cent proof Old Foresters Why Not Indeed.

Sexual love: Burneau sailed for the prison isle of Miscobar, a free man, a man alone, but a man apparently cheered by the salt spray as he cleared the last of the jetties, for he was singing as he headed out to the open sea, towards the smaller of the two islands ghosting into view now on the hazed horizon.

Sexual love: the diminishment of all choices and all freedom to a size perfect for humans.

The voyage took much longer than one might have expected,

considering that the two islands were visible all the time. Apart from being a voyage from Badeo to these two outlying rocks, and a journey from the clamour of man and seagull to lapping near-silence, it was also a progression from a toughly sunny midday into a cooler and spider-webbed afternoon mist. Burneau, long after his singing had subsided and stopped, looked back anxiously towards Badeo on more than one occasion. The great island sat like a haughty lady in the fading of the sun, brushing off all regrets, and rendered by her indignation indifferent to all homecomings. Then, as the young man turned again, his face mottled with the cold spray, Cobar loomed up suddenly, green and black, so close on the left side, white gulls flecking its shoreline, above that nothing but trees, then a building jutting up at its highest point, masts, a fence, the prison from which Burneau had freed a thousand men. Steering the *Dantelle* further around the larger island, Burneau was afforded a clear view of the minehead, and a quarry gashing the woodland, some burned-out trucks and huts. Something ugly might well have happened. There was no sign of life.

Miscobar turned out to be some way behind: distant as well as much smaller. No habitation or structure could be made out on the smaller island, not even as it grew nearer, not even as Burneau almost lost control of the motor boat, letting it veer back towards the west shore of Cobar, because he was distracted with peering into the thickening mist at its bleaker sister.

By the time he had got the measure of the helm again, visibility was very poor. He could see both islands as he glanced about in panic, but even if he had been able to see Badeo itself through such a fog, the dark side of Cobar would have blocked his view entirely. He blew out his cheeks, grimaced, and steered directly for the Miscobar shore.

It was only when he cut the engine, about thirty yards from the shoreline, that the unpractised mariner Burneau realised there was nowhere to tie the boat: no jetty, no quay,

303

no harbour of any kind. He cursed the *Dantelle*'s owner aloud for not warning him of this obstacle to his quest, but it is only fair to say that one has a distinct recollection of Burneau telling the man he wanted to sail to Cobar, which does have a little harbour, not to Miscobar, which has nothing. From this vantage, certainly, it did not appear to have a prison, not even a secret one.

The silenced *Dantelle* slowed in the water, and bobbed for a time, very gradually turning around in a circle, so that Burneau kept on having to move around the tiny deck to keep his stiff, drenched face aligned with the shore. He disappeared into the little cabin and reappeared with a coil of rope, as if hoping that would somehow conjure up on the island some pole to which he could attach it.

Instead it conjured up a man, hooded against the wet mist, standing quite still on the beach, except that he was waving the whole of his right arm at Burneau.

Burneau gave a little cry when he saw him, and peered into what was developing into heavy rain, as the mist cloud confessed its true mundane identity.

'Hello there? Paol? Paol Maricolo?' Burneau croaked out quite absurdly in the circumstances.

The man continued to wave his arm. As this was all he had been doing since Burneau set eyes on him, it meant the same as giving no answer. The poor sailor tried again: 'I have this boat and I've nowhere to land it, you see?'

The man waved a little more, then stopped. Burneau shouted: 'I'm looking for the prison!'

The hooded man seemed to nod at that. Then he pointed with his right arm away along the shore, where there seemed to be a cove of some kind. Burneau stared in that direction, and must have made out at last the thin finger of brown rock that stuck out to sea, obviously a place where he could tie his rope. He waved back to the hooded man and started the motor.

As the *Dantelle* sputtered into life and set off for the landing place, it kept a more or less parallel course with the hooded man, who walked quickly along the stony beach, his hands deep in the pockets of his foul-weather clothes. Burneau, who had made no such provision, clung grimly to the helm, getting soaked to the skin. He timed the cutting of the engine well – for a novice – and the *Dantelle* drifted to a point about twenty yards from the rocky needle, beside which the strange man stood, arms folded. Burneau took up a position at the bow of the boat, and hurled his coil of rope as far as he could, so that it landed a few yards away from the shore. The hooded man walked into the sea to retrieve it, and began tying it around the rock while Burneau, wholly unprepared for the prospect of having to swim ashore, was trying to improvise, with little success, a sealed dry bag to carry his belongings in. All he included were his gun, his government identification and a cream wallet into which he stuffed about half of his remaining sick pay. Gingerly he eased himself down into the green salted swell, shrieked as he slowly plunged, held on to the side with one hand for about a minute, then kicked off and swam, discovering he could stand in the water almost at once.

He still appeared pleased by this achievement when he reached the shallows and the wet shingle. Even when Mace (of course) had drawn a gun and was pointing it at him, Burneau must have considered this to be some precautionary measure related to the fact that Miscobar was after all a prison, rather than an early indication of implacable hom-icidal hatred.

He stumbled to his knees on dry land and panted for breath. Mace waited.

'Hokay,' said Burneau, 'Phew ... Well, I'm from the Badean Free Government, I've got papers, I've come to effect the release of one – '

'Paol Maricolo, formerly of Avenue Hali, Badeo,' said Mace.

Burneau got up properly.

'That's right, that's him. How do you know?'

''Cos he's innocent, ain't he, Blue?'

Now Mace, with a rather crude sense of dramatic timing, threw back his hood so Burneau could see him.

Burneau saw him.

'Guardsman Mace,' he went, 'from the old days.'

'Guardsman Burneau, so-called,' Mace sneered, 'from the old days. Minister Burneau, so-called. Oh, I like the boat.'

'It's not mine,' said Burneau weakly. 'I loaned it from a man.'

'He'll have it back by sundown.'

Burneau swallowed and started explaining: 'I always, Mace, always wanted to explain about that day with the Viceroy . . .'

'Do what you bloody want, mate, but bear in mind if you say another word I'll shoot your face off.'

Burneau suddenly knelt down again, but kept his hands near his sides. Too near, because Mace walked over, keeping his gun trained on Burneau's head, picked Burneau's dry bundle out of his pocket, stashed the money and documents and tossed the gun spinning into the shallows. 'Standard issue sodding island hixie shit,' he noted. Then he stepped back, and gestured for Burneau to get up and follow him.

They walked away from the ocean. Mace treading backwards, Burneau forwards, to a clump of dead trees and boulders, which they moved behind. Mace threw Burneau a black rag and told him to blindfold himself with it, which he fumblingly did, the rain streaming down his cheeks.

When Burneau was blindfolded, Mace pulled him forward at the elbow, pushed him down to a kneeling position, then grabbed his right hand and slammed it down on a ledge of mud-brown rock.

'Nod for yes,' said Mace. 'You feel the rock?'

Burneau nodded.

'That's our playing field. You know what we're going to play?'

Burneau nodded.

306

'Here's Mace's Rules, not yours. Mace's Rules. You beat me, you win. We play again. We match, we play again. I beat you, you hurt, Burneau. Mace's Rules. Best of seven, not so far from the old days. Winner gets the boat. Loser stays here, lunches on birdshit, in time starves. Mace's Rules. Round One. One – Two – Three!'

Burneau clenched his fist. Mace didn't do anything. He didn't have to, since Burneau couldn't see what was happening. He didn't tell Burneau the score either, and Burneau didn't ask.

'Round Two. One – Two – Three!'

Burneau made the scissor shape. Mace did nothing.

'Round Three. One – Two – Three!'

Burneau flattened his hand into paper, whereupon Mace drew a pair of scissors from his pocket, parted the blades, raised up the sharper one and hacked it deep into Burneau's palm so that he screamed. The gulls scattered.

'Scissors cut Paper. It's very, very close, Blue, I can tell you. Round Four. One – Two – Three!'

Burneau's hand made the scissor shape and began to bleed on the rock. Mace picked up a fist-sized stone and brought it down on the spread fingers. The thud had a crack down it. Burneau howled in the rain.

'Oh, bad luck, mate. Stone breaks Scissors. So near, so near. Round Five. One – Two – Three!'

Burneau's hand feebly, slowly, flattened itself again. Mace watched it, did nothing.

'This could decide it, pretty green boat or deep blue sea . . . Round Six. One – Two – Three!'

Burneau howled again and shrivelled his fractured hand into what was closer to Stone than anything. Mace watched it trying to do that, then took a piece of paper out of the side of his hood and slipped it between two of Burneau's crooked fingers.

'That's it then, son. Paper wraps Stone. Pleasure boat trip for Freeman Mace. Who knows? Might make it home to the

Domain. That's your home too, ain't it? Well, now it's this dead shitheap. You thought there was a prison here. Reckon you were right, 'cause let's see you get out of this one. Oh, I forgot. You can't read, can ya, Blue? Not like now, you can't. Let me read you the story . . .'

Mace plucked the bloody piece of paper out from between Burneau's fingers, flattened it and read: '"Dear Miss Maricolo, your brother is on the island of Miscobar, working the diamond swamp. Only the Government will let him out, 'cause it's a secret jail. No one knows about it. You have to pay some money to the right top person. I was there with him but I got out in a boat I made out of wood. I tell you this 'cause you was good friends to my wife Sulsi at your hostel. Can't say my name. Burn this letter. Sincerely, your friend." Course, this is just a copy. By the way, it's all true, that last bit. Your schoolgirl puss was mates with my wife, always talking about you she was, how she loved you and all that shit, and how you was in the government now and you'd help her, seeing as how she thought you loved her as well. Too bad, ain't it, Blue, 'cause you, mate, are fuck-all help out here with a fucked hand and no boat and no way home to your happy ever afters. Eh?'

Burneau groaned.

'What d'you say?'

Burneau said nothing.

'As I say, Burneau. As I always fuckin' say, Blue, Paper wraps Stone. Bye now.'

Mace drew back his lower leg and shoved Burneau in the chest with the sole of his foot, so that he slumped against a sand-coloured dead tree and lay still.

He would have heard Mace's footsteps crunching across the stone. He would have heard him walk into the water, and kick for the boat. He would have heard the engine of the *Dantelle* cough into life: he must have done, because he too coughed at that instant, though he didn't make a move to remove his blindfold, get up, protect his broken hand, or his drenched and frozen body, or do anything.

308

Nor did he react when the engine suddenly cut out again, there was a short cry, a pause, then something went into the sea.

Nor did he flinch or attempt to see what was happening when footsteps crunched towards him again.

But he screamed the loudest, longest scream in the island's ancient memory when a warm wet hand clutched his good hand, and the second loudest, second longest when he lifted his own hand and the warm hand came with it, light as a glove.

'Shadow Angel beats Argeline Shit-For-Brains,' said Tragolani, untying Burneau's blindfold. 'No offence.'

'B-b-b-' Burneau gibbered to no purpose, as Tragolani picked up the rapidly draining white hand with his left and shook it with his right. Then he said, 'Say goodbye to your partner, Maris,' and threw the hand into the woods by the shore. 'Grow a whole fuck-off forest.'

Tragolani supported Burneau across the beach to the needle of rock, then went off into the trees, leaving his boss shivering and mumbling in the incessant rain. He came back with a large piece of bark and unhooked the rope from the rock on Miscobar. Then they waded towards the boat together, holding on to their raft. Tragolani hauled himself over the side of the *Dantelle* and dragged the sodden weight of his friend aboard after him.

He stripped Burneau and wrapped him in the bedding from one bed, then helped him into the other, swathing his smashed hand in a sling made of pillowcases. Then he took the helm, and recounted his side of the story at the top of his voice all the way back to the wharves of Badeo, while Burneau slipped into fever and delirium and missed it all.

What those forlornly crying gulls and petrels naive enough to imagine there might be some tasty pickings from the *Dantelle* heard was a long, ranging, slightly exaggerated account of how Tragolani, having been hired by Burneau to protect him when he was a Minister, had never technically been discharged from that duty, even though it was widely known in ex-Organ Liberat circles that Burneau was 'washed up' in government, that his secret gift had evaporated, that with Nunez gone he had no real supporter among the upper echelons. . . . How Tragolani had therefore kept a close eye on his erstwhile boss, having so nearly failed to save him in the toilet facilities at All Afternoons that terrible night, and had sworn off alcohol so as better to accomplish his task, a task made quadruply difficult now that the four government bodyguards had been discharged from the Reconciliation Ministry, and now that the whereabouts of the man himself were increasingly hard to predict, him having no responsibilities in the Palace of Popular Valour. . . . How Tragolani had therefore stalked him as before, called himself the 'Shadow Angel', seen through Burneau's frankly pathetic attempts at disguise, stalked him through the narrow alleys of the market district, stalked him down to the wharves that morning and seen him pay off the skipper of the motor boat *Dantelle* . . . How, while Burneau distracted the man with bribes and bottles, Tragolani had soundlessly slipped into the cabin of the boat, cleared some storage space for himself under one of the beds and waited. . . . How they had sailed together heaven knew where . . .

And how he had hard Burneau cut the motor, and shout to the man on shore. . . . Tragolani's astonishment at where he was when he emerged from under the bed! His dismay at the desperate weather! And his horror at what he saw on the beach of whatever unearthly island Burneau had lunatically steered them to!

What could he do? What could he do? By the time he realised what was happening, by the time he realised that the man with the hood was forcing Burneau to walk up the beach, the man was out of Tragolani's range. There was no way he could go splashing ashore – the man would cut him down in the shallows! He waited a time of agony, heard

Burneau's cries of pain, saw the hooded man do up his coat and make his way to the needle of rock. Tragolani drew his twelve-inch blade – motivated by pure vengeance, for he thought his friend had died by now – huddled down behind some matting on the deck, and waited for the man to take the helm. The moment he did so, Tragolani leapt out, stole up behind him and jerked his head back. Unfortunately, all he jerked back was the hood. The man, however, was too surprised to react to his last chance, so Tragolani stuck him through the throat as he turned, and several times through the chest as he made his way gargling to the deck. When he was definitely dead, Tragolani sawed the man's hand off and threw the rest of him in the sea.

'What was his name?' Tragolani roared into the rain.

Hearing nothing, he nodded to himself, then shouted: 'You better get some sleep, boss, that's best!'

After about five minutes, he said: 'Didn't half bleed, the barbarian, would you look at this fucking craft? Hope your skipper enjoys his rum!'

The gulls at the harbour spotted them, and hung close by Tragolani as he steered the last sea mile. There were great stone-coloured clouds rumbling low all over Badeo. They made the boats and sails in the harbour a luminous piercing white, and cowled the bony head of Mount San Timotheo far off to the south-west.

Tragolani shouted again: 'You sleep while you can, boss! Almost got you home!'

V

Storms came, and a long spell of warm unsettled weather on Badeo. The thick summer trees waited a fortnight or so for signs of a return to what they had become so sleepily fond of, but, as no return seemed forthcoming, they took one night their collective annual choice and began to redden and brown in the rain. The human population followed, altering modes of dress, walk, work and conversation in line with the appearance of things rather than the temperature or the time of year. A general briskness occupied the people, a sense that it was time to put the memory of war, the carnival feel of victory and the ensuing idle hangover behind them. It was time to pick up the ordinary where it had left off, at the point where history had haughtily donned its capital H and made legends of half-truths and heroes of all but those who had doggedly, bravely, survived defeat. The island continued to exchange prisoners with the Domain, like an elaborate accelerating courtship of matching gifts that would end in a loveless marriage of convenience. The removal of physical threat somehow raised in every family the level of economic expectations, as if survival was to be celebrated with limitless plenty. After all, it was not so difficult to resent the whimsical dictats of President Iaio Gabril every bit as much as the faceless unaccountable legislature of the far-off Domain, to bemoan the economic chaos of Free Badeo in terms strikingly similar to those with which one had bemoaned the political impotence of the Island in its sullen Dominion days. The accent was on the betterness of the past, the greater moral probity of those who had formerly held authority, the parlous state of the next generation and the woeful condition of municipal works. The times were steeped like old fruit in the born Islander's conviction that all things decline, all things slope away from the high, caring self to the flat, loutish indifference of the ocean. The Badeans descended into their damp autumn relishing to the full the irritability of the free.

And the season so suddenly gone, one cast about in search of a foothold, a handhold against that slide into winter, for something or somebody whose little history one knew, by whose progress or demise one could measure one's private hopes. One searched for a soul through which to interpret Time, with whom to cling to youthful lightness, or to age with in dignity or, at the worst, to mourn and outlive, but somebody, somebody, carting a known name stressfully home across this silent plain. Alone was not enough for a god, with the season so suddenly gone.

One has seen Badeo, one has seen Furasol, Tatri, Gamor, Saldeo, Laquilla. The most beautiful girl on the island is, really, Juilla Maricolo, nineteen, working half the night and half the day at the pamphlet works on the very outskirts of the Capital, just off the dirty wide Highway Gamor, where it skirts the ocean to the north. The workers' elevated train leaves from FABRICO, the industrial terminus, at noon, but MARICOLO J. sits there midnight-eyed in her grey-blue smock, her sixth week completed now, watching the flats crumble and the empty new villas sprout in the east of Badeo, the Way of Full Flagons, Avenue Lazard, STADIO, the first stop, where she sees thousands of boys and men in their red-and-white cloaks, pushing through Avenue Naheen on their way to the game; SANCRISTO, the second stop, beneath where the cheapest seafront hotels are scaffolded from war damage, and the coalfish sellers ply the last of the year's trade, bolted into their thick dark aprons. She gazes out at the colourless ocean, then rolls her eyes away to the other side, where she sees two Urban Watch cadets nudging each other, and, opposite them, the object of their amused distaste, a wiry, tangle-haired individual (only and no less than

313

Tragolani, the Shadow Angel) reading and sniggering aloud at one of the pale blue pamphlets they produce where Juilla works: *The Responsibilities of Freedom*, written by the President himself. She turns her head back again and closes her eyes for the odd moment, jolting awake every time, suddenly, then sinking back again when she sees the view has not changed.

It must be considered likely that between them they will establish co-ordinates by which one can relocate the wounded and redundant Maris Burneau, who disappeared from a small flat in the northern dock area of Badeo one night, and has not turned up in any of the predicted places. All Afternoons, the Palace of Popular Valour, the luxury homes on the new Boulevard Nunez: these have continued to grow agelessly and proceed nowhere quite contentedly without him, while Tragolani drives around the island at the wheel of a filthy red van, sleeping in the back of it on the sodden byways of main roads, looking for someone, and then, one day on an elevated train, just as it is about to plunge underground, finding her there.

Her hair was matted and greasy, she wore no make-up. She looked dark and despondent, but peaceful when her eyes were closed and her dry lips parted as if in faint surprise or pleasure almost. Dozing and waking, dozing and waking, she took the Green Line and Blue Line all the way to UNIVERSITY, where she stood up, yawned behind both hands and got off the train.

Tragolani followed her some way west along the Promenad Furasol towards Allalong, taking in the dull sea view whenever she did, then advanced abreast of her, waved the blue government pamphlet and said: 'You print this shit, honey?'

She glanced across to see who was addressing whom, then lowered her eyes and kept moving.

'Look at this,' said Tragolani cheerfully, riffling through the pages to show her: '"No victory has ever been attained

314

without the application of superior intelligence to the question of love." What does that mean? Zero!'

Juilla kept walking, turning right into the Avenue Maldeau, with her unwanted escort hurrying to beat the stagger and stay at her side.

'And this,' he said scornfully: '"It is the misfortune of all colonial powers that they are founded not upon a vision of love, but a vision of power. A vision of power cannot see behind the enemy that it seeks to overcome, but a vision of love has no limits, and can therefore observe all angles." I don't think that's true geometrically, let alone philosophically. It's just a drawn-out gloat. How do you let this stuff slide by?'

'I don't know you,' said Juilla after a moment.

'Yeah, but I found you. I been looking for you.'

Juilla stopped and stared blankly at him. His clothes were even dirtier than hers, but they evidently had nothing to do with an honest night's work. He stank a bit.

'For me? Why? I don't know you.'

'I'm a friend of Burneau's. He needs to see you.'

Juilla gazed away down the Promenad, which glistened wet with a morning's rain. It seemed so sadly abandoned after all those blazing afternoons. Nobody who was there had anything better to do. She murmured: 'Why does Burneau need to see me? Got some news, has he?'

'Sort of.'

'About someone?'

'Sort of about you, really.'

She sniffed: 'He doesn't care about me. He said he'd help me but then I don't see him all this time. I got work, I got some money to pay a top man in the government. So I don't need his help. Tell him. Where is he so you can tell him?'

'It doesn't matter. He's out of the government. He's not a well man, Burneau.'

'Not well? That's rich. He's a born liar. Not well means he's well. Well means there's something wrong. Love? That always means he wants something.'

315

'Yes,' said Tragolani, 'true. But he does want something. Look, let's get a swig here. They know me.'

Without waiting for an answer, Tragolani hurried Juilla down some stone steps to a below-ground café, Under The Influence, and, rather as he had done to Burneau on the *Dantelle*, responded to the captivity of his one auditor by giving an extremely detailed and often quite digressive account of how the comatose shock-victim Burneau had fared since surviving – a survival owed entirely to Tragolani's shadow-angelic intercession – his fearful ordeal on the island of Miscobar, a narrative which can be abbreviated with no exclusion of worthwhile matter. Some people talk too much, and Tragolani, though challenged by Juilla's inclination to yawn almost constantly – she was, after all, a shift worker trying to get home to bed – evidently swore by the sound of his own voice making observations. He talked for the duration of two Fortifieds and three coffees, while Juilla sipped one single lemon cordial, and wept unnoticed with pure fatigue.

Tragolani could talk about 'the day summer ended'; Juilla, like any Badean islander that year, knew which day he meant. On that day, he had moored the *Dantelle* on the wharf at Badeo, paid the owner off with the rest of Burneau's sick pay in recompense for the stains all over his boat – 'Caught this moonfin – devil of a struggle!' – then hurried Burneau away to a government flat on the Avenue Inkhol. Having some rudimentary medical knowhow, Tragolani disinfected the palm wound and attached splints to the broken fingers, then propped Burneau up in a bed, sedated him with spirits and string music and waited for the fever to pass.

It took a long time to do so, and his patient kept him alert all day and awake all night with the most curious observations and most unexpected words. Eventually, however, Burneau's colour returned, his sleep patterns became normal and he began to make sense again, at least when not inebriated by the sedatives.

316

Two things had become abundantly clear to Tragolani. One was that Burneau would not rest nor resume his placidity of old until Tragolani had located Juilla Maricolo and explained the business on Miscobar, thereby exonerating him from blame for her brother's continuing absence. This might restore Burneau's good name in her heart. The other was that Burneau, for reasons which one would presume are obvious, had risen from his fever with a morbid and implacable dread of everything in the world that was stone.

Stone, stones, things made of stone, things looking or sounding or smelling like stone. Iron, copper, lead, brass; lime, terra-cotta, sandstone, chalk; gold, silver, platinum, all gems of any kind; anything found by the sea, by a lake, by rivers; keys and all coinage, medals, badges, rings. The earth, the ground, paths, steps, tiles, walls, houses, doors, any gathering cloud Tragolani could see through the blinds that might conceivably cause it to hail, any stoneware pots he used to prepare Burneau's dinner, utensils which might conceivably have contaminated it and so poisoned him. The former Minister of Reconciliation lay shivering in a strange bed in a strange part of Badeo Town, paralysed by fear but fixated by his vision of love requited in a soft, yielding, predominantly plastic milieu.

'There's one still out there, you see,' Tragolani whispered to Juilla. 'He says there's one still out there, the most terrible of all . . .'

Juilla tried to disguise a yawn by sipping her lemon drink, but the yawn was so great she had to hold the glass to her lips for some ten seconds, and replace it on the table with as much in it as there had been when she lifted it.

Thus Tragolani did what he frequently repeated he had promised Burneau he would do. Explain that Juilla's news of her brother was a falsehood invented by the vengeful Mace as a way of luring Burneau on to Miscobar to die. Swear on the most implausible of oaths that Burneau had indeed risked his life to sail there for her, and would have lost it had it not

317

been for Tragolani (though he said it himself). Show how Burneau's subsequent silence and disappearance were now wholly explicable in terms of his recovery from shock and fever, not to mention his advanced condition of 'pernicious lithophobia' ('I don't rate doctors so I consulted a dictionary,' Tragolani confided, ordering another coffee). Finally, leave Juilla with the strongest impression of Burneau's abiding ('and hardly surprising,' his friend added courteously, 'if you don't mind me saying, sugar') love and affection, and his intention not only to find Paol Maricolo if it was the last thing he did ('Those were his very words, sweetness') but to bring him to Juilla so that all three, brother and sister and husband one day, might remain together thereafter and live out their lives in what Tragolani, seemingly somewhat embarrassed by the ending of his account, glossed offhandedly as 'the usual old etcetera . . .'

Juilla looked at him, then looked at her lemon drink.

'I don't believe any of that.'

Tragolani shrugged and became brisk.

'Well, that was the news. Done my bit. It's a large island, you know. But I found you. Maybe that'll be enough. Maybe that'll cheer him up, poor wounded bastard.'

He took out some ten-marker notes and spread them right across the table. It was not a very hard currency any more.

'Nice of you to chat,' he said. 'I'll say you told him Hi.'

As he stood up, Juilla said suddenly: 'Tell him he promised me. Tell him he promised he'd get my brother home.'

Tragolani looked at her with a rare expression of seriousness. 'Is there any point? I figure he meant that he loved you, friend.'

'I loved him too,' she whispered, 'but he always goes, you know, he always goes away.'

'Yeah, well. I'll say you said Hi. It was big of you to say so much. Take care out there.'

With that he left her. Juilla stared down at her table for a good long while, then suddenly looked up and about her as if she'd sleepwalked in and had no idea where she was. When the door of Under The Influence slammed behind her, each man in the room was smiling the best smile he reckoned he had, and six of them had made a distinct movement towards her table.

Tragolani picked his van up from a garage under the Hotel Imperion, slammed it into life and got on the Promenad Furasol heading south, barging the most hard-nosed of drivers swearing into the slow lanes.

He sped along the Promenad into the Way of Sperice, followed that as it curved around the Bay and swept south, then crossed the Rumol at the Brade Infan and was out of the city, whistling. In an hour he reached the outer edge of Laquilla, the elegant lake-town in the middle of the island, but took a right at a T-junction and sped away from the built-up area along the lakeside instead, eastward.

He left the main road and the lakeside and arrived at last at a meadow fringed with tall red trees. Leaving his van by the side of the lane, he climbed over a stile and made his way quickly along the meadow's edge until he came to the woodland. Turning his attention to the branches above him, he walked for about a hundred yards alongside the trees, and finally got to the largest one of all. A rope was hanging down from it. Tragolani took hold of the rope with both hands, as if to begin climbing, but appeared to have second thoughts about it and stayed where he was, holding the rope and shouting aloft: 'Boss? It's Federico!'

Having received no answer for some time, he was just putting his right foot up on the lowest knot of the tree when a very small voice from high above said: 'Did you find her?'

'I found her!' yelled the Shadow Angel. 'She's a beauty, Burneau!'

The whoop of joy that disturbed several unlikely collective nouns of woodland birds from their late afternoon pursuits was emitted by Tragolani, for delivering the glad tidings, rather than the concealed Burneau, to whom they were most pertinent, but for the next half-hour, from high up in the tree, where an expert hand had built a tiny wooden house across some sturdy branches, there was much happiness to be overheard, men's happiness with all its sounds – shouts becoming songs, songs becoming shouts, corks thumping gassily out of flagons, the knocking of wooden drinking mugs. To anyone walking beneath the red trees, beside this mild unattended meadow in the heart of the island, they would have been inordinately puzzling, the human sounds from high above, but also, surely, mysteriously gladdening.

The extremely young and muscular man who was indeed walking beneath the red trees did not appear to find it so. He tilted his head back slowly and pondered, listening hard. Then he backed softly behind the next tree, drew a pistol, and waited.

Tragolani came scrabbling down the trunk of the tree about an hour later, somewhat unsteady, and fumbling for a key somewhere in his clothes. When he had walked about ten yards away from Burneau's tree, the very young man stepped out behind him and said loudly: 'Excuse me!'

Tragolani whipped round with a gun already in his hand. 'Who the flaming fuck are you?'

The youth, clearly taken aback, lifted his hands up slightly to suggest peaceful intent, and to show he was not armed – or at least to show Tragolani that it was possible to believe he was not armed.

'Keep still, son, there,' slurred Tragolani. 'You're looking at the Shadow Angel.'

'No troubles, man. I'm looking for a friend.'

'No friends here, son. It's the country. Look. Nobody.'

'There's nobody up that fine old tree?'

Tragolani looked up at the tree, as if seeing it for the first time.

'That one? No! Course not. Somebody up that tree? What are you, some kind of squirrel-catcher?'

'Not me, man,' said the youth, starting to return his hands to his pockets.

'Keep 'em out!' barked Tragolani.

'Keep what out?'

'Your hands, son, your hands!'

The youth spread his hands away from his body, and sighed.

'I was told you might be able to help me. Would your name be Federico Trag – '

'Could be!'

'What do you mean it could be, man?'

Tragolani looked incredulous that he had to clarify the point. He said it with emphasis: 'I mean I might not want to tell you.'

The youth looked perplexed. 'You might not want to tell me? Oh . . . when'll you figure if you want to? I'll wait.'

'Don't. I've decided. Sod off, kid. It's not your field.'

'So. Yes. True,' confirmed the youth. Then he seemed to think of something: 'I wonder if I might ask . . . do you know a man named Maris Burneau? From the Argeline?'

'I might do.'

'I'll wait,' said the youth again.

'No, I don't, come to think of it,' said Tragolani irritably.

'I'm looking for him.'

'Happy fucking.'

'Thank you, man.'

'Go away now.' Tragolani gestured away across the field to a small white truck parked a few yards from his van. 'That your truck?'

'That's so.'

'What is it. Cruiser?'

'VK7. Dauberman.'

'Applecart.'

'Hardly.'

'Sod off in it anyway,' said Tragolani, nudging his gun in the air, as if that might shift the intruder.

The extremely young man sighed and set off ruefully towards his Dauberman VK7. As he passed Tragolani, he stopped one last time to ask him: 'And your name's not Tra-golani?'

'No.'

'Fine. What is then?'

Tragolani stared hard at the youth in surprise and said with a snigger, 'It's Maricolo.'

The youth stared right back, then turned and resumed his walk, murmuring, by way of goodbye, 'Wild. That's mine.'

Ten minutes later, in the gloom of Burneau's lofty habitat, the reclusive ex-Minister received the muscular youth with a joyful embrace, having peered at him uncomprehendingly for some moments.

'Because you look nothing like him!' he exclaimed.

'We all grow,' said Paol Maricolo. 'We none of us stay the age I was.'

'He must have grown half his size again!' Burneau told Tragolani excitedly, while the latter, who had climbed only half-way into the treehouse, nodded and said: 'Uh-huh. More Pilgrim, boss?'

As Burneau waved Tragolani out into the branches again to collect the wine from wherever they kept it, Maricolo put his hand into his coat and brought out a little bottle of his own. Burneau visibly shrank away.

'What kind of glass is that, Paoli?'

'Not glass, plastic,' said the young man. 'Why?'

'No reason,' Burneau said hoarsely. 'How did you find me?'

'Asked around. Doesn't matter. Heard a rumour. Who cares? Found you.'

'Have you seen your sister? Tragolani found her, she's all right, she's now working in – '

'This is what you want, man; we lived on this in the war.'

Burneau gave him an odd look, then gingerly took the bottle and held it up to see. The liquid was viscous, yellow-brown, slow to move. The label, which was handwritten, read simply 'Spirit of the Front'.

322

'Spirit of the Front,' said Burneau. 'This isn't an Argeline drink, is it?'

'It's a gypsy drink. Recipe's a secret. We used to swipe it from the encampments round Tatri when our wine ran out. Play games, kind of thing. Last man to down it, first man to heave it, you know . . . Have a go, man. Have a go, then tell me what gives with the old house in a tree. I knew you were crazy, but this?'

Burneau sniffed the stuff, blinked twice, then took a hesitant sip. Maricolo watched him, smiling.

'Smooth at first, freezes up, then it cracks, then it bleeds . . .'

Tragolani reappeared with a bottle of purple wine.

'What's the prince of the byways forcing down you, boss?'

'Spirit of the Front,' said Burneau. 'It's smooth, then it — cracks?'

'Freezes up,' Maricolo corrected, 'then it cracks.'

'Then it bleeds,' Burneau added. 'But it's still smooth . . . oh no, it's starting to freeze a bit now . . .'

Maricolo grinned. 'That's how I grew up, man, you're drinking it.'

Burneau took a larger swig, flushed and announced: 'We are all going to drink a toast to the reunion of Paol and Juilla Maricolo forthwith!'

'You seen her lately?' Maricolo asked.

'Federico has.'

'I saw her,' said Tragolani: 'She's fine, she's got shift work. Might be nice if you told her you were back on the rock, my friend. You know women.'

'The women can wait,' said Maricolo. 'First, a drink to — enemies in wartime, friends in peacetime . . .'

Burneau filled his mug half full with the slow thick concoction, then said loudly: 'That is something I would be delighted to drink to!'

'Can you drink as much as him?' Maricolo asked Tragolani.

'Dole me some of that slug-trail and I'll show you.' He took the bottle from Burneau, filled his own beaker and raised it, demanding of Maricolo, 'Where's your drink, Mr Dauberman Wheelbarrow VK7?'

Maricolo emptied the remains into the mug Burneau passed him, and the three men drank together, high up in that tree.

Then they set their mugs down empty on the planks of the floor, all licked their lips, made the various sounds by which men signify the successful despatch of very strong drink, and waited for the liquor to determine what each would find to say next.

But the next thing that happened seemed to contradict what had gone before. The swaggering army drinker Maricolo's cheeks bulged, then he jerked his head forward, seemed to hiccup, then splattered a mug's worth of completely unreconstituted foamy spirit all over the floor of Burneau's arboreal retreat. The howls and jeers of contempt that might have been expected from the older men were caught, however, in their throats. The eyes of both Burneau and Tragolani had quite glazed over, and nothing moved for a whole three minutes at the top of the tree, until Tragolani slumped forwards comatose into the mess, and Maricolo sprang into action, hoisting the equally unconscious Burneau across his broad shoulder, and beginning the long, complicated climb down to the meadow.

Outside of sexual love, it is virtually unheard of on this island for a human ever to do for another human exactly what the other would like done. Outside of sexual love, it is also exceedingly rare for a human to do to another the precise opposite of his or her desire. But what Maricolo now did to Burneau was an approximation of the opposite of Burneau's desire.

For one had found Burneau at what had clearly been the best place for him: peaceful, harmonious, solitudinous, stone-free.

Now, when the once-popular, once-powerful Minister of Reconciliation, drugged, dragged and grimy with dust, stiffly reopened his eyes upon life, he was greeted by the sight of Paol Maricolo opposite, squatting down in army fatigues, chewing, pointing a gun at him. All around was waste-ground, dust, rubbish, detritus. Maricolo sat on a great rusty canister. Beyond him, the nearest human life was packed into vans and flashing across a distant flyover. Nothing here looked like anything Burneau had ever wanted or hoped, not since one began to want and hope on his behalf. Accordingly, he thought he was in the hands of his destroyer, and sat up quivering in a stone world.

'You're with him, aren't you?'

'Who?' demanded Maricolo.

'Yung. You're with Yung!'

'Yung? I'm not with anyone. I'm free, man.'

'Your gun's made of stone, bullets are made of stone, they *are* stone! Ground is made of stone if you want me to fall against it, in fact it's all of it all of it — '

'Shut up, Burneau, shut up, man and listen! Then you can talk whatever crap you got still for brains.'

Burneau blinked, and mumbled: 'I've got some power, Paoli, I can make things happen . . .'

'You got no power, man. I got the power. I got my own gun like you had, and you got nothing.'

'You don't know Yung . . .'

'Shut up about him whoever. I want to talk about my sister.'

'What about your sister?'

'You remember her then? That's man of you.'

Burneau shook his head.

'I do remember your sister. I saw her, I've seen her since the war ended, she asked to see me, she — '

Maricolo got off the canister and strode up to Burneau, brandishing the pistol right in his face. The youth was seething. 'Liar! She don't want you, she don't want you, man, she don't want to see you!'

'What do you mean?'

'I know you! I know about you was in the room that day – the time you were with us, man, the time you were having my mother also!'

'No I never, Paoli, I – '

'My ma sling you out for it, so don't give me that nothing, man! I tell 'em that day, I tell my mother and sister I say if I ever find that fucker Burneau I'll kill him with my two hands for raping my sister! Look at yourself now, man!'

Burneau cried: 'I didn't do that! You were lied to, Paoli!'

As Maricolo put his free hand round Burneau's throat, Burneau's hands lifted reflexively in self-protection, but they glided down again when Maricolo desisted, spitting. 'Sevenfolds a liar, man, sevenfolds! You wait your chance that time, then you go for her, when we're keeping you alive in our place! We saved your hide, man, keeping you in our place, making out you was our father. You remember that? And you all the time making on to my ma, then you come after my sister and rape her? You're evil, man, no wonder them fucking bandits love you!'

'We love each other, Paoli – your sister and I – that's the truth of it!'

Maricolo glared, and backed away a couple of steps, stumbling, muttering: 'Believe it's not so, man, believe it's not so . . .'

'Why shouldn't it be so?' Burneau pleaded. 'She loved me then and loves me now!'

'Not you. Not you.'

'I love her, Paol, I know that's true!'

'Oh no, you got no love. You're a terrorist, man, you're a killer and a cheat and a war criminal. Only you get on the winning side. I fight when I'm told and I get two years in the hole with dead men! You raped the island and now you run it . . .'

'You ask her if I raped her, Paol. She'll tell you.'

Maricolo cackled, then retreated a few yards and stopped. He wiped his gun on his brow.

'You think my sister'd love a dog like you?'

'I know she does. Ask her.'

Maricolo stared for a long time at the traffic on the flyover. Then he looked back at Burneau. 'Fine. You show me. You ask her. Let me hear her tell you she loves you.'

'Tell me? She can't, she's – '

'So she can't? You mean she won't, you shit, man!'

'It's the stone, Paol, you got to believe me, it's the stone! I can't stay outside, I can't go to Badeo, a man is trying to kill me with stone – that's why I live in the tree, you see, because this lunatic is – '

'Hey, what's this shit?' yelled Maricolo, rushing at him with the gun again. 'You think this is, what, a water fight? I don't care about no lunatic, *I'm* the lunatic, *I'm* trying to kill you. You give me some respect or maybe I will do!'

'All right, all right!' cried Burneau, raising his arms to the youth. 'It's just that I can't go anywhere near your sister now because of this man out there, the man with the stone. If it wasn't for him, I'd go straight to her! If it wasn't – '

Maricolo roared into his face: 'You shit, you snake, Burneau! – you care more about your evil rebel hide than about my sister! You send your drunk out to look for her while you swing through the trees? You down below everyone, man, you way down in the swamp!'

'Oh, I'm not!' roared Blue Burneau. 'I'll show you, little brother Paoli, I'll find her, you'll see us, you'll hear her tell me to my face she loves me – right? Then you'll be happy, yes? That what you want to hear? You'll hear it, I swear it!'

'She'll never say it.'

'She'll say it!'

'She better, man, or I'll kill you.'

'She'll say it anywhere, Paol, any time, just tell me where and when! You want to see love you'll see it! You want to hear lovers you'll hear us! You'll be happy then, Paol. I'll tell her you're free!'

'The fuck you will, Burneau. She thinks I'm dead and it stays like that till this deal is done.'

327

'My friend, you're mad, you're – '

'I'm not your fucking friend, man. You know the Falls Taverna?'

'What?'

'The Falls Taverna! Rich man's dining house.'

'Above F-Furasol, under the c-cliffs?' Burneau stammered.

'Take her there. Tomorrow night.'

'That's – that's – that's a m-m-mountain, Paol, it's – '

'It's full of fucking stone, yeah right, and the Taverna's built into the cliff. We used the place in the war, we fired at you bastards from the roof. We threw your dead sloper dogs down the Manzini Falls. Stone everywhere, man. We'll see how much you love . . .'

'You – are asking me to take your sister to the F-F-Falls Taverna?'

'And let me hear her tell you she loves you.'

'In the Taverna? The Falls Taverna?'

'You want money? I can get money.'

'I don't need your money. What if she won't come?'

'You're dead.'

'What if she can't come?'

'You're dead.'

'What if she won't say it in public?'

'You're dead. You take her to the Falls Taverna, you buy her dinner, you make her tell you she loves you so that I can hear it – and I'll be right by your side, man, all the evening – then fine, I'll be waiting for her when she gets home, and everyone's happy, and see you at the wedding. Else, she don't come with you, or she comes and she don't eat, or she eats and she don't love you – then you're dead dog by sunrise, Burneau, and that ain't 'cos you gave the island over to the bandits, or 'cos you shot a good man down, or 'cos you lie that you didn't do it – so long to all that fighting shit – you take the long drop 'cos you trampled on my ma and sister, and came on like you was father to us all. My ma saved your hide, Burneau. Now you better hope my sister feels the same. I'm out of here. You better start moving.'

328

'I don't know where I am!' cried Burneau, dragging himself to his feet.

'Make something up. It's what you always do.'

With that, Maricolo walked over to his white truck, climbed in and drove off. By the time his truck had joined the traffic on the highway, Burneau was nowhere to be seen.

Then he was a distant blue speck inching over the wasteland.

Then he was waving his arms on the very edge of the highway!

VI

One drifts through the streets of cities and lanes of towns. One hangs off the fences at the sides of villages, ghosts through the yards of chapels, one walks by the sea. The young loving couples go staring and chuckling by with their special jokes and gifts and belongings, and they ornament the time with innocence and wildness and hopeful feeling, just as they have ornamented every time and each country with their indifference to the covert hatreds of the empowered, their obliviousness to the gravitational drag of want and boredom, their murmured defiance of the clock. Their numbers rise as cities grow in knowledge. The parklands fill with them in the wisest of countries. The freedom of young loving couples is the good upbringing of the nation. Scorn of sexual love is a country's second childhood.

So what could have been better than to see a young man catch the elevated train, carrying a small bouquet of yellow roses under his arm, and walk the length of that train to find a lovely young woman dozing in a corner? What more beautiful than the look on his face as he found her, what more tender than the care with which he sat down beside her before she noticed him? Had this been one's first encounter with the life of Maris Burneau, one would have smiled at the unfolding generosity of his day, felt warmth at the realisation of his dreams and hopes, noted him down among the thousands of others, and moved on softly to find a different story, not even waiting long enough to see the sand-edged eyes of the girl fluttering open, or hear her first sounds of recollected bliss.

As it was, Juilla opened her red eyes and stared hotly at him.

'You're back,' she said.

'Have these,' he said, holding up the flowers.

'Why? Where can I put them?'

'In water,' said Burneau.

'What water?' said Juilla.

They proceeded along these lines to her stop, where they disembarked and walked along Promenad Furasol. It was a warm but gusty autumn day, dry so far. Burneau still had the flowers. Juilla was yawning.

'Why you want to take me there?' she yawned.

'It is a very beautiful place, Jula, and I've something I have to tell you.'

She stopped.

'You got news?'

'Yes!' said Burneau.

'About Paoli?'

'Well . . . Yes!'

'Tell me now, here.'

'I can't. Come to dinner.'

'I can't. I have work.'

Burneau seized her by the upper arms and said urgently: 'It's terribly important, Jula, it's a matter of life and death that you have dinner with me tonight! I've got some government money left, I'll pay your wage!'

'That's so sexy, Mr Blue Devil. How much?'

They walked on, arguing for a time, Burneau yielding no details of his news, Juilla making no commitment. Burneau tried to convince Juilla that he was taking her to the most beautiful place on Badeo; Juilla asked him not to call her 'Jula', it was a child's name. Burneau asked her what she wanted from life. Sleep, she said.

'Sleep, then, Juilla,' he said. 'Sleep until six, then I'll come to your place and we'll go to Furasol.'

'How will we get to Furasol *if*, that is, *if* I go. Can you drive?'

Burneau said: 'Yes.'

'. . . But my van is at the workshop,' he explained, when he arrived early that evening at a tiny one-room flat on the Plaza Nuneval. 'There is, however, a very good coach service that departs from the University Lodge . . .'

'I'll need 570 markers against losing that job, I worked it out. Did you say coach service?'

'You don't want that job, Juilla, it's all lies.'

'I don't want to ride on a coach service with you.'

'We'll take separate seats.'

She looked at how he was dressed.

'Just now you're Blue Burneau,' she observed.

Burneau was indeed wearing an ironed blue suit, which very pleasantly set off the red roses he had brought. Juilla took them and went back into her room, leaving him standing uneasily on the Plaza, which was filled with little sneering groups of children. When she returned she was wearing a simple white dress with a black sash and ribbons in her hair. She was the most beautiful girl on the island in those days, and that was the best she had ever looked.

'I've changed my mind,' she said, 'I'm staying in.'

Because they rode in separate seats on the crowded Furasol coach, both had to endure the conversation of slightly inebriated students out for a relaxing weekend on the Bay. The coach made an infinite number of request stops as it followed the line of the coast, however, so these travel-companions changed by the minute. Burneau kept standing up in his seat to keep an eye on Juilla, a few rows ahead. She was always ignoring her seat partners, staring out of her window at the yachts on the Bay, the sun going down in yellow clouds behind them, making their hulls gleam goldenly while blackening their sails.

'Sit down,' said Burneau's next student, who was Paoli Maricolo in dark glasses and a wide-brimmed hat. 'You're drawing attention to yourself.'

'It's not easy, Paoli. One day you'll be in love. You'll understand.'

'In love?' Maricolo snorted. 'Don't make me heave. You paid her to come, man, I saw you, now she won't even sit with you.'

'I paid her because she'll lose her job at National.'

'Fuck, man, if you paid me to stuff myself at the Falls Taverna out of a bandit's wages, I'd come, job or no job. You slime, Burneau, you're going to lose it all. That's a terrible suit. I'm off.'

Maricolo moved towards the back of the coach. Burneau stood up again, smoothed his suit jacket, and watched Juilla watch the sun go down over the Bay.

'There's a seat underneath you, sir,' said a polite student who had eased in next to him, having had to stand in the aisle all this time.

When the coach stopped in the middle of Furasol it was dark. Juilla got out first and stood shivering under a lamp-post in what was in fact quite warm night air. Burneau joined her by the lamp-post, and glanced back to see who else was getting out of the coach.

'Made a friend, did you, Blue Devil?' Juilla mocked.

'That's right,' said Burneau. 'We're engaged to be married.'

Burneau led Juilla through the bright streets, along the main drag, then they took a left up a narrow steep incline, a dark cobbled avenue.

'Super part of the world,' said Juilla. 'This is where you rebels used to eat each other?'

'You got that off the television. Look: we're going to take a ride.'

The top of the little avenue was also the DOWN terminus of a funicular railway that stretched its taut cables up the side of Mount San Timotheo into impenetrable darkness, but for the warm lonely lamp of the UP terminus, and, next to it, an illuminated house.

'That's where we're going to eat,' said Burneau. 'I hope you're hungry.'

'Hey, in that hanging car? I hope you're joking.'

The two of them had the cabin to themselves, and could see below them the twinkling lights of Furasol all the way to the dark Bay. Beyond the black water was the bright long strip of Badeo Town itself.

'I'm somewhere there, asleep,' said Juilla.

'I'm somewhere there, alive,' said Burneau, though he appeared to be looking even further out, perhaps remembering his Argeline origins, though the great Mainland was beyond his horizon.

'I'm not hungry,' said Juilla.

'I am,' said Burneau.

At the Falls Taverna he ordered the largest steak, which was called a 'Galido Granda', and every vegetable option there was. Juilla chose rice with a sauce and three big salads, because she was unable to choose between them. 'The three things I like are yellow tomatoes, drawbeans and whiteroot mash. So of course you see they have to spread those things over three completely different salads. You must be rich now, mister, because I have to have them all.'

Burneau nodded and traced his finger down the wine list.

'Castel Karol-Lajessi,' he said. The waiter took the booklet away, and Burneau sighed. 'We drank that at the Camp. It was near here. It was on this mountain.'

'I know that, Blue Devil. I watch the news.'

'It was a bad time,' Burneau recalled.

'Sounds like, if you drank that stuff. That was the wine at the bottom, it had millions of markers by it.'

'The President is a connoisseur.'

'He's a murdering slime.'

'He was a professor, you know, a Professor of Wines.'

'He's a lying dog. He says there are no more prisoners anywhere. So where's Paoli?'

334

Burneau, who had evidently noticed Maricolo in a corner of the aperitif bar, wearing sunglasses and unfolding a giant newspaper, said: 'I don't know, Juilla. Maybe he didn't make it.'

'He made it, mister. He's the king of escapers.'

'That's me, Juilla. Here's our wine.'

They drank a whole bottle before the food arrived, and Burneau ordered another one with it. He became animated, by turns nervous and amusing, while she said very little, concentrating on the splendour of her food, and the hugeness of the wine glasses.

'They may as well be tankards being this thick.'

'They may as well. You like the wine?'

'It's gorgeous, Blue Devil.'

'Are you enjoying yourself?'

'I'm enjoying the food and wine. You would if you'd got through the war on black bread and eggs instead of this Castle Carol'n'Jesse. What's your news then? That's why I came.'

'Oh, that can wait,' said Burneau with his mouth full. 'Can't we just – enjoy each other's company?'

Juilla put her fork down neatly.

'I'm telling you, Mr Burneau, I didn't come here for company. I came to hear how you're still looking for Paoli, and that's all. It's your bloody old war, isn't it? You shot the Viceroy, you started it. You sat up in that old Camp and took our soldiers out. You're why my brother went. And my ma, come to think, but she always had it in for me . . . No, you're why everything. You and no one else but you, Mr Bandit Blue Devil.'

Burneau stared. It looked perfectly impossible for him to prevent himself doing what he had just thought of doing.

'I love you, Juilla.'

Their waiter arrived suddenly. 'Is everything fine, sir?'

'No,' said Juilla.

'Yes,' said Burneau.

'Very good, sir,' said the waiter drifting off with a smile.

Juilla rested her upper teeth on her lower lip, shook her head, and said: 'No, no way, no how, no do. All so long ago. No way. Doomed.'

'I would have stayed for ever,' Burneau persisted, 'but we fell asleep and she found us. Don't you remember?'

'Wasn't like that. You planned it all. Lies of Blue Burneau. Paol told me.'

'What, planned what? What lies? I fell in love with you!'

'Then moved to a mountain and started a war against my whole world. What's that, wedding present, Blue Devil?'

'I was a wanted man, Juilla!'

'Not by me.'

'Hell, yes!'

'Hell no. You believe what you want. It's a Free Island, as you're aware.'

'I'll believe what I want!'

'Any desserts required, sir?' asked the waiter, who appeared to have seeped up out of the carpet like steam.

'No,' said Burneau.

'Yes,' said Juilla. 'What's this Zokolat de Larola?'

'It's a thin pastry base, my lady, covered in thick mocha chocolate and strawberries, then a layer of banana cream, then the chef's own secret almond topping. It's exquisite, my lady, if you don't mind me saying.'

'No. Can I have cream on it as well?'

'Cream,' noted the waiter, dematerialising with a bow.

Juilla looked happy. 'You're always so hasty, you are, mister, so serious. You should cheer up more. Look at you.'

'You'll make yourself sick with all that cream,' said Burneau sulkily.

'After black bread and eggs for two years, I'll throw up anything.'

As the mountainous dessert arrived and Juilla Maricolo tucked into it with relish, Burneau glanced across the bar where he saw her brother, still in dark glasses, grinning and

336

shaking his head. He waited for Juilla to finish off a mouthful of chocolate-coated strawberries, then said: 'Juilla, if you don't want me around in your life, I'll go, I'll go far away. I wouldn't want to stay.'

She licked her lips and smiled pleasantly. 'I'll miss these dinners, Mr Burneau.'

'Tragolani said you said you loved me.'

'I don't like him.'

'He's a good friend. He looks after me. Or – he did.'

'I don't like him. Sorry.'

'Do you – do you think you love me?'

Juilla made a muffled noise to emphasise how much her mouth was full of pudding. Burneau forged on.

'If you were just to say it once, I'd go, I'd leave you alone. If you just said you loved me, Juilla, here, now, you'd never have to see me again, nor hear my lies or troubles.'

'You can't go,' munched the girl. 'You've not paid.'

'Lie to me, Juilla, lie to me, I don't care. Just say it once!'

'Say what.'

'Say you love me.'

'Just to get rid of you?'

'Just to get rid of me. Quite loudly, though.'

'In front of all these people?' she wondered, heaping almonds on her spoon.

'Just once, then never again.'

'Coffee?' asked the waiter, who this time had slithered out of the Zokolat de Larola. 'Spirits?'

When Maricolo saw his sister throw down her fork and spoon, stand up and storm out of the Falls Taverna crying, 'I don't love you, mister, I hate you!' he himself stood up and let his newspaper float to the ground. He took off his sunglasses, folded his arms and grinned at what had happened. Burneau fumbled several hundred 100-marker notes out of his blue suit on to the table, so that the money completely swamped the remains of their candlelit dinner, then hurried out after her, past the courteous smiles of the waiting staff, and the stares of the smart astonished guests. Maricolo, obviously cast in whatever drama was about to unfold, gave a grim public laugh, and went after his quarry.

The silence that sheeted every table in the dining room of the Falls Taverna was finally broken by the whisper of a wife to her husband.

'Did you see his face, Roberto? That was Blue Burneau.'

'I saw him,' said the husband, 'and I guarantee it wasn't.'

Juilla Maricolo was walking curiously slowly, away from the Taverna but not towards the UP terminus of the funicular railway. She was taking the dirt road that wound around Mount San Timotheo, the path used by slopers on the mountainside and intrepid walkers from all corners of the island. She continued to move at this painfully retarded pace until Burneau burst into the light outside the restaurant. As soon as he saw her, she quickened and went into the dark. Burneau peered ahead and set off in pursuit. Then Maricolo burst into the same pool of light, and saw him, likewise, just as he disappeared up the track.

As soon as all three of them had passed behind an outcrop of the mountain, the last faint spill from Furasol was cut off and they had only starlight to go by. It was just about light enough to see how narrow the path was, too slight for motor vehicles, and how steep was the plunge on the right-hand side, down into an abysmal blackness of rocks and wild woodland.

'Juilla!' yelled Burneau. 'You don't understand!'

'I do!' came a faint cry, much further ahead than one would have expected.

'You're steak, man, you're Galida Granda,' said the voice of Maricolo, much closer behind than Burneau would have wanted.

'Juilla, I love you!' he roared into the night.

Now nothing came from far ahead.

'Leave her the fuck alone,' came the grunt from close behind.

Heavens, the starry heavens alone, know what went through Burneau's mind as he ran, but, whatever it was, some kindness in the past or forgiveness in the future, some glad morning or golden evening, some long-forgotten face or long-remembered voice – or the pure blue terror of the hunted human man – from somewhere deep in his soul he found the strength to run faster. With his stomach a swag-bag of food and wine, he ran; with his mind streaming and his eyes seeing nothing, he ran the fastest he could ever have run, and gradually, ever so gradually, he began to pull back the yards between Juilla and himself, and to widen the gap between himself and Maricolo.

'Believe I love you!' he howled through his gasping.

'All too long ago!' cried the girl, some twenty yards ahead now.

'I got you, I got you!' came the heavy splutter of his pursuer, some thirty, forty yards back and stumbling as he spoke.

And then it started. Gravel and pebbles, rocks and stones, scuffing down the cliffs above them, breaking on the road and leaping in fragments over the edge into the dark below.

'Murder!' screamed Burneau, the first to be hit.

'Landslide!' roared Maricolo, and fell to his knees.

Juilla looked up blankly as the pebbles began raining down around them.

Burneau put his hand to his face, which was cut and beginning to bleed.

'Run under the cliff!' he cried ahead to Juilla. 'Run under the cliff and wait for me!'

Juilla, still uninjured, ran against the cliff and hugged it. Burneau, also flattened against it, crept along its rough face. The stone shower had eased off slightly, giving Maricolo a chance likewise to shelter in the mountain's overhang. Further along the cliff-face, other slides were beginning, as pebbles dislodged stones that knocked small boulders from their ancient moorings. Wherever he stood, giant against the starlight, the Guardsman Yung – for one does not believe in coincidences – had found the perfect place from where to bring every loose rock on the north face of Mount San Timotheo pelting down on Furasol, that wounded heartland of the independence struggle.

Burneau finally reached Juilla, wedged against the face of the cliff as the stones began to rain once more on the path.

'The Falls!' he yelled. 'The Falls! We can make it to the Falls!'

'What?' she cried out, as a flint scuffed her shoulder and cut the sleeve of her dress with a red tear.

'We'll go in the water there – no more stones!'

'What?' she cried again, as a rock the size of a man's head missed Burneau by inches. 'Watch out!'

'Come on, Jula, it's not far to run!'

Burneau stepped round her, took her hand and began to pull her along, both still sliding right up against the cold face of the cliff.

Maricolo, afforded better shelter where he was, had already crawled half the distance towards them, cursing as one rock thumped his fingers and some fragments cannoned off his cheek.

The great gorge of the Manzini Falls split Mount San Timotheo at its north-western spur: the river Manzini was the widest and strongest in the Furasolian delta, having plummeted so far down a sheer drop. Here its spray was a ghostly white shroud between two thunderous drums of destruction, as the terrible landslide started shearing away ledges and pathways, snapping off outcrops like twigs, forming new rubbles of chaos for as long as they had a place to settle.

Now one could hear the first stones raining on the mountainside villages of the wealthy, the first human cries, the first wails of emergency klaxons. Those trapped high up on the north face itself would be lucky to be remembered. Already the lamps at the UP terminus of the funicular railway

340

had been smashed off, and the Falls Taverna, with its roof stove in, was ominously dark and quiet.

Tiny from this vantage, Maris Burneau staggered, bleeding, round the ankles of the mountain, tugging his distraught beloved behind him as her dangerous brother crawled and stumbled doggedly in pursuit, and the stones of Mount San Timotheo hurtled past into unlimited darkness.

'We'll jump, we'll have to, love!' Burneau howled over the noise.

'Where, into what? Jump where?' wept the girl.

'There!' he shouted, as they reached the sudden edge. 'That!'

Juilla almost fell past him into the spray in her horror. The tumult of the landslide must have drowned out the waterfall's own thunder, for she stared down and screamed with panic as Burneau caught her and held on.

Maricolo was getting closer, wiping blood off his brow. Only one sharp jut of rock now obscured his view of the two of them, and, standing up and shielding his face with his arms, the youth peered upwards into the dreadful hail. As it seemed to be thinner and lighter so close to the edge of the waterfall, he advanced steadily away from the cliff-face to get a better angle. Then the first of the silhouettes came into view, Burneau's, then Juilla's, two silhouettes clutched tightly together before the impossible white and hurling foam. He stepped towards them, almost doubled up, his arms locked over his head. He would have heard Burneau roaring from there.

'You have to jump! There's no stone! We'll float, we'll come out on the banks below! There's no more stone!'

'I can't! We'll die!'

'You won't die, Jula! I love you, you can't!'

Maricolo glared through blood, and took out his pistol.

Juilla screamed at Burneau: 'But you can die! You can die, mister! What about me then!'

'No, I can't die, love! I'm Blue Burneau! I can't die, I love you!'

'Blue Devil – will you hold me?'

Burneau held her even tighter.

'No,' she yelled, 'when I jump, you donkey!'

'I will, I will hold you!'

Now Juilla held him, as stones ricocheted around their battered feet, and when they parted they rejoined and kissed for what as far as one knows was the first time, or the first time for a long time, and then – and it was not clear which of the two initiated this, which in this angelically bewildering world one may take to be some token of true love – they rocked over the edge together with a protracted and harmonious scream.

Maricolo saw the embrace, and he saw the kiss, but he'd gone so far to learn to learn so little, and was much too near the edge when he saw what he had come to see. A huge boulder was seven yards above his head when a smile began to form on his face, seven feet above when he nodded to himself, seven inches above when he began a word that began with *S*, which, had there been life enough to say it, had promised volume enough to attract the attention of both his sister and his briefly new-found brother.

The naked sprawled bodies of Maris Burneau and Juilla Maricolo were found tangled together on a little mossy bank in a quiet backwater of the River Muzau, about two miles downriver from the Falls.

The holy sisters who found them had been busy all morning tending Furasolians injured in what everybody was excitedly calling the Great Slide. The women had been praying for the recovery of their sixteen patients, and were on their way to fetch water from the river when they spotted the bodies.

The man was on his back, his eyes open, his arms and legs spread out in every direction. The woman – no more than a girl, for sure – was lying face down across him, so that they formed an X (something for which the holy sisters could be

342

thankful, perhaps, since each was concealing the other's most private regions). They were curiously bloodless. They did not appear to have drowned.

The first sister to find them knelt down on the mossy bank. Her companion said: 'Mercy on them, lost in a vengeful rain.'

Burneau, for want of anything better to say, said: 'Good morning there.'

The holy sisters ran screaming back to their hospital and contacted the authorities. By mid-afternoon Burneau and Juilla were in jail in Badeo Town.

And this time they had gone too far. The President sent a stranger to see them, a police commander called Gremish, who told them, tonelessly but with emphasis, that, though it much grieved President Iaio Gabril, he could not see former Minister Burneau in person. He was too preoccupied with the aftermath of the Great Slide at Furasol, which had triggered off a minor insurrection in Eastern Badeo, where anti-Government forces had gathered to feed off the superstitions of villagers convinced that the rockfall was a divine vengeance upon Furasol for the Rebellion. Regiments were on the move. These were troubled times, again.

'I quite understand,' said Burneau, who was handcuffed to Juilla, both of them now in blue prison clothes, having been brought from the Delta in bits of rough sacking. 'I do quite understand. But what have we done wrong?'

'We can set aside gross indecency committed on private grounds,' said Commander Gremish. 'We can overlook your underpaying the bill at the Falls Taverna by 3,568 markers and seven cents, since the Falls Taverna is not now in any position to prosecute, having neither fixed assets nor securities. We are not overly concerned with the arboreal violence committed against a guaranteed tree in the region of Laquilla. Nor with simple vandalism of a boat called *Dantelle*, registered to a Captain Quan of Badeo. No, those are minor matters. The way I understand it, Mr Burneau, is that the President senses about your good self a whole climate of unease and unpredictability. There was the War, of course, and I, in brackets, for one salute your contribution to that, Mr Burneau, on a personal note ending the brackets, but he feels that since the War you have not been at your best. Overworked, Mr Burneau, tired. There was the business with the Amnesty, he mentioned, and then the unpleasantness in the market district. He stated that he was not interested in why the mountain should start to crumble to pieces and crush half the luxury homes in Little Fura at the exact moment you decide to dine in the area, Mr Burneau, but he wished me to relay to you his disquiet at the coincidence. He very much wanted me to say this: "The taste of mine and taste of yours are not the same, so pass . . . The cup between and taste anew and . . ." something something glass. Then – '

'It wouldn't be glass,' muttered Burneau, 'it would rhyme with "yours".'

'Right. "The taste of mine and taste of yours are not the same, so pass . . . The cup between and taste anew," er – '

'"The origin and cause",' said Burneau: '"For every drop in every glass is changing into you."'

'Well,' said Gremish tersely. 'He did want that said.'

'It got said,' said Juilla.

'And,' the Commander continued, 'that he thanks you from the bottom of the cask for your help in the Heroic Struggle of the Badean people, and trusts that you understand that he can do no more for you than grant you the considerable mercy of this sentence upon you and your female accomplice, namely you, miss, and so.'

Burneau, whose fingers were now entwined with Juilla's as they sat there manacled, said brightly: 'I understand what he thinks I understand, and trust what he thinks I trust, and thank him for whatever he grants us. I always liked him.'

Commander Gremish wrote something down on his own document, then said briskly: 'Good. Then we shall proceed to the harbour.'

344

'The harbour?' asked Juilla. 'What for, chum?'

'That's where the boats sail from, miss. The harbour.'

Burneau and Juilla were taken to a large underground garage and helped into the back of a sealed van by some young Urban Watch cadets.

'Watch your step there,' said the leader of them.

Burneau thanked him.

Commander Gremish unlocked a little window at the back of the van, shook Burneau's free hand and wished them well.

Then off they were driven, through Badeo to that same wharf from which Burneau had steered the *Dantelle* on his perilous voyage to Miscobar. The Watch cadets helped them down into wet, dark, autumnal daylight, for it was by now late afternoon, and led them along the wharf to a blue motor craft, the *Gleam in the Eye*, some twenty yards long, a boat for a crew of six, it looked.

'Blue ship for a blue man,' said Juilla.

'I'm not good at steering these,' Burneau answered in tears.

Once aboard, the leader of the cadets unlocked them from their handcuffs and escorted them down into the boat, showing them the galley, their living space, two sets of narrow bunk beds, a tiny bathroom near the bow.

Burneau sat down on one of the beds and said nothing, but Juilla demanded of the cadet: 'Shouldn't you teach us how to sail the boat?'

'No need,' said the cadet with a smile. 'If you look, love, I think you'll find your helmsman is aboard.'

'Anyone for Spirit of the Front?' said Tragolani, stepping down into the galley quite engulfed in a rugged sea sweater. He'd been arrested that afternoon in a bar called The Livelihood. 'No one loves us any more, boss.'

And the cadet soon departed from the *Gleam in the Eye*, for he was very young and inexperienced in working with criminal types, and had been, as he told his colleagues later in the bar they frequented, both surprised and embarrassed by the unabashed joy and vigour with which the three – the helmsman, the 'honey' and the disgraced ex-Minister – hugged each other and cried. The sentence of 'Perpetual Banishment from Badeo' was just a sentence to the cadet, a sentence that was merciful because it was not prison and not death. He would say the words over and over again that night, when the *Gleam in the Eye* was far out to sea, far from sight of Badeo Island, but he could not make them strong enough to carry the weight of emotion he had witnessed, and he staggered home inebriated but insisting to his friends that no, never again would he dwell on the personal.

In the darkness of the night, before one too must leave the island – for Maris Burneau, his was the story one chose in one's innocence to follow and remember – in the darkness of the night, as the *Gleam in the Eye* rolls and heaves on the ocean, and a hooded figure can be seen distinctly holding on by its one green lamp, it falls to one, in the absence of a Badeo Present, to observe how there endured two curious phenomena on the island far into Badeo To-Come.

Burneau left his name behind. After he was gone, a character in one of the long-running television dramas (it was called *The Return of Carli* and set in the remote past) began frequently to refer to a range of dark blue colours as being 'blue as Burneau'. The phrase caught on, though nobody who said it found it easy to define. Some meant 'blue' to mean 'unhappy', and some meant it to mean 'naive'. Some meant it to mean 'gone away for ever', others 'beautiful', and to children it merely felt lucky on the tongue.

But to most people, it was a shade of sky: late evening sky on a good clear day, a spectrum of blues from a rich purple to the pale blue of a boy's eye, and one would say to his companions, 'That's a sky that's blue as burneau,' without really knowing what burneau was, or why it was blue, or what he meant at all. It was his companions who would know what he meant, each knowing something different, each knowing

346

that the one who had looked up and remarked upon the sky had in reality some ache in his heart, and that at the moment he had spoken it had suddenly intensified, and for the moment it intensified it didn't ache at all.

The north face of Mount San Timotheo continued for years afterwards to behave in the most treacherous and erratic manner. Once or twice a year – usually at the turn of a season – it would rain rocks upon the communities beneath, until people simply ceased to build their homes there. Several expeditions were mounted high above the tree-line, to search for evidence of what was causing this chronic geological instability, but nothing was ever scientifically proven. And no importance could be attached to two or three uncorroborated sightings of a shy colossus who kicked boulders as he walked, and whose hands moved so fast they were nothing but clouds.

VII

When night fell on that first evening, Tragolani could still see the shape of Badeo on the horizon, with Cobar and Miscobar two black eggs close by it. He called Burneau and Juilla to the deck to see, but neither could make out what he was showing them. They had wasted too much time trying to open a third bottle of Mauette, and by the time they had filled three glasses the land was gone.

'Plenty more where that came from,' said Burneau.

'What's that, boss?' said Tragolani.

'Mauette. He gave us crates of it.'

'The Mauette,' Tragolani said blankly. Then: 'There goes home, you people.'

Burneau's conversation since they arrived on the *Gleam in the Eye* had been conducted entirely in terms of wine, as if he had lost his grip on their situation, and was trying to diminish all experience to what was in front of his face. Juilla seemed gay and excited, like a schoolgirl on a day trip; Tragolani was grave and wry. He locked the boat on to what he reckoned was a north-western course (the boat had been diligently stripped by the young cadets of all navigational facilities, so he declared he would rely on sunlight and stars) and then he joined the inebriated couple in the living space.

'North-western?' said Burneau with a frown. 'What's north-western?'

'I don't know,' said Tragolani, cutting up some bread for the three of them, 'but north is the Domain and we can't go there.'

'Why can't we go there?' wondered Juilla.

'Small matter of him,' said Tragolani, putting his hand on

Burneau's slumped shoulder. 'The Great Blue Devil, the Unmentionable Bandit Betrayer. Damned in Perpetuity. No going there.'

'Is that right . . . ' murmured Juilla.

'That's quite enough peppertutity for one night,' said Burneau. Juilla looked quizzically at Tragolani.

'So you don't know where we're going?'

'Who wants the crust? I'll have it. No, I'm going where I think it might be warm, dear. That's something. Whether there'll be any land to be warm on is another. Welcome to Perpetual Banishment, Miss Maricolo. Bread?'

They had planned to take it in turns at the helm, but by the end of that first evening they were all so tired that Tragolani just cut the engine and let them drift.

Burneau awoke naked in the double fold-out bed they had. Juilla was looking at him.

'Good morning,' he said.

'It's sunny, you know. Maybe we found somewhere.'

He kissed her. She was still looking at him, then she kissed him back.

They could hear the low throb of the engine, and sitting up in their small bed they could see Tragolani at the helm, drinking wine from a beer glass. All around him was brilliant blue sky, and the ocean flat and glittering with it.

They embraced together, and fell inside each other, and stayed inside each other while the morning grew sleepy. Burneau would try to speak, but Juilla would kiss him, then lie back and close her eyes.

Later they went out with breakfast for Tragolani. They sat together on a wooden ledge while he locked the wheel again. Then they told stories until they were hungry.

Burneau told them the truth about the Viceroy. That Nunez was the one who killed him. That he had been distracted by the colour of her hair, and had lost the Viceregal party. That he was not a rebel at heart, but a crossing-sentry.

349

Only, one thing had rather led to another. It was interesting to hear this.

Tragolani was not surprised. He told them he wasn't really a rebel either. He'd signed up for Gabril's vinicultural courses in order to meet Kalula Reynard, a girl from his home town, who had subsequently quit the University and become a piano singer. 'Like you say, boss, one thing rather leading to another.'

Juilla, who was extremely impressed by Tragolani's tale because she had heard of Kalula Reynard, told them the plot of *Amador the Wine-Grower*, during which recitation Tragolani and Burneau stared at each other sadly.

'Amador is basically a good person,' Juilla explained, 'but she has terrible demands, and it gets her into bad places with bad men.'

'How bad?' asked Tragolani.

'Desperate,' she told him. 'Nothing-to-lose men.'

'Does she survive?' Burneau wondered.

Juilla obviously found this such a daft question she looked at Tragolani for support.

'Does she survive? he goes. And it's only called *Amador the Wine-Grower*!'

'I hope she survives,' said Tragolani.

In the afternoons they would sleep, rising groggily at what they guessed was about six – Tragolani's watch was now showing a different time to the boat's clock – and at which time they would play games, or read one of the dozen or so worn-out history books the cadets had thoughtfully placed on board, or they would write diaries, or draw. It was only Burneau who drew, starting to fill a notebook with maps of fabulous islands, as if to compensate for the emptiness of the horizon.

Tragolani, rather tactlessly, still wanted to play Scissors-Paper-Stone (plus all the features he had imposed on it himself) and found an enthusiastic opponent in Juilla, who was every bit as ready as he was to manipulate the laws of the game. That would annoy Tragolani. 'Laws are laws, dear,' he would say. Burneau declined to participate, and went on crayoning in his islands.

After about a week of such days (six or seven days: Burneau had been scratching them up but Tragolani reckoned he'd missed one) they began to worry about their supplies. Juilla organised a system for eating less food, Burneau decided he would never drink again – after downing two bottles of bad Sutai in a morning – and Tragolani saved fuel more frequently, letting the boat drift ever further to what he said was the north-west.

They could not agree on that either.

'It's slipped,' Burneau said one afternoon in the galley. 'The lock's slipped because now we're moving east by the sun.'

'The sun declines in autumn, Maris,' said Tragolani. 'It's not as east as you think it is.'

'It's not east at all,' Juilla pointed out, 'as it's afternoon now.'

'It's not afternoon,' grumbled Burneau. 'We haven't had lunch yet.'

'And whose fault is that, mister?' she teased.

'It's not my lunch day!' Burneau retorted. 'It's Federico's!'

'It would be if you hadn't forgotten to scratch up that day,' said Tragolani.

'Scratch up what day?' said Burneau.

Burneau and Juilla woke up in the middle of the night staring at each other.

'What will happen?' said Juilla.

'We'll find somewhere,' said Burneau.

'When, mister?'

'Soon.'

'If we went to the Domain, maybe we could find Paol.'

'I can't go there, Juilla.'

'So what will happen?'

'We'll find somewhere.'

Juilla closed her eyes. Burneau took a long time to sleep again. When he woke again, she was looking at him again.

Tragolani had grown quiet and thoughtful. He read more, played fewer games, contented himself with maintenance of the boat and never asked for help from his companions. One night in about four, he would drink as if he was fixing to die of it, and let his mind flutter home, settle on his childhood, which he would relate to Burneau and Juilla in such rambling, ramifying detail it became a new drama serial for them.

They would sit together in the galley, trying to guess what would happen next to the characters in Tragolani's past.

'Do you think he gets together with the farmer's girl?' Burneau began one day.

Juilla shook her head.

'No chance. She loves the new man Eustace.'

'Can't see it ending well for him,' said Burneau.

'Oh it will, he's Tragolani.'

But they would have to wait until the next time they heard the engine cut out, and Tragolani roll in from the deck with a broad grin, saying, 'Where's that box of Pilgrim, children? Let's banish ourselves *perpetually*!'

'What will happen?'

'We'll find somewhere,' said Burneau.

'When, mister?'

'Mister. Why do you always call me mister?'

'When, Maris? I can't bear this ship.'

'Well. Soon, I should think. I never heard of an ocean going on this long. There'll be something belonging to the Ptopolinos, maybe, like the Grand Reef Islands . . . or, what is it, Urada.'

'That's south, not north-west. I got a Five in Geography.'

'When we go where we're going, Juilla, we'll never have to

352

lie about anything again. We'll introduce ourselves as lovers from a faraway island. The first person we see, we'll ask where we can get married.'

'All right, Mr Blue.'

'It won't be long now.'

'What about Federico?'

'He'll be our friend, love. Our first dinner guest.'

'His manners are no good. He'll have to improve them.'

'You didn't use to like him.'

'He's all right. I like his stories, but I don't believe them. Like I never believed your stories.'

'You did,' said Burneau, touching her face.

She lay back and stared at the low ceiling.

'I don't believe he ever loved the farmer's girl.'

'Who?'

'Federico. In his story.'

'He says he did. It's his past.'

'Exactly. I just can't imagine him loving anyone. He doesn't care enough?'

'Do I care enough?'

'Certainly enough. You certainly care enough.'

Burneau closed his eyes. This time she touched his face and he opened them again.

'Tell me we'll find land tomorrow. Give me a story to believe.'

'We'll find land tomorrow.'

She stared at him. Then she broke up laughing and cried: 'It's no good, old Mr Blue, I can't believe that one!'

They did find land. Or Juilla found it. She had stood alone for about two hours, gazing mournfully into the bright clouds before the sun, gazing so intently at those clouds that by the time she noticed the hyphen of land beneath it was quite a considerable size. She screamed with delight, as Burneau and Tragolani crawled up from a drunken bout of the Game of Confessions to contemplate finally, in masks of tearful silence, the shape of their distant salvation.

353

But it took hours to get much closer, and, as they approached the land, it seemed as though a curious disquiet began to overtake the two men.

'You know something,' said Tragolani softly, as he steered the *Gleam in the Eye* alongside a dark, wooded coast, 'I think I know this place.'

'Do you think we're back where we were?' Juilla said with a frown, searching for something familiar.

'Not Badeo, no,' he muttered. 'I remember it from the Camp, from Camp Liberat, from photographs we had to study every time your boyfriend here had his dreams.'

Juilla said: 'We're just friends, really, we don't – '

'Hey, boss, what do you reckon?'

As there was no reply, Tragolani and Juilla both turned round to see if Burneau was all right. He'd gone below deck.

'I'll go,' said Juilla.

'What's wrong, Mr Blue, what's the matter?'

He looked up at her bleakly.

She sat beside him. 'Is it anything I said?'

He swallowed, inhaled deeply, then finally stammered: 'T-Tragolani – says he can steer this thing. He's only taken me right back home.'

When they all felt they could, the three of them sat together around the table in the living space. Tragolani confirmed that he recognised the land as a remote western strip of the Argeline Domain.

'The Rezion Irispar,' whispered Burneau.

'Swear on my dead mother, Maris,' said Tragolani. 'I thought we were far from here. That's not the sun I was brought up with. Or the stars, for that matter. It's like someone just made them up, like one of your sodding islands.'

'If it's remote, no one will know him,' Juilla suggested. 'No one will know you, love,' she said to Burneau.

'Maybe,' said Tragolani. 'That's possible.'

'I can't go there,' Burneau repeated miserably. 'It's only

forty miles to home from here. If the sun shines tomorrow I'll be able to see the Folded Mountain. But if anyone finds me we'll all be slaughtered.'

'Also possible,' Tragolani allowed.

'It seems so unfair,' said Juilla, 'seeing as it's his home. He didn't mean to do what he did.'

'Tell that to your damn Arselickos,' said Tragolani.

They sighed together, then Juilla rose briskly and fetched a dark black bottle of the best Krem-Billiger.

Tragolani said tiredly: 'We were saving that till we found a place to stop, sweetheart.'

'I say we've found a place,' said Juilla. 'We can make up a name for Maris – it won't be the first time!'

Burneau looked dully at the fizzy wine she poured into his glass.

'I'll be Mr Krem-Billiger,' he mumbled. 'More wigs, more lies.'

'If it's our only chance!'

'I can't set foot ashore, love. If I do that I'll walk all the way home and they'll hang me at my own crossing post.'

Juilla stared at him for some time, then looked at Tragolani, who looked away. She sat back. 'So we have to sail on.'

'Yep,' Tragolani agreed. 'We have to sail on. Maris has no chance on the Mainland.'

Juilla lifted up her glass and drained it in one go.

'We'll find you another home, dear,' she said quietly, reaching for the bottle.

That night they drank heavily. Dark wines, light wines, beers and many spirits. Tragolani hatched a plan to forage ashore for food and drink.

'There's no village for miles,' Burneau warned him. 'Irispar means "mosquito-place".'

'They can have my blood,' said Tragolani, 'Arselicko insect bastards.'

'Do you know what "Gispar" means?' Burneau demanded.

355

'Haven't a clue,' said Tragolani.
'Bird-place.'

Burneau became increasingly sentimental.

'Can you believe it? Of all, all the places in the world you have to steer us to? The Argeline Domain? Your worst enemy and my own home!'

'My mother lives on the same bit of land as the bit of land we can see out there,' Juilla expounded, 'but she's a cow so I doubt if I'll find her and she hates me.'

'Least you're home, Maris,' said Tragolani. 'Home's what saving your hide cost me.'

'File a complaint,' Burneau snarled. 'File it with the Minister of Reconciliation.'

'You mean the Minister of Banishment, eh?' Tragolani snapped back.

Juilla raised her hand. 'Did you ever hear about a claim for bomb damage? Dr Fencile helped me to file it.'

Tragolani stood on the table and growled like an old man: 'The wine is bad, my cock is small, remember I've no hair./I don't know what the fuck that means, I'm pissing up a wall./Badeo's broke, who gives a shit, so pass the vintage wines.'

'Weens,' said Burneau, 'it should be, for the rhyme.'

'It's a tragolette, you arsehole, it doesn't have to do that.'

'I'm going to sing!' Juilla decided.

'Sing!' cried Blue Burneau.

It was their wildest party yet. By the end of the night they had sung, danced, danced naked, swum around the boat, fought, thrown food around and cooked a three-course meal (one course each) that nobody wanted to eat. Tragolani had climbed out of the sea with a harvest of shells in his hand. He clattered them down on the table and said, 'Arselicko, souvenir, boss!'

By that time Juilla had somehow managed to fold down

the double bed, stretch out on it, calling to them, 'I'm taking a rest for some minutes now,' and fall instantly asleep.

Burneau and Tragolani covered her with blankets and went back to the galley. They played the Game of Confessions until there was nothing left to confess. They were drinking apple stow out of great thimbles.

'I've got one,' said Burneau after a long silence.

'So have I,' said his friend.

'What is it?'

'You first, Maris.'

'No, you.'

'Chop for it,' said Tragolani.

'All right.'

'Tragolani played Paper. Burneau held up a finger.

'That's not in the game,' said Tragolani.

'Pen,' said Burneau. 'Pen writes on Paper.'

Tragolani sniffed and told his secret.

'That farmer's girl. It never did work out the way I said it did. Just wanted to keep you two happy with the story, you know?'

'You liar, you had us! She never loved you, Federico!'

'She never did, boss.'

They both drank.

Burneau's last secret was that he had killed the captain called Nunez, so, in the spirit of the game, he took a swig and told it.

As Tragolani just sat there for so long, not commenting on Burneau's last secret, Burneau said: 'Where is she now, your farmer's girl, Federico?'

Tragolani still said nothing. He was staring at the wall.

Burneau's face seemed suddenly to freeze. He stood up and stepped quietly away to his bed, taking off all his clothes and easing himself in beside Juilla, who was dressed in nothing but a sailor's sweater, and had curled up so tightly that her hands were clasping the soles of her feet.

357

Burneau opened his eyes, saw that it was broad daylight outside, and saw that he was alone in his bed. He could smell
Juilla's scent all over the sheets, because he buried his face in
them and went back to sleep.

Burneau opened his eyes again, and this time he sat up. He
realised that the engine was running and the boat was moving quite fast. Naked and unsteady, he climbed out of bed
and went crouching through the living space and the filthy
galley, to emerge blinking into sunlight.

The wheel was locked on course. The land was gone.
North, south, east, west, whichever way they were now, the
land was gone from them all.

'Hmm,' said Burneau, then he went below deck again and
made his way towards the door of Tragolani's tiny cabin, a
frown on his face. He gently opened the door.

Tragolani had gone, so had all his belongings.

So had Juilla, and all hers.

Burneau sat for hours beside the helm, but he never unlocked
it. He looked from side to side, he looked up at the blue sky,
he looked down at his hands. He didn't eat or drink or uri-
nate. Neither did he speak or sing or cry.

When he did all those things he did them all in a matter of
minutes, and then he was by the helm again, looking from
side to side, up at the blue sky as it halved gloriously into
golden and purple, then down at his hands, first the backs
then the palms, then out to sea.

Soon he drank more, cried much, laughed for a time. He
sang a bit, ate some bread and cheese, threw it up in the
ocean. The next time he was to be seen sitting beside the
locked helm he had two letters in his hands, and he read one,
then the other. Then the first again, then the other.

The first:

Dear Mister Blue, I'm sorry to go without saying but I can't bear the old Gleam any more and Fedrico thinks I have a chance of being happy if I go ashore now. He says also you will be safe at the next islands, so I can go away feeling OK. But I don't feel OK. You should have said about finding Paol because I most wanted to see him in the world Maris and you never said. But I still love you a lot Mr Blue and I wish we will meet again and hope you don't forget me ever because I never forgot you. I am your Juilla, signed Juilla Cristina Maricolo. xxx.

Then the other:

Dear Maris, by the time you get this we will of gone ashore. We did not wake you because it is too dangerus for you in your country you come from as you know. I think us two will be alright. You have got feul enough easy to get to the next islands which I think maybe called the finch islands or island. You better stay on that course I locked on. There is food for ages still, plus there is beer. I am really sorry to have left you, but I had a long think boss and what I thought was that it was not really very fair on the girl who is only young to drift for ever like this when you know as well as I do I had no idea what I was at. But you cannot let the women panic thogh. She is a nice girl I think and I can see why you looked out for her. I promise I will make sure she gets settled in a nice town where no one can hurt her. Then you will not ever have to worry. We had some good times together didnt we Maris and I will always remember them but you do not need your SHADOW ANGEL any more because you are in no danger I can think of. I am not much good with words and punchuation spelling and so on so I do not know how to finish my letter but I have got to now so we can get ashore. Juwila has finished her letter. She is very sad to go but thinks it is best also for you. We will leave our letters on the side in the gally. So just to say good luck Maris but you do not need it because you always find it somewhere! from F. E. Tragolani with love.

   PS I almost forgot! Your letter to the monk you wanted me to take that time. I found it in your map book and I took it. I promise as well that he will get it and if he has died your people will get it. That is all my boss unless I remember an other thing!

The next time Burneau sat beside the helm, on the next

beautifully sunny morning, he had his colouring book with him and was hard at work.

He had imagined so many islands that he was running out of pages, was using the backs of pages he had drawn on already, so that faint splotchy imprints showed through and began his new drawings for him.

The way he worked, the patterns he made, these in the absence of anyone to talk to were the only clues to his state of mind, alone on the vast silver ocean.

One island was hot and shady, and a stickman sat on the porch of one house, drinking from a big glass. The sky was green.

One island was long and so slender you could see the ocean from anywhere. Half the island was the stickman's house, and the other half was his garden.

A third island was all a kind of room, like a bar room, where the stickman was being served two drinks. All the other stickmen in the bar were smiling. Through the window one could see the sea looming.

On several islands the stickman was dressed in smart clothes, and was accompanied everywhere by a stickwoman in a triangle dress. These islands were variously hilly, wooded, mountainous, or filled with lakes. There were always high rectangular buildings, and they were always in the distance.

One island was bleak and black, and the stickman and stickwoman were alone on it with their red pet that could have been anything, but if one looked carefully one could see boats arriving across a sloping green sea.

Burneau was not the greatest sketcher, though every day he got better and more adventurous, as he wove his way through the imaginary archipelagos, adding fine details.

But who can tell what passes through another's mind? Not even a god. Maybe they were places the young man had been to, maybe they were places he wanted to see, or merely places he believed he would see. He worked by day and night, as the

360

Gleam in the Eye sliced through the stillness. He worked when the engine cut itself for good, and the boat drifted from its locked course. He worked with a smile, he worked with a frown. He worked in tears, because his tears could be islands too, grey islands, and he worked with his head all but asleep on the page.

When he ran out of paper he used the sides of boxes, he used the shell of the boat, or he worked on old islands, turning his rivers to streets, or his trees to more stickmen, or his stickmen to stout jacketed citizens. The last canvases he used were the backs of the letters his two friends had left him, but he needed them so he used them.

What did he wish? Can a god not guess?

That such islands were there, around, at some point in the direction he was drifting. That there were islands of friends, islands of wine-growers, islands of story-tellers and islands of lovers. That one such as Juilla Cristina Maricolo might be found on one island, and another such as her on another. That on those islands he would never have to lie, because nobody expected him to guard them, fight for them, win their wars, think for them, believe them or save them, murder them or love them. That every island he had drawn was somewhere he would be welcome.

He turned another page to an island he was working on.

It was his favourite island yet, judging by the hours he spent on it, how many times he changed his mind about it, and how many different things seemed possible there.

He hoped, and one knows he hoped, because one heard his clear voice addressing one by name on a windless night, that somewhere in his world, somewhere over that vast bright starlit ocean whose horizon is three times as far from you as any horizon you have seen or imagined, there might be two or three such islands for him, or just one, one even, one was all he would need. But it was a beautiful, brilliant blue day by now and one could see there were nine thousand.